A Class of Her Own

Thornback Society
Book Two

By

Aspen Hadley

Printed in the United States of America
First Printing, 2022
ISBN: 9798364341174

Cover Design by Nicole Brown and Aspen Hadley
Proofread by Sophie Young

OTHER BOOKS BY ASPEN HADLEY

<u>Stand Alone</u>

Simply Starstruck
Blind Dates, Bridesmaids & Other Disasters
Suits and Spark Plugs
Halstead House

<u>Just Enough Duology</u>

Just Enough Luck
Just Enough Magic

<u>Thornback Society</u>

Class Act

If you're interested in writing updates, and sharing a few laughs, you can sign up for Aspen's newsletter through her website www.aspenmariehadley.come

Aspen also loves to connect with readers and friends on social media. You can find her on Instagram (@aspenhadley_author) or on Facebook (Aspen Hadley Author)

DEDICATION

To Lowell and Susie,
my father and mother-in-law,
True examples of dedication to family!!

And . . . since this book is releasing in December
"Christmas Gift!"

PROLOGUE

Last week of May
The Thornback Beginning—from Meredith's point of view

I concentrated on slicing my sandwich into even, bite-sized squares—the whole wheat bread fighting against my cheap plastic knife as I sawed back and forth. I shouldn't have gone with the thick sliced turkey; it was making things difficult.

"My life, represented in food." Lizzie's morose words brought my attention back to the table I was sitting at with my friends in the faculty lunchroom.

Lizzie's nose wrinkled up as she stared at the limp noodle dangling off the end of her spoon. It looked like some kind of chicken noodle soup. *Probably homemade*, I thought as she wiggled the noodle at us until it slopped lazily back into her bowl. If I was any sort of cook, I'd ask for the recipe. Everyone had stopped talking at Lizzie's pronouncement about her life relating to the noodle, and our eyes were all on her, curious about her uncharacteristically dramatic mood.

She continued, "School's out for summer next week, and I need to do something that makes me feel alive. I'm in danger of disappearing into the void of monotony."

Only boring people get bored, I thought to myself. For the most part, I had little sympathy for any sort of self-pity. Although I could empathize with needing a change in the routine.

Ruby was the first to reply. "I felt alive when I was catching vomit in a trash can earlier." She chuckled, her dark eyes nearly disappearing as they crinkled up.

The rest of us groaned, and Hailey—never one to deal with 'yucky stuff'—pushed her plate of leftover stir-fry away while muttering under her breath about proper table manners and conversation topics.

Lizzie sighed, which had the desired result of reclaiming our attention. "Am I the only one watching the clock tick and realizing how fast time is passing while I sit inside a schoolroom?" She speared us all with a look. "I'm about to finish my tenth year of teaching here and am in serious danger of becoming a vicious stereotype." She pointed at us one by one with her now noodle-less spoon. "You should all be worried, too. We're in our thirties, never been married, and teaching school. Eventually someone is going to accuse us of being old maids. Certain parts inside of me are actually turning to dust."

"Old maid is an insulting term," I replied, my darkly lined blue eyes flashing in offense. The last thing we needed was to all be roped into her pity party. Maybe I liked being single. Maybe it was the only truly safe and free way to live. And I didn't appreciate being told there was something wrong with me.

"I could have called us spinsters, which isn't any better," Lizzie replied with a shrug.

"Who says we need a label?" I continued, pausing to pop a piece of my sandwich into my mouth before reaching up to tuck a lock of jet-black hair behind my ear. "Labels are limiting."

"I heard a new term. Thornback," Aryn stated as she bit into her crisp salad. At our blank stares Aryn hurried to swallow and then leaned forward with a cheery, amused expression. "I read an article the other day that said the word spinster was for women who were like twenty-three to twenty-six. But Thornback was what they called unmarried women over the age of twenty-six. It was some sort of reference to a hideous fish with thorns down its back, meaning those women were ugly and prickly."

Ruby's brow furrowed and her lips pouted slightly. "That doesn't sound any better."

Aryn held up her hand. "I know. It was terrible. But . . . there's a movement on social media right now to resurrect the word in more of a dragon-like way. Like saying, 'Who needs a man? We're thornback dragon women, and we rule the entire kingdom.'"

The five of us were silent for a beat—something that certainly didn't happen often—before Hailey sputtered out a laugh, her white-blonde bob swaying against her chin as she shook her head. "It's perfect," she said. "See, Lizzie, we're not old maids. We're a bunch of thornback dragon women, thriving without men."

Lizzie leaned across the table to give her a high five as her mood lightened. "I love it."

Ruby squared her shoulders playfully and stated, "I'll stand with you Lizzie, and so will your sisters of the lunchroom table." She set down the soda she'd been nursing and gestured widely. "We, the Thornback Five, must seek adventure in the great wilderness outside of this school. Each of us will find our fortunes, and happiness will be ours."

I rolled my eyes at Ruby's theatrical speech while everyone else chuckled, drawing the attention of other faculty members who had been peacefully eating. Someone cleared their throat, and I turned my head slightly, clearing my own throat loudly. Since when was laughter and happiness outlawed in an elementary school? This throat clearing passive-aggressiveness was something that happened frequently, which made it easy to brush it off and refocus on each other.

"We should form The Thornback Society," Aryn said, raising her water bottle. "To fierce woman!"

We all agreed by picking up our various drinks and tapping them together.

"What kind of adventure are we talking about here?" Hailey asked after we'd all taken a swig.

Lizzie shrugged. "I'm not totally sure. All I know is that I need something to happen before I lose myself."

The ticking of a clock and the squeaking of plastic chairs could be heard while we thought. Across the hall the sounds of children eating and talking wound their way to us, and I wondered if I'd ever felt as carefree as they sounded.

"I need to be outside," Lizzie said thoughtfully.

"Oh," Aryn squealed softly. "My brother went on one of those river rafting trips last summer. It was a week long, and you raft and camp as you make your way along a section of river. Maybe we could do something like that?" Her curly red hair caught the light as her blue eyes grew wide with excitement

Lizzie's expression lit up, and she nodded. "Yes. I've never done anything like that. It's perfect. Who's with me?"

She looked around the table that was crammed into the small faculty room and surrounded by vending machines that were never used and a kitchenette original to the school from the 1970s. My group of best friends sat there, looking back at her with thoughtful expressions. Aryn—cheery and kind; Ruby—the nicest and silliest; and Hailey—too classy to be here but still one of us. In the past four years, since the last of us had found a position here, we'd all clicked into place and found the home we'd been missing. Somehow, they'd even been willing to take me on, a rarity I didn't take for granted.

"I'm definitely in," Aryn said.

Surprisingly, it was Hailey who was next. "Okay, Lizzie, I'm in."

Lizzie held off celebrating until she'd heard from all of us. She looked to me. "It'll be amazing. The five of us, out in the wild, nobody calling us 'teacher, teacher.' No routine, no long days of trudging along."

It did sound nice. I didn't vacation often, and maybe it would be good for me. "You plan something, and I'll come," I agreed.

It was only a matter of moments before Ruby joined up. Lizzie clapped her hands together, her tight honey-blonde curls bouncing against her forehead as she nodded with excitement. Her expression held the promise of something fun and something different . . . which were probably the two things I most feared in this world.

CHAPTER 1

November

Let's pretend for a second that I'm the type of person who would go to a psychic, and while gazing into a crystal ball, I'd be told that someday I'd buy a six-foot tall, inflatable turkey wearing a Pilgrim hat and spend an entire Saturday night after dark trying to stake its stubborn bubble-like feet into my front lawn. Well . . . I'd have asked for my money back and called her a kook while loudly proclaiming my disbelief to anyone within ear shot.

Yet, here I was, holding a stake while a stupid six-foot bird tried to blow away in the truly annoying east wind that came blowing over the top of the mountains and straight into my yard. If I didn't know better, I'd think a cosmic funnel existed upwind from my property and that someone was having a laugh at my expense. My neighbors' leaves appeared to be hardly blowing while my trees were attempting to fall to the ground. Plus, it was cold.

"Do you think we could try again during daylight tomorrow?" Lizzie asked, her voice muffled by both the turkey's gigantic plastic feathers shoved up against her face and by the scarf she'd moved up from her neck to cover her from chin to eyes. She looked hysterical with her curls poking out from under her cap and her hands flailing to push the feathers away.

"The goal is for everyone to wake up to this little surprise," I replied with some effort. I had a stake between my teeth and was trying my best to tug the bird's feet back toward the ground. "If they see me doing this, I'll have to answer too many questions."

"I think you'll be answering questions regardless," Ruby piped up from my front porch, where she was sipping something steamy while wrapped in winter clothing and a blanket she'd stolen from the back of my couch after announcing that it was colder than a brass toilet seat on the shady side of an iceberg.

She'd originally been totally on board with this yard decorating plan of mine, but upon stepping out of her car and experiencing the frigid wind, she'd flat out refused to get involved. However, that didn't mean she was leaving because she definitely still wanted to watch it all unfold. Just . . . from a place of warmth.

"My yard, my choice," I stated, a mantra I'd been saying to myself all afternoon.

Did I really want a gargantuan turkey, complete with an LED light-up bow tie, towering in my yard? No. Did I really, really want to passive-aggressively get under the skin of my HOA board? Yes. I had a point to prove, and if it took a little bit

1

of tacky yard decor to accomplish it, well, I was game. And exactly what was that point? Well, it was still percolating. I hadn't landed on a firm creed yet, only that it was time to go overboard if I wanted them to start seeing the world outside of their meetings.

Another gust of wind hit, and I heard Lizzie squeak as she tumbled to the ground. She was now being mauled by the turkey, which made Ruby laugh out loud, and I bit my lip to keep from joining her. All I could see of poor Lizzie was her mittened hands and her kicking feet. The struggles of her short stature never stopped being funny to me. I grabbed one of the winged, arm-looking things and heaved it toward me, but it insisted on going back down and disrespecting Lizzie once more.

"Ruby, a little help?" I called as I tried to wrestle the bird.

Ruby thankfully set down her mug and joined me, lifting from the other side. The problem was that we'd started laughing while Lizzie begged for mercy, and it made it harder to get a firm grip and lift. Before too long, though, Lizzie's head popped around, and the look she gave me was anything but amused as she straightened her cap and tucked her springy curls back into place. She stood, unwrapping the scarf from her face, and put her hands on her curvy hips.

"I'm done here," she grumped. "I was on board with making your yard into a haunted house last month, and I'll definitely be back to set up Christmas next month if you're still at war, but this turkey crossed a line with me, and I'm out." She huffed a little as she marched to the porch to retrieve her purse and then headed toward her car. Her coat was bubble gum pink, and her curls bounced against the collar like the period at the end of her statement. "You'd better pray I don't have a black eye from that battery pack that just tried to knock me out cold. I have my bridal pictures next week."

"Don't worry, it's so cold out it's like putting ice on your face. Maybe drive home with your window down?" Ruby called.

The two of us watched her drive away as we held onto the wings and struggled against the beast. When Lizzie's taillights were out of sight, I turned to Ruby, who had been unusually quiet for the past couple of minutes.

"I feel like I shouldn't enjoy her anger so much," Ruby stated thoughtfully. "The problem is that she bounces around like an irritated oompa-loompa, and I can't take anything she says seriously."

The description was spot on, and with Ruby's deadpan delivery I couldn't help but laugh out loud. "You want to help me finish this?" I asked.

She reached out a hand, and I gave her a stake and the hammer I'd been using. Ruby made short work of it, staking the bird as competently as I'd known she could. Ruby had a strange and varied set of skills that made her quite handy to have around. We stood, both of us putting our hands on our hips and taking a few steps back to see the finished product—which ended up being different than I'd imagined. The bird was facing the house and its tail feathers were facing the street. With the breeze blowing, it looked like it was wiggling its bum at the neighborhood in a taunting and sassy manner.

2

Ruby laughed and bent over to tug at a stake, most likely thinking I'd want to fix it.

"No, leave it," I said before she could loosen anything. "It's perfect."

*****

A knock on the door sounded right as my toaster popped the next morning. I smiled smugly to myself, buttering the bread and spreading on some homemade raspberry preserves I'd made from last summer's harvest at my dad's house. The tart and sweet scent mixed with the warm butter, and I inhaled as a second knock came. I put it on a paper towel and rounded the corner out of my kitchen into the small entry hallway of my home. After a quick hand smoothed my hair to make sure nothing was sticking up where it shouldn't be, I opened the door and held out the toast in offering.

Brooks VanOrman, HOA president and pain in my backside, looked at the toast and back at me with an inscrutable expression. His dark hair was still wet from his shower, and his black beard looked freshly trimmed. As usual, he was wearing a button-down shirt and jeans, but in concession to the cold morning air, he had a jacket unzipped over the top.

"You're right on time," I said, wiggling the toast. "So predictable that the toast popped up right as you knocked. I made it for you. The raspberries are organic."

His dark eyes looked at the toast again before moving up to my face. "I don't want your toast."

I ignored the involuntary way my traitorous ears seemed determined to love the sound of his voice. He always spoke carefully, his voice deep and almost hypnotic—as though he'd been taught how to speak by a grandfather sitting on the front porch with all the time in the world. Sometimes, during HOA meetings, his words would slow down as he thought, and I had to cross my toes back and forth over each other to keep myself from trying to finish his sentences. Slowness was not a quality I admired.

"What do you want, then?" I asked, both of us knowing exactly why he was here.

He jerked a thumb over his shoulder at my turkey, standing proud and wiggling its bum at the world. He sighed, already weary of this conversation.

"Miss Atwood, the HOA bylaws clearly state you can't have horrendous inflatable turkeys twerking in your front yard."

I raised my eyebrows and took a bite of the toast he wasn't going to eat. I didn't bother with good manners, talking through my food as I replied, "Could you please explain what twerking is? I'm unfamiliar with this term."

He blinked the slow blink of deep skepticism. "You don't know what twerking is?"

I took another bite. "Sure don't."

He nodded and stuffed his hands into his pockets, the movement giving me a sneak peek of that mystery tattoo near his collar bone before it disappeared again.

3

He took in a deep breath and focused on me as I continued eating. I held his gaze as he tilted his head, watching him try to decide what angle to hit this from. Brooks VanOrman was a lawyer of some sort. I wasn't really clear on what his specialty was, or whatever, but he was probably used to having to face down difficult people and argue his case.

"Miss Atwood," he started, and I grinned.

"Please, call me Meredith. Miss Atwood sounds so formal."

"This is a formal complaint."

"From whom?" I asked, eyes wide as though I didn't know that Hazel next door, loyal HOA board member and snoop extraordinaire, had to have called him at sunrise.

Hazel was in charge of distributing tickets to people who'd broken bylaws, and she loved her job with a rabid commitment I begrudgingly admired. She also loved her blue hair—on purpose—and telling everyone that her seventieth birthday was coming. Two things I admired less, mostly because I'd put her age closer to eighty-plus and her alleged seventieth birthday never seemed to materialize.

"Hazel," Brooks answered. "She also texted me a picture of the exact bylaw you're breaking."

I brushed the toast crumbs off my fingertips. "Hazel knows how to text pictures?"

"She does," he muttered. "And she seems to consider the bylaws good reading material."

I was suddenly intrigued by just how many text pictures Hazel had sent him and what they were of. From where I was sitting, Hazel didn't do anything but snoop and knit. I doubted Brooks was interested in pictures of her latest hot pad or of candid shots of neighbors going about their lives. I glanced at Hazel's house, wondering how many pictures (with white lines slashing through them where her blinds got in the way) of me she'd sent to Brooks.

"Hmm. Maybe she's the one I should ask about this twerking thing then? She seems to be pretty up-to-date on stuff."

Brooks rolled his eyes. "Look, you and I both know that *you know* that this turkey thing is completely ridiculous. You did it to, once again, irritate me and waste my time. Are you going to take it down, or do I need to set Hazel free with her ticket book?"

I folded my arms. "First of all, Mr. VanOrman, I don't spend all my time thinking up ways to irritate you, and I don't care how you spend your time."

"Right." His tone was clipped, suspicious and annoyed.

"Second of all, I happen to love Thanksgiving, and this is how I choose to honor the day our great nation came together to . . ."

He held up a hand, and I stumbled to a stop. "Meredith?" He leaned slightly forward, close enough for me to catch the scent of his toothpaste. "The turkey is tacky, and you know it. What will it take to get you to remove it?"

4

Maybe stop treating me like roadkill at the HOA meetings and start discussing things of actual consequence, is what I wanted to yell at him. Instead I balled my hands into fists and met him head on. "You veto the idea of charging overnight guest fees."

"This isn't congress. I don't actually have veto power."

"But you do have sway. Charm them into voting against it."

His head bobbed once, sharply. "Done."

"See, that wasn't so hard."

His hands came out of his pockets, and he tugged at one of his sleeves. "It would be great if we didn't have to bicker every month."

I smiled sweetly at him. "You're the one who wanted to be president so bad."

"Actually, I didn't want it at all. But I've heard that you did, and that explains a lot."

Not much in life managed to steal words from my mouth, but that last little dig did it. Before I could summon a response, he spun on his heel and was off my property in a matter of seconds. I watched him go next door to knock on Hazel's door, but I wasn't able to see her or hear the conversation thanks to one very large bird and his inappropriate dance moves.

*****

The scent of my reheated chicken casserole was giving off tuna fish vibes the next day at lunch, and I thought about apologizing to my friends, but that would mean acknowledging that the smell was me. Right now Ruby was shooting daggers at Peter Jarmin, fellow teacher, who had a bad habit of bringing stinky foods into the faculty lunchroom. Peter and I weren't fans of each other, so I was letting him take the fall. I also wondered if there was some sort of food poisoning risk in eating the casserole, but I was never one to waste food, so I took a cautious bite. It was sort of chewy in a bad way. I reached for my bag of celery slices.

"You told him you didn't know what twerking is?" Lizzie laughed as she stirred a thermos of reheated soup. "That's so perfect. I wish my brain worked as quickly as yours does. I only have great comebacks an hour later, which is never actually helpful."

Pleased with her compliment, I offered a small smile around my bite of celery. I hate celery, for the record, but adults are supposed to eat healthy, so it kept making its way into my lunch bag. Plus, it's cheap, which is like a unicorn. Cheap and healthy isn't a partnership easy to find.

"One Meredith brain is enough, Liz," Aryn teased from her place at the table. "Imagine what would happen if there were two of them out in the world? It would probably create a vortex through which time and space ceased to exist."

I stabbed Aryn in the arm with the celery. "Science obviously isn't your specialty," I replied with a smirk, "and you'd be lucky to have more than one of me."

"I may not be a scientist," she smirked, "but I did study psychology. I'm considering going back to school and writing my master's thesis on you."

The others laughed, and I rolled my eyes—the same routine we'd done thousands of times. In fact, I couldn't imagine a world where I wasn't rolling my eyes every day. Not for the first time, I considered getting my eyeballs examined by an ophthalmologist. Maybe my eye muscles would win an award or something. This was, of course, an idea Ruby had put into my head one afternoon after studying me closely enough that I asked her what was going on. She'd replied that she'd love to study my eyes and their musculature, and that strange idea popped into my mind on occasion. I was warming to it.

"I couldn't have had that beautiful moment without the help of Lizzie and Ruby," I wiggled my celery and snapped off another bite.

"Twerking turkey," Hailey said softly on a chuckle. "It really is perfect."

"Please tell me you didn't deflate it," Ruby said as she peeled off the lid of a pudding cup.

While I think pudding cups are gross, I admired Ruby's ability to do what she wanted to do and eat what she wanted to eat without any sign of concern over it. Sort of strange for a nurse. She should have been firmly in my camp where healthy mattered.

"Are you kidding? Until Hazel actually delivers a ticket, that bird is there to stay," I replied, watching her scoop out a mouthful of chocolate-flavored gelatin.

"You need to send us a picture," Aryn stated before biting into her sandwich, "before a ticket arrives and you have to take it down."

"Something tells me a ticket isn't going to get you to back down." Hailey watched me with her typical quiet expression.

"You assume I can afford to keep paying extra fees to the HOA board," I muttered. "I'm a schoolteacher. I'm not made of money."

"No," Hailey nodded, her blue eyes sparking suddenly. "But I might be willing to pitch in . . . you know, for a righteous cause."

"Twerking turkeys are a righteous cause?" Lizzie asked, her curls bouncing as she laughed. "This gets better and better every day."

"Have you thought about what you'll be doing for Christmas yet?" Ruby asked me.

I shrugged and slowly finished chewing that diabolically disgusting celery stick, purposely drawing out their interest. "I have a few thoughts."

The truth was, I had thoughts, but it was currently fifty/fifty on whether I actually put it up or not. It wasn't cheap to thumb my nose at the community rules—and I wasn't making much headway with inflatables.

"Complete with drawings?" Lizzie's head popped up, her smile growing. I nodded.

"Did you color code our assignments?" Aryn asked me as the first lunch bell rang, signaling that it was time to head back into teacher mode.

"The fact you said that with a straight face worries me," I replied, putting my food containers in my lunch box.

"The fact that you probably did is what worries me," she retorted, pushing back her chair to stand. She brushed her long red curls over her shoulder and smiled down at me. "You're getting predictable in your old age, Atwood."

I stood but still had to look up to meet her eyes. "I still have to assign porta potty duty."

Her laughter was her only reply as she headed out the door.

CHAPTER 2

It's a well-known fact among schoolteachers that there really is no perfect month for student behavior. September brings the back-to-school giddiness. October is chatter about Halloween. November is looking forward to Thanksgiving break and discussing who'll be eating the most pie or who is going on the most exotic vacation. Makes it hard to teach math when all they want to do is discuss whether pumpkin pie is actually made from jack-o-lanterns or from cans. The current stats in my classroom were fifteen for canned and ten for the actual gourd itself. I was partial to apple and thought the mushiness of pumpkin was nasty, but there was no way I'd be mentioning that and derailing our language arts lessons, too. I only had seven more school days to get through before these kids would be released into the food-filled arms of their families, and while I found some of it entertaining, it couldn't go fast enough as far as I was concerned.

"Have you ever been to Hawaii?" Jasmine asked as I walked around the classroom, checking their progress on a grammar lesson we were working through.

I raised my head and shook it. "No." Apparently that's where she'd be going for the holiday. It was a concept so foreign to me that she may as well have asked me if I'd ever trekked to the top of Mount Everest and had a spa day with a Sherpa. "I'll be staying in town for Thanksgiving."

"Sad," Tyson sighed, and I watched as he and Jasmine exchanged pitying glances.

The familiar tightening of my stomach and chest caused me to bite my lips together. I hustled to mentally run through the thoughts I'd long ago learned to use when pitying glances were sent my way. I instantly worked to reframe it. This wasn't a judgment; this was them caring for me and genuinely feeling sad that I didn't get to go somewhere so beautiful. *There is absolutely nothing lacking in me.*

"I prefer it, actually," I replied kindly as my chest loosened, and I was grateful that it had happened so quickly this time. "It's nice to be home for holidays."

"That's like me," Katie piped up. "I stay here, and my cousins come to see us."

I watched her set her pencil down and noticed the others following suit. Apparently lesson time was over. I glanced at the clock and caved. We only had five more minutes left, anyhow, and then it was time to pack up and head home.

"What kinds of food do you make?" Katie continued.

Little faces glanced my way, open with curiosity about their teacher. It never ceased to amaze me how much students wanted a glimpse into my personal life. I remembered being both in awe of and slightly wary about my teachers. As a motherless child they'd seemed almost like fairytale creatures to me, but I'd also kept them at arm's length, fearing questions that I didn't want to answer. Adults had always drawn mixed reactions from me until I became one myself.

I pasted on a warm expression, and the practiced lies rolled off my tongue easily. "Oh, my dad starts cooking the turkey early in the morning, so it's tender and juicy with crispy skin . . . " I continued painting a scene of yeasty rolls, warm potatoes with melting butter, homemade jams and pies, and everything else that I knew would keep them entertained. "So, I feel pretty lucky." I finished and then pointed to the clock. "Let's get packed up."

The children, always motivated by getting out of school for the day, were quick to clean their desks and begin moving around the room, gathering end-of-day items. As they snagged their lunch boxes from the cafeteria bucket and zipped their backpacks closed, I glanced out the window to see fat, heavy snowflakes beginning to fall. We'd only had a dusting of snow up to this point, but the gray clouds gathering outside, shutting the sun out and making the world appear gloomy, were a sure sign that this storm would really deliver. The good news was that the students would get home before it got too deep. The bad news was that the teachers would probably be driving home in the thick of it—in run-down cars with teacher's salary tires.

I briefly wondered if my inflatable yard turkey could dance in the falling snow or if the cold air would deflate it. My spirits lifted at the image of that glorious thing. It had been proudly dancing in my yard for three days now, and Hazel still hadn't been by to deliver a ticket. I'd caught a couple people walking by and taking pictures, which made me wonder if there was an underground movement of support for my actions. My lips twitched as I told the students to line up, and we marched down the hall to the front door.

I may not get a turkey cooked by my dad for Thanksgiving, but I had an inflatable protest sign proudly shaking its tail feathers in my front yard, so things were going just fine.

✳✳✳✳✳

I'd been wrong — things were not just fine. Three hours later the snow in my driveway was so deep that my little car couldn't blaze a trail through it. I looked around and balled fists in annoyance. In my row of six attached townhouses, all the other driveways and sidewalks were clear. Hazel's next door? Clear. Across the street from me, Leland, another HOA board member, also had cleared walks, and his driveway looked pretty welcoming under the lights of his townhouse.

In fact, as I sat there and counted, I discovered eleven welcoming townhouses and one icy, dark tundra.

That one was mine.

It not only looked abandoned, but I'd argue that the snow removal company had decided to deposit all the extra snow directly at my door. It was also possible

9

that power had been cut to my place, because the timed outdoor lights that typically shone above my garage were off. To add to the depressing portrait, my inflatable turkey was a shapeless blob. The snow had covered the blower fan, and the poor fella was sagging in the middle, causing his top hat to repeatedly tap the walkway that led to my door. He was bent in half, looking like he was bowing to some unseen royalty so deeply that his brow swiped the ground.

Game point, Brooks VanOrman, I thought.

I put my car in reverse and got in a position where I could park near the curb—an illegal move on snow days. HOA rules clearly stated that cars had to be off the streets in order to keep it clear for plows to have access. Too bad it was after six o'clock and no plows would be coming my way tonight. I'd be shoveling this mess myself, which was a bitter disappointment. I knew from driving across town that it was a wet, heavy snowfall. My back hurt already.

Even more disappointing was knowing that as soon as I finished here, I'd have to drive out to the small town of Paradise to shovel my dad out. He probably hadn't even noticed the storm. He never did. I'd long ago stopped asking myself why I bothered when he didn't care how much snow piled up around him. There were simply some things a person did for family and some habits that had been set for years.

With my car parked, I lugged my work items in the house, hissing as snow fell into the tops of my shoes and against my ankles. I made quick work of putting on snow gear and heading back out with my shovel. As I worked my way back and forth across my single-wide driveway in a pattern I believed to be the most efficient, I thought about all the ways I could make this pay off for me. Technically, denying me snow removal was a genuine safety hazard, unlike a big turkey, which was a minor annoyance. I paid money to have my yard kept clear. What would the board say if I asked for a reimbursement this month?

I heated up quickly, both from frustration and the hard work of shoveling the heavy snow. I occasionally got teased about being all pointy elbows and knees. Yes, I had no real meat on my bones, nothing curvy or soft, nothing inviting. Because of that, people assumed that I had no muscle, but muscle was the one thing I did have. In spades. I'd never backed off from a physical challenge, and I wasn't about to start now.

An hour later I'd finished my own house and was pulling up to my dad's place. The run-down, two-bedroom house I'd grown up in was dark—no surprise there—but the shed behind the house had light peeking through the tiny slits between boards. It had originally been a barn, and, according to family lore, it was the reason my parents had chosen this house. At the time they'd had me and my younger sister Willow, and they weren't expecting to have more children. Dad needed a studio workspace, and Mom loved the cozy, little, white house that went along with it.

I occasionally tried to picture it how it would have looked thirty-two years before, the way Mom would have seen it, but it never quite materialized in my mind. It had never been spruced up the way my mom had planned, and a third daughter had arrived, filling up the tiny room that the three of us would share until I moved out after getting my college degree. The house was now gray and peeling, the roof in need of repair, and the front door was so off-kilter that no one bothered using it.

One set of tire tracks led up the gravel drive to the back door of the house, proof that Willow had dropped off dinner as she'd promised. It was her week to feed him, and I was thankful for that little mercy as I followed her tire tracks in the snow, parking where she had.

The doors of the shed were open with no regard for the storm, and I could see Dad's head bent over his workbench. The past couple of times I'd been out to his house I'd noticed how white his hair had become. His shoulders had always been a little stooped, a byproduct of a life spent hunched over a bench as he created whatever spoke to him at the time. He'd dabbled in everything from glass blowing to portrait painting to wood carving, and the remains of every art form lay scattered around the shop, the edges of the tools throwing shadows across his face.

None of them had come close to making enough money, in spite of the fact that he was very talented at whatever he picked up. But they'd all fed his soul.

I'd have appreciated it feeding mine and my sisters' stomachs, but you can't have everything. Mom had been the marketing and budgeting side of their duo, and without her, well . . .

I mentally shrugged off the thoughts as I followed what had to be Willow's footprints into the shed.

"Hey, Dad," I called as I entered the circle of light. "What are you working on?"

His dark eyes flashed over his shoulder briefly before turning back to his work. "Mosaic," he stated. "Found some glass bottles at the thrift store. I came home and shattered them into pieces."

I couldn't help but notice that his voice wasn't scratchy from disuse tonight, and I was relieved at the proof that he'd interacted with other humans today. Dad was the type of artist who went on a deep dive with every new creation. Sometimes he disappeared for days at a time. I had a few wispy memories of him spending time with us, but most of my memories involved me hunting him down before I became old enough to accept he didn't always remember we existed.

"Willow made beef stew for dinner," he continued, using his head to point toward a plastic container on the counter. "I don't eat beef."

Yeah. This week. Last week he'd been on a keto diet kick and got annoyed when I brought grilled cheese sandwiches. The carbs were out to kill him.

"Quite the storm," I commented, heading to the corner, where I knew I'd find the snow shovel. "Thought I'd get your walkways cleared."

"Thanks, Evergreen," he said absently.

I stiffened at the detested name but didn't bother to correct him. I hated my given name with unreasonable passion. Can you imagine naming a child Evergreen Atwood? Just because my father had changed his name to Forest in his twenties, 'in order to better align with his personal views while still honoring his surname,' didn't mean he had to give tree names to his three daughters. Willow and our youngest sister, Ash, had at least gotten monikers they could live with. Evergreen? It wasn't even a specific tree—it was a broad classification. He said it was because him and my mom thought I could use the inspiration of the evergreen and its ability to survive year-round.

Why they'd looked at a newborn and thought she'd need a fighting name was a sick kind of foreboding, but they'd gotten that one thing right. I was a survivor. However, when I'd gone to public school for the first time and realized precisely how strange that name was—and we're not talking quirky strange—I'd quickly switched to my middle name, Meredith, and never looked back. When Mom had passed during that first schoolyear, I'd said a permanent goodbye to Evergreen. That girl had ceased to exist. Heck, my best friends didn't even know Meredith wasn't my first name. Dad, however, during unfocused times, would still slip up and use the old name. It gave me the shivers every time, as though he was still talking to that little five-year-old girl. I often thought time had frozen for him the minute Mom had died.

My father was the last person anyone would have pegged as the marrying type. He'd lived a nomadic and artistic lifestyle until somehow my practical and beautiful mother, Judith, had caught him in his late thirties. Together they'd settled down and had three girls. After she was gone his anchor was too, and now he was a solitary old man, in his late seventies, with dwindling attachments to the world.

I dragged the shovel around to the house and began the work of digging out the back steps and walkways that would never be used. Dad didn't host guests. The only people he spoke to were cashiers at the store, unless he was in a grunting mood that day, and our family members. His only walking path was from the house to the shed or to his truck. But I shoveled until my shoulders ached and my lower back screamed because I was not interested in having to nurse him through an injury caused by icy, snow-covered paths.

I caught a glimpse of his mosaic cat as I returned the shovel to the shed and had to admit it was beautiful. Oranges and yellows, with bright green eyes and slivers of whiskers. If he decided to put it up for sale, I had no doubt it would make him some money. Money he'd never cared about.

"I'm done," I said as I spun to head back down the gravel driveway to my car. I didn't bother to shovel that, because, seriously, shoveling gravel would be a wasted effort and Dad's truck could plow down it in the same tracks Willow had created and I'd used. "I'll see you next week for Thanksgiving."

"What?" he actually turned to face me.

I stopped and looked back at him. "Thanksgiving. Next week. Ash is bringing her boyfriend home to meet us." Heaven help the man. "We're eating at my place."

His large, bushy white brows sunk into his weathered face. "I don't want to eat at your house."

I put my hands on my hips, ignoring the soreness in my arms. "I know that. But my house has a little more room, and I thought since we have another guest this year . . ."

He was shaking his head before I finished. "The Atwoods always have Thanksgiving at the family home."

What family home? I thought, shooting the sagging building a glare. But I only nodded at my dad. "Okay. I'll talk to the girls."

"Good."

And with that, we turned our backs on each other and walked in separate directions.

*****

When I arrived home it was to find Brooks VanOrman standing on my porch. My mood was shot, my back was in agony, and just . . . no. I pushed the button to open my garage door and parked my car. When I got out, he was standing in the open doorway of the garage, watching me from underneath a dark beanie pulled low over his eyes. Between that and his beard, it looked like his face was a small strip of flesh with two dark eyes peeking out.

"You look like a murderer," I said flatly. "Come to gloat?"

"Gloat?" he asked.

"The blow-up turkey is dead, thanks to this storm, and I shoveled my own driveway." I slammed my car door and cocked my head. "I can applaud your resourcefulness. Rather than ticketing me for the turkey, you somehow made sure the snow removal company skipped me. Nice."

He shook his head. "Actually, I didn't ticket you for the bird because Hazel said she was hoping to run a social media campaign about it and thought it would increase the attractiveness of our community to potential homeowners. Something about making us look fun."

I blinked. "Hazel runs social media campaigns?" Some of my bluster washed out, and my tired mind went down that rabbit hole for a second.

"I haven't actually looked at it."

"Afraid you'd end up having to ticket your own ticket master?" I asked, my mouth quirking.

"Something like that. Listen, I came to check in, actually. Leland told me your drive wasn't shoveled, so I called the snow removal company. Turns out their machines ran out of gas, and they didn't get the last few houses."

"Hmmm. That excuse would make sense to me if I wasn't the only house on this block who was missed. You'd think it would have been a few houses in a row."

He nodded and looked around. "You'd think."

I pursed my lips. "I shoveled it myself. But I'd like a discount on my next HOA payment."

Now it was his turn to cock his head. "I've only been doing this a little while, but I'm quite sure we don't run a discount program."

"I pay for snow removal, and I ended up doing it myself."

"That was your choice, I guess."

He tucked his hands in his pockets, and it was the type of relaxed, *I'm not taking you seriously*, move that spiked my heart rate.

"My choice? Do you see what I drive? I couldn't get in my driveway without shoveling. And heaven forbid I parked on the street. Hazel would have triple ticketed me for that infraction."

"Hazel only has single-ticket authority."

"Brooks!" I groaned out his name. Why was he always like this stone I was beating upon? Never reacting, always immovable, never ruffled. I wanted him ruffled! "You get my point."

"Yes. As exaggerated as it might have been."

I glared. He stared right back, minus the emotion. It grew silent as we both watched each other, me waiting for any sign of weakness I could exploit, him most likely wondering what weakness of his I'd try to exploit.

"Oh, Meredith, dear, how sad you must be." A squeaky voice pulled our attention away from each other.

Hazel marched up my driveway, bundled in a fur-lined parka and some sort of tall boots that hit her above the knee. She had a knitted scarf around her neck and held one end in her hand, pressed to her mouth. She'd moved it to speak before pressing it back against her mouth. I couldn't for the life of me figure out why she didn't have it wrapped up around her mouth too if she was that cold.

"Sad?" I asked, knowing full well it was a mistake.

She moved the scarf. "To find out yours was the only house missed by the snow people. It must feel like you've been targeted," she said and then pressed it back against her pink lips.

I looked back at Brooks and raised my eyebrows, even though I spoke to Hazel. "Brooks here was telling me there were several homes missed."

Hazel shook her head and waved her free hand before pulling the scarf away from her mouth. "Oh, no. I don't think that's true. I've contacted everyone, and it looks like it was only you."

"You called all one hundred and twenty homes?" I asked, my jaw feeling lose with shock.

"You know how many residences there are?" Brooks asked with raised eyebrows.

"Don't you?" I shot back.

"Moving on. The snow removal company told me . . . " Brooks started, but Hazel waved her hand at him and he stopped midsentence.

"Oh, no," she giggled. "I blitzed it out on the interwebs and heard back from everyone."

I didn't trust her information. At all. For starters, her verbiage was suspect. For all I knew, she'd messaged a group of Japanese noodle houses, and they'd all reported back that they were happy with their snow removal. I also didn't believe for one minute that all the other homeowners had responded. I knew people too well to believe that statistic. I did, however, believe that my house was the only one skipped, although the reasons were a little fuzzy at the moment.

14

"Thanks, Hazel," I sighed. Then I changed tactics. "I am sad, actually. You know my dad's a widower, right?" I softened my stance and made my eyes large. "He's mostly homebound, so I had to go shovel him out after I finished here. Thankfully my sister had brought him dinner, but I haven't had mine yet. And I'm so cold and hungry. It's been a hard night."

Hazel's eyes grew round, and she dropped the scarf down to her chest, pressing it against herself as her mouth rounded too. "Oh, now we can't have that. Brooks will call that nasty snow company immediately, and we'll get this figured out. In the meantime, I have some delicious stew left over from dinner. Why don't you come over and get a bowl, huh?"

"Beef stew?" I asked, thinking of my dad and his sudden issue with beef.

"Yes, dear."

I threw Brooks a smirk over my shoulder as I followed Hazel to her house. "I love beef stew."

CHAPTER 3

I needed to run. I needed to blow off some steam and feel the burn of my muscles as they worked. It was the best way I'd found to manage stress, and I was under a whole lot of that now that Hazel had decided I was her personal project. The beef stew and sob story had backfired, and, for the past two nights, I'd come home to find Hazel waiting on my porch with a casserole dish and two plates. Thanks to my efforts to make Brooks squirm, I'd ended up dining with Hazel for three nights in a row. I didn't like it one bit. Hazel was fine as far as neighborly relationships go—I never heard her through our shared wall, which was all I really needed—but I craved my alone time. Not only did I spend my entire day with twenty-five children and co-workers, but I thought of alone time as something I'd earned after years and years of caring for others and putting myself at the bottom of the list.

Adding to the annoyance of my unwanted dinner company was the fact that my inflatable turkey was a lost cause. At some point one of the sides had torn. Twerking Tom was no more. Hazel tried to comfort me about his demise. However, I found myself more relieved than upset when she pulled out her phone and started showing me how the pictures she'd taken of my twerking turkey were going viral along with the hashtag #letturkeysbeturkeys. There had been a disturbing upswing in the amount of applicants waiting for a home in our community to open up. I didn't want to tell her that she probably wasn't attracting the type of crowd she'd been going for with her marketing efforts.

I'd been only too happy to take the turkey down—well, more like roll up his pathetic carcass—and deposit him in the dumpster at the clubhouse. Hazel sympathetically looked the other way rather than ticketing me for dumping on private property, although she assured me the fine would have been steep had she chosen to write me up.

My salvation came in the form of the annual YMCA Turkey Trot held the Saturday before Thanksgiving, which was thankfully today. They used to do it on Thanksgiving morning, but it turns out that the people in my city would rather start stealing tastes of the stuffing and pie while watching the Macy's Thanksgiving Day Parade than run. That was fine by me because today I was in the mood to pound the pavement.

I arrived at precisely 8:45 a.m. at the lineup, ready with my number pinned to my black, long-sleeved athletic shirt and my running bag strapped across my hips.

I had chapstick, water, sunscreen, bandaids, and some gum, although I didn't often chew gum while running thanks to an unfortunate incident when I'd tried to both swallow and reject swallowing gum during a 10k. People had tried to save me from my non-choking, and it hadn't been pretty.

The air was still chilly as I found a place to stand and tugged my foot up towards my bum to give my quads a good stretch while scoping out the competition. With my hair slicked back and my normal grumpy resting face, not many people were meeting my eyes. In the past I'd tried to look more friendly, but it didn't come naturally and there was freedom in hitting my mid-thirties and learning to stop caring so much. Besides, I wouldn't have known what to do with peppy women attempting to chat me up pre-run. It was best this way.

"You know that this is a relaxing family affair," Aryn's familiar voice had me looking over my shoulder. "You're not supposed to stare them down like you're about to enter the wrestling ring and settle for nothing less than total surrender."

"Speaking of wrestling, I see the gladiators have arrived," I replied as I glanced behind her to see her strapping brothers pinning their numbers to their chests.

She grinned. "Don't worry, they'll be running with the men in their age division."

"I wasn't worried."

She tugged at the safety pin on the corner of her own number. "Makes sense. They may have a solid foot of height on you, but you're spry and have that killer instinct." I rolled my eyes but chuckled as she waved them over. "Sean, Rory, Patrick," she said, pointing to each of her red-headed, muscled-up siblings, "you remember my good friend Meredith."

Patrick and Rory grunted, offering me jock nods and almost smiles. Sean, the nicest of the bunch, held out his hand to shake mine. "Good morning for a race," he said.

"Every morning is a good morning to race," I replied, squeezing his hand in return. I'd go to my grave before admitting I squeezed it extra hard to see if there was any type of reaction. There wasn't.

"Alright, place your bets before the races get started," Sean said to his siblings.

When I'd first met the Murphy siblings, I couldn't understand their bet-happy ways, but over the years Aryn had placed some pretty hysterical bets with our group of friends, and I'd revised my opinion. Betting, especially when the stakes were more about a good laugh than anything else, was kind of fun.

"Aryn is definitely losing to Meredith, but she'll come in second in the women's race," I replied, even though it hadn't been directed at me.

The three brothers all grinned, looking at me like I'd appeared out of nowhere and was suddenly interesting.

"I'd put money on that," Rory chuckled.

"Don't bother. This is a 10k and Meredith is a sprinter, not a marathoner," Aryn teased.

"Loser buys lunch?" I pointed at her.

She nodded once, her ponytail swinging, and her brothers all clapped her on her back, wishing her luck as they moved on to placing bets about their own outcomes. Those claps would have thrown me to the pavement, but as the youngest sibling and only girl, Aryn was tough. I didn't envy her that. It had been hard enough in a house of only girls, but at least the physical stuff had only consisted of throwing clothing at each other and name calling. Her brother's voices faded as they moved to where the men were lining up, but I watched as they continued to push, elbow, and slap each other good-naturedly.

"I still don't understand how your teeny, tiny parents produced you four. When I think of your poor mother and the childbirth she endured . . . " I shook my head, and Aryn laughed.

"Mom says we're all big and strong because there's a secret ingredient in her shepherd's pie. I've looked, and it's not steroids."

A sharp whistle blew, and we walked to line up with the other women in our age division. Now that we were in our thirties, it seemed like the numbers were smaller, but the women were more serious runners. I thought it made things more interesting, but Aryn always maintained an air of being out for a relaxing morning. Only her and her family would think of this the same way most people thought of teatime.

"I'm glad you're here," I said to her as I readjusted my running bag and stretched my arms. "I didn't want to run alone this morning."

She glanced down at me with a surprised look. "Really? I thought you preferred to pound the pavement solo."

"Usually, yes."

She studied my face, her blue eyes—a lighter shade than mine—were filled with a sympathy I only accepted from my closest friends. "Rough week?"

"Yes. With another one looming."

"Yeah, the holidays aren't your favorite, plus you're meeting Ash's boyfriend this year. I also know you've been fighting the HOA board again, but is something else going on?"

I shrugged. "Not really. Although Hazel has been feeding me dinner every night like I'm a stray cat."

She smiled. "Good thing I brought my listening ears this morning," she said as the flag was raised. "Think you can talk and keep up with me at the same time?"

I grinned and nodded as the flag dropped. "I'm thinking burgers for lunch."

*****

"Just pour the water over my head. Pour it," I said less than an hour later as I bent over at the waist, chest heaving, slick hands braced on my thighs.

"Excuse me?" A woman's hesitant voice answered me.

I gestured, making a wide circle over my head. "Dump it all here."

"Are you talking to me?" The voice sounded even more hesitant, if possible.

18

I stood straight, and a lock of my thick, black hair fell out of my bobby-pinned hairstyle and into my eyes. "Are you the water lady at the finish line?" I asked. She nodded. "Then I'm asking you to drench me from head to toe with that cold water you're holding."

She looked at her cup and then back at me. I reached for the cup, but before I could grab it, another hand with bright blue fingernails snagged it and splashed the whole thing towards me, hitting partially on my face. The sound of Aryn's laughter accompanied me wiping my eyes. When I opened them, she was standing in front of me with a giant smile on her face. She was as sweaty as I was, her cheeks nearly matching her red hair.

"Why do you always have to scare the water people?" she asked, reaching for a second glass of water and tipping it over the top of my head.

I closed my eyes and sighed as it ran down my neck and into my exercise clothes. "Why do they always have scaredy cats at the finish line? If someone says, 'drench me,' then for heaven's sake, drench the person."

"You are literally the only person who makes that request. It takes a minute to process."

I glanced around and spotted a blond man pouring water over his own head a few yards away and pointed. "He's got the same idea."

"He's doing it to himself, though. It isn't that you want water poured over you, it's that you're requesting a stranger do it for you."

I shrugged. "No difference in my mind."

The blond man turned with a smile on his face for whomever was approaching him in the distance, and I recognized Ford Whittaker, our friend Hailey's boyfriend. Sure enough, a quick scan of the area showed Hailey walking toward him, holding hands with his daughter, Hillary, while his son, Henry, walked alongside them. Hailey looked as polished as ever, her platinum blonde bob swaying against her jaw as she walked. She was wearing athletic clothes, but seeing as she was a devotee of yoga, I doubted she'd run any of the races. Then again, she had a knack for remaining sweat- and dirt-free at all times regardless of the activity. When we'd gone on our river rafting adventure this past summer, she'd always looked ready for a photo shoot, even without make-up or having had a real shower for days.

"It's Ford," I said to Aryn. "I always knew I liked him."

I nodded in their direction, and Aryn and I fell into step, heading their way.

"You like Ford because he pours water over his head?"

"Among other, more important reasons. But that clinched it, yes."

"You have a strange way of vetting people."

I slid a glance at her. "I vetted you, you know."

"I've always wondered what the deciding factor was for letting me into your world," Aryn smiled down at me, her eyes alight with humor.

"The fact that I've won every race we've ever run," I smirked, bumping her arm with my shoulder.

19

She laughed out loud, and Hailey and Ford turned to watch us walk the last few steps.

"Let me guess, Meredith won?" Hailey dimpled.

"I can't figure out how she does it," Aryn playfully sighed, reaching up with a cloth she'd produced out of her own running bag to wipe sweat from her face. "She does that terrible spin class a few times a week, which has nothing to do with running, and suddenly on race day she's an Olympian. Meanwhile I'm playing sports and jogging the entire city every week, and I can't keep up with her tiny legs."

Ford chuckled. "Spin class isn't for pansies."

"One spin class is the equivalent of running 6.2 miles. So, this was like a regular Tuesday to me," I stated, and Hailey laughed.

"She took me to one a few months ago," Hailey nodded. "It almost killed me."

"I remember," Ford said, looking down at her and sharing a moment that brought color to Hailey's face.

I looked to Aryn, slightly uncomfortable with the emotion between them. "Plus, as you said earlier, I have that killer instinct."

"How was your race?" Aryn asked Ford after giving me an eye roll.

My mind wandered as the rest of them discussed how Ford had done in his age division. I took in the activity around the park where the race had ended. Families were gathering to congratulate each other under the bare branches of century-old trees. The sounds of cheering and happy chatter was always a little bittersweet to me. I appreciated families and was very grateful for my two sisters, but it had never been as warm and solid as these moments showed. There was so much hugging. So much.

I shivered a little as my body began to cool in the November chill, my wet clothes stealing heat away from me. Motion from the side of my eye had me glancing to my right only to find Hazel waving one arm and coming my way like a terrier after a rat. Even though my legs felt like rubber bands, my initial reaction was to run away. However, right as I made a move to turn, I noticed a very familiar man walking alongside her. He was tall to her short, dark clothing to her bright outfit, and quiet patience to her bubbly exuberance. Amusement skated through me when I noticed that she had her hand wrapped around his wrist, tugging him along forcibly. I knew that Brooks could break the hold if he wanted to, which somehow made the whole thing funnier. I had no idea how Hazel and Brooks were at the Turkey Trot together, but I found myself delighted by the development.

Hazel's blue hair matched the clear, freezing cold sky, as well as the leggings she was wearing. Her bright pink running shoes must have had poor traction, because she suddenly slipped, which had Brooks reaching out to steady her even though she had an iron grip on his wrist already. The expression on his face could be found in the dictionary under 'grin and bear it.' He had on his typical jeans and flannel shirt, with an army green military-style jacket over it and work boots with plenty of tread. He definitely wasn't here for workout time.

I waved my hand behind me to signal to my friends, and said quietly, "We're about to have company."

Their chatter died down as they looked toward the mismatched couple making their way to us.

"Who are they?" Hillary asked.

I only had a split second to glance back at my friends and whisper, "Brooks VanOrman and Hazel."

A very, *very* interested silence fell from behind me, and I could feel the weight of their curiosity as Hazel came to a skipping stop firmly inside my personal space bubble. They'd heard of Hazel, seeing as we'd been neighbors for a long time. They'd also heard about Brooks, and I didn't need to ask to know which one they were focusing on.

"Well, Meredith Atwood, what a pleasant surprise to see you here on this lovely winter morning," Hazel crooned, releasing Brooks and clutching at my hands. "Don't you look refreshed after your run."

I looked at Brooks over her head in time to see a flash of something in his eyes, letting me know that we both understood exactly how un-fresh I was in that moment. Ugh. Rule number one, never let your enemies see you looking less than perfect.

"It's so nice of you to get Brooks out of his cave and into the fresh air," I replied sweetly, releasing Hazel's hands to wipe my wet hair back out of my face.

"Who do we have here?" Aryn asked as she eased around to stand next to me.

Her voice was bright and cheery, and I could imagine her eyes running up and down Brooks as she soaked up the first chance any of my friends had had to see him in person after months of me complaining about him. I wondered what she thought and if he lived up to my descriptions of him. I could also imagine Brooks taking her in, thinking that a tall, beautiful, friendly woman like her would be preferable to a shrew like me. Well, joke was on him, because I wasn't a shrew to everyone. Mostly.

"Hailey, come meet Mer's friends," Aryn added with a wave at Hailey.

Hailey's dimples flashed, deeply, as she came to stand on my other side. I felt Ford move up closer behind us and the two kids hovered somewhere nearby too. This was just great.

"I'm Hazel." My elderly neighbor dove right in. "I've been feeding Meredith this week. She's really had a hard time."

Aryn already knew the story, but Hailey looked at me. I knew her mind was whirling. "*Meredith? Having a hard time?*" Followed up quickly by "*Meredith accepted home-cooked food from a neighbor?*"

In my defense, unless I've been in a person's home and know for a fact that they keep things tidy and wash their hands correctly, I'm not touching their food. I'd rather starve than try something that might have sticky hand germs in it. It's a quirk of mine, but I have it on good authority that there are other people who feel this way too.

21

When Hazel realized that she'd caught my friend off guard, she hurried to fill the surprised silence with more words. "Oh, maybe you aren't aware, but Meredith's father is an elderly, helpless widower, and she's had to spend some time with him this week, on account of all the snow we've gotten."

Hazel nodded as she spoke, a sympathetic expression on her wrinkled face. If she didn't see the irony of the fact that she herself was an elderly widow, I wasn't about to point it out to her.

"Is Forest sick?" Hailey asked, referring to my dad. Because while, yes, my dad was a widower and, yes, I helped him out all the time, my friends knew he wasn't helpless. He was simply distracted. "You didn't mention it."

"I offered to take him some dinner yesterday," Aryn added. "I had all that extra stroganoff left over."

"Forest is off beef," I muttered.

"Are you his Grandma?" Hillary piped in, pointing between Brooks and Hazel, which had the satisfying effect of shutting everyone up.

I watched while Brooks and Hazel looked at each other and then at my group and then back at each other. It was clear that Hazel wanted to claim him and that Brooks was trying to avoid offending her.

"They're just really, really good friends," I said to Hillary with a smile. "Like me and Hailey and Aryn. They go everywhere together."

Brooks cleared his throat and gave me a look as Hazel reached out and attempted to weave her arm through his. This was the most gratifying moment of my entire battle with Mr. VanOrman. I bit my lower lip to keep from smiling too broadly.

"What brings you two besties out this morning?" I asked, managing to tamp down on a chuckle.

"Oh, well, I always walk the 3k and with all the extra snow this week I was feeling a little worried about slipping and falling. You can't be too careful about that," Hazel replied. "I cornered Brooks here and recruited him to keep me safe. He walked the 3k with me."

"In those boots?" I asked. "Your feet must be dead."

Brooks simply shrugged as Hazel turned to him and tilted her head. "I never did ask where you were going when I waylaid you. I hope I didn't interrupt your plans for the day."

Brooks managed somewhat of a kind look in her direction before he muttered, "I was getting supplies for . . ."

"Well, anyway," Hazel interrupted with a breezy laugh, "I suppose that ship has sailed. He's not much of a talker, you know. But that works fine, because I am."

Aryn was radiating pure enjoyment over this entire interaction, and I desperately wanted to shout, "*This is gold!*" but instead I shot her a look I knew she'd be able to read as clearly as if I'd actually said the words. She nodded at the same time I felt Hailey reach out with one hand and pinch me lightly on the elbow. She was enjoying this too.

"It's getting pretty cold standing here," Brooks said. "Let's get you home, Hazel."

We said our goodbyes, and as soon as my neighbors were out of earshot, Aryn and Hailey descended on me.

"He doesn't have horns," Hailey mused.

"And he doesn't seem to be missing nearly as many brain cells as you'd described," Aryn teased.

"Who's missing brain cells?" Aryn's brother, Sean, asked as the giant trio arrived on scene.

"That guy," Aryn pointed to Brooks's back as he and Hazel rounded a corner of the YMCA building. "Only his brain cells aren't missing. Meredith was telling fibs."

"Girls do that when a guy isn't interested in them," Rory shrugged—as if this was a thing I would do, as if he knew me at all.

"Rory, just . . . no," Aryn shoved him. "Stop being such a dude. The last thing Meredith wants is to date him."

"Then what does she want?" Sean asked.

"Only to strip him of his title and make him beg for mercy," I replied with pinched eyes.

The others were silent for a minute until Ford said, "And that's the opening line of every great love story."

CHAPTER 4

The monthly HOA meetings were hosted in the main room at the community clubhouse, and tonight it smelled like leftover pizza and chlorine. It wasn't a great mix. But the mood in the room, well, it stunk way more than the leftover food and pool smells. I'd been sitting in that place of stink and disappointment for a solid twenty minutes while absurd topics were raised. Finally, I couldn't take it anymore, and I raised my hand. Brooks's eyes moved to where I was sitting in the front row of folding chairs. He immediately shook his head and mouthed the word *no* to me before looking away. I pinched my lips and raised my hand higher, wiggling my bottom slightly off the seat. Hey, my fourth graders seemed to think it worked, so why not give it a try?

Brooks—somewhat desperately, if you ask me—turned to look down the long front table at the other members of the board. None of them seemed inclined to say anything. Hazel was motioning with her eyebrows in my direction. Leland, the HOA vice president, was cleaning out his nails with a pocketknife. That just left Shayla, the treasurer. Shayla glanced at Brooks and then back at me, unsure who was the bigger threat here. Her blonde ponytail swung across her face, and I couldn't help but sympathize with her a little. She was so young. Too young, really, to be thrown into the lions' den this way. Her raging crush on Brooks wasn't helping.

"I'm sorry, Brooks," she mouthed with a shrug, her eyes immediately shifting to the paper in front of her.

"Anyone else?" Brooks looked around the crowded room, and I watched him deflate when no other hands went up.

The meeting was well attended. In fact, this was the biggest crowd we'd seen yet. I preferred to assume people were becoming civically minded rather than admitting that word was beginning to spread about the epic battles between me and the board. I wasn't interested in providing a sideshow for everyone. What I really wanted was for people to get involved and help improve things. However, while it may not have been the reason I'd want more attendees, I could use the numbers to my advantage. I was wearing the board down, that much was obvious, but I still had a ways to go.

"Miss Atwood, I suppose," Brooks said with a long-suffering sigh.

"Thank you." I stood and positioned myself directly in front of the table. No one else did this, but I felt it offered up a little special something to the viewers.

"Regarding the motion to prevent people from sharing towels in the pool area," I turned to glare down Vicki Waters, who had brought it up in the first place. She lifted her chin and held my gaze. I looked back to Brooks. "It seems to me that hiring someone whose sole purpose is to monitor towel usage is a frivolous use of money. Secondly, if people want to share, who are we to care? Share or don't share as long as you don't increase my monthly association fees and turn this place into a police state where towel sharers are shamed."

Vicki jumped to her feet. "Towel sharing is how germs spread. It's a disgusting habit, and it devalues our community."

Leland looked up from picking the dirt out from under his thumb nail. "Hear, hear, nasty business."

"Do you have data to back up your claims?" I asked.

"Meredith," Brooks interceded, "we aren't here to ask for scientific back up. We're here to discuss improvements to community living."

My eyes grew large. "You're disregarding science now?"

Brooks's shoulders moved up and down as he breathed in and out slowly. "Science—if needed—comes later in the process. For now we're simply chatting about if this is an issue we need to investigate more."

I threw my hands up. "Come on. I've been a schoolteacher for twelve years now, and one thing I can tell you is that kids don't remember which towel they brought to the pool. To try to assign malicious intent to towel sharing is beyond ridiculous."

"What about the adults who do it?" Vicki cried.

I turned partially to meet her head on. "Most married couples share far more than an occasional towel. Are you proposing to go into their homes and make sure they stop?"

There was an audible gasp followed by whispers and some laughter. I held back a smirk as Vicki's face turned red.

"That's not the same thing at all," she whined.

I shifted my shoulders, the very picture of unbothered, and turned back to the table. "Let's spend less time on these types of things and more time on important matters. Did you know that one in four children in our community are dealing with insufficient food? I'm sure some of our neighbors are counted in that number. Instead of towel police, let's use extra funds to provide lunch on the weekends, or over school breaks, to the children in our neighborhood who could use the support."

Hazel nodded at me, pleased and grandmotherly. Leland's mouth tugged down into what I hoped was a thinking expression. Shayla was putting on lip gloss and stealing glances at Brooks, who clasped his hands in front of him and looked at me for a moment. I couldn't tell if he was touched by my suggestion or plotting ways to drive me out with a pitchfork. His dark eyes were unreadable, and his mouth was a flat line.

"If they can afford to live here, they can afford food," Vicki harrumphed before sitting down. "We aren't here to vote on food. We're here to vote on towels," she added.

I shook my head at Brooks, but he only nodded. "She's right. If you'd like to put in a motion to discuss hunger needs in our area, we can discuss that next month."

"I should stop coming to these things," I muttered and sat down with a thud. These meetings were simply more proof that I was always fighting a losing battle.

"That might not be a bad idea," I heard someone behind me whisper to their seatmate.

I managed to keep my head high and my shoulders firm, but the statement sneaked into that soft place I kept well hidden . . . the spot that reminded me I was too much for most people.

"Now, Hazel had a matter to discuss," Brooks said, moving on.

Hazel preened, fluffing up her blue hair and smiling at what felt like every person in the room. "As the enforcer of bylaws, I'd like to discuss the matter of garbage and recycling cans being kept out of view from the street," she said. "It's come to the attention of the board that the Holt residence has been keeping their bins next to their garage door where they are clearly visible."

I rolled my eyes. It had come to her attention because she regularly trolled the neighborhood in her car, driving idle speed and peeping at everyone's homes to find infractions of the law while licking the tip of her pen and keeping her ticket book on her lap.

"This comes with a $600 fine," Hazel stated.

I wasn't the only person who gasped. "That's ridiculous and excessive," I blurted out.

My gosh, think about how many meals that could provide, or how many warm coats it could buy.

"Hear, hear," a few others called.

Hazel held up a wrinkled hand. "Maybe, but it's clearly in the contract that all of you signed as homeowners. The Holts have been given warnings." She flipped through her ticket book and did some quick counting. "Three warnings with no change. At this point I'll be writing an actual ticket, and they will be fined." She glanced around the room again, this time not smiling at everyone. "Let this be a firm reminder that our bylaws are to be followed."

"What will you do with that money?" I asked. "It could buy a lot of lunches for kids." Even knowing better, I couldn't help the hopeful tone in my voice.

"Or enough towels to prevent sharing," Vicki piped up.

I groaned. Hope squashed once more as Leland pointed at Vicki with his knife and nodded and Shayla blew a bubble. How old was she, anyway? Didn't bubble blowing stop in adulthood? Especially at meetings?

Brooks held up a hand. "We'll discuss what to do with it once the fine is received by Shayla."

He was actually going to let that fine go through? I balled my hands into fists in order to avoid causing another scene.

Shayla immediately brightened up at the use of her name and offered Brooks a smile that made my insides churn. It was gross. I shouldn't have cared that she flirted with him, but something about it made my stomach heave. Something about all of this made my stomach heave, and I withdrew inside myself, not really listening as the meeting wrapped up.

*****

Snow was falling again when I left the clubhouse to start walking home. I'd tuned back in during the vote on towel sharing, and I was grateful it didn't pass. Good grief, these people were legitimately bonkers to think up these things—and then to assume they mattered. But I couldn't stop thinking about that absurd fine for cans being seen from the road, or the fact that there wasn't a clear answer about how those funds would be spent after they were collected. I wanted wisdom and transparency, but all I was getting were fools blowing bubbles.

I tugged my coat tighter around me, not for the first time wondering how nice it must be to carry a little insulation as part of your body makeup. I'd been a chubby toddler, with rolls upon rolls, and a sweet, rounded tummy. In all my baby pictures, my eyes were nearly covered by cherubic cheeks when I smiled. I'd often wondered where all that padding had gone in later years. After my mom had passed, it was like my body simply didn't produce anything squishy anymore.

"For the record," Brooks's voice startled me out of my reflective moment, "and I've deeply questioned saying this to you—I thought your idea about hungry kids was the best thing I've heard in that room in months."

He'd managed to fall into step next to me without me noticing. Strange. I was usually pretty aware of my surroundings.

"Then why did you brush it off?" I asked, ignoring the pleasure his compliment brought.

He slowed his steps to match mine and tucked his hands into that same military style jacket he'd been wearing a few days before at the turkey run. "Because if I allowed every meeting to be a launching pad for suggestions, we'd be there all night. Making people submit them ahead of time keeps things moving along."

I wished I didn't appreciate him having a logical explanation. Logic was my favorite thing.

"You don't live this direction," I stated, instead.

"I'm walking your way to make sure that the snow removal guys got your driveway done this time."

"Sure." I pulled my hands out of my pockets to rub them together briskly. "Because it was such an honest mistake last time."

"It was."

"The truth is probably that Hazel invited you over to knit tonight. Besties do that."

He huffed out a breath. "Don't you think I'd be walking with Hazel right now if that were the case? And I really doubt that best friendship automatically means knitting. I can't really see you and those two friends of yours knitting anything. It's too soft. You'd be more into working with iron and steel." I didn't bother replying but offered him a sour expression. "Speaking of, I never did catch their names the other day."

I nearly smiled. "I didn't tell you their names on purpose. You're the enemy, and they're both spoken for."

This was a slight fib in that Aryn was not spoken for, although I had a feeling that wasn't going to last long based on the sudden return of a high school friend who gave me serious long-lost crush vibes—vibes that she was currently denying.

"I'm not looking for a setup," he stated.

"Of course you're not. You have Hazel."

"And how, exactly, am I the enemy when you started this little . . ." His lips pursed as he thought and waved a hand between us ". . . battle?"

We reached my driveway, and I was happy to note that it was clear. A few doors down the crew was working their way along the street. My outdoor lights were on, and the place didn't look too shabby.

"I don't start battles, VanOrman, I only win them," I said. "The driveway is all clear, so you can go home now and sleep well knowing you've served your constituents." When he didn't reply I looked his way to find he was staring at the living room window of my house. "What is it?" I asked.

"That's my question. What is that thing in your window?"

That *thing* was my cat, and I didn't appreciate his tone. "For your information, that's my cat, Betty."

"You named it?" he took a few steps closer, and Betty proceeded to arch her back and press her bum to the window.

"She only shows her backside to her enemies." I tried to say it with a straight face, but a giggle slipped out and I clamped my mouth shut.

"What . . . breed is she?"

" I don't know. Mixed."

"Between a cat and a mole rat?"

I gasped. "No. And what is a mole rat?"

"Lumpy, tiny eyes, two really large front teeth." He hooked two fingers in front of his mouth to demonstrate.

"Go home, Brooks. I'm not sure I can keep my attack feline from gnawing off your face with her huge front teeth if you come any closer." I tugged my key out of my pocket and unlocked the door, but he was still watching Betty walk along the back of my couch. "Holy Paprika, man. It's a cat. Pull yourself together," I cried.

I slammed the door behind me and then walked directly to where my fuzzy gray and white cat was lounging. Brooks was still watching through the window, so I picked her up and snuggled her under my chin. She immediately started purring, while Brooks's eyes grew large, and he pretended to heave like he was going to throw up. I yanked the drapes closed and then moved further into the house, cooing to my beautiful Betty while fighting down a smile over his antics.

"You're such a good girl," I said to her as I sat her on my bed. "Giving that mean man a direct cut that way."

I continued telling Betty about my day while I changed into a thick flannel pajama set and washed my face. She was always a good listening ear, and she never took the other side regardless of what it was. I'd found Betty three years ago in a box behind the elementary school where I worked. I'd asked a lot of questions, and when no one had answers, I'd claimed her for myself. Betty was definitely not a suave and sophisticated looking cat, but she had pride and honor. She had grit and strength. Which is exactly why I'd chosen the name Betty, in honor of women's rights activist Betty Friedan. As far as I was concerned, both my cat and the real Betty were tough cookies who inspired me to keep going strong.

Also, my Betty was fuzzy and kept my lap warm.

My phone rang, interrupting my monologue to the cat, and I found it in my purse. It was my sister Willow, which didn't really surprise me. Thanksgiving was only a few days away, and we hadn't talked details yet.

"Hey," I answered, flopping down on my bed next to Betty.

"Did you hear dad's back on beef and off of poultry?" Willow said without greeting. "Poultry. As in turkey. At Thanksgiving."

"It's still a few days away; he'll come around," I replied.

"And Ash says her boyfriend . . . Jasper? Josh? Jake? . . . Whatever his name is, he's vegetarian." Willow sounded more tired than truly annoyed, something I couldn't relate to as I was typically actually annoyed. "So, what does that mean for us? We're doing a tofurkey, or whatever it's called, and pretending we're all happy about that?"

"His name is Jake, and how is he vegetarian? Doesn't he run a fishing expedition, outdoor shop thing? People hire him to catch, gut, and cook fish."

"Maybe he's one of those people who doesn't consider fish to be meat?" Willow offered.

I laughed. "Look, we're still going to cook a turkey. We'll make sure there are plenty of side dishes and other choices for Jake. Ash doesn't expect us to cater to him."

Now it was her turn to laugh. "I'm sorry, are we both talking about Ash? She absolutely expects us to cater. That's all we've done, every day of her life. That's what happens when you're the baby with no mom. We spoiled her rotten."

"Well, someone had to be spoiled," I retorted lightly. "Might as well have been her."

"I guess." We were both lost in our thoughts and memories for a second before Willow pressed on. "So, assignments. Same as usual?"

"Yeah. Tell Ash to bring drinks. Those are easy with traveling. When will she be here?"

"Tomorrow night. She wants to stay with you."

I was caught off guard by the request. "She always stays with Dad, though."

"Says she doesn't want to this year, with Jake and all."

"What about you?" I asked.

Ash had always gravitated toward Willow. It made sense. Willow was like her name, flowing wherever the breeze blew with strong roots that kept her grounded. She was practically my twin in physical traits, small and dark with sharp edges and bright blue eyes, but my opposite on the inside. While I wore business clothing and kept my hair short and straight, she wore flowing pants and scarves, her hair hanging in beachy waves down her back. While I'd been busy making chore charts, paying bills, and keeping everyone in line, Willow had been Ash's soft spot and place of comfort. She'd been that for me too when I'd needed it. Of the three of us, Willow had been the one with Dad's artistic tendencies, but she'd never left reality to pursue them.

"I can clear out some space above my shop if you'd rather they stay with me," she offered.

Willow owned a clothing boutique on Main Street called Willow Wood. Yep. That's right. Dropping a few letters off our last name had produced a cutesy sounding store name. Go Mom and Dad. Anyhow, she lived in a studio apartment above the shop, which meant tight quarters.

"Sorry," I replied, "I'm surprised, I guess, but they're totally welcome here."

"I think she's hoping to ease Jake into the whole Forest Atwood situation, you know. Better to stay off site and give him some breathing room between interactions."

"Yeah. I can see that. Hey, Jake isn't allergic to cats, is he?"

Willow made a humming noise. "No idea. But even if he is, it's like two or three nights; he'll be okay."

"Cat allergies can be rough, Willow," I chuckled.

"So can staying with Forest."

We wrapped up the conversation, and I turned off the lamp when we were finished.

"Well, Betty," I said as I stroked her fur in the darkness. "Looks like we're having guests this week. I hope they like you."

CHAPTER 5

I should have been more worried about Betty hating Jake than about whatever allergies Jake might have had to cats.

Immediately upon my opening the door to Ash's bright smile with Jake standing behind her, Betty launched herself onto Jake's leg and bit his kneecap before letting out some sort of jungle call and zigzagging across the room and under the couch.

After getting over the shock, Jake, who proved to be a forgiving soul, carried their luggage to the guest room where Betty had launched out of the closet and onto his back as he bent over to set down the bags. How she'd gotten from the living room to the guest closet was a mystery. Nevertheless, she wrapped her front legs around his neck and screeched to raise the roof while Jake ran out of the guest room and into my kitchen screaming as loud as the cat was. Gray fuzz flew, and so did some spittle from Jake's mouth, although I'd never dream of mentioning it.

As Ash and I chased the whirling pair around the room, trying to pry Betty off before she managed to mangle his jugular and send him to the hospital, I started to wonder if Betty might have slipped from the pro-feminist movement straight into anti-male rhetoric. It was a troubling thought, for sure. Man-hating was a slippery slope.

Jake's neck was now bandaged, and he had a scratch over one hazel eye. Luckily, his hair was a little long in the front, so I figured he could cover it. It wasn't easy, but we got Betty firmly closed in my bathroom where she seemed to be going through some sort of mental breakdown. I doubted I'd find my towels all in one piece.

Ash sat on my couch, Jake next to her as she squeezed his hand, and he tried to offer her a smile. We were all breathing heavily, my navy shirt sticking to my back with nerve sweat followed by horrified sweat followed by relieved sweat. My body was probably on the verge of dehydration at this point.

"You, uh, have a nice home," Jake finally said.

A hysterical laugh I'd been trying to tamp down on forced itself out of my throat, and I gave into it. "It's really nice to meet you."

As the three of us laughed, I finally had a chance to inspect my youngest sister's boyfriend. Jake was on the shorter side, which had been convenient for reaching the cat wrapped around his neck, with the muscular build of a man whose entire existence was built around being outdoors. His skin was tan, with laugh lines around his hazel eyes, and his hair had a few last summer sun streaks in the darker locks that were coming on with the winter. All in all, he looked solid and kind, dependable—a guy you'd rely on during an emergency. It was really all I'd ever hoped my sisters would find.

"That wasn't quite the welcome I'd expected," Ash wiped some makeup from under her amused eyes. "I didn't know Jake was going to cause a crack in the force."

"I think Betty might be going through puberty," I grinned.

"I had no idea she hated men," Ash added. "Then again, I doubt you've had much of a chance to test that theory."

The look she gave me was sly and so sister-ish that she deserved the pillow I threw at her. "I've had guys here before."

"Sure. The plumber, the furniture delivery guy, the appliance repairman." She turned to Jake with a giggle. "Meredith hates men. That's probably where her cat gets it."

My jaw flew open, and I reacted in spite of knowing she was purposely pushing my buttons and didn't mean a word of it. "That's not true. I love men. I think they're very . . ." I shook my head, digging for words, which only made Ash laugh again. "Good looking. They're good looking and, handy to . . . have . . around . . . with their, you know, muscles and, um . . ."

"Like I said. No men for Meredith. She wouldn't date a guy if I paid her to."

I leaned back into the chair cushion and folded my arms across my chest. "Not true. I'd accept your money, but I've dated without it."

"Name one guy, just one, that you've gone out with since Ron."

I pouted, and Jake's eyes grew large. "Ron sounds interesting."

"Ron couldn't handle this," I gestured at myself. "He tucked tail and ran."

"He lasted a year, though," Ash said, as though he deserved an award for sticking it out.

"So, I can be a lot," I said.

"Some guys like 'a lot'," Jake replied easily.

I nodded. "I like this one, Ash. Does he have any brothers?"

Ash laughed and kissed him on the cheek. "No. But he does have a sister who trains dogs. She may be able to consult with you about your rabid cat."

"Betty isn't rabid." I pursed my lips in thought. "You know, she did show a guy her bum the other day. Maybe that was a sign."

Ash and Jake both looked at me like I should be in the bathroom shredding towels with my cat. "Please, go on," Ash said at last.

"Well, I was talking to a neighbor outside, and she turned and pushed her bum to the window," I smiled remembering. "He said she was hideous."

"He called Betty ugly?" Ash frowned. "She's adorable."

"I know."

"Terrifying, but adorable. Who was this guy?" Ash asked. "The guy you were talking to?"

32

I shrugged. "The HOA president. He's a royal pain." An extra loud yowl came from my room, and I jumped to my feet. "I think I'd better go check on her."

"Do you have any little kitty handcuffs to put on her? Maybe a kitty straightjacket?" Ash asked.

"Oh, stop. You're getting to stay here for free, so you can't complain," I retorted.

"Uh . . . I think a price has already been paid. In blood." She patted Jake's shoulder.

I stuck my tongue out at her right as a crash sounded. Straightjacket indeed.

*****

The next morning I awoke with Betty laying on my face and the sounds of laughter coming from my kitchen. I'd eventually gotten the poor animal settled down, but she refused to leave my room, and so I'd had to move the litter box into the corner. She really, really did not want anything to do with Jake. I couldn't say that I understood her aversion. Jake was nice enough, totally non-threatening with his big, warm smile. Everything he'd said so far had been friendly, and he watched Ash like he'd won the lottery.

Willow's soft laugh floated to my room, and I realized my sisters were already starting to cook without me. I gently removed Betty from my forehead and climbed out from under the covers. After a quick splash of water on my face and some mouthwash, I made my way into the kitchen where my two sisters were still in their pajamas too. Jake was dressed in actual day clothing, but that was okay. If he was still around next year, we'd get him some flannel pajamas to wear. We may always eat at Dad's house, but we always cooked at mine. And we always did it wearing pj's.

Dad's appliances were worn out, with only one burner working, and only one of the heating coils in his oven ever showed up to help. The problem was you never knew which heating coil it was going to be. We wanted delicious food to help balance out the day. Plus, Dad never joined us in cooking and chatting, so what did it matter where we prepared?

"I hear you're a vegetarian," I said to Jake as I rounded the corner into the warm room. He nodded. "That sucks on Thanksgiving."

He smiled, as I hoped he would, and shook his head. "There's so much food planned that I won't even miss the turkey."

"Well, when you only see each other once a year, you tend to throw a big party."

Willow looked up from where she was taking groceries out of a bag, her long hair tied behind her with a bandanna. "Hey, I see you way more than once a year."

"And I feel so lucky," I said in a robotic voice that had her tossing a mixing spoon at me.

Ash laughed, her teeth flashing as she worked to braid her long, light brown hair down the side. "I brought some herbs from my garden to use this year," she said, nodding toward a basket she'd placed on my counter. "They're so good."

My phone dinged several times in a row from the kitchen counter, where I charged it at night. I took seriously the warning to keep screens out of the bedroom. It seemed logical to me. As my sisters circled around Ash's herb stash, I picked up the device and unlocked the screen.

Hailey: Happy Thanksgiving everyone. Whip, whip, hooray!
Aryn: Let's give them pumpkin to talk about
Ruby: Pie am so grateful for you ladies
Lizzie: Let's get basted

Ah, the annual pun parade had arrived. A smiled tugged at my lips as I thought about how to respond. None of them would be satisfied until we'd all contributed. And really, it might be silly, but it was so like my group of friends that an affectionate tug behind my rib cage had me laughing as a pun popped into my head.

Me: Nobody puts gravy in a corner
Aryn: How's Ash's boyfriend?
Me: I like him, but Betty attacked him. Mercilessly
Ruby: Does he need stitches? I'm free to consult over the phone. Dad is currently shoving the turkey into hot oil, so I won't be free after the explosion, but I can call you now

I laughed silently as I replied.

Me: No stitches. Betty won't leave my room though
Lizzie: I always knew your cat was a man-hater
Me: She is not
Lizzie: She is
Ruby: Definite man-hater
Aryn: She might be a people-hater in general. She scares me

Time for a subject change.

Me: My dad says he's off turkey
Aryn: I thought it was beef
Ruby: Forest likes to switch up his aversions
Me: I'm cooking turkey anyway
Aryn: Good for you. He'll probably eat it
Lizzie: Turkeys are so cute, I do feel a little bad every year
Ruby: Did you know they're actually really smart and good at geography
Hailey: They taste good too

I laughed at Hailey's reply, which had my sisters looking my way. I hurried to sign off with my friends, knowing these conversations could last a while and also knowing that my focus needed to be on this rare family time.

Me: Love you guys. Hope there's nothing fowl about your day. Bye

Everyone chimed in with one last goodbye, and I put my phone down. Clapping my hands together, I looked to the trio waiting for me, and smiled.
"Game on."
"Game on," my sisters replied.

*****

Dad's house was cold when our party entered through the back door. It had snowed a little more since I'd been by to shovel, but the slim walkway from the driveway up the back steps was still usable. Dad's truck was parked in the rickety carport; however, the house was dark and quiet, with all the drapes closed.

"Heat off again?" Willow asked as she pushed passed me to set her armload of food on the green kitchen counter. She swiped her bangs off her forehead and put her hands on her hips as she surveyed everything. "It was on when I fed him last week."

"A lot can change in a week," I muttered, unloading my own items onto the scarred wooden table and trying to keep my tone light and airy.

I glanced at Ash's face and then at Jake's, concerned that this was going to make Ash uncomfortable, having Jake see the place in all its glory. But Ash seemed to be taking it in stride—head high, smile in place as she walked to the range and put the still-warm stuffing on the cooktop. She threw open the oven door, the screeching of unused hinges deafening in the silence, and motioned for Jake to put the foil-covered bird inside.

"Jake, do you mind grabbing the rest?" Ash asked him as she fiddled with the knobs on the oven, trying to set it to warm.

Jake lightly tugged at her braid and gave her shoulder a squeeze. She looked his way, and I watched as a world of unspoken things passed between them. Not for the first time, I wondered how that would feel, to have someone be able to understand and speak to you without words . . . to be part of a unit that didn't even require actual sound in order to communicate. I pressed a hand against my stomach to ward off the unwanted emotion and flipped the light switch, grateful for the buzz of fluorescents.

"Power's on," I whispered to Willow who mouthed, *"That's something"* in response.

"He knows we're coming, right?" Ash asked through tight lips the moment Jake was out of earshot. Her cheerful facade slipped as she turned and leaned her back against the stove. Her green eyes had become frosty, and I thought maybe I *could* communicate without words because I understood exactly what she was

35

thinking. "It's Thanksgiving today. I drove a boatload of hours to be here. Oh, and the oven doesn't want to kick on."

Willow was quick to soothe. "Of course he knows. He's probably getting cleaned up right now."

"I don't hear the groaning of water running upstairs," Ash stated. Now she crossed her arms across her narrow chest. "I brought Jake here, against my better judgment, because we've been together for a while now, and it's time."

"Hey, now." It was my turn to jump in. "He still got to meet me and Willow, right? And we're worth coming to see."

Ash's stance relaxed, and she nodded, reaching up to pull her braid over her shoulder and fidget with the ends. "Yeah. You're right. It's just so . . . embarrassing sometimes."

The three of us nodded, completely understanding the years of emotion behind this moment. Embarrassment gets exhausting. You'd think at some point you'd lose the capacity to be humiliated, but none of us had found that stopping point yet. We jumped back into motion when Jake returned, his arms loaded up, his smile still in place.

"I'll go find Dad." I forced a nonchalant tone and left the kitchen.

I snagged my phone, knowing I needed an outlet for my own frustration and that it couldn't be my sisters. It was never my sisters because of choices I'd made long ago. While none of my friends had grown up in my house, they knew enough to be supportive and had proven many times that I could depend on them for a quick vent.

Me: House is dark and cold. No sign of my dad. Ash is mad
Ruby: Does it smell like dead people?
Me: No. But it might soon
Aryn: Is he in his workshop?
Hailey: Shoot, did the power get turned off again?
Me: Workshop doors are closed. House lights are working. Gas might be off though. It's chilly and the oven isn't working
Aryn: Sorry about Ash
Me: Jake is being cool. Poor guy
Ruby: Do you need blankets?
Me: No. I need Forest to show his face and explain himself

At the top of the stairs, I knocked on my dad's closed bedroom door. When there was no reply, I opened it and entered the darkened space. Dad had always slept with light dampening shades because, as a dedicated artist, he created whenever the mood hit and slept when he could. As a result, although it was sunny outside, my eyes were having a hard time making sense of anything in the room.

"Dad?" I called. There was a moaning sound from the direction of the bed. "We're all here. The food is ready."

"Food?" he mumbled.

"It's Thanksgiving. Ash is here with her boyfriend."

"Ash?"

"Your youngest daughter." My tone was deeply sarcastic, and I knew it. My phone dinged, saving him from my sharp tongue.

Aryn: Any luck?

Me: Found him in bed. How illegal is patricide?

Ruby: I think you have a case

Lizzie: Is he sick?

Me: No. Probably stayed up too late

Hailey: Can you get heat going in the house?

Me: Still figuring that out

"Dad, why is the house so cold?" I asked. My eyes had adjusted enough that I watched as he moved into a sitting position. "Did the gas get turned off?"

He rubbed his face. "Maybe."

"Maybe?" I asked, striving to keep my tone light.

"You know I'm not good at keeping up with bills, and I'm usually outside anyway."

I sucked in my lips and took a deep breath. "Dad. It's Thanksgiving. Take a shower, wake up a little, and then you're going to eat some turkey with your daughters and meet Jake."

"I don't eat . . ."

I held up a hand. "Today, you eat turkey, okay?"

He actually looked at me and nodded. "Always loved a good turkey."

A smart choice on his part.

When I arrived back down in the living spaces, there was a fire crackling in the wood burning stove, and someone had placed the bowl of mashed potatoes on top of it. At least we all agreed that if something had to go cold, it would not be the potatoes. Cold potatoes are the total worst.

I walked into the kitchen with loose limbs and an easy smile. "Dad had a late night and overslept. He's going to take a quick shower and be right down." They all smiled back and offered words of relief, although my sisters' eyes held some questions. "I'm going to run down to the basement and see if the furnace went out overnight."

I hated the basement of this old house. As a child it had been the stuff of nightmares. As a teen I'd conquered my fears, mostly by channeling them into anger, and made peace with the place. But I still hated going down into the dank space. I knew it was a lost cause and that Dad had forgotten to pay the bill—or possibly didn't have the funds to cover it—but I loved putting on a good show. The *Meredith Can Do It* show had been playing for about a million seasons with no series end in sight. I startled as the pipes gave a loud groan, signaling that Dad had turned on the upstairs shower. The water heater sputtered, and I realized that with no gas, his shower would probably be short and cold.

So, sue me if I smiled a little about that.

It only took me about three seconds to discern that the gas was definitely off, and I pushed down my frustration as I went back upstairs. The others were in the living area gathered around the stove. The table had been set while I'd harassed Dad and checked the basement, and the food was waiting in the kitchen, laid out along the counter with serving spoons ready.

"Okay, we don't have gas today," I said in the most 'isn't this silly' tone I could muster. "So, we'll hang around in this room. The fire will keep us warm enough."

"Cool. It'll be kind of like camping," Jake stated, rubbing a hand down Ash's stiff back.

She relaxed a bit and smiled at him. "Yeah. Only with better food and a flushing toilet." Then Ash jokingly looked at me. "The toilet does flush, right?"

We laughed, even if it was stilted, and all fell into our practiced roles of forced cheer. The thing was that over the years we'd come to realize that forced cheer often turned into genuine cheer, so we got comfortable and settled in.

"You'll call the gas company?" Willow asked me quietly. I nodded. "He's got to be a couple of months behind. They don't turn it off after the first missed month."

"Sad that we know that," I replied.

"Agreed."

"I'm ready for some turkey," Dad's voice broke into the room followed by his body itself. He was wearing an old green knit sweater and corduroy pants—some sort of artist's throwback outfit. His white hair was long around his shoulders, and his facial hair was scruffy, but he looked awake and alert and somewhat present in the moment. "Who's carving?"

"Meredith," Ash and Willow said in unison. "It's tradition."

And it had been, ever since I'd carved my first turkey at the ripe old age of eight. Nothing dangerous about that.

"Mr. Atwood," Jake piped up, standing from the couch as Dad fully entered. "I'm Jake Baird. So nice to finally meet you."

Dad shook his hand and then tugged him close, inspecting the face that was slightly below eye level with his. "Your eyes are the perfect example of russet brown."

Jake blinked. "Thank you. I always thought they were hazel."

Dad let him go and nodded. "Too many browns to be truly hazel, but what do I know about eyes? I've been working on a mosaic and been having a hard time nailing down the right color of brown. I think it's russet."

He looked at the back door and began to head that way, but Willow snagged his sleeve and sat him down at the table. "Food first, Dad. Russet later."

"Sure, of course. Sorry. You girls know how it is when I get an idea in my head." He looked around at us as we each took our seats. His smile was warm and kind, and I remembered many times feeling like my dad's focus was the same as a sunbeam shining down on you. It was so glorious, so warming when it happened, that you managed to hang on until it happened again, no matter how cold it was in between. "Your mom would be so proud of all of you." He didn't mention Mom much, so when he did, we all tuned in. "She had a lot of hopes for you three."

When he didn't continue, I watched Ash's shoulders slump before she forced a smile back onto her face and said, "I think we've smelled this food for long enough. I'm starving. Let's eat."

"Carve it up, Mer," Willow added.

"Don't forget to save the wishbone," Dad added. "Wishes are too important to throw away."

If only I still believed in them at all.

CHAPTER 6

B lack Friday found me where it always did—helping at Willow's boutique during the morning rush. Usually I had time to go to breakfast at Angie's, where I got the Benedict Arnold breakfast—add avocado, thank you—and sipped hot cocoa while pepping myself up for the onslaught of cheery shoppers in a tiny space. Today, however, I'd overslept, thanks to Ash and Jake challenging me to a game of Monopoly after we'd returned from Thanksgiving dinner.

Here's the thing about me and games: I'm out to win. I *will* read the rule book, I *will* adhere to every single printed word, and I *will* call you on it if you try to deviate. I'm totally unwilling to use shortcuts or give up after several consecutive hours because others are bored. The game must be played to conclusion.

Yes, I have enough self-awareness to understand that I can be rigid and suck the joy out of game playing. Ash knows this about me, and she still challenged me to a game. This is because Ash is the cutthroat of the family and likes to try to bring me and Willow to our knees. Between the two of us games aren't good fun— they're more like military matches. Still, the blame lay firmly on her shoulders, which is exactly what I told Willow when I slipped through the doorway separating the back of her shop from the sales floor and found her at the register.

I was dressed in a sweatshirt and leggings, which did not fit the shop's aesthetic, and I was expecting to hear about it, so I headed it off with a shrug. "Yeah, I know," I said, gesturing to my outfit with a quick, jerky movement. "Not Willow Wood dress code."

"You're late," she said with a fake smile in case customers were watching. "I thought we said 7:00."

I smiled back, as plastic looking as her. "Ash made me play Monopoly."

Willow rolled her blue eyes in the same exact pattern I always did. "She should know better. Jake will never stay with her now that he's seen her in evil mode."

I shrugged. "Her own fault. She knew what she was getting into."

Willow tugged at a green and red-checked headband that was slipping down her forehead. "You know, just once you could have called the game and gone to bed." I pressed my lips together and slitted my eyes. She threw up her hands, bright silver rings sparkling on every finger. "Fine, fine. I know." She sighed and smiled when it caught the attention of a shopper nearby. "Anyhow, can you clear out the dressing rooms? They're already sloppy."

"At 7:45 in the morning?"

"Happy Black Friday," she chirped before moving toward a pair of women who seemed to be arguing over a tote bag in the corner.

I moved to the side of the store where two makeshift dressing rooms had been created using curtains. Sure enough, there were heaps of flowing tunics and breezy pants dotting the floor. Skirts and dresses in patterns I'd never agree to wear were dangling from hooks with their hangers on the floor. Scarves of every color were thrown over the curtain walls. Basically, people can be the worst sometimes. All my life I'd heard the phrase, "Their mother surely raised them better than that" and I'd thought to myself, I only had a mother until I was six, and I'm not lazy or messy. My point? People control themselves. Their mothers aren't to blame. (Okay, some mothers are, but that's not the majority.) I maintain that people should take responsibility for their own actions.

I started by wrapping the scarves in layers around my neck until I could barely move my head and their extra length dangled down each side of my body. Then I grabbed clothing items and hung them over my arms until I could hardly waddle. I completed the look by gathering hangers in my empty hands and holding onto them as I headed toward the back of the store, where I could spread it all out on a big table, sort it, fold or rehang, and then bring them back into the main area. As I was walking I felt a tug on the end of one of the scarves. I barely had time to register that one of them had slipped and someone was standing on it before I was pitching forward. I reached out my hands to break the fall, which only ended in a pile of nice, pointy hangers covered by all the clothing on my arms creating a seriously sharp nest for me to land on. Sadly, the scarf was pulling at my neck, and so while I was on my hands and knees, I was looking straight up. It was not a comfortable position to be in.

I tried to turn my head to call attention to my predicament because clearly the person responsible for my torture was oblivious to the fact that they were standing on the scarf.

"Hey, can you move your feet?" I called over my shoulder. Nothing happened. "Hello?" I called louder. "I'm being slowly suffocated here."

"That seems to be a slight exaggeration," a mellow, deep voice replied as the scarf loosened and I was able to let my head fall forward. "No loss of color, your lips aren't blue, and you're still yelling at people."

I sat back on my knees and yanked the offending scarf toward me as I turned, already knowing I'd find Brooks standing there. I was sure it was my imagination, but the temperature in the store seemed to heat by several degrees, and I fought off an unwanted blossom of warmth as he looked down at me.

"Why?" popped out of my mouth without forethought.

He shrugged. "I'm not sure. I've been paying attention, though, and yelling seems to be your primary communication method."

I struggled to my feet and shook my head, tugging the scarves free now that I knew they were a literal death trap. "No, I mean why are you here? This isn't the type of place I'd expect you to shop," I said to him. "But if you're in the market for lounge pants, I think black would be a good color for you. You know, to match your heart." His face remained expressionless, but I noticed a spark in his eyes that I wasn't sure how to read.

"Can I help with that pile of clothing and hangers you dropped?"

"Absolutely not. But it's nice to know you can be so helpful in an emergency," I said as I bent to scoop the pile.

"In an actual emergency, I'm very helpful."

I wrestled the outfits and hangers, giving up on separating them, and held them in a bundle against my chest as he disregarded my instructions and bent to pick up an armful himself. In the small store we were sharing a miniature space, and I noticed the smell of spice and mint coming off him. I whipped my head around, not wanting to know what he smelled like, and a piece of my hair got stuck in my mouth. I blew at it, but it was lodged, and he chuckled as I fought with it. The sound reminded me that others were probably watching our little interaction, so I cleared my throat and turned to walk away. I blew at the hair in my mouth again, and it didn't want to budge. Aggravating.

Brooks followed me through the door into the back of the shop.

I slammed the clothing/hanger pile onto the table and spun to face him as I tugged that blasted hair out of my teeth. "You can't be back here."

He set his armload of things next to mine and leaned a hip against the table. "Is this where you come when you aren't polluting young minds?" he asked.

He shrugged out of his jacket and rolled up his sleeves, giving me a flash of a forearm tattoo that I was suddenly ravenously curious about. His jeans were wet around the ankles as though he'd walked through some slush this morning, and his hair seemed a little damp. He looked . . . relaxed. Completely at home here, maybe even entertained by the situation. To borrow an old phrase of my grandmother's— may she rest in peace—it got my dander up. This was my world, and he did not get to find it a comfy place to be.

I scowled, folding my own arms, which made the big sleeves on my sweatshirt puff out oddly. "Polluting young minds? Please. No one cares more about those kids than I do. I don't know where you get your ideas."

"I've been wondering when you'll bring your little ten-year-old army to one of the HOA meetings and stage a coup."

He was smiling. It wasn't big, and his lips had barely shifted, but his eyes were dancing a jig. He was enjoying this. Why? Men didn't usually react this way to me. In fact, they typically ran, accused me of being a harpy, or fought back twice as hard. I didn't know what to make of him. He raised his eyebrows as I continued to analyze him. It was as though he didn't realize that we had an unspoken 'avoid each other at all costs' understanding. I was baffled by his continuing to hang around and by the fact that this interaction, while annoying for sure, wasn't exactly terrible.

"Do you truly not realize that customers aren't allowed back here?" I gestured around me. "You need to get back to selecting a pretty bracelet to match your tunic."

He pushed his hands into his pockets, and I did not try to sneak another peek at that tattoo. "Bracelets look really good on me, and I can pull off a tunic like you wouldn't believe. If it hits me midthigh, watch out ladies."

A laugh huffed out of me without asking permission, and I clamped down on it. "Brooks."

"Meredith."

"Why are you here?"

"I like to make sure that my strangulation victims are okay before I take my leave."

I put my hands on my hips. "I'm fine. Besides, I'd have thought you'd want to applaud yourself for strangling me."

"You lived, so there's really nothing to applaud."

I sucked in my lips and shook my head. "Why are in you in my sister's shop?"

He glanced around. "Your sister owns this?"

"Yes."

"I always figured you were an only child."

I blinked. *Don't ask, don't ask, it's a trap* . . . "Why?"

"Temper tantrums, insisting on things being your way, general moodiness. It's really fascinating stuff."

It certainly wasn't the first time someone had listed out my boorish qualities, so I was unruffled. "Joke's on you, those are my best qualities. Your inability to stand up to ridiculous ideas tells me you're a middle child."

His teeth looked white against his black beard. "Actually, I'm the baby. Just an older brother."

"As the oldest child myself, I feel for him."

He chuckled. "You know, the management here might be interested to know that you're not treating the customers very kindly."

I batted my lashes. "Welcome to Willow Wood." I pointed. "Now go before my sister gets after me for you being back here. Sisters are much scarier than management."

He lifted his hands, palms outs, surrendering with good cheer. "I'm going, I'm going. Fashion calls." He made it to the doorway and turned back toward me. "By the way, this is one of Hazel's favorite stores. I'm getting her something for Christmas."

"You buy Hazel Christmas presents?"

One shoulder lifted in time with the side of his mouth. "I find that keeping on her good side has its advantages."

And with that, the singularly strangest interaction I'd had with him came to a close. I was left standing by the clothing pile I'd hauled in, watching him walk to the register to make a purchase. Had he been holding something this whole time and I hadn't noticed? I watched as he spoke to Willow, her smile broad and welcoming in a way I'd never be capable of. He said something that made her laugh, and my shoulders sagged. Why was everyone so bewitched by the man that had stolen my dream and sparred with me on several occasions?

Heck, why was I a little bewitched myself?

He glanced back at me, catching me watching, and offered a wave before exiting the store. I shook my head, blinked a few times, and put him back into his slot as evil job stealer. It was more comfortable if he stayed in his assigned category.

As soon as he was gone, Willow hustled back to where I was standing.

"He said he knows you," she stated, eyes alight. "Who is he?"

"He's the HOA president I've been at war with." My voice was gloomy even to my own ears. "His name is Brooks."

"That's him? Your main opponent?" Her brows wrinkled. "But he's nice and gives off such a sunny vibe."

"Of course he is and does. It's all part of the persona he puts on."

"Hmm. Well, at least while you're engaged in battle the view is pretty." She pinched my upper arm. "Because that man is easy to look at."

"Easy to look at might be a stretch," I replied.

Willow gave me a knowing look. "Mer, he may not be textbook handsome, but there's something really appealing about him."

"I'm ignoring you," I said. She laughed and left to go help more customers.

I got to work sorting the clothing items in front of me. The image of Brooks standing there with his little half-smile didn't want to dissipate. If I really concentrated I could still smell that spicy scent he'd brought with him. His eyes were a little too hooded for my taste, his brow strong. And if one felt like being unkind, they could mention that he had thick eyebrows that were in danger of unifying at some point. But, yeah, his build was okay, and his height was, you know, not terrible. He could consider doing something about the curly hair on his head that wasn't ever totally tamed. I'd also really like to stop wondering what his two tattoos were of and why he'd chosen to get them.

A few minutes later a flurry of activity caught my attention as Lizzie and Aryn arrived.

"Willow said Brooks was here," Lizzie said, grabbing my arm and tugging me in for a hug. "What did he want?"

I allowed her to hug me because Lizzie always thought hugs were the answer before gently pulling back. "He said he was shopping for Christmas gifts."

"Do you believe him? Or is he stalking you to get more ammo for your next HOA meeting?" Lizzie asked.

For the first time that morning, my face split into a full smile. "I love, love, love that you went dark like that."

Aryn cracked up too. "We have reason to be suspicious."

I turned back to the clothes that needed to be hung. "True, but I believe him. It is Black Friday, after all, and he had no idea I'd be here."

"Was he a jerk?" Lizzie asked.

"He must have been nice, Liz, considering Willow was floating a bit out there," Aryn piped in.

I swallowed hard, an unfamiliar tingle starting in my chest. "Do you think Willow liked him, liked him?" I asked.

Aryn tipped her head back and forth. "Hard to say. Does she giggle a lot?"
My family was not known for its giggling. "No. Not really."
 Her face grew speculative. "At the very least, she found him interesting."
"And cute," Lizzie added. "She mentioned he was cute. What does he look like?"

"He's cute," Aryn confirmed, and the tingling in my chest changed to a rock in my stomach. "It catches you by surprise. Like, if you passed him on the street you'd maybe not look twice, but when you have a few minutes to look at him you start to think, 'Hey, this guy's kind of . . .'" She trailed off as she looked down at me.

"No, please go on telling me how cute you think my enemy is," I grumped, accidentally dropping the garment from the hanger I was holding.

Aryn's expression was pensive, and she patted me on the shoulder. I didn't like the way she looked like she was unlocking a mystery, so I spun away to pick up the dropped item.

"Anyhooooow . . ." Lizzie jumped in. "Does Willow have any of those kid jumpers left? I want to get Sally something for Christmas," she said, referring to her soon-to-be stepdaughter. Lizzie was getting married to her secret high school crush in less than a month.

I nodded. "Yeah. I saw some by the front window."

Lizzie zipped out. "I gotta get them before they sell out."

"You okay?" Aryn asked as Lizzie's honey blonde curls bounced out of sight.

I shook my head, clearing the haze that hadn't lifted since Brooks's appearance. "Yeah. Just . . . feels like my two worlds collided, and suddenly everyone is on Team Brooks, and I'm struggling to catch up." She offered a sympathetic smile. "He tried to choke me with a scarf, you know."

Her eyebrows rose. "Total truth or embellishment?"

"Embellishment."

"So, what are you going to do about it?"

A smile bloomed on my face, and I was reminded once again exactly why I'd chosen the group of friends I had.

*****

Monday morning found me in the last place anyone wants to be—even as an adult: the principal's office. Sure, it's spelled with 'pal' on the end because you're supposed to be tricked into thinking they're your ally. But some things never change from childhood. He's still the boss, he's still a little stern, and you still leave feeling like you did something wrong. Maybe it's just me. My friends didn't seem to share the same feeling. They thought he was a great boss. I was used to having a different opinion, though, and wasn't letting peer pressure cloud my judgment.

Regardless, I was sitting across the desk from John Wall after school when I was supposed to be enjoying Recap and Recoup with my friends. I found myself wishing Brooks had stepped a little harder on that scarf.

45

"Miss Atwood," he began, offering me a smile. That's another thing—he never called me by my first name. He called my friends by their first names. With me, it was always so formal. "We've officially entered the holiday season, and this year the Parent Teacher Association would like to put on an evening of cookies and Santa for the families."

He'd lost me as soon as he said PTA. Sure, they did great work and the school couldn't run without them, but the keyword here was *work*. Whenever I got roped in by the PTA, it was going to mean busting my chops and putting on a happy face about it. Another thing my friends didn't agree with me on. They wholeheartedly supported the PTA, which made me wonder how I'd gotten called in.

"Is this a new thing?" I asked, for something to say. It seemed benign enough.

"Yes. This year. We'll try it out, and if it's successful, we'll make it a new tradition."

How special, I thought. I'd spent half my life trying not to hate the idea of Santa and the other half trying to pretend I thought it was good fun. The truth is that Santa is really painful for kids who learn early on not to expect him to come. Even more painful for kids trying to play Santa for their younger siblings. I was definitely not the right fit for whatever Mr. Wall had up his sleeves. I didn't have much holiday spirit.

"We'd like you to head it up," he stated, folding his hands over his stomach.

I smacked my lips together. "I see."

"Is that something you can do? We'll let you select a committee from the staff, and, of course, there are some members of the PTA to assist as well."

Oh, they'd *let* me. How kind. "I think it's only fair I warn you that I have an extreme aversion to the fat man in red."

Mr. Wall ran his tongue over his teeth, making his lips pop out. "You're telling me you don't like Santa?" Obviously his tone was one of disbelief. Nobody hates Santa.

"Yes."

"And this would prevent you from overseeing a family event involving him?"

"Without getting too much into my life history, I lack the holiday cheer necessary to dive in."

He nodded. "Okay. Well, I have to be honest with you. It's your turn to head up something from the staff side of things, and it's this or the end-of-year carnival. Since you seem to have an aversion to PTA events in general, I had felt this was the lesser of the two evils. But I'll let you decide."

What kind of choice was that, really? I could throw together some cookies and arrange a visit by Santa with the help of a committee, or I could run the always over the top end-of-year carnival. Ten hours of work verses one million.

"I'll take Santa," I replied.

"I thought you might. Choose your committee from the staff, and I'll get you the info on the PTA members who signed up. Let me know who will be helping you." He sat up and scribbled a note on a pad of paper.

"Is there a date for this event?"

"Saturday, December 17th."

Only three days before Lizzie's wedding. Bad luck. I was sure I'd be helping with last-minute bride freak-outs and emotional meltdowns at that same point in time. Still . . . it was this or the carnival. Even the word carnival made me shudder.

"Okay." I stood. "I'll keep you posted."

I hustled directly across the hall to Ruby's health nurse room, hoping my friends were there and hadn't already dispersed to their own classrooms. Thankfully, when I opened the door, they were still lounging around with big smiles, laughing at something I'd missed. Drat. I hated missing out.

"What did John want?" Hailey asked.

"Mr. Wall wants me to throw a cookies and Santa party for the school and community on December 17th."

Lizzie's nose wrinkled. "That's so close to my wedding."

"And you don't like Santa," Ruby added.

"It was this or heading up the end-of-year carnival." I pulled a face, and they all shivered.

"Good call," Aryn stated. "The carnival will suck out your life force."

"I get a committee. So, consider yourselves members," I pointed at each of them, skipping Lizzie. "Except you, Liz. You'll be too busy with last minute wedding and packing. I'm not adding to your list."

Lizzie beamed. "Only one more month until I marry Jackson and move down to Moab. My world is about to change, big time."

They all launched into chatter about the wedding, and I only half listened. Weddings didn't hold much interest for me, although I was trying really hard to stay present and celebrate with Lizzie because I loved her so much. I had no interest in the dresses, the food, the venue, and rarely thought about relationships myself. So, while they oohed and aahed over Lizzie's plans, adding happy commentary, I wondered where on earth I'd find a Santa and how I'd dredge up the energy to care.

CHAPTER 7

I may have issues with Santa, but that wasn't holding me back from decorating my front yard to the hilt this year. After the success of the inflatable turkey, I couldn't wait to get started. There had, unfortunately, been the slight speed bump of cost. After wandering several stores I'd quickly realized that holiday yard decor—particularly the hideous kind—wasn't cheap. I should have known this, considering what I'd spent on the Thanksgiving turkey, but I'd let hope take the reins and possibly blacked it out of my memory. Regardless, I'd taken the issue to my friends, who had offered to pitch in. In the end I purchased the biggest Rudolph the Red-Nosed Reindeer in the history of reindeer, and they said they'd show up on the appointed night with some things to supplement.

My friends came through big time. They'd taken my Rudolph and leveled up with a Frosty the Snowman, some spinning Christmas trees, storage bins filled with old strands of Christmas lights, and some sort of homemade, light-up candy canes to dot the lawn. Had we all gone into debt for these items? Possibly. But there are some things in life that are more important than money. Honor being one of them.

"Honor for the Thornback woman," I joked as I watched things being unloaded out of Aryn's and Ruby's cars.

"Dragon warrior women!" Ruby cried into the cold air.

A beep pulled our attention to Hailey's car as she parked against the curb. I watched as four people climbed out. Hailey and Lizzie had brought their men to help. For about two seconds I wanted to cheer as my army showed up to go to battle, but then things started to feel a bit fishy. They'd not been this excited at Halloween when I'd told them my plans for Christmas, and I had a sneaky suspicion that they'd been discussing Brooks behind my back and thought that if they went really big on breaking the HOA rules it would throw us into some sort of forced proximity love story.

I mostly blamed Ruby, who read romance novels the same way I read non-fiction books—taking all the words on the pages as facts. I wouldn't put it past her to be imagining me tearfully receiving an HOA ticket as I was mercilessly thrown in handcuffs by a broody and terribly attractive Brooks, whose shirt was ripped open as his eyes couldn't help watching my trembling lips. As for the others, well, Ruby can be really persuasive, even when we totally disagree with her, simply because her ideas make us laugh so much.

I'd be willing to bet money that the phrase "heaving bosom" had been thrown around.

"Rubes," I called to where she was unrolling the inflatable Frosty on my driveway. She looked up, her long, dark hair flipping over one shoulder. "You're not trying to play matchmaker here are you?"

She made her eyes big and round. "Me?"

"You."

She licked her lips. "Nope. Just over here doing my civic duty against tyranny."

I chuckled and turned back to help Aryn untangle the third strand of lights we'd come across in the big bin she'd hauled over. "Tell me the truth," I said to her. "What's Ruby plotting, and why are you all suddenly on board with decorating my yard?"

She kept working at the knots in the strand, not bother to look up. "She's not plotting anything that I know about. Although it was her idea for us to all bring more decor. I thought she was being supportive."

"She's trying to get me and Brooks together."

"Why would she do that? She knows you don't like him."

"She's the queen of lost causes. A good enemies-to-lovers romance gets her juices flowing. Plus, Jackson and Ford got recruited." I threw Aryn a look. "Now try to tell me nothing's up."

"Nothing's up," Aryn said, but she only made it halfway through without cracking a smile.

"Oh my gosh," I blew out a breath.

"Relax. I really don't think anyone is plotting. We all think it's funny how this battle keeps getting bigger, and we want to be in the middle of it, not watching from the sidelines. It's amusing stuff."

"You can't tell me that Jackson really drove up from Moab to help me tick off my HOA president."

"No," Lizzie cheerfully replied from over my shoulder, "he came up to see me. And when I mentioned that I had plans for vengeance tonight, he came along."

"No man in his right mind passes up a chance to participate in vengeance," Jackson added with a grin as he slung his arm around Lizzie's shoulders.

I turned and offered Jackson a smile. He looked exactly the same as he did every time I saw him. Tanned and outdoorsy with confidence and good humor. He was so perfect for Lizzie, and they were adorable in their reconnected love. I was genuinely happy for them, but I still felt bad that he'd gotten roped in to decorating my yard on his vacation time.

I gestured to Ford as he and Hailey joined our circle. "And Ford too? Isn't he too busy selling organic products to the world to be here?"

Ford chuckled as he zipped up a slim fitting coat. "I agree with Jackson. This is more important. It's not every day we get to stick it to the man."

"We're warriors of justice," Hailey laughed. "Though I don't quite understand how breaking HOA law by decorating your yard for the holidays is going to get the HOA president booted so that you can have his job, I'm here to support however I can."

All of us blinked at her for a second, and my heart sank at the complete, quiet logic behind her words.

"I . . ." I opened my mouth, unsure of what to say, when Aryn and Ruby joined our circle.

"There's no way we're going unnoticed right now. Seven adults setting up giant Christmas decorations isn't exactly sneaky," Aryn stated. "Hazel is probably peeking out her window this very second."

Ruby looked around. "Which house is Hazel's?" she asked.

I pointed next door. And my diabolical friend group, as though guided by puppet strings, turned as a unit and all smiled and waved at Hazel's house. Her curtains twitched, they laughed, and I groaned and slapped my mittened hands over my face. Hailey was right—this made no sense. What was I doing?

"So," Jackson clapped his hands together. "What's my assignment? I'm kind of excited about this."

I took a deep breath, licked my lips, and nodded. Everyone was here, we were committed, this was going to be funny and rebellious, and there was some sort of message in it. So, yeah, it was happening.

I pointed to Rudolph, who was still in his box. "Someone needs to figure him out." Jackson grabbed Lizzie's hand, and they headed that way while Ford and Hailey looked at me expectantly, their two blond heads bent toward one another. "How about you two take on the swirly trees?"

"Great," Hailey chirped. "Do you have a map of your yard so we know where you want them set up?"

"No," I scoffed. Hailey raised an eyebrow. "It's on the trunk of my car." I glanced at Ford, and he offered me a nod.

"I like a person who thinks through the details," he complimented. "It shows dedication to your cause."

I smiled, appreciating his appreciation.

"And Mer," Hailey's voice grew quiet. "Sorry I sort of burst your bubble. I'm not trying to . . ."

I pasted on a smile and chuckled. "You couldn't stop this train if you wanted to."

She smiled back, although the look in her eyes said she knew I'd lost some steam and let doubts creep in.

Her and Ford headed into my open garage, Ford's hand against the small of Hailey's back, to consult the map and then picked up the boxes with the twirling trees and headed to their designated section of the yard. I paused for a moment, watching as my friends dragged extension cords and inflated things, all the while chatting and laughing. It was a strange little version of the North Pole, with everyone wearing coats and hats, their cheeks rosy from the cold. Warm affection melted through my chest. They were all here for *me*, taking time out of their busy lives and away from kids and family to help me with a silly revenge project. I'd felt these sensations before, the sense of awe that I had this kind of support and the aching gratitude that came with it, always followed by a sliver of feeling unworthy. I wasn't as cheerful and easy as the rest of them, and I knew it. Thankfully those unworthy thoughts faded more each year as I settled into and trusted the bond we shared.

"We should be listening to holiday music while we do this," Ruby said, huffing slightly as she dragged Frosty to where Hailey had told her to put him. "Oh, even better, we could carol while we work."

"Carol?" I asked.

"You know, singing songs about Christmastime?" Aryn teased as she handed me another knot of cords to unravel.

"I understand what caroling is," I stated. "Just not why people want to do it."

"Something about Christmas spirit," Aryn replied.

"I thought we were trying to be sneaky about this?" Lizzie asked as she walked passed me, holding a red bulb that was going to be Rudolph's nose.

"A few people missed the sneaky memo. Did you polish that?" I asked with a grin. The thing was shiny enough to see my reflection.

Lizzie gave a quick nod that made a curl fall over her eyes. "We are not here to do things halfway, Atwood."

"You know Dasher and Dancer and Prancer and Vixen . . ." Ruby suddenly started singing, loud and clear, and before I had any control over it, the entire group had joined in.

It was currently ten o'clock at night, and no one in this party was under thirty years old. I had purposely turned off all outside lights at my house and told everyone to dress in dark colors. And they were singing at the top of their lungs. To say this particular problem had never crossed my mind was an understatement.

"This is madness," I said under my breath, although I did have to swallow down a laugh.

As they sang I took the strand of lights I'd untangled and walked to the end of my driveway to get a good overall look and decide where to hang them. With my hands holding the strands and my ears totally focused on the off-key singing of my friends, I didn't hear Hazel approaching until she was standing right next to me.

"Oh, dear, Meredith. I'm afraid this isn't going to turn out well for you," she said.

I glanced over to find her dressed in a puffy, marshmallow-man style coat and earmuffs, with her blue hair sticking up around them.

"Mr. VanOrman and the board won't be pleased," she muttered. Then she looked up to meet my eyes. "I love what you're doing here, really, I do. The holidays should be celebrated. It's just that, maybe you've gone a little too far." Her left hand twitched, and I noticed she was carrying something in it . . . something that looked suspiciously like a ticket book. "I have to be honest and tell you that this was the first time Thanksgiving decor was such an issue. There was a pretty mixed response from the community to your dancing turkey, and that will be addressed at the next board meeting. But this, well, Christmas holiday code states only a wreath on the door and a single line of lights along the roofline." She grew quiet for a second and then pointed at Frosty. "Does he sing?"

"Sing? No."

"Do any of them play music?"

I shook my head. "They're silent as far as I know."

She pursed her lips in thought. "Well, that's something then. We do have an ordinance against excessive noise."

My friends had stopped singing when Hazel walked over and were still going about their duties but with one ear clearly turned toward the conversation. Lizzie was currently on Jackson's shoulders attempting to screw in Rudolph's nose, and I doubted noise was going to be the real problem when all was said and done. A ticket for light pollution was much more likely when that whole thing came together.

"There goes my wish to start a garage band," I replied, sarcastically.

She spun and put a hand on my forearm. "Don't even joke about that. You're on thin ice already."

I ran my tongue over my lips. "Is this really a big deal?" I gestured at my friends stringing lights and having whispered conversations.

"Let's cut to the chase. You're doing this in the dark, which means you know exactly how it's going to be received. What's your long game here?" Hazel smacked two lips together. "This," she gestured to my friends in the same way I had, "is a waste of time and money. There are easier ways to get your point across. Ways that make sense."

"I've tried attending meetings, and I get booed out of the room." I shook my head, annoyed.

"You'd catch more flies with honey."

I tilted my head and gave her a look. "You expect me to go into those meetings and try to kiss up to get my way?"

"No. I expect you to be nice. Brooks is popular around here because he's a nice man."

"Brooks also approved that rule about wearing a uniform when hosting a garage sale."

She shook her head. "Because that bought him the leverage to turn down overnight guest fees and the ordinance against letting pets on the common area lawns. He gave up a little thing to get more, and he did it while keeping the peace."

Lizzie gave out a squeal, and our attention was immediately caught by a giant ray of red light, rivaling a lighthouse in a storm. It spun in circles, casting its beam all around the neighborhood before landing on my own front door and then doing it all over again.

"Oh, boy," Hazel said, flipping open that ticket book.

Ruby burst out singing, and the others joined in as Hazel wrote out her ticket and handed it to me. I watched her walk back to her house, marching along to the tune of "Joy to the World," all my friends screeching it into the night air. I knew I was doomed, I knew this was stupid, but somehow it didn't keep me from joining in on the chorus.

*****

A white paper was taped to my kitchen window the next morning. I wasn't dressed for the cold, but I went outside in bare feet and snatched it off, shivering as I hustled back inside while reading it. It was on legal size paper, typed up precisely, and signed by Brooks VanOrman, HOA president. Things had officially gone belly up. While I was familiar with hopeless causes and had never shied away from them, I knew it wasn't going to be a fun road.

I dressed hurriedly in jeans and a sweater, wrapping my coat around me and tugging a cap down over my ears before I walked the two blocks over to Brooks's house in the section of the neighborhood with single family homes. Moving my body always helped me with anxiousness, and I thought I could use the exercise before facing him down. I banged on the front door and waited for him to answer. I had his threatening little note in my hand, wrinkled and a little worse for the wear. When he didn't answer, I knocked harder and called his name. Still nothing. I took a few steps back from the door and peeked into the front window. The house looked quiet. I called his name once more, and, this time, I was answered by the sound of his garage door opening.

I walked toward the garage and waited. He was standing near the back of his car, wearing a heavy-duty apron of some sort and pushing safety goggles up onto his head. His curly black hair got snagged on the goggles and stood up straight in places, giving him a childlike look. There were wood shavings dusting the top of his work boots, and a sweet burning smell with little puffs of smoke rose from a worktable off to the side.

"What a surprise to see you this morning," he said with a slanted smile.

My throat felt suddenly thick at the familiar sight of all the artist's tools. My eyes couldn't seem to stop scouring the place. His big work bench was filled with different shapes of wood with hand-carving tools hung on a rack above it. Different sizes of wood planes rested innocently nearby. Saws hung from nails on the wall, and chisels stood upright in an old coffee can on the corner of the bench near where clamps were attached to the edge. But these weren't the only things my eyes cataloged. There was an air compressor and a large red standing toolbox with drawers left open showing screwdrivers and hammers, measuring tapes, and marking pencils. His garage was filled with crafting tools, artist's tools . . . the tools of my childhood.

My face must have shown something, because his stance adjusted into one less prepared for battle, and he cleared his throat. I didn't dare look at his face, but I imagined from his tone of voice that he'd look concerned.

"I'm making a few toys to send to my nieces and nephew for Christmas."

53

I nodded, feeling my head wobble as my heart started to beat hard. It didn't make sense to have this discovery affect me so much. "You're a lawyer, though. Right?"

When he didn't answer right away, I finally looked at him. He was watching me with a furrowed expression. His nod was slow, and I tamped down on a scream while I waited for his reply. My hands shook, and I tucked them into my pockets.

"Yes. I'm a lawyer. This is a side hobby during the cold months when I'm not doing as much outdoors."

His voice was low and gentle, the way someone would try to talk to a wild animal or a person on the brink. I suddenly saw myself through his eyes and realized that my intensity over this was absurd and confusing to both of us. For some reason I'd been triggered over something that didn't actually matter. Sure, I'd recently started to dislike him a little less than before, but Brooks and his chosen lifestyle meant nothing to me. I swallowed hard and worked to shrug casually as I reminded myself that there were many, many people with artistic hobbies who managed to live full lives and not sacrifice their children for their art. Again, didn't matter what he did with his time. It wasn't like we were chummy or that I depended on him for anything.

"That's . . . whatever." I pulled the now destroyed note from my pocket and flapped it in the air. "Care to explain this?"

He continued to watch me for a moment, and I waited with prickly skin for him to ask what that had been all about. His eyes were kind and curious, and, if I'd been another type of woman, he'd probably have pressed. But he seemed to recognize the barriers I had in place, and, instead, his shoulders relaxed and his expression shifted into unbothered innocence.

"It's pretty self-explanatory," he said. "It's what we in the biz call a cease and desist notice."

"The biz, huh?"

He nodded. "The biz."

"I was unaware that HOAs have the power to deliver this type of letter."

"Oh, we have all sorts of power. This, however, is a non-binding letter with no legal effect, but it can be used as evidence if litigation becomes necessary." He ended with a smirk.

"If litigation becomes necessary? Are you going to sue me for an excess of holiday spirit?" I huffed.

"If the misconduct continues."

"Alleged misconduct."

He bit on his lower lip for a second, and I was suddenly sure he was trying not to laugh. "Trust me, there's nothing alleged about what's happening in your yard. Did you miss the traffic jam this morning?"

"So, I had to dodge a few cars on my way over here. People want to get into the holiday spirit by driving by. That's called fun, Brooks."

It actually hadn't been fun. There had been at least five cars parked along my curb, and for someone as private as me, it felt like a total breech. I wasn't exactly loving the consequences of my choices today. But, again, backing down wasn't part of my genetic code.

"They're stopping to take selfies," he continued.

I nodded. "Because it's such an awesome attraction that they want to be seen there."

He tugged off his safety goggles and put them on the bench next to whatever he'd been working on. Running a hand through his thick hair, he shook his head and sat down on a stool nearby.

"Meredith. Let's be real. In the several years you've lived here, you've never once decorated for any holiday until that first Halloween after I became president. Now you've become this neighborhood's number one holiday enthusiast."

"You haven't been here long enough to know that for sure."

"I've lived here for four years, and your house is near the community entrance. I would know if it had been decorated like this before."

That sort of deflated me for a second. He'd been here that long? "How did I never see or notice you before?"

"I'm going to ignore you pointing out how unworthy of notice I am and tell you that I avoided involvement like the plague. I paid my monthly fees, and, other than that I did not have any interest in how this place ran or what the retired population wants to spend their time worrying about. I laid low, kept my house tidy, and that's how I liked it. Then one day Hazel dragged Leland and Shayla over here, begging me to take on the HOA presidency just because they'd heard I'm a lawyer."

It hurt, like it always did, hearing that they'd begged him to take the job when I'd been more than willing. So willing that I'd set up a meeting with them and offered to take on the position. Sometimes I wondered if they'd gone directly from meeting with me to his doorstep. What had I done so wrong?

"What kind of lawyer are you?" I asked, pushing down the questions and hurt.

"I handle property law."

"What, exactly, is that?"

"Real estate and property disputes. I help with things like foreclosures, deed transfers, zoning restrictions, wills, and coordination with lending agents involved in the sale of a property."

"Seems to me that an HOA would fall neatly into your profession then. You're the property pro."

"I'm not."

Now it was my turn to smirk. "You sort of are. But if you didn't want to do it, why did you say yes?"

"I didn't think it would be that big of a deal."

I laughed. "Why on earth would you think that?"

"I hadn't met you yet."

My face froze, and I glared at him. "Those decorations are staying up."

He nodded. "I kind of figured." He ran one finger through a pile of sawdust that had collected on the bench. "Those tickets are going to get pretty costly. I'm not sure you're going to have a happy holiday season."

"Not the first time I've heard that phrase, yet I'm still standing."

CHAPTER 8

The noise in the school cafeteria was deafening, but over the years I'd become a pro at either sorting through the chaos for important sounds or blocking it all together. I stood on the stage, raised above the general mayhem, and surveyed the area for any spills, choking issues, or kids who were trying to thieve food from others.

Yep, it was my day for lunchroom duty. Rather than hiring extra workers to come in and assist, the principal had worked it out for teachers to take turns every couple of weeks while their students were in other classrooms. Today mine were at their weekly music class, and I was doing one of the many non-educational things required of us. I watched as Ruby, who often volunteered to be in the cafeteria at lunch, walked up and down the rows of tables. She chatted brightly with the kids, gave out high-fives and smiles, and carried a tube of wipes that she used to wipe faces or hands as needed. We were the school version of good cop/bad cop. Guess which one I was?

I did a sweep of the tables and was working my way back when Ruby's head suddenly popped up, and she blinked down at a first grader she'd been walking past. The kids around him were giggling, and Ruby said a few things to him before moving on. Curious as to what had happened, I left my perch and met up with her in the second-grade table section.

"What went down with the first graders?" I asked quietly enough for kids to not hear, which, in this situation, meant I said it at normal voice volume, not bothering to whisper.

Ruby laughed. "That first grader kissed me right on the bum."

My eyebrows rose, and I grinned. "Seriously?"

"Yeah. He said, 'I love you, Nurse Ruby' and gave me a smacker straight on." She tugged a wipe out and handed it to a child next to her. "I told him that we don't kiss people on the bottom, and he felt a little embarrassed, so I told him I wasn't angry."

"I definitely don't condone bum kisses, but I think it's pretty sweet that he likes you so much," I replied.

Ruby nodded, and we started walking again. "Last week when I had to quickly spin around to try to catch a kid before they dropped their whole tray, one of the third graders got hit in the head with my backside. She turned around and called me Big Booty Judy. So, I think I'll take the kisses over that."

I bit my lips to keep from chuckling. "Creative."

"Yeah. The whole third-grade table likes to whisper 'Big Booty Judy' now when I walk by. It's both embarrassing and hysterical. I finally get a nickname at school, but it's because my rear end knocked a kid in the head."

"Would that be considered bullying and name calling?" I asked. "Do we need to put a stop to it?"

Ruby shrugged and picked up an empty tray that someone had left. "If it lasts more than a few more days, I'll address it. For now they seem to think of it as an inside joke between us, and there's no intent to hurt my feelings."

I tugged at the cuffs of my button-down shirt as I thought about how my natural inclination was to look for offense and then react to it. Ruby's was to assume good intent. She was the type of person I could learn from, and I was trying. I liked to think that I was improving under the good influence of all the women in my friend group.

The first lunch bell rang, and the entire table of first graders whooped, gathered their things, and thundered out of the lunchroom. We had five minutes before the fourth graders—including my class—would arrive to take their place, so Ruby and I went to the wash station and gathered rags and sanitizing spray to get the table cleaned up. We worked quickly, starting on opposite ends and making good time. Honestly, I considered it a success if I didn't spill anything on my slacks or accidentally bleach them somehow. We finished right as I saw the next wave line up at the cafeteria doors. I signaled to them that we were ready, and the students with home lunch came streaming directly in while the school lunch kids got in line at the serving window.

"So, I went to Brooks's house yesterday to confront him about a warning letter he left at my house," I told Ruby as we stood off to the side, monitoring the second graders who were getting ready to be released into the playground. "He's a woodworker, and, for some reason, it knocked me flat."

Ruby's eyes grew large as she looked over at me. "Really? I'm surprised it bothered you."

"Yeah. I stood there like a frozen dummy for ten entire seconds, looking around and feeling like I'd fallen into a black hole. In what world do my dad and my . . ." Stumped on what to call him for a second, I waved my hands. ". . . enemy neighbor person have the same hobby?"

"I can imagine that brought a tidal wave of thoughts."

"Yeah. None of them flattering."

Ruby released my shoulder when we heard the particular squeal that accompanies spilled drinks. It came from the third graders, and Ruby headed straight over while I moved to the side of the room to get a mop and rags. Ruby got the student cleaned up while I mopped the chocolate milk that had pooled on the table and under her chair. Her white pants weren't going to survive this, and I wondered for the millionth time why white pants, shirts, dresses, skirts, or anything were made for kids. I couldn't even keep white clean as an adult.

We finished right as the next bell rang and the second graders one table over herded out. Now we had five minutes before the fifth graders arrived to claim their spots. It was a never-ending cycle of quick transitions. I still had to finish mopping, and Ruby was helping the girl who'd burst into tears, so I knew it was going to be tight. I was right. We pulled it off, but by the time the fifth graders came in, I was sweating. I hated getting sweaty at school and having to wear the same clothes all afternoon.

Eventually things were as settled as they could be in the lunchroom, and Ruby came to where I was standing under the basketball hoop. The good thing about older grades was there was a little less spilling. The bad thing was there were a lot more reminders to stay in seats and keep hands to yourselves. The first graders might keep dumping their trays over, but the fifth graders liked to pinch, poke, tug, and generally irritate each other. It was definitely early attempts at flirting.

"Okay," Ruby picked up our conversation. "So, Brooks likes to be creative. Doesn't mean anything. Lots of people do woodworking."

I nodded. "That's true."

"It's like how a lot of people read romance novels."

I called to two boys to quit wrestling and then looked to Ruby. "I'm sorry, but I don't see the connection."

She smiled. "Some people say that romance novels lead to unrealistic expectations. But thousands of people read them and don't leave their husbands or children to go seek their one true love."

"Riiiight . . ."

"So, stands to reason that a lot of people woodwork, but it doesn't take over their entire existence."

"True."

"I like to draw blood, but you don't see me going around trying to stab everyone."

"Gratefully," I replied.

"Okay. So, we can agree it's a fact about him and not a big deal?"

"Yes," I nodded, feeling that particular mix of slightly confused and also strangely lighter about everything that came from chatting with Rubes. "But you know that it's really not a big deal to me what he chooses to do with his free time. I'm not sure why I even mentioned it or why it caused any sort of reaction."

"Because you don't hate him as much as you thought you did." She offered me a smile, and then a noise caught both of our attention. "Griffin," she yelled, her voice carrying above the fray, "tables are for sitting at, not standing on."

*****

One of my favorite things about being an adult is the ability to avoid things I don't like. Sure, on occasion I get forced into a situation, but for the most part I don't do things I don't want to do. I don't eat mustard, I don't accept invitations to go out for seafood, and I don't try on frilly dresses while standing in front of a mirror and having my four best friends commenting on it.

Yet, there I was, in a bridal dress shop being forced to select a bridal party dress for Lizzie's wedding—and the color palette was shades of pink. The room was filled with mirrors and painted in white with about two bazillion lights pointing at one pedestal. White couches and chairs, along with a glass coffee table, surrounded the pedestal. The only color in the room came from the clothes we were wearing and from an entire rack filled with hanging dresses in pretty much the same color. I stared at the rack as Lizzie told us that her theme was rose and rosewood, which was, uh, the same thing.

She called me up first, and I lightly touched one of the dresses before pulling my hand away like I'd been burned. "So . . . pink then?" I said.

"No," Lizzie shook her head. "Rose and rose*wood*. Two different colors." She pulled out two dresses in very slightly different shades. "See, this lighter one is rose, and this darker one is . . ."

"Rose*wood*," I replied with more sarcasm than I'd liked to have.

Lizzie looked up at me with a squinty-eyed expression that her future children would fear. "Just like your heart is currently being shades of burnt and ash."

Stifled laughter came from the rest of the ladies, and a smile tugged at my mouth. "Dibs on rosewood," I said.

Lizzie nodded and sorted through the rack before pulling out a gown and holding it up to me. "This gown would look nice on you. It's got straight lines and fitted sleeves. You've got the body for it. Try it on."

I took it out of her hands and moved to a dressing room while exchanging looks with Hailey and Aryn. Ruby, who had been next in line, was busy with Lizzie. Hailey gave me a thumbs up, and Aryn shrugged while she mouthed 'good luck' to me. Well, at least I'd be making Lizzie happy, I supposed, even if my soul was hissing like a vampire in the sun at the thought of wearing pink.

I put the gown on and zipped it as far as I could without help. Turning side-to-side in the mirror, I had to admit that the cut suited me. If only it had been a navy blue or deep green. I'd have even supported a rich purple. But this made me feel like a package of smarties or a pixie stick. People I knew would be at the wedding. People who would be astonished to see me like this. I pulled a face in the mirror.

"Are you ready, Mer?" Lizzie called excitedly.

I groaned under my breath, reminded myself how much I adored that curly-headed lady, and swept the door open. "Yep."

"Come stand on the pedestal," Lizzie directed.

I did my level best not to meet anyone's eyes as I crossed the room and climbed up onto the raised platform in front of a half circle of mirrors. I blinked a few times as the beams of light tried to burn my eyeballs out of their sockets.

"Um, do I really need to stand here? Isn't this reserved for wedding gowns and brides?" I asked.

Lizzie's eyes met mine in the mirror. "It's for whatever I want it to be for."

Okey-dokey. I nodded. Lizzie walked around me a few times, stepping up next to me to finish zipping the dress, before moving back down to circle again. After her third pass I looked to see how my friends were reacting. They were all smiling at me. Hailey looked like a proud mom. Aryn looked amused, and Ruby had glowing hearts for eyes.

"It suits you," Lizzie pronounced.

Ruby clapped. "You're beautiful in pink."

I took a closer look at myself. "Really? I never saw pink as my color."

"You actually have curves in that dress," Aryn teased.

I ran my hands over hips that had appeared out of nowhere. And my chest, usually so ignorable, didn't look like it would need padding. My eyes grew larger, and I blinked a few times. Okay. This was a surprise.

"It's so pink, though," I said with less bite.

"Lizzie's right; it suits you. Or do you want to try on a couple more?" Hailey asked, and I could tell by the way her eyes gleamed that she knew exactly what my answer would be.

"Nope," I hopped down. "Unzip me, and let's call it good. Onto the next victim."

Lizzie tugged the zipper down. "No victims here. Just my best friends participating in my dream wedding."

Cold water would have felt better than that statement. I turned and grabbed Lizzie's hands before she moved away to the next dress.

"Liz," I said genuinely, "I'm so happy you want me in your wedding, and I'm sorry to be a brat. Forgive me?"

She actually teared up before wrapping her arms around my waist and giving me a hug. "I knew you'd be a pain, but I also knew you'd come through. Thanks, Meredith."

I patted her back and shared a look with Aryn. "She knew I'd be a pain?"

Aryn shrugged and grinned. "Come on, even you knew you wouldn't go down without a fight."

I frowned as I thought about it and then nodded. "Guess so."

I moved into the dressing room with the frown still on my face. I hated that my friends assumed I'd fight them on everything. Yes, fighting was as natural as breathing to me. I'd always had to fight for every scrap in life, and, I guess in my strange way, I'd come to think of fighting as a communication style. I vowed to work on it, and by the time I was back in my regular clothes—hello, blue blouse and black slacks—I was determined to be better.

Ruby was dressed and up on the pedestal when I rejoined the group. The dress she was wearing had floating layers and big puff sleeves. It was the lightest shade of pink, and Ruby looked like a princess. Something she mentioned no less than twenty times. Aryn and Hailey, both being pretty easygoing and matter-of-fact, were a breeze to choose dresses for. By the time we were all finished, my stomach was growling, and I was ready for some alone time.

61

"Tomorrow is my bridal shower," Lizzie squealed as we made our way to the parking lot, tugging on coats and thin driving-style gloves. "The wedding is getting so close."

"Only fifteen days," I supplied.

"Mrs. Elizabeth Duncan Walker," Lizzie sighed, a hand to her chest. "Has anything ever sounded more perfect?"

Aryn smiled as she unlocked her car. "It's all coming together, Lizzie. It'll be a beautiful wedding."

"See you tomorrow," Hailey waved. "I'm off to have dinner with Ford and the kids." She offered Lizzie a hand squeeze. "I love the dresses."

"I looked like a princess," Ruby preened.

"Yes," I laughed along with the others. "You really did."

"Now I need to find me a prince," Ruby added, gliding to where her car was parked. "He'll sweep me off my feet and carry me into the sunset."

"You'll find him," Lizzie responded.

"I know," Ruby nodded. "I'm sure the universe has someone especially for me."

Funny, I thought as I started up my car, *I'd always figured the universe had no idea where to find the kind of man I would need.*

CHAPTER 9

"What I don't understand, no matter how many times we discuss this, is why you ever wanted to be the HOA president in the first place," Lizzie said to me around a mouthful of cheese the next night. "You've got your hands full teaching school and helping out your dad. Why do you want to get involved with more things?"

She took a seat on the warm gray couch in my little family room and tucked her legs up under her. The "I'm the Bride" sash she was wearing slipped off one shoulder, and Hailey leaned over to tug it back into place. Today was Lizzie's bridal shower, and we were all gathered in my house to celebrate. The other guests would be arriving soon, but for these blissful moments it was just the five of us. The dress fitting the night before had been a wake-up call in a way, and I tried not to get overly sentimental as I looked at each of them, understanding that the little band would be breaking up as Lizzie moved in a few short weeks. The five of us were so different, but together we'd formed a well-rounded unit that had taken forever for me to find, and I had no interest in goodbyes.

If I was being deeply honest, these women had mentored me and taught me so much that I'd missed out on by not having a woman's influence growing up. I was attached to them, big time.

Aryn sat next to me in a pair of chairs, her long legs crossed, and flipped a strawberry into her mouth. "Lizzie, listen, Meredith doesn't appreciate things that aren't working how they're meant to work. The HOA was in total disarray, and she offered to step in and get them moving in the right direction."

Lizzie made a face. "Sounds painful."

I shrugged, not bothering to hide my true feelings from my friends. "You guys are my best friends, so you already know that I have certain weaknesses—like patience and charm—but I also have strengths, such as organizing, seeing needs and filling them, and making good use of funds and time. So, I put together a case for how I could revamp the community, and they said they'd think about it and then ran to Brooks." I scowled. "It's incredibly insulting."

"Hurt your feelings, too," Hailey said softly, and I nodded.

My friends had been told several versions of the same spiel I'd just given, but I hadn't ever told them the details of the meeting or how humiliated I'd felt when I'd heard they hadn't even bothered to think about my proposal other than to find someone—anyone really—other than me. I hadn't dared to ask even Hazel where

I'd gone wrong in my presentation. Had I come on too strong? Had I scared them somehow? It was a failure and embarrassment that nagged nearly every day.

"Which is what kicked off the entire feud," Ruby added as she dumped ice into the punch bowl. "I really think you're punishing the wrong person. Brooks is as much a victim of this whole thing as you are. How was he supposed to know that you'd offered to take the position?"

"Ruby, you're missing out on the bigger picture here," Hailey added from where she was arranging a tray of vegetables.

"What's that?" Ruby asked, moving back into my kitchen to get the punch itself.

"We're Team Meredith all the way."

Ruby pursed her lips as she poured the bright pink punch into the waiting ice. "But Meredith likes logic, and it's illogical for her to be taking this out on him."

Aryn slitted a grin my way. "Your response?"

I rolled my eyes. "This has nothing to do with logic. That flew out the window when Hazel and Leland ran screaming away from me and begged someone else to do it."

"So, punish *them*, instead," Ruby stated.

I laughed. "I am. Rudolph shines directly on both of their houses. All night."

"How many more tickets have you received?" Hailey asked.

She set her veggies on the table and came to sit by Lizzie on the couch. She was wearing a pearl necklace and reached up to run her fingers along each pearl, a sure sign she was worried for me. It made it hard to meet her eyes as I gave an honest answer.

"Three. One per day," I replied, tugging down my shirt sleeves and smoothing out my pant legs.

"How much are they, each?" Lizzie's tone was concerned.

I shook my head and brushed it off. "Not much." Aryn gave me a knowing look, and I ignored her. "I'll take the stuff down when the season is over."

"Is there any chance you could be evicted for this?" Lizzie asked.

"Nah. Don't worry about me."

My doorbell rang, and I went to answer it, relieved to set aside this line of questioning. If they kept at it, they'd eventually unearth the truth that the tickets were more than I could afford, and there was actually a chance I could be evicted. It didn't help that Ruby had a point about the logic behind continuing to punish Brooks. Honestly, I'd take it down that very night if I thought I could, but I felt trapped in this stupid plan, especially since I'd dragged my friends in and caused some sort of social media frenzy. It had gotten out of hand, and I didn't see a way out. I was going to go bankrupt for pride.

My stomach was heavy as I answered the door to find a handful of Lizzie's childhood friends smiling in the cold. I did my best to smile warmly and invite them in. I followed them back toward the family room, already suffocating from the conversations I'd be listening to this evening. It was hard for me to pretend interest in strangers. I could listen to Hailey discuss opera, even though I don't like it, because I love Hailey. Listening to Kathy down the street discuss her horror over rising grocery prices was enough to make my brain melt.

Tonight was definitely going to be a brain melter. Lizzie deserved to be celebrated, though, so I squared my shoulders and pasted on a smile as I followed after the gaggle of giggling girlfriends. However, before I got very far, another knock at the door pulled me away. I was happy to have an excuse to fall back. I was less happy when I opened it to find Brooks standing there. He was holding another ticket, and my stomach met my toes as I took it out of his hand.

His body filled up the doorway, blocking what little light was provided by my porch light, as he said, "This game is getting expensive, Atwood."

"Cost doesn't matter when you're fighting for a cause," I lied. I lied so hard. My cause was losing its allure. It was a tainted and decaying beast that I had to sleep with every night.

He leaned one shoulder against my door jam and crossed his arms. "And what, exactly, is your cause? Because from where I'm standing, all you're doing is repeatedly violating HOA codes and racking up some serious fines. How is that helping your platform?"

I managed to keep from stumbling over my words as I thought about how to answer. The facts were that the yard decor was tacky, the fines were piling up, and nothing was changing with the HOA board. They still didn't want to hear from me, and they still wasted time on ridiculous things when there was so much more they could be doing.

"My issue is that I think the HOA board isn't in tune," I finally said.

He nodded. "Okay. What are they not understanding?"

"Real things, actual issues."

"Like?"

A burst of laughter drifted down the hallway, and I looked over my shoulder. Aryn was standing near my table, looking towards me. Her expression asked if I was okay, and I returned a small nod, letting her know I was fine and to keep the party going. Friend telepathy was the best.

I turned back to Brooks. "I'm hosting a party right now; I don't have time for this."

"I did a little sleuthing, you know."

"I'm assuming you're telling me this because the sleuthing was about me?" I folded my arms.

"Bingo. Any lawyer worth his salt can dig up facts on people, so I dug."

"And what super interesting tidbits did you find out?"

"High achiever, little bit of a loner, single dad and two younger sisters."

"None of those fact required much digging, and I'm not a loner. Do you hear this house full of people?"

One side of his mouth tugged up. "What's the party for?"

"None of your business."

"I'm getting married!" Lizzie called, having heard him . . . mostly because all my friends were now innocently hovering in view of me and Brooks. "I'm so excited."

Brooks shot her the type of warm smile that he'd never directed my way. My toes curled as he offered her a "Congrats."

This was, apparently, the invitation they needed to join us in my tiny entryway. I looked heavenward and mentally took a few deep breaths. I adored these ladies, but honestly.

"You did it to me with Ford. Ax throwing," Hailey whispered in my ear as she lightly touched my back. "Payback is rough."

I wondered if the expression on my face was similar to the horrified one she'd been wearing when I'd gone up to Ford that night. The thought helped me relax and find the actual humor in the situation.

"Guys, this is my HOA president, Brooks VanOrman," I said, even though I knew for a fact that they already knew that. Some of them had already met him. But it seemed like the proper thing to do. "He's here to kill dreams and suck all the joy out of hearts."

"That feels a little like a pot and kettle situation," Brooks replied, one side of his mouth tugging into a crooked smile.

My friends laughed at his comeback, and I shook my head. "He's leaving," I replied.

"First I need to ask you a question," Brooks held up one finger.

"What's your question?" Ruby asked. "She's not an open book, but I am, and I'll tell you anything you want to know about her."

"Did you guys ditch all the other guests?" I asked them.

"They're eating and talking. This is more interesting," Ruby replied.

"Besides, we can't start gifts without you," Lizzie added.

I snapped my fingers. "Oh, sorry, Brooks. I'm needed elsewhere. Your question will have to wait."

"One question, and then I'll go." His eyes were coaxing, his voice was low, and it hit me as though he'd actually reached out and tugged on my chest.

My friends, those naive fools, all nodded. I sighed. "Fine. One."

"Your idea about helping hungry kids in our neighborhood, that wasn't the only idea you'd been working on, right?"

"Oh, Mer, that's so thoughtful," Lizzie squeezed my shoulder.

"That crusty exterior is an act," Ruby said to Brooks, and I groaned as his eyebrows rose with amusement. "She only wanted to help others like she should have been helped."

"Go back to the party," I said firmly to my friends.

With grins and a few laughs, they walked down the hall and disappeared into the family room. Brooks was still waiting when I turned back to him. I silently prayed that he hadn't picked up on Ruby's little tidbit about me having needed help in my younger years.

I pursed my lips and did my best to relax. This wasn't a battle, and I could communicate kindly. "I had a few ideas, yes, about ways the HOA board could make better use of their time and funds. The community needs a leader with some sort of vision. Towel sharing protocols is a total waste of time and resources. I made a presentation to the board, or at least to Hazel and Leland, and they ran screaming to you to save them from me and my ideas."

"What other ideas did you have?"

I felt suddenly vulnerable, as though we'd shifted our positions. "You said one question."

"I'm guessing you know from firsthand experience how it feels to be hungry as a child?" Oh great, he'd heard. He said it softly, as though it had the power to blow me over. Which it did, actually. I nodded but didn't reply verbally. We weren't to a place of sharing childhood traumas. He stood up straight. "When you're ready to talk again, which might not be for a while after you see that last ticket, I'd be interested in hearing more of your thoughts on what the board could do to help the community."

Surprised and a little flustered, I managed to say okay, and then I shut the door quietly behind him.

****

A few days later I stood in Willow's boutique, a victim of her inability to do year-end inventory without me badgering her and keeping things on track. She strongly disagreed that she was victimizing me and instead said it was my sisterly duty. She was currently holding up a bright yellow jumper with a floral pattern, trying to press it against me as I squirmed away. Tonight I was apparently a double victim as she'd been hitting me hard with her ideas of how I should be dressing. Make that a triple victim because she was also diffusing oils that didn't smell good together.

"This would be darling on you. With your thin build and dark coloring, you could really pull this off," she said brightly, leaning toward me.

I backed away. "It's yellow. With flowers. No."

I headed behind the check-out counter to boot up the scanner we used to catalog how many of each item she had. She, predictably, followed. Willow couldn't seem to stay on track with *boring* things, but she was like a dog with a bone when it came to things that interested her. And dressing me had always been high on her list of dreams. Probably because I was on year thirty-something of not letting her do it.

"Mer, come on. You always dress so . . ."

"Professionally?" I smirked when she couldn't come up with the right word.

"Stoically."

I blinked as she waved the jumper toward me again, trying to see if it would be long enough. "Stoic is not a way of dressing," I replied.

"No, it's a way of being that's showcased by the way you dress. Your clothing says boring, lacking creativity, uptight."

I glanced over her outfit of a long, shapeless dress cinched by a scarf around her waist and earrings that touched her shoulders.

"The way you dress is great, for you. But my preferred style is practical for covering the body and looking put together without drawing attention to oneself."

Her own eyes rolled, and she marched back toward the rack of jumpers. "Maybe a different color?"

"Pass."

"Ugh. You're the worst."

I waved the scanner at her. "Yes, the definite worst. So terrible that I've come down here to help you do inventory even though it's the most tedious thing I have to do all year while getting nauseated at the smell of those oils. What mix did you throw together? My eyes burn."

"If your eyes are burning it's because they needed to purge toxins from your soul," she chirped. "How's the Santa and cookies planning coming?" She redirected, and I knew I'd won the clothing battle for now.

I picked up the stack of flowery notebooks she kept by the register and began scanning each one into the system. "It's in six days, and I don't have a Santa."

Willow stopped riffling through the clothing she was separating into colors. "What? But you've advertised the event to the community already."

"Yep."

"And have no Santa."

"Have you ever tried to hire a Santa? Do you have contacts in the land of jolly elves?"

Willow put her hands on her hips, her deep purple nail polish catching enough light to show off some sparkles. "Meredith, if there's one thing I know about you it's that you get the job done. So, pardon me for calling bunk on this Santa thing. You haven't even tried yet."

I moved on to a collection of bracelets on a spinning rack. "Not true," I sighed. "I've actually called several people whose names I was given. They're all booked or dead. The dead thing feels suspicious. I wouldn't be surprised to find out that 'Playing Santa' is listed as the cause of death on their death certificates."

"How many have you called? Ballpark figure?"

"Five in Cache Valley, another four in the Ogden area. I even reached out to a handful in Salt Lake. There's no hope."

"Yikes," Willow pulled a sympathetic face.

"It's me. The holidays are never nice to me."

Willow laughed and went back to sorting clothing. "You know, someday you'll be a mom, and you'll have to pretend to enjoy holidays."

"I'm thirty-five, and, seeing as I'm not one of those spontaneously reproducing reptiles, I'd need a man for that. I don't have one of those, as you've noticed. Besides, I already raised you and Ash, and you pounded my maternal instincts into dust. Parenthood is not happening."

"I've been manifesting someone to you."

There was a jingle of chains as I accidentally bumped the bracelet rack. "What are you talking about?"

"I'm talking about sending powerful thoughts for a desired outcome into the universe. I'm using laws of positive attraction to bring your man into reality."

I laughed. "How long have you been doing that? Because, so far, nothing."

"Not long. It occurred to me recently."

"How about manifesting yourself a date?" I teased, moving away from the check-out counter to the shelves next to it. "You're no better off than I am in that department."

"You're wrong," she said in a sing-song tone that had me letting the scanner dip down as I looked at her. "I've gone on five dates with the same guy. This month."

My mouth dropped open. "Are you serious?"

"I am. His name is Steve, and he's really great."

"Did you manifest him into being?"

She nodded without a single hint of joking or embarrassment. "I did. Which is how I knew it would work for you."

We worked in silence as I tried to decide if I wanted to hear more or not. Willow hummed softly, happily, knowing me well enough to let me process while she separated out colors and sizes of clothing for us to scan into the system. Willow had always been one to hum while working. On one rare occasion when Dad had felt the need to share, he'd told us our mother did the same thing. Willow had beamed and been a committed hummer ever since.

My memories of Mom were foggy at best. Flashes of a dark-haired, warm presence. Everything I knew about Judith Atwood pointed to someone sturdy and practical compared with our father. And while she'd gone along with giving us nature names, she'd insisted we all had a middle name to tether us to earth. I was always grateful to her for that, otherwise I'd have been stuck with Evergreen Atwood my entire life. Willow and Ash both had sturdy middle names too, but they liked their first names well enough to use them.

"How, exactly, does a person go about manifesting?" I asked ten minutes later.

Willow was kind enough to not react over the small victory she'd won. She simply stopped humming and answered matter-of-factly. "Well, it's a process. First, you make a list of qualities you want in this person. For you I listed smart, hardworking, and kind. Because you'd walk all over someone with a low IQ, you'd kill a lazy person, and you need more sweetness than you're willing to admit. Next, you visualize how you'd feel with that person. I imagined you'd feel settled, finally. I imagined you feeling secure and safe. Then, you . . ."

This was too much, and I held up my hand as my skin began to feel too tight for my body. "It sounds insane." What was really insane, though, was the way she'd gone to the effort to see me and ponder what she thought I'd need. It frightened me.

Here's the thing: Men do not like me; men get nowhere near loving me. Men had always called me words like abrasive, bossy, cold, and humorless. I'd tried dating, but that had been in my twenties when I was still working through my very real issues with my dad and his neglect. I'd had no good measuring tool for what I wanted, and being myself had only ended in fights and clashes that had left me frozen on the outside and broken on the inside. I was not cut out to be in a relationship, even if I had grown and come to better understand myself in my thirties.

I knew this because every man I'd ever tried with had told me that I was a total failure at being part of a couple. Every man had run away . . . from me, specifically.

"No more," I said in a raspy voice.

Willow pressed on anyhow, like she always did, possibly not even hearing me as she folded some pants. "Let me finish. Once you've laid that groundwork, start by focusing your thoughts on a desired outcome. Then you make statements to yourself like, 'I wonder where Meredith and her new guy will go on their first date' or 'I'd better tell Ash to set an extra plate at Thanksgiving next year' type thing. You never manifest with even a hint of doubt. You can't say things like 'I hope Meredith has someone by next Thanksgiving' or it won't work. Make sense?"

I'd gathered myself as she'd spoken, and now I shook my head. "Not at all."

"That's because you're not a dreamer, Mer. You're too practical. But I know for a fact that if you put out good into the universe, you'll get good back."

I wasn't against that concept. If you're a jerk to people, people will be a jerk to you. I mostly thought of it more as actions and consequences. I'd never thought to level up by putting certain thoughts into the world. It gave me something to chew on as we finished inventory. Like, how could I use this manifesting thing to help me with social change in my area.

I asked Willow a few questions about Steve, and that was all it took to get her talking cheerily about him and her plans for the holidays. She was hoping to meet his son, JB, but didn't know if it was too soon or not, yada, yada, yada.

As I pulled into my driveway several hours later, I felt a sense of bad juju coming from all those holiday decorations. It was time for this to end. So, even though I was bone tired from helping Willow all day, I bundled up and went to work at taking down the tacky, overdone revenge decor. Maybe this one good action would send some of those good vibes back my way.

When I finished, I delivered my tickets and fees to Hazel, who accepted them, and my empty yard, with a kind and slightly sad smile. I'd be eating ramen noodles for the holiday season, and maybe into the new year, but at least my record was clean. Hopefully the universe would reward my good behavior.

CHAPTER 10

I could tell from the sunlight streaming through my blinds the next morning that today was going to be one of those slightly warmer, delicious winter days. It was early, but I'd never been good at sleeping in, even on weekends, so I stretched and scratched at Betty's soft fur for a moment before I threw back my covers and made my way to my bedroom window. I opened the blinds, intending to take in the view of the sunrise, but my eyes were caught by something black and white, waddling along the top of the snow before disappearing under the trampoline in my backyard.

When I'd purchased this little two-bedroom townhouse a few years back, it had been from a family who had outgrown it. But during their time here, they'd installed an in-ground trampoline that took up practically the entire sliver of back yard. I typically took it down for the winter, but this year I hadn't gotten around to it. Because of that, I'd inadvertently created a booby trap for woodland creatures as it appeared that a skunk had fallen between the springs and was now residing—perhaps against his will—underneath.

Either that, or a neighbor cat was down there. I hadn't gotten a real close look before it disappeared. I bit my lip and watched to see if anything popped back out. Cats were climbers, so it should be able to rescue itself. But, then again, the springs weren't terribly far apart, so if the poor cat's aim was off at all, it could be repeatedly slamming its head against a spring and getting shot back down into the darkness beneath.

Spurred on by this thought, I hustled to the bathroom to use the facilities before slipping on a knit cap and my big winter coat. I had to investigate, and it was always best to do that with an empty bladder. I may not have birthed children, but at thirty-five I no longer trusted my bladder to withstand jump scares.

Betty followed lazily alongside me as she always did in the mornings, brushing against my ankles as I walked and doing her level best to trip me up. But today I was moving faster than usual, and she was left behind with a soft meow as I went into the kitchen, slipped on my boots, and went out the back sliding door. From here I could see the pawprints and maybe what looked to be a dusted trail behind it. Cats didn't typically drag their tails, so it was pretty likely I was dealing with a skunk.

Did skunks live around here? I wasn't that close to the mountains, living down on the west side of the city where the roads were flat and packed with homes. I wasn't used to seeing creatures in my neighborhood. I reached into my pocket, glad I'd grabbed my phone. I was hoping I could stay far enough away to be out of spray range but use the camera feature to zoom in and see what was going on.

When I was as close as I dared to get, I heard a shuffling noise under the trampoline, and I jumped back several inches, holding my phone out in front of me like a shield. A tiny, six-inch-long shield. Rolling my eyes at myself, I turned it around and turned on the camera, zooming in until I could see two eyes in the shadows. It was looking at me. It wasn't hissing or making a sound, and its backside seemed to be pointing away, so I dared to creep forward until I could confirm that, yeah, it was a skunk. And it was bigger than Betty. I snapped a fuzzy picture and headed back into my house to figure out next steps.

After hanging up my winter gear and making a cup of hot tea to warm up, I got online and did a little research. Turns out skunks are happy to live anywhere because they're garbage eaters and opportunists. They usually slept in the winter, but it's not a full hibernation, and, when temps aren't too cold, they'll forage in the night. My best guess is that the little trampoline prisoner had been making his way back to his den when he was bamboozled by the springs and slipped through the cracks. There was a lot of unhelpful but concerning advice about how they carry rabies and you don't want them in your yard because they're territorial. Also, a huge section on how to get the stink off your body and clothes should they spray. But probably the worst bit of information was when I read that they're not good climbers.

The skunk was stuck, and I was his only hope. I couldn't let him starve under there. I couldn't trap him and relocate because getting a skunk trap under there without disturbing him and getting a face full of skunk gland juice sounded impossible. So, while I made some toast and cut up some fruit, I thought about all my options. The one I landed on was pretty out there, but after looking up critter catchers in the area and finding out it costs hundreds of dollars to have them come out, I was desperate enough to attempt it.

Desperate enough that I threw on clothes, put back on my knit cap, and drove over to Brooks's house with determination. I was dirt poor thanks to paying all those HOA fees, and I was about to do some good old-fashioned begging from the one person I knew for sure would have what I needed.

He answered after a few knocks, looking sleep rumbled and disappointingly adorable in a snug white tee and flannel pajama pants. His hair was standing up, and a yawn filled up his face as he leaned against his doorframe and looked at me. I'd seen him do that lean before and was starting to think it was his favorite position to stand in. He looked warm and cuddly, and I had to step back a little to keep from reaching out to touch him.

I swallowed and shoved that absurd thought down. "Hey. I need wood. Specifically, two long thin pieces and several shorter pieces. I'm building a ladder."

He yawned again and nodded. "Of course you are. It's like 6:30 in the morning."

"Uh-huh."

"On a Sunday."

"Yeah."

"It's still dark outside."

I glanced up and pulled a face, putting on a show of confidence I wasn't really feeling. "Not true. The sun has risen. Either way, I'm too broke to go to the store, and I know you have supplies. I'll go pop my trunk." I spun around and headed to where I'd backed my car in. "Hey, could you open your garage?"

He shook his head and closed the front door, but he hadn't said no, so I popped my trunk and then turned to face his garage door, waiting. It took him a minute or two, during which time I questioned every single thing about this situation. It was pretty brazen of me to show up here, asking for him to supply my project. We weren't even really friends. Of course, we weren't exactly enemies anymore either, but . . . yeah.

I stomped my feet and rubbed my hands together, then paced a few steps to get some heat moving in my limbs and to help with the worries that I'd done something rash. As I moved I looked up at the sky and took a deep breath. It was shaping up to be sunny, and I was here for it.

The squeaking of his garage door had me turning back around. He appeared wearing jeans and that military jacket along with boots. His soft white tee had stayed as part of the outfit, and he hadn't bothered to fix his hair. He could easily be on the cover of one of Ruby's romance books and a flutter raced through my stomach.

"Okay, what exactly are you looking for, and why is this immediately necessary?" he asked, his voice still sleep roughened. Cue another flutter.

"I'm thinking two long pieces, maybe four feet long. They need to be small, though, like one by one, if you have anything that size."

He nodded, rubbing his hand over his beard, as he moved to a back corner of his garage. "I have a few scraps that might work. What's this ladder for? A garden gnome? It's not going to hold much weight."

"Yeah, I know. It's just . . . a thing I'm making. Doesn't need to hold more than, maybe, fifteen pounds?"

He glanced over his shoulder at me, his eyebrows raised. "Wait. It's going to actually be used for something? Are you hanging things on it? Or . . ."

I shrugged, super casually, and joined him in the scrap area to see if I could find small pieces of wood that could be used as rungs. "Yeah, I'm still figuring out the details."

"So, you simply woke up this morning, with the sun, and thought, *I'll build a tiny ladder*?" Now he was sounding a little put out.

I opened my mouth, sighed, and pinched my lips. "Not exactly." Would he make fun of me for rescuing skunks?

"You're being sketchy."

I smiled. "Something you should be used to by now.'"

He tugged out two boards that were around the length and width I'd pictured in my head. "These work?"

73

"Yeah." I snagged them out of his hands and headed toward my trunk. "Now I either need another one to cut into rungs or other scraps to create them out of."

"How many rungs do you need?" he called.

I deposited the poles in my trunk and went back into the garage. This part I wasn't sure about.

"Um, let's pretend I was building this for Betty. How far do you think her cat legs can reach between rungs?"

He stopped looking around the pile and stood straight, hands on hips. "Is this for Betty?"

I shook my head. "No. I'm using her as a hypothetical measurement tool."

"For planning out rung distance? That's a very specific hypothetical tool."

I licked my lips and then clamped down, biting them together and offering nothing more than a nod. He folded his arms. We locked eyes, and I recognized that he was going to want some answers before this continued. Most people's advice would be to dispose of a skunk, but I was not in the business of disposing of creatures, nor did I want to be. I wanted them to live out their lives with zero interference from me.

Only, something strange happened the longer we watched each other. I started to think about the face I was looking at. His eyes really were very interesting. Kind of like dark chocolate with milk chocolate swirl. His face was the kind I'd never call boring. Eyebrows I'd once made fun of were now expressive as they moved into various positions, and I watched him go from curious to annoyed to worried and cycle back again. His mouth was . . .

Oh, this had to stop. Flutters were starting for the third time that morning, and, no. Just, no.

So, I blurted out, "I'm building a skunk ladder," followed by swallowing and putting a hand over my mouth.

At first his expression was caught off guard, but laugh lines began to form around his eyes and then move to his mouth. "Liar."

I rolled my eyes and crossed my own arms. "I'm not lying. I watched one cross my yard and fall under my sunken trampoline this morning. I did a ton of research, and a ladder is the only way to get him out. So, I'm building one."

A smile broke out on his face, and he leaned back over the scrap pile. "I'm impressed. Not many people would try to rescue it." His tone was warm and complimentary, and I wanted to smile back at him until he said, "There's no way you're building this without me."

"Yes, without you."

He didn't bother looking back at me as he plucked a few blocks from the floor. "I know you can, but I'm too interested in how this is going to play out. Go grab those poles you put in your car. We can build it here really easily. My garage is set up for it."

I didn't immediately move to do what he asked, mostly because I didn't want to share this with him, and he was totally butting in. However, I could see the logic in having a helping hand, and he definitely had all the tools and space that I was lacking. So, with a loud huff to make sure he knew I wasn't happy about it, I retrieved the two long pieces from my car and brought them back into the garage.

He had moved to the work bench, and, as I came through the doors, he reached up and hit the button to close them. Then he flicked on lights and a space heater to keep us warm while we worked. I scooted close to the heater, putting some space between us as he took the posts and laid them across the table. While I watched him get things prepared, I thought about Ruby telling me that not all creative, woodworking men were deadbeats. I tried not to think about the countless hours I'd sat in a workshop and wished my dad would acknowledge I was there. Brooks was talking to me and bustling about, not checked out and wary of my company.

"Tell me how you came to the conclusion that a skunk ladder was the way to go," he said.

I could hear the amusement in his tone, but it didn't feel like he was making fun of me, only that he found the situation itself funny. I relaxed when it became apparent that no mocking was going to happen. As I told him about my research and reasoning, he laid out the smaller blocks between the poles and adjusted them a few times while asking follow-up questions about my thought process. It was, by far, the most laid-back interaction we'd ever had. When he was done I stepped closer to see the layout.

"That's too far apart," I said thoughtfully.

"Betty could make that distance," he argued. "I've seen cats stretch out."

"Yes, but we're not talking about a cat. We're talking about a skunk. Do they stretch? Do they have short legs? What's hidden under that fur?"

"Okay. Did you get a good look at it?"

I took out my phone and showed him the picture I'd snapped. "See. It's pretty good sized."

He grinned. "I can't tell anything from that blurry picture. You should submit it to a gossip site and tell them Big Foot is living under your tramp."

I pulled my phone back and tucked it in my pocket. "I watched it cross the yard. It's probably the same size as Betty."

He made big eyes. "Betty is a monster. We need a bigger ladder."

"Make fun of her again and I'll trap the skunk and leave it in your bed," I cracked.

"Leaving me gifts in bed? I think you need to slow down a little, Atwood. We're barely on speaking terms."

I blushed against my will and turned away under the pretense of finding more chunks to create rungs out of. When my exasperation had faded and I had two more rungs in hand, I came to the table again and scooted him over by pushing my hip against his until he gave me some room at the table.

I rearranged the rungs. Then he adjusted them to his liking. Then I shot him a glare and moved them to my favorite spacing. His lips twitched, and he reached to adjust them again. I put my hand over his before he had a chance to move it and made a growling noise that caused him to actually laugh.

"Build it like this," I said. "I think it's the right size."

We didn't talk over the noise of his cordless drill screwing the pieces together until a little, skunk-sized ladder had been formed. He took it off the table and held it up between us. It came to mid-chest on me, and I gave a satisfied nod.

Reaching for it, I offered him a small smile. "Thanks."

He grabbed it back toward him. "I'm coming with you."

I shook my head and reached for it once more. "No way. I don't need a man to help me drop a ladder between the springs on my trampoline. I can handle it."

He allowed me to take it. "Has nothing to do with what you can or can't do, and everything to do with me wanting to see this. It's the most entertainment I've had in weeks."

"There's not going to be anything to see. They're nocturnal. Most likely, he'll cower under there until dark tonight and then come out."

He turned off the garage heater and the lights and then opened the big main door. "Still coming."

I picked up the ladder and went to put it in my trunk. By the time I had it settled, he'd closed his garage door and was sitting in the passenger seat of my car with a ridiculously satisfied look on his face. I didn't bother saying anything but started the car and drove back to my place.

"What are your plans for bait?" he asked.

"Apple slices."

He grinned. "What time did you get up this morning that you've had time to see him, do research, and formulate a rescue plan?"

"I'm an early riser."

"Obviously."

We pulled into my driveway and into my garage, where I lifted out the ladder and propped it against the garage wall before leading the way inside my house to prepare some apple slices. Brooks followed along, shrugging out of his coat and hanging it next to mine. I'd had other people in my home, many times, but it had never felt as small as it did with Brooks leaning up against one kitchen counter area while I worked at the other. His coat hanging next to mine was like an itch I couldn't scratch. My eyes kept catching on it, and before too long I was noticing his scent filling up the little space.

My hands fumbled with the apple, catching it before it rolled onto the floor, as I opened a drawer to get a knife. He watched it all in silence, and I could hardly stand it.

"If you look out the sliding door you can see the path he left," I said, using the paring knife to point.

Brooks, either actually interested or taking the hint, moved across the small space to look outside. "Yep. I see it."

I hurried to finish with the apple, and soon we were dressed warm again and approaching the trampoline. He was carrying the apples, and I was carrying the ladder, a power move he'd acknowledged with nothing more than a crinkling around the eyes. We didn't talk, both of us understanding that we didn't want to scare the little guy. However, when we were standing next to the tramp, we realized there was a small issue. A spring or two was going to need to come out in order to leave room for him to actually use the ladder because the ladder itself took up all the space between springs.

I gestured at the springs, then to the bowl of apples, then the ground, then to Brooks, then to the springs again. He grinned and pointed at himself, the bowl of apples, the ground, and the springs. I rolled my eyes, picking up on his sarcasm even in the silence. His grin broadened, but he put the apples down and knelt slowly, peeking under the trampoline as he tugged a couple springs free. He set them off to the side and looked at me, holding his hands apart to show me about how big he thought the skunk was. My eyes grew large. Definitely bigger than Betty.

Brooks gestured for me to hand him the ladder, and at this point I simply gave it to him. There was no hill to die on here. He was already soaking his knees by kneeling in the snow. He slid the ladder into place and then placed a few apples slices around the top. He looked up to me, and I gave him two thumbs up before he looked back down under the tramp. When he did, he made a noise and jumped back, landing on his bottom before scrambling to his feet. I immediately understood the issue and made short work of jogging a few feet away. When we were out of firing range, we stopped and looked back at the tramp.

"Are you sure you don't want to call animal control?" he asked.

"It's a few hundred dollars," I replied.

"Ah, money you don't have on account of paying all those HOA tickets, huh?"

I clicked my tongue. "And to think we were just barely getting to be on speaking terms, and you had to bring that up."

He chuckled. "What's your plan after he's gone? And how are you going to know he's gone?"

"I'll know. And then I'm going to spray white vinegar around the perimeter of my yard to keep him away."

"What if his winter den is here?"

I hadn't considered that, and, now that I was considering it, I felt bad about it. "How do I know?" I asked.

He patted my arm. "Don't worry about it. You said he was crossing your yard. His den is probably somewhere else. Speaking of dens, you crawled into mine this morning. And now, I think I'll invite myself to have something warm to drink while we watch for Rocky to relocate."

He moved toward my house, easily covering the distance with his long legs as I hustled behind him. "You're not staying here all day. He won't be out until later, when the sun goes down. And Rocky? Who says you get to name him?"

Brooks held open my sliding glass door to let me pass through first, stomping snow off his boots before he came in. "Meredith, that skunk looked me right in the eye and told me his name. I'm simply trying to honor that shared experience."

I started to shrug out of my coat, and his hands were there, gently helping me out of it and hanging it up on the hook. "Look, I don't . . ."

He laughed. "I'm not really going to stay. I just really, really love the reaction I'm getting out of you over it."

I flashed to those fifth graders in the lunchroom, poking and tugging on hair and generally annoying the girls to get a reaction out of them. Apparently, men did the same thing, only in a more nuanced way. I refused to categorize it as flirting like I did with the school kids. I clasped my hands together to help center myself. Because Brooks was right, I was coming unglued over every word that came out of that man's mouth this morning. And I had been the one to get him involved.

"My jumpiness this morning is simply because I'm deeply concerned about Rocky."

He nodded. "Rocky is a pretty great name. I'll come back at dusk tonight, and we can see what happens." When I opened my mouth to argue, for what point I did not know, he lifted a finger. "It's the cost of using my wood to make the ladder."

I nodded and walked him to the door, then watched as he headed down the street back towards his house, both dreading and strangely looking forward to the night ahead.

CHAPTER 11

Brooks was not the only one who showed up for a skunk viewing party that night. It was my own fault for telling my friends about the day's adventures. Only Aryn and Ruby had been free that night, but they'd both come over right as the afternoon grew dusky.

"This is so exciting," Ruby said, clapping her hands against her chest. "I took extra time with my hair and makeup tonight."

"You do look especially cute tonight," I said kindly. I mean, she did look really cute with her high ponytail, warm leggings, and long wool sweater. "Is there a certain reason why?"

She gave me a look. "Um, I've never been to a viewing party before. I'm assuming there will be pictures taken."

A knock at my door announced Brooks's arrival, and Ruby gave a little squeak.

"The cute neighbor is here," she said.

I'd been walking toward the door to answer it, but at that comment I turned, and Ruby almost slammed into me. "I have no idea what's happening with you, but do not make this weird, please."

Bless her, she did her best to smooth out her expression, but those eyes were still dancing a jig that would not be stopped. "I'm here to support you and the skunk, and maybe stare at Brooks when he isn't paying attention to see how he looks at you when *you're* not paying attention."

"Oh my gosh," I sighed, but had to slam my lips together to keep from laughing at the bizarre conversation I was having. "He doesn't stare at me."

Aryn was down the short entrance hall, one hip cocked against the table, her hands in her pockets. We exchanged a look, and she grinned as I turned to open the door. Brooks was standing there looking much nicer than he had earlier. His hair was combed, his clothes fresh, and a nice scent came off him—different from the warm, natural way he'd smelled that morning.

Ruby was getting impatient behind me, and, before I had a chance to greet Brooks myself, her hand jutted over my shoulder.

"I'm Ruby Jenkins, and I'm so looking forward to watching for a skunk together," she chirped. "We met when you came during our friend's bridal shower."

Brooks smiled and took her hand, which meant they were shaking hands in front of my chin. "So nice to see you again."

79

"Isn't this exciting? I had no idea Meredith was so invested in skunks, but I can't wait to see what happens tonight," Ruby said.

She then stepped around me and reached out to help Brooks out of his coat while I watched. She didn't even try to pretend she wasn't giving him a once over as his back was turned, and before he could see her, she looked at me and wiggled her eyebrows while making her mouth into an O shape. I had to clench my jaw to keep from rolling my eyes or sputtering out a laugh at her antics. She was going whole hog on the matchmaking tonight.

"Brooks, nice to see you again," Aryn said as he headed that direction, leaving Ruby and I alone for a second.

I nudged Ruby with my elbow. "Knock it off. What are you trying to do?"

She nudged me back, causing me to stumble to the side. "He has a nice build, and he smells great. And that hair." She made a humming noise. "Running your fingers through that could be the only plan you need for an entire weekend. I give him two thumbs up."

"I have no need to run my hands through his hair," I hissed as we neared the kitchen, where Aryn and Brooks were lightly chatting.

She sighed. "That's a shame, because I think your entire mood would brighten after a few minutes."

"So, skunks," I called when we came into the open living area. "Who's in the mood?"

Aryn, used to Ruby and understanding that she'd probably thrown me for a loop, nodded and picked right up. "Me. Totally in the mood for skunk watching."

Brooks looked bemused. "Did he take any apples? Or are they still there?"

He and I wandered to the window, where the last bit of daylight was still shining through.

"No new tracks, and the apples are still there. Aryn brought over a motion detecting camera, and we braced it in the tree nearby. So, we should be able to watch for movement on the monitor and not have to stand with our faces pressed to the glass door all night."

"Unless you want to stand there, close together, faces pressed to the glass," Ruby joked, motioning to the two of us.

I smacked my lips. "Pass. Let's go sit on the couch."

Brooks chuckled softly as he followed, and I had the feeling Ruby had winked directly at him this time.

We all took seats, and I was grateful that Ruby hadn't been able to maneuver Brooks onto the couch next to me. He seemed to find her amusing rather than weird, and I was grateful. With Ruby, it was always best to operate from a place of humor.

Ruby crossed her curvy legs and plated her fingers together before looking right at Brooks. "So, what do you do for a living?"

"I'm a property lawyer."

"Convenient," Ruby replied. "For, you know, being an HOA president."

Brooks nodded. "Can be."

"I'm a nurse. Convenient for untraceable poisons." She held her face in some scary serial killer expression for three whole seconds before her eyes betrayed her and laughter followed. "I'm kidding."

Brooks nodded. "I'm impressed, you had me convinced I needed to keep an eye on my veins."

Ruby beamed, and I forced a laugh. "Aryn, do we have that monitor up and running?" I asked.

Aryn came out of the kitchen with a small screen, about ten inches wide, and propped it on my coffee table. "If I got all the instructions right, this should do it." She pushed a power button and knelt down in front of it to watch. "It's supposed to be wireless, and I already know your password."

Ruby leaned toward Brooks and stage whispered, "Her password is sexy minx, all lower case. I reprogrammed it when she wasn't paying attention."

My eyes shot to Ruby's right as a burst of laughter left Brooks's mouth. He hurried to slam his lips closed, but his shoulders were still shaking as I shot eye darts at Ruby. She was not supposed to be playing so chummy with Brooks and poking fun at me. And Brooks was not supposed to be so charmed by her. This was getting out of control.

"Where did you get this stuff?" I asked Aryn as I forced myself to settle back into the couch and play it cool. "I didn't know you were into home security."

Aryn's answer was mumbled, so I asked again. This time she looked up from her kneeling position and met each of our eyes as though daring us to say a word about it as she stated, "Wesley."

"The computer guy at school?" Ruby asked with her trademark 'oh, isn't this interesting' smirk. "That was awfully nice of him to loan out his *personal assets*."

This time it was me clamping down on a laugh because that had been hysterical when it wasn't aimed at me. I can be a hypocrite, but so can everyone else. "It's a weekend, so did you already have this stuff or did you, like, contact him on his private line to discuss?" I asked.

Aryn's lips pinched. "You already know Wesley and I went to school together. It's not that strange that I'd have his phone number and know he's into electronic gadgets."

"This is true," Ruby said, scratching at her jawline. "But I'd never heard of him until this year when he showed up at school, so pardon me if I'm suspicious of your alleged longstanding friendship. Is there, maybe, a recharged flame happening in our midst?"

"Rubes?" Aryn muttered.

"Yes, pal?" Ruby replied sweetly.

Aryn shot her a look over her shoulder that said we would not be discussing any of that. "Zip it."

Brooks, for his part, was watching our discussion with interest, and I'd nearly forgotten he was there. Well, sort of. He'd done a fantastic job of blending into the background, at least. But when I looked his way, it felt peculiar to have him there, like he'd stumbled into something personal. He was in my house, with my friends, participating in one of our many oddball shenanigans, and I wasn't having an easy time keeping up with this transition.

"So, what do we do while we wait?" Ruby asked as Aryn took her seat in a side chair. "We could play a game."

"Pass," I replied.

"You don't like games?" Brooks asked.

"I like them, we just don't have time tonight, and we need to be paying attention to the monitor."

Aryn smiled easily. "Meredith is competitive, and games can take a long time when she plays."

"I like rules. And following them," I stated.

His expression warmed. "Finally, someone who gets me. I'm going to read that rule book from cover to cover and make sure we play correctly. Drives my brother and sister-in-law mad. They've decided they'll never play with me again." He chuckled as my eyes lit up. "But this is interesting information coming from the twerking turkey, Rudolph woman. I could have sworn you tore up rule books for fun."

My friends laughed, but I playfully scowled. "I only break dumb rules."

He nodded. "Of course."

"She follows all the rules she believes in, though, to the letter," Ruby stated, obviously trying to have my back.

"I'd be interested in hearing about your system of deciding what to follow and what not to follow," Brooks said, crossing one leg over the other to rest his booted foot on a knee.

"That's easy. It comes down to logical versus illogical," Aryn replied. "It's not a bad system. I borrow it sometimes myself." Aryn gave me a fist bump, and I smiled at her.

"Okay, let's have an example," Brooks said.

"You've had several recently," I replied. "Yard decor mandates are illogical. Not parking my car on the curb during winter months is logical."

"Hmm. How about the rule that your lawn can only be three inches tall?" he asked.

I frowned. "There's a rule about that?"

He nodded. "I didn't know either, but I've recently become very interested in what the codes are. I had a feeling Hazel was getting a little ticket happy, so I've been doing some light reading of the bylaws in the evenings."

"Talk about downer reading. You must be sleeping like a baby," Ruby stated. "I'd never make it through the first page without it making me conk out."

"You made it through nursing school," Aryn replied. "Give yourself some credit."

Ruby giggled. "Because bodies are interesting. All that blood and fluid and muscle and tissue."

"You literally sound like a serial killer right now," I stated with a smile.

Ruby smiled big. "Really? Maybe creepy could be my new thing."

"It suits you," Aryn laughed.

Brooks was smiling in his chair again, watching as our conversation devolved completely. "My mom is a doctor," he said. "I have a feeling she'd really like you, Ruby. My dad's a CPA and about as squeamish as they come. Mom always loved to try to make him squirm with stories from her day."

"Did she succeed a lot?" I asked, intrigued by any information I could get about him.

"Oh, yeah. Not to mention me and my brother. All three of us would be feeling faint and Mom would be grinning at her seat, watching us all set down our forks and take deep breaths."

It took me a minute to realize that I was matching his smile, my eyes fixed to his face, but when the room grew quiet, I cleared my throat and got back to business.

"Okay, so it's basically dark now," I redirected. "Operation Rocky Retrieval is on."

"Rocky? What a cute name," Ruby said, leaning forward to watch the screen closer.

"I named him," Brooks said proudly. The man looked like he'd gotten a gold star in school.

"Let's place a bet on how long it takes for him to come out," Aryn said. "I'm guessing he'll be out within thirty minutes."

"I think he'll wait until the moon is high and then come out. So, midnight," Ruby stated.

"I'm betting even faster than Aryn says, because I have faith in the ladder plan," I said. "So, about fifteen short minutes."

We looked at Brooks. He shrugged. "I say he doesn't come out at all, and you have to call animal control to deal with it."

"Ugh," I said to my friends. "Do you see this?"

Ruby shocked me by throwing a pillow at Brooks and howling, "No pessimists allowed."

That was the kind of thing you'd do with a friend, and, as far as I could tell, Brooks wasn't in that territory yet. But he caught the pillow with a grin and held it close on his lap.

"I stand by it. What does the winner get aside from bragging rights, which is a given?" Brooks questioned.

We all looked to Aryn. It was her idea after all. "I'm not sure. I'll have to think about it," she replied.

"I have an idea," Ruby wiggled in her seat. "I'll draw a portrait of Rocky for the winner to have as a memento of this night."

Aryn and I blinked at each other and then at Ruby. "Rubes, you don't draw," Aryn said.

She nodded. "Exactly."

Exactly? What did that mean?

Brooks seemed to find everything that came out of Ruby's mouth to be a total delight because he was wearing a wide smile.

"I wholeheartedly accept," he said. "One portrait of Rocky, drawn by Ruby."

Pleased, Ruby looked back at the screen. "It would help if I could get a good image of him first."

"He's a skunk. So, you can just draw a skunk," I stated.

She shook her head. "You clearly don't know much about drawing, Mer. I need to get his personality, his essence, on the page."

"But . . . you don't draw," Aryn reminded her.

"I'm not drawing him; I'm capturing him in a timeless way on paper." Ruby opened her phone and started scrolling through skunk images. "Oh, hey, did you guys know that people can domesticate skunks? You have their glands removed, and they'll use a litter box. It says here they're very similar to cats."

"No," the three of us called at the same time.

Ruby startled and then rolled her eyes at us before looking back at her phone.

"Oh my gosh!" Aryn cried two minutes later. "Look."

We followed where she was pointing at the monitor and saw a skunk poke its nose out from the trampoline springs.

"He's on the ladder," Brooks breathed.

I fell off the couch onto my knees and got close to the screen. "It's working. It's totally working."

Rocky the skunk, apparently sensing it was safe, climbed the rest of the way out and stopped to eat an apple slice. He picked up the second slice in his mouth and meandered away. The four of us sat in silence for a few moments, waiting—I suppose—for the other shoe to drop. That couldn't be it, right? Just a three second ladder climb, apple snatch, and head out?

"I . . . think . . . we're done here," Brooks broke the silence with halting words.

"That was a lot of work for very little drama," Ruby said. "I was hoping maybe there would be a skunk battle or suddenly an owl would swoop down and carry Rocky away. It would have made for a really great portrait."

"I didn't get a picture," Aryn moaned. "It was so fast, and I was so surprised that I forgot."

Silence again as we all processed that news, but then . . .

"Wait," I looked around, a smile blooming on my face. "I won! My ladder worked, and I won!" I looked to Brooks. "I'd like to submit an item for next month's HOA meeting."

He groaned, but it was teasing, and the tip-tilted smile on his face caused those flutters to rise again. "What?"

"Skunk ladder. I have one and will happily rent it for a fee to neighbors who need help ridding their yards of nuisance animals. The money will be used to pay off all my tickets."

Brooks laughed, and I found myself sharing a smile with him.

"Rocky was not a nuisance," Ruby huffed.

Brooks and I laughed harder.

I walked him to the door while Ruby helped Aryn gather up her camera and monitor supplies. The feeling between us was more friendly than it had ever been, and I was sort of glad he'd been around for the skunk situation. He paused in the doorway after putting his coat on.

"You know, you have great friends," he said.

Pleased, I smiled and nodded. "I really do."

"Seems to me like friends say a lot about a person, don't you think?"

"Depends on where you're going with this," I teased.

"Only that you can tell a lot about someone by the company they keep."

I raised my eyebrows. "And what do you think my friends say about me?"

His lips rose in a mysterious half-smile that made my kneecaps feel squishy. "Probably more than you'd like for me to know."

CHAPTER 12

Monday morning came with a strong sense of guilt. While I'd confessed to Willow days ago that there was no Santa for the upcoming school party, I hadn't had the guts to tell my committee. My main reasoning was that I thought I could still pull it off. However, with it being the very week of the event, I was forced to admit I was in a spot of trouble. I'd tried—I truly had—because I hated failure and worshiped follow-through, but even my stubbornness hadn't made a Santa appear. So, bright and early I shot off texts to my friends. I didn't include the PTA committee members because I wasn't trying to start a whole thing. My thornback sisters and I could handle it.

Me: Emergency meeting in my classroom this morning
Ruby: What's the emergency?
Aryn: Can you text us?
Me: This needs to be in person
Hailey: Topic of the emergency?
Me: Santa and cookies party
Hailey: Did you text the PTA part of the committee?
Me: No. Just us
Aryn: That's a bad omen
Me: Please get to the school early today

The worst part of this was that they'd all done their jobs. Posters were hung, fliers had been sent home, cookies had been ordered, families were planning to attend, and assignments for set-up and clean-up had been given. In short, everything was a go. Except for one really big issue—there was a real possibility of no 'ho, ho, ho's' ringing through the school hallways. They weren't going to be happy with me, and they loved me. I couldn't stomach the thought of what Principal Wall and the PTA were going to do.

I haphazardly straightened my hair, did minimal make up, and didn't worry about ironing my clothing before heading to work—the anxiety rushing through me in a way that prevented me from eating breakfast. I sat behind my desk, nauseated and tapping my fingertips against it, while they all took a seat in the front row of small desks. No one liked having to be in early on a Monday, and their attitudes showed it. I painted on a welcoming smile, which only seemed to create suspicion.

"We're here," Aryn muttered, letting her head flop down onto the desk, "What did you do?"

I put a hand on my chest and attempted an innocent smile. "Me? Nothing."

"Your smile is chilling," Ruby said. "And your text used the E word."

"Emergency is not a word to throw around on Mondays," Aryn stated.

"Now, let's not be hasty. Maybe Meredith just wants a quick update since the Santa and cookies night is on Saturday, which is in only a few short days." Hailey offered me an encouraging and supportive look. I gritted my teeth. Her smile faltered. "What happened?"

I held up my hands and stood to walk around and sit on the front of my desk. "Okay, let's take a breath here. Nothing to overreact about."

"We aren't overacting. You said the word emergency," Ruby reminded. She'd not had time to do her hair at home, so she was currently sitting at the desk brushing and braiding while watching me. "And you didn't want to include the PTA."

"Meredith, you are the last person I'd ever suspect to issue an SOS. You handle stuff, and you don't get ruffled. The fact that you said, and I quote . . ." Aryn pulled out her phone and read my text. "'Emergency meeting in my classroom this morning,' that's like watching the news and being told a volcano erupted, and you'll need to evacuate within thirty seconds." She sat her phone down on the desk and gave me a look.

I held up my hands. "I, um, well, sometimes things are harder than they seem like they're going to be."

"You had one assignment," Hailey said thoughtfully.

"She didn't get a Santa," Ruby groaned. "We have no fat guy in a red suit."

My expression must have shown both my surprise and guilt over her guessing it, because there were several sharp intakes of breath before Hailey spoke.

"No . . ." Hailey looked at me with wide eyes. "That can't be it. He's the whole point . . ."

Aryn pointed at me. "Look at her expression. Oh my gosh, Ruby is right. We have no Santa."

Conversation erupted, and I let them get it out of their systems. Mostly it consisted of wondering what my problem was and accusing me of being a holiday dream buzzard, out to find joy in the scraps of happiness I'd left shredded on the proverbial holiday highway.

"Okay," I waved my hands after a second. "First, I have to defend myself. You guys know me. I tried. I would never fail on purpose. I've been stressing about this for weeks, making calls all over the state, and nothing worked out. So, now that you all know what the issue is, let's discuss solutions, please. Do any of you know someone who could play Santa?"

Ruby glared, Aryn wasn't amused, and Hailey looked concerned—not with Santa, but with me. She, alone, probably saw enough of the real me to know I'd punish myself much harder for this than they realized.

"Ford, maybe?" Hailey offered.

"Ford is too fit to pull it off without major stuffing," Ruby stated. "Plus, Santa isn't here as eye-candy for the moms."

"You have a point." Hailey looked pleased—as she should—and shrugged her shoulders.

"Maybe one of my brothers?" Aryn said hesitantly.

"No offense, Aryn, but they're kind of the opposite of welcoming," I muttered, picturing one of them just staring at children from their looming height.

"And again, too thin," Ruby said.

"Um, my brothers are far from thin," Aryn retaliated. "They're straight muscle."

"Let's go over the description of Santa once again, shall we?" Ruby said. "'He had a broad face, and a round little belly, that shook when he laughed, like a bowl full of jelly.' Nowhere in there does it say, 'He had huge biceps, and a firm little belly, that flexed when he laughed, and ate protein jelly.'"

We all laughed, which helped ease some of the tension.

Aryn shook her head. "You win. Plus, Meredith is right; my brothers' eyes don't twinkle at all."

"My dad could maybe do it," Ruby said when the laughter died down. "He's a big guy. I don't think he could grow a beard by Saturday though."

"We can get a fake beard, but your dad lives out of state," I responded. Ruby nodded glumly. "I think he'd be great, but we do need someone more local. I'm not sure what to do. I've exhausted all my ideas." We sat in thoughtful silence for another minute before I muttered morosely, "Maybe we should manifest a Santa into our lives."

Hailey cocked her head. "Did you suggest we *manifest* a Santa?"

I blew out a breath. "It's something Willow mentioned the other day when I was helping her with inventory. She's manifesting a man into my life."

They sat up straight, all thoughts of Santa flying out the window.

"Interesting. Why is she doing that?" Hailey asked.

"She thinks I'm a lonely spinster who deserves love, I guess." I pulled a face. "Who knows what goes on in Willow's head."

"How does one go about manifesting?" Aryn asked, more intrigued than I'd have expected.

"You do a bunch of visualizing and imagining and then show no doubt that it will happen," I replied with a wave of my hand.

"What kind of guy is she trying to visualize?" Hailey asked.

I rubbed my hand over the bridge of my nose, wanting to drop it but knowing they never would until I gave them an answer. "Someone smart, hardworking, kind, who would make me feel safe. Now, can we please get back on task?"

Ruby wrinkled her nose. "I had an aunt one time who swore she was going to have a new house by her birthday. There was no way it was happening, because she was broke and lazy, but she walked around talking about it all the time. 'I'll hang blue curtains in my new house; I'll buy red towels for my new bathroom.' Then, all of a sudden, two days before her birthday, someone shows up offering her an RV to live in. She hung those curtains and bought those towels like she'd never doubted it for a minute."

"I'm not buying it," I replied, not to be mean, but because I didn't believe in this whole business of attracting things to oneself. "There has to be a logical reason someone did that for her." Because there were once things I'd needed very much, and no amount of wishing had changed my circumstances. Getting up and working hard were the only truly reliable things. "It's a bunch of hocus pocus."

Ruby smiled. "This stuff works." She patted her stomach as it rumbled. "I'm about to manifest myself a philly cheesesteak."

"At eight o'clock in the morning?" Hailey laughed. "I can't digest meat until noon."

"I'm going to manifest myself a new car," Aryn added. "I wonder what time my new car will arrive next week?"

A bell rang, alerting us to the fact that the students would be arriving soon. My friends all stood, laughing and chatting about what they'd be manifesting themselves.

"What about Santa?" I called after them.

"Better start manifesting," Aryn offered as they rounded the doorframe and disappeared from sight.

I was in trouble.

*****

It was time to tuck my tail between my legs and beg for mercy two days later when no Santa had materialized, regardless of the fact my friends had told me that Thornback manifesting was twice as strong as regular manifesting, and that they knew it would come together. They had actually put in some work, making a few calls, and coming up as empty-handed as I had.

Desperate times occasionally birth desperate answers, and at lunch that day, I'd had an idea pop into my head that was so abhorrent I'd had to push away the rest of my lunch and try to stop a cold sweat from trickling down my spine. However, by the time the students went home, I'd realized I had nothing to lose. So, I walked the long walk to the principal's office to ask Mr. Wall if he wanted to play Santa.

I sat rigidly facing his desk as he leaned forward and templed his fingers in front of him. "Let me see if I understand this," he said.

I hated that phrase. People only said that phrase when they fully and completely understood something but wanted to say it out loud one more time to make sure that *you* understood how displeased they were with the situation.

"We have a Santa and cookies party scheduled for Saturday. It is now Wednesday, and we have no Santa. So, what we do have is a cookie party and decorations. But no Santa for the Santa part of the party." He said this all very calmly.

I nodded. "That's the basic idea, yeah."

He smacked his lips. "I don't think I have to tell you what a problem that is."

"I'm very aware."

"I overheard students in the hall today saying how excited they were to sit on Santa's lap and ask for a gift." His tone was becoming less calm.

"I totally understand your frustration, and I take full responsibility for it," I soothed.

He blinked slowly at me. "Yet I have no Santa, so what good does your acceptance of responsibility do me? You accept that you failed?"

I felt like a hot poker was being driven into my stomach. I hated failing. Deeply. "I did have an idea, actually, that came to me during lunch today."

He raised his eyebrows and leaned back. "Okay."

Now, I'm not suggesting here that what I said next was fully truthful. However, I have found that the occasional white lie to smooth things over isn't a terrible idea. "I know how much the students here like you," I began, watching as his mouth lifted at the corners. He unclenched his fingers and nodded. "Kids love time with the principal. For example, when you walk around the cafeteria and greet them at lunch or go outside at recess and shoot some basketball or hold the jump ropes—those kinds of things."

Now he was nodding. "The students seem to enjoy that, yes."

"So, what if you played Santa? What if you got to be the hero of the night? You know a lot of their names, which would make them feel special. The parents would get a kick out of seeing you dressed up, and I think it would bring an element of school spirit to the event." That last part might have laid it on too thick, but I held my breath and didn't say anything else.

He seemed to be recovering from the horror of my announcement and actually considering being Santa. "I don't have a costume."

"I'll find one."

"In three days?"

"Definitely." I'd sew one myself if I had to.

I would sheer a stinking sheep, process the wool, figure out looming, and sew it with strands of my own hair.

"Alright. If you'll provide a costume, I'll be Santa."

He actually smiled, pleased, ego stroked, and a wave of relief washed over me. Yes, I still had to find a costume, but at least there would be someone to put in it.

It was nearly dark by the time I left the school to make my way home. Snow had dumped once more, and it matched my mood. While Mr. Wall had agreed to be Santa and didn't seem totally angry with me anymore, his initial annoyed words still rang in my ears. Sure, he had a valid reason to have been frustrated with me. Still, nothing he said about it could compare to the way I'd already berated myself.

I didn't do this type of thing. I didn't let people down or not follow through with my duties. I was the woman who had the assignment finished far in advance. I did not leave things to chance. Procrastination gave me hives.

My hands were numb from using my coat sleeve to wipe snow off the windshield and having half of it go down into my coat. Dejection was my companion as I turned into my neighborhood. I didn't want to deal with the cold or the ice that sometimes built up on my front porch or the fact that I'd had to work late after groveling and ego stroking in Mr. Wall's office. This entire week had been a total bust.

I saw a male shape scattering handfuls of ice melt on my front porch steps as I turned into my driveway. I figured it was the snow removal people until I caught sight of the dark beard and realized it was Brooks. I watched for a moment, feeling mixed emotions about him doing a kindness for me. It wasn't logical for him to be here. The HOA hired people to do this. If I was one to analyze my feelings more, I'd probably be forced to add a smidgen of guilt to the equation. I did not deserve this. I'd had zero contact with him since the skunk viewing party, and I'd kind of figured we'd go back to our respective corners.

But logic and guilt aside, it felt amazing to have someone think of me and to check up on me.

I parked my car in the garage and gathered my things before going out onto the driveway, my arms loaded with my lunchbox and laptop bag.

"What are you doing?" I asked when he neared.

His breath created a cloud between us when he spoke. "I'm trying to prevent you from suing the HOA because of a slip and fall injury."

"Well, consider this my cease and desist letter," I replied.

His eyes scraped over my face. "You're asking me to cease and desist spreading ice melt?"

I bit my lips together and nodded once. "Go do it for some person who can't do it themselves."

"All the homebound are taken care of. Now I'm working down the list of . . ."

"If you say single women, I'll kick your shins," I growled, offended for capable women everywhere.

He closed his eyes for a moment and took a breath. When he opened them again, his expression was patient and maybe a little amused. "I was going to say, the list of people the snow company missed last time. I wanted to take inventory and make sure they're getting everyone done. I brought ice melt for the north-facing houses to be safe."

Logical. North-facing homes tended to get really icy walkways, and he was just double checking that the contract was being fulfilled. He didn't have to look so happy about making me look ungrateful and rude though. Then again, I'd done that to myself. Again. Sigh.

"Okay. I retract my cease and desist."

He brushed at some snow on his sleeve. "You're usually so delightful to talk to, but you seem to be upset tonight. What happened?"

91

I wanted to tell him not to worry about it, that he had more people in the neighborhood to check on, and that he had no reason to listen to me, but instead I met his dark-as-night eyes, and my shoulders sagged. I dove straight into the situation with Santa and how much I hated throwing parties for the school because it was a lot of people to make nice with but that when I said I'd do something, I did it. The entire time I talked he stood perfectly still. He didn't shuffle his feet or try to add anything in. He didn't tune me out. And when the words ran out, and my hands felt so tired that I almost dropped my lunchbox and laptop, he finally spoke.

"At least you've never tattooed the name of your ex on your body."

"I . . ." My mouth opened and then shut. Then, oddly enough, I laughed. "That's the best 'hey, cheer up' thought you had?"

He lifted one shoulder. "Yeah. Things are never really rock bottom until you've permanently put someone's name on your backside and then they break up with you."

"How do you know I don't have a secret tattoo somewhere?"

"Let's say I have a hunch."

"I have to say, if you've chosen the butt as the location to place the name, then things were pretty doomed."

"Exactly. So, you had a hard time finding a Santa, and you still don't have a costume, and getting together with a bunch of strangers to eat cookies on a perfectly good Saturday night in December is a total waste of time and energy? Look on the bright side."

"My bottom is pristine?"

Now he laughed, with shining eyes and full teeth showing as they caught the lights from my garage. A chill chased up my spine, and I shivered as warmth moved through me. I hadn't seen him laugh often because I'd always been out to get him and bring him down. We'd both said rude things to each other, and we'd both dug in our heels, but now I stood there wondering if I really had any idea of who this man was at all.

"Thanks for the really unusual pep talk." I paused, pulling a face. "And, I guess, for the ice melt too."

He held up his little bag of ice melt as though raising a toast. "You bet. I'm off to fight ice on other porches. Have a good night."

I went inside feeling oddly lighter, although, when I saw a voice message alert from Willow on my phone, some of the tension crept back in. Dad probably needed to be shoveled out again. I couldn't consider addressing it until I'd had a cup of hot tea, so I got my kettle going, shrugged out of my coat, and sat down at my table before listening to the message.

"Hey, Mer, I've already been to Dad's house tonight. He has dinner and clear pathways. Special thanks to Steve for helping me. I'm telling you, manifesting works. You're off the hook tonight, but you're it for the next big storm." Her voice was cheery, and I heard a man laugh in the background. That must be the mysterious Steve.

I deleted the message and leaned my forehead against the cool wood surface, where I attempted to manifest broccoli cheese soup into my life.

It never arrived.

CHAPTER 13

Santa and cookies night was a roaring success, and my friends deserved all the credit. The school cafeteria had been transformed into a North Pole wonderland. Walls were covered in black paper with stars and snowflakes covering them to look like a night sky. There were candy cane decorations hanging from the ceiling and a large Christmas tree next to a fake fireplace where a cozy recliner waited for Santa. Fake presents sat under the tree while a large velvet bag filled with candy canes sat nearby for Santa to hand out. The entire place smelled like cookies and hot cocoa and nothing at all like school lunch, which was a holiday miracle itself.

It had taken us all morning to pull it off, and I felt humbled and incredibly thankful for my friend group and the community parent volunteers. I'd kept things cheerful other than one measly little temper tantrum moment when Ruby informed me I'd be dressing up. My fellow committee members were dressed up festively, sure, but I'd made it pretty clear during planning that I'd wear regular clothing, thank you very much. My nod to the evening was a red sweater and black jeans. I'd even worn a green headband.

"Put this on," Ruby said as she came to stand by me on the stage, where I was surveying everything.

I looked down and pulled a face. "I'm not dressing up. And if I *were* dressing up, I wouldn't be wearing a candy cane on my head."

She pushed it against my stomach. "You are because you owe us big time for helping you pull this off."

I looked around at my friends, down at the costume Ruby had handed me and then back to Ruby. "How come Hailey gets to be Mrs. Claus? She looks classy and cute in that red dress."

"Because Hailey *is* classy and cute and really nice and all the kids aren't afraid of her," Ruby replied. "You, however, could use a big dose of sweetness, thus the candy cane outfit."

"Fine." I yanked it out of her hand and frowned down at the horrid red-and-white-striped sweater. "Maybe you should have had me dress as The Grinch."

"I'm dressing up as the Grinch," Ruby grinned. "He's the most interesting character in the holiday scene. Lizzie's an elf, which is perfect for her, and Aryn is an adorable snowman."

Of course my friends all had fun costumes. The PTA members were also dressed as elves or snowmen. "Why don't I get to blend in with the other elves?" I asked.

She gave me a look. "You're wearing that."

"Well, I'm not wearing the hat."

"Who found you a Santa costume?" Ruby bared her teeth at me.

"Aryn," I replied. Aryn's neighbor, it turned out, had a Santa costume from when his children were little, and he'd been willing to loan it to me for the night. I owed him big time for the favor. "Are you trying to tell me this is how I'm paying her back?"

"All I know is that Aryn says you're wearing the hat."

The hat in question was a vertical candy cane, rising off the top of my head, and making me at least two feet taller. It was humiliating. I shook my head, but Ruby raised her eyebrows, and, somehow, mind-melded with me, sending me images of how unafraid she'd be to use modern medicine to get her way. I offered one deep sigh and disappeared into the faculty bathroom to change.

The striped sweater was too big, which wasn't much of a surprise, and the scratchiness was annoying but survivable. The hat, however? Oh my heavens, the hat. It sat on top of my head, snapping snugly beneath my chin so that I looked like a face peeking out of a candy cane. It was snug to my cheeks and chin, so no hair showed—just my giant face, sticking out as a long contraption rose above me, forming a hook. I stared in the mirror for a while, and when I'd been there long enough to see the humor in it, I snapped a picture with my phone and sent it to my sisters.

Ash: Framing it

Willow: Checking outside to see if pigs are flying

I still had a small smile on my face when I arrived back in the cafeteria, which shrunk when I realized I had to duck to make it through the door. I found my friends talking a few feet away and knew they'd seen it because they were trying very hard not to laugh. I rolled my eyes at them and turned back toward the door when the sounds of families arriving caught my attention. We'd advertised it as a party, so people had come wearing all sorts of holiday things, including jingle bells, which really added to the chaotic feeling.

Good news: no one was going to pay me much mind.

Bad news: I should have taken some preventative headache medication before coming.

I made my way to where Principal Wall was taking his place in Santa's recliner and had to admit that the costume had turned out well.

"Looks like you managed to pull it off," he said when I was standing near him with my gigantic candy cane head. "I hope we have a good turn out."

"The holidays are busy, and Christmas is less than a week away, so we'll see," I mumbled, distracted by trying to keep an eye on everything going on.

"That's what I like—that positive attitude. You really have a gift for putting a Pollyanna spin on things," he muttered back.

I glanced at him, and he returned the look. Stalemate. I'd been in a few of those, but when it came to staring contests with bosses, I tried to keep it to a minimum.

"Thanks for being Santa," I forced some genuine gratitude into my tone.

"Thank your committee for making tonight happen."

His tone said he doubted I'd helped at all. I was about ready to launch into a snippy reply when Hailey popped into view. Up close she looked even more beautiful in a red velvet dress with a white, fake-fur collar and a pearl necklace. She had snowflakes dangling from her ears and a big, warm smile. Ford and his two kids, Henry and Hillary, were a step behind her as they took everything in.

"John," she smiled at our boss, "you look wonderful. The students will be so excited."

Principal Wall returned her warm greeting. "The cafeteria is transformed. You did a great job."

Hailey looked to me. "It was Meredith's doing. She ran the committee."

He didn't bother to look at me when he made a noncommittal noise. "Looks like we have people arriving. Are you all ready to go, Mrs. Claus?"

She nodded and turned to greet some children who had run straight to the big man. "I am."

Ford worked his way around the kids between them and leaned to rest a hand lightly on Hailey's waist as he placed a kiss on her cheek. He whispered something that made her face turn pink. It sounded like "under my Christmas tree," but I couldn't be sure. All I did know was that watching that tiny interaction brought up the sharp pain in my ribs I'd been experiencing lately.

I immediately slid into my place of comfort and took charge, forming a line to see Santa, making sure the cookies and milk were ready to go, picking up any garbage people dropped, and generally observing everything. These types of gatherings weren't really my scene. I was a pro at hanging on the sidelines and avoiding getting tangled in any lengthy conversations by always staying busy, but a few parents came to chat with me about their student, and I met them with openness. After all, I understood how much they loved their children and cared about their education. We were on the same team there.

"We have a situation by the cookies," Ruby hissed in my ear as she brushed past me.

"What's going on?"

"Milk puddle at ten o'clock, growing into nine o'clock, now taking over eight o'clock . . ."

I pushed off the wall where I'd been leaning and darted after her, only my stupid candy cane hat somehow got hooked on the basketball net hanging above me. I was moving so swiftly and the cane got caught so tightly that I actually came off the floor and swung feet forward by my head for a second before my momentum stopped and I flew backwards, stumbling as my feet touched the ground again. A tearing sound released me from the choke hold, and I dropped to my bum under the hoop.

96

I blinked a few times and then looked up to see the candy cane still wedged in the net, dangling there mocking me.

"Meredith!" Lizzie immediately knelt by me, causing her elf hat to tip forward. "Are you okay?"

I nodded. "Yeah."

Aryn came over next, her eyes dancing. "Oh my gosh. I wish so much I'd gotten that on film. It's not every day I get to watch your feet fly out from under you."

"I almost experienced death thanks to you and that hat," I retorted. I rubbed at the spot under my chin that had momentarily born my entire weight. "Thank goodness the snaps came free."

Aryn sputtered out a laugh and slapped her hand over her mouth. "Where were you off to in such a hurry?"

"Ruby said there was a milk puddle forming."

"I'll go help her." Aryn darted away, and I could see her shoulders shaking from laughter as she hurried to the other side of the gym.

"This might qualify for workman's comp if you're seriously injured." Lizzie patted my arm.

"Is the candy cane still up there?" I asked, embarrassment washing over me as I realized how many eyes were directed our way.

Lizzie looked up, her elf cap slipping backwards over her curls. "Yep."

"Care to guess on a percentage of people here that just watched me hook a hat in a basketball net and swing from it by my head?"

It took her a few seconds to shove down the giggles, but she finally answered as she stood and reached down to help me up. "No more than sixty percent."

"What a relief."

✶✶✶✶✶

The snow was really dumping again as I drove through my neighborhood in the dark after the party and cleanup were all done. Why did winter have to be so crummy? Both dark and snowy? Come on Mother Nature, throw us a bone here. Let's have sunlit snow days every now and again. It's bad enough that people get off work at 5:30 p.m. and have to head home in the icy tundra, but throwing darkness into the mixture is plain rude.

I was grateful that my driveway was at least clear when I arrived, but I could see the shape of Brooks as he walked by, tossing ice melt again. This time he was also carrying a snow shovel with him. I pulled into my garage right as he arrived at Hazel's house next door. I parked my car and popped open the trunk to retrieve some of the things I'd contributed to the decor, which didn't really amount to much. I glanced up to see him wave at me and turned to face him.

A tiny, almost unnoticeable bubble of happiness tried to float up under my sternum at the sight of him standing there with a smile that was meant for me. Frightened, I squashed it. I may not be trying to make him pay for all the injustices of the world anymore, but I certainly couldn't be happy to see him.

"How long until you fire the snow removal company?" I called across the snow-covered lawn. "Aren't they supposed to be spreading ice melt?"

He tossed a handful of pebbles onto Hazel's porch. "It's not as easy as that."

"I'd have fired them several weeks ago when they started skipping peoples' houses."

"You'd have fired Mother Teresa for too much self-sacrifice and encouraged her to have a little 'me time,'" he retorted with a laugh.

A delighted feeling swirled through my chest at the sound, and I bit the inside of my cheek. I was going to go over there and tick him off so that we could take this situation between us back to places I felt comfortable with. I tugged my mittens out of my coat pockets—because all Northern Utah women know to keep mittens in pockets from October to April—and closed my trunk, leaving the decor where it had been sitting. Moving out of the garage, I used the key code pad to close the big door behind me. Brooks stood still and watched as I broke trail through the snowy yard rather than taking the shoveled sidewalks. His breath came out in light puffs of white around his face, and I could see condensation in his dark beard as I came to a stop near him.

"You're not even wearing boots," he muttered, looking down at my loafers.

"I'm fine." I actually hated that I'd forgotten about my footwear and that snow had fallen in and was melting around the soles of my feet but admitting that was not happening.

He nodded, a tiny smile still tugging at his mouth. "I forgot, your feet probably stay warm from the heat of crushing dreams beneath your heels."

I laughed. I'd meant for it to sound sarcastic, but I'd been so caught off guard by his statement that it was accidentally kind of a real laugh. "That's big coming from the guy who placates everyone so delicately all the time."

He sprinkled a tiny handful of ice melt over the tops of my shoes, and when I was done looking down at my loafers in shock, I glanced up to see him grinning from ear to ear. His smile was particularly bright in the soft glow of Hazel's porch lights, and he looked like a young boy who'd just hit his first home run.

"Don't want ice forming on your toes," he said in an amused tone.

My mouth opened, knowing that in this verbal dance the next move was mine, but I was at a loss for words. I'd come over here feeling irritated, and now I felt . . . something else. My lack of reply seemed to make him even more happy, and he reached for the snow shovel that had been leaning on Hazel's railing.

"Here. Let's see if you can do something besides attack me," he said. "If you have the energy to come after me, you have energy to help."

I grabbed the shovel. "This is for Hazel, who can't afford an injury if she's going to get your new sweater knitted by Christmas."

"I asked her for stripes this year. They're such a classic look."

He moved to the porch stairs, and I found the distance helpful. I was used to him giving as good as he got, but I wasn't used to enjoying it. Other men hadn't wanted to spar with me—they'd wanted to break me down and win a battle. It was never fun or clever, and it was always painful. I was used to banter with my friends, but Brooks was the first man to banter with me who seemed to enjoy my sharpness, and it was throwing me into a tailspin.

While I thought about that, I finished shoveling a few stubborn spots on the walkway that had been flattened underfoot and turned to find Brooks standing at the end of Hazel's driveway, simply watching me.

"Good, you're done. We're going to the Parker's house now. Keep up, and don't slip in those shoes."

He turned and walked down the street, his dark coat and hoodie helping him blend into the darkness. He was being bossy, but I didn't argue—just fell into step a few paces behind. The Parkers lived the next block over, and Brooks wasn't slowing his pace for me even if his legs were longer. I didn't hustle to keep up. I'd been walking around all afternoon and evening and didn't feel the need to tap into my nearly depleted reserves.

For the next hour—for no good reason I could decipher—I followed Brooks from house to house in some order only his brain knew. My shoes were soaked, my hands were cold, and my nose was beginning to drip when we finished the last house. I felt good tired, like the mindless exertion had helped me let go of the unpleasant day. It was nice.

"That's it," he said as we stood at the end of the Brown's driveway and looked at their festive home.

I wondered, out of the blue, how many times my dad had shoveled snow for others or even known someone else might need something from him. Yet, here was this man, wandering about after dark, secretly serving people. It tugged at my emotions, so I focused on the white lights sparkling on the roofline and the full evergreen wreath on the door that added a beautiful last touch. It was all so classy and well done that I once again had to face how over-the-top my own inflatable decor had been.

"What a boring holiday display," I joked, gesturing at the house and breaking the comfortable quiet.

"Agreed. How is the International Space Station supposed to see it?" Brooks replied in a dry tone.

I chuckled as I spun to hand him his shovel so I could head home. Unfortunately, I hit a patch of non-melted ice and reached for his coat with my free hand, hoping to stop my fall. It was total instinct, because if I'd thought it out, I would have simply let myself fall rather than take him down, too. Brooks, not expecting the sudden tug on his torso, grunted as we landed with a thud, the air knocked out of my lungs as my arms flopped to my side. I was slow to register the weight of him on top of me and the way his beard was tickling my cheek as our faces pressed close. When I did process it, heat crept along my skin and over my frozen nose. Our eyes caught for a split second before Brooks shifted, pushing up onto his arms until he could roll off me.

"You okay?" he asked as we both looked up at the night sky.

"I've breathed better," I replied, trying to ignore the way my senses were still filled with the scent of peppermint on his breath and that particular smell that woodworkers carry with them always. It was at once familiar and new. "That's the second time I've fallen today."

"Really?" He sat up and looked down at me.

"Yep. The other one involved a candy cane hat and an attempted murder by hanging," I replied.

"There's a story there." He continued to watch me, but I kept looking straight up, too scared to meet his eyes.

"You'll have to wait for the full-page spread in the Washington Elementary School yearbook this spring."

He smiled softly. "Ah, so it was public."

"They usually are."

We were silent for a beat before I sat up, too. He jumped to his feet and reached down a hand, which I took. His grip was strong, and he pulled me up quicker than either of us expected. I came up hard against his chest, my hands pressed between us. The very moment I'd been trying to avoid happened as I tilted my head back to find him looking down at me. The dark hid some things, but not his curiosity as his eyes skated over my face. I didn't want him to be curious about me, and I sort of hated that I'd become curious about him. Curiosity killed the cat, if I recall. I pressed against his chest, and he released me quickly.

I tucked my hands in my coat pockets and made a face. "So . . . you going to find a new snow removal company?"

He nodded and a smile peeked out. "Sure am."

CHAPTER 14

The origins of a bachelor or bachelorette party has always been lost on me. If you want to party with your friends before your wedding, that's great. Do it. But to plan something for the express purpose of celebrating your 'final night of freedom'? If going into marriage feels the same as going to prison, then you may want to rethink the situation. Also, does life really change that much after getting married? I understand the concept of pledging yourself to someone as far as loyalty and a commitment to support each other, but I do not remember anyone ever pledging to give up their entire self for the other person. If your fiancé is like, "*Hey, hope you can squeeze out that last drop of fun tonight before we say our vows tomorrow, because after that you can plan to say goodbye to life and stare at me on the couch for the next fifty years,*" well, that's a hard pass for me.

Don't even get me started on this idea of two halves making a whole. If you are only half a person, you have no business entering a marriage. I'm certainly not interested in schlepping around that kind of mess for the rest of my life. If, and I mean *if*, I ever consented to get married, we'd have to be real clear about the fact that I would still be me and he would still be him and no one would be suddenly expected to change entirely.

This entire principle of mine is probably a big factor in why I'm not married nor looking to be. It may also be why my few attempts at a relationship never really worked. Guys say they like independent women, but, in my experience they actually like women who put on a good show but are happy to follow their lead in the end.

These were the somewhat inappropriate thoughts I was having as I slowly swirled a tiny cocktail straw around in my drink at Lizzie's bachelorette party. One of my hands propped up my head as I did so. There was a lot of laughing going on around me, but I didn't bother to look away from the soda I was nursing along. My bare shoulders were chilled in the hotel bar area, where we were kicking off what promised to be a somewhat unappealing night.

Because I'd thrown the bridal shower, I had not been required to help plan said party, so I couldn't say for sure it was going to be horrifying. I was simply going off past experiences combined with my current setting. I was in a bar, wearing a slinky black dress, swirling a non-alcoholic beverage. According to my fun rating system, where bars and dresses receive a zero and mystery activities get a two, well, I don't really need to expound.

"Meredith, you look amazing in that dress," Ruby sidled up next to me and sat on a tall stool. "Did Willow dress you?"

I shifted my eyes from my drink to her face. "Yes, Willow loaned me the dress. I have to say, your makeup is leveled up tonight." She'd drawn huge cat-eyed liner with bold green shadow, and her eyes looked far different than what I was used to seeing on her.

"Is it too much? I'm not trying to pull off a Halloween costume vibe."

I straightened my head and patted her arm. "You look exotic and mysterious. It's too bad this is a girls' night thing, because if there were men around, they'd be all over you tonight."

Her smile flashed. "Thanks. I do like to imagine a little macho drooling going on around me. Hailey and Aryn really know how to plan an event."

I glanced around. "Who are all these women, and why do more keep coming?"

The small bar area had originally held just the five of us—with Lizzie wearing a white cocktail dress and a little tiara. I'd been relieved and thought maybe my group of favorites was going to spend a night pampering ourselves and dressing up fancy. But more people had started arriving, and now there had to be at least fifteen people gathered around. I knew only two of them. Lizzie's mom, Jan, and sister-in-law, Abby. The rest were total strangers, which only made me want to find the darkest corner possible and build a fort in it until everything was done.

Look—I'm not a total people hater. It's more that people don't really understand me and, over the years, I've learned it's best to keep my distance for all our sakes. Social situations have always been awkward. As a child I didn't relate to kids my age because, while they were playing dolls and riding bikes, I was a caretaker. As a young adult I didn't relate to the whole 'taking chances' and 'going boy crazy' stuff because, yeah, I was paying bills and raising Ash. In my twenties I didn't understand why people were still trying to act young. Things were getting better as my peers aged, and my rough edges were smoothing out, but things don't magically adjust overnight.

"Lizzie grew up here," Ruby said, answering my question. "She knows a lot of people. Plus her family is here." She waved at Aryn, who looked like a supermodel in her sparkling dress with heels. "When Aryn wears heels it's like her legs become extendo-legs, up to the sky. She looks great."

I grinned at the image of the rubber-band mom from that kids' movie. "She's got legs for days."

Aryn moved to where we were sitting and leaned up against the table, surveying the crowd. "I think everyone is here. Right on time. Hailey was right about timing."

"She always is," I replied.

"Can you believe Lizzie gets married in only two days?" Ruby sighed. "She's so lucky."

"She was lucky before she met Jackson, too," I reminded Ruby. "Because Lizzie is a whole person who does not need a man to make her complete."

Aryn smirked and walked away, uninterested in engaging with me. Plus, she probably had business to attend to.

Ruby, however, engaged. "You're right, of course," she said, looking at me with those glowing cat eyes. "But she's happier now than I've ever seen her. Jackson makes her braver and lighter and she seems surer of herself with him in her corner. So, no more grumpy words about it. Just because you love being single and indestructible doesn't mean the rest of us do."

"You're all indestructible too," I muttered.

She nodded. "That's true. But even strong things benefit from a support system. One piece of wood can lift a lot, but when you nail a second board alongside it, it can carry a lot more. Having a partner in life doesn't take anything away from a person."

"You've got the wrong idea," I defended, feeling slightly uncomfortable suddenly. "I think it's wonderful that Lizzie's happy and Hailey has Ford. I'm really happy for them both. It's a good thing."

"It's just not for you?"

I swallowed. "Exactly."

A small smile tugged at her lips. "We'll see, Meredith."

Hailey called the room to order by clinking a knife against her glass. She too looked amazing in a turquoise dress with a short, flirty skirt, her light hair held back by gold clips. She was smiling at everyone, and I saw the same things in her that Ruby had mentioned about Lizzie. Hailey—at thirty years old—was coming out of her shell, and I had to admit that Ford had started that metamorphosis in her. She was growing into the potential the rest of us had always seen.

"Thank you all for coming to help us celebrate Lizzie and her upcoming marriage to Jackson," Hailey called. There were some cheers, and Lizzie pumped her fists in the air, which made everyone laugh. "For our first stop we'll be walking a few doors down to Bella's where we'll be taking a private cooking class."

Lizzie cheered again and led the herd as they moved toward the doors, laughing and squealing and leaving their drink glasses anywhere they could find a place.

"We're doing a cooking class in cocktail dresses?" I said to Ruby.

Her eyes fell to her own dress. "Oh boy. I have a spilling problem."

"I have a sister problem—as in she loaned me this dress. I don't want to have to pay for it if it gets stained."

A warm hand landed between my shoulder blades. "Pep up, dear, and paste a smile on that mug," Aryn said as she herded Ruby and I after the others.

"Cooking in fancy clothes?" I raised an eyebrow as I started walking.

Aryn nodded slowly. "We do what the bride wants. When you get married we'll dig up graves."

Ruby sputtered, "Or hand out pencils to little children who think they're getting candy."

I held up a hand. "Hey, I did that one Halloween. One, okay. And it was only because I didn't think I'd get trick-or-treaters in my neighborhood full of old people and hadn't bought candy."

Ruby sighed. "It would have been better to turn them away."

I laughed and shook my head. "I hope it's pasta and you spill red sauce all over your dress."

"She's bloodthirsty, just like I always thought," Ruby said to Aryn.

We joked and jabbed as we followed the rest of the women into Bella's restaurant. The front end had a few diners, but many fewer than usual, and I asked Aryn how they'd managed to pull this off. Bella's was a delicious Italian restaurant in a town that really needed one. It was busy all the time with long wait times that no one bothered to complain about.

"Ford and Hailey pulled some strings," Aryn replied. "I didn't ask too many details. My part of the evening comes after this."

"There's more than just cooking?" Ruby clapped her hands together. "I hope it's a tour of a candy factory. Or maybe go-cart racing."

Aryn chuckled. "It's neither of those things, but I'll keep them in mind for your bachelorette party someday."

"Or for my birthday, whichever comes first," Ruby replied cheerfully.

We followed the group through a set of doors and into a cavernous kitchen, which we passed through into a back area that was set up with eight tables and cook tops. It didn't look like something that had been there long-term, and I wondered what kind of strings Hailey and Ford were dealing with, because the strings I'd been given in life did not tug the same way.

"Everyone pick a partner," Hailey said when we were all together. "Two to a table. I'll go let Tori know we're here."

"We should be partners," Ruby said to me as Aryn was called over by a woman I didn't know.

I looked at Ruby and the way she'd gone directly to the knife block, and then I glanced around to see if there were any other empty spots open. I heard the specific sliding sound of a knife coming out and spun to face her.

"This feels well balanced," Ruby grinned.

"Something at this table has to be," I replied. "I'll go see if they have aprons."

Ruby waved the knife around and then tossed it lightly in the air and caught it again by the handle. "Yeah. I can definitely cut stuff with this."

Ruby was a great cook and knew her way around the kitchen, but I didn't think she should be handling that knife like she was warming up for a circus act. I backed away and went to where Hailey had returned and was chatting with Aryn.

"Ruby is tossing knives," I tattled.

Aryn and Hailey glanced over at Ruby in time for the three of us to see her pick up another and start some sort of juggling thing. I looked back at them with a 'see what I mean' expression. Aryn bit her lips together, and Hailey covered her mouth with one perfectly manicured hand.

I gestured to Ruby. "Well? Maybe one of you should be her partner."

Neither of them said a word but kept biting and covering their mouths until Aryn accidentally snorted, and then both of them burst out laughing.

I blinked. "So, you're telling me I'm her partner?" They nodded. "I'm going to need an apron, some towels, a mop, safety goggles, and a Kevlar vest."

This really set them off, and even I couldn't help laughing as we glanced Ruby's way in time to see her move over to the table next to us and test out their knives while the poor strangers watched in total confusion with a smidgen of alarm.

"There are aprons on that hook by the door," Hailey pointed to the side.

I marched over and snagged two before retrieving Ruby from yet another table, offering up apologies and nudging her back to our station.

"Word is that Tori is the original owner's great-granddaughter, that they look eerily the same, and some people think she might actually be Bella reincarnated because this restaurant was her heart and soul and even death couldn't keep her away," Ruby said as she tied on her apron.

"Bella's opened the same year I graduated high school, Rubes. It hasn't been around long enough for Tori to be a great-granddaughter." Ruby snorted, so I shook my head and opened the proverbial door. "Okay, what do you believe?" I asked, tying my own apron and wondering who would have told her all of that in the three minutes I was gone.

"I can't say for sure because I've seen some strange things. But I do know, for a fact, that this place has the best fettuccine alfredo in town." She smoothed her hand over the metal table in front of us. "I'm hungry." She pointed a knife at the front of the room. "I wonder what we'll be making, and I wonder what Tori will look like. I'm thinking she's got to be maybe twenty-five years old, short curly brown hair, big soulful eyes. I'd imagine she looks content because she's where she loves to be."

"Did you say soulful eyes?"

Ruby nodded. "Big and soulful."

I smacked my lips together. "Like a basset hound?" Ruby playfully hit my arm. "Great. Hope those big eyes get here soon because I'm ready to get going."

Tori, it turned out, was the daughter—not great- or grand—of the original owner, whose name was Salvatore. He'd named the restaurant after his grandmother, whom Tori had never met, and he was still alive. Tori was probably fifty-five; she had long, gray hair; and her eyes were kind of squinty. There was nothing soulful about them. But she was warm and funny and charming in a way that helped me relax and pay attention.

I'd never been an actual cook. I could throw together basic meals, but it was about function and necessity, never about expressing love or care in some way. Tori made me want to be different. As we mixed with our hands and she talked us through the process of pasta from scratch, I thought about how much it would have meant to learn to cook from my mother. I'd simply been too young when she passed, and that old familiar wanting rose in my chest—the grief of losing things you'd never had.

A slap across my cheek pulled me out of my thoughts, and I glanced up to see Ruby whipping her pasta around her head like it was pizza crust and she was in the cartoons.

"What are you doing?" I ducked as spaghetti came at my face.

"I'm keeping it loose and elongating it," she said, looking up with intense concentration as her noodles became helicopter blades.

"No one else is doing that," I pointed out. "But now they're watching."

"They are?" Ruby looked away from her noodles, and they flew off her hands, across the room, and landed with a flop near Tori's demonstration area.

"What an interesting technique," Tori commented placidly. "What did we learn from that, Ruby?"

She knew Ruby's name? Of course she did.

Ruby hurried forward to pick up the mess. "We learned that this is not the proper way to handle noodles."

The class laughed as Tori chuckled. "Exactly. Mistakes can be very helpful. Now, Ruby, go back to your station and try again."

Ruby dropped her pile of pasta into a trash can and met up with me again, a big grin on her face. "She's much nicer than my mom. Whenever I launched a wok full of veggies into the ceiling fan, she'd always yell down the house."

"So, you have a history of throwing food and it failing?"

"Yep."

"Then why do you keep doing it?"

"Because one of these days the idea in my head will work, and when it does it's going to be awesome."

I watched, working my own pasta and following Tori's instructions explicitly as Ruby went about her business with careless glee. Eventually we both had pasta dishes: mine pristine and hers a little lumpy. But they both tasted great, and at the end Lizzie laughingly awarded Ruby the gold star for creativity—an award that the whole group clapped for.

After we ate our creations, Aryn led us another few doors down to a large salon where we'd receive after-hours pedicures. Everyone sighed happily as we kicked off the heels we'd been standing in for two hours and dipped our feet in hot water. I was happy to see I'd been seated next to Lizzie. She was beaming. In fact, she'd beamed the entire night.

"Not as horrible as you expected, right?" She turned to face me, her tight curls falling over her eyes.

I smiled. "Not at all. It was a great activity requiring no social involvement from me. The people thank you."

Lizzie laughed. "I was thinking about asking you to do the main toast at the wedding, but I was afraid you'd steal the show and never give the mic back."

"You're smart to keep me out of the spotlight; I crave it so."

She leaned her head back, and I watched as a secret, little smile landed on her lips. "Only two more days, Mer. Can you believe it? What are the odds that we'd have gone on the very river rafting trip that he was guiding?" She sighed. "Have you ever wanted something for so long and thought you'd never get it?"

"Yeah," I replied quietly. A lot of things.

"I got it. I got Jackson, and we're going to build this whole life together. I'm so happy."

I reached out for her hand, and she wrapped her fingers around mine tightly. "I'm going to miss you," I admitted. After the wedding she'd move hours away, and we wouldn't see each other hardly at all.

"It's going to be so strange to be teaching at a new school and be the new girl, in a way. I've lived here my entire life, but now my world will change so much. New city, new family, new daughter, new job."

"That's a lot of new things," I squeezed her hand.

"I know you hate sappy things, but tonight is my night, so you have to accept it. I think it will surprise you to learn that I needed you as much as you needed me," Lizzie said. "You taught me how to be stronger and fight for my cause."

I shook my head. "I'm lucky you guys let me tag along. I know I'm not always easy."

"We do it strictly for entertainment," she replied.

"Yeah, I'm a barrel of laughs."

She squeezed her fingers against mine again. "Don't sell yourself short, Mer. We know who you are on the inside."

A cork popping stole our quiet moment, and I let go of Lizzie's hand as she sat up a little straighter. Little plastic fluted cups were passed around along with some sparkling cider and chocolates. Lizzie clapped and made a comment that had everyone laughing along with her as I leaned back in my chair and felt my shoulders give up some tension for the first time in a long time.

As far as bachelorette parties go, this one hadn't been bad at all.

CHAPTER 15

The clubhouse smelled like fish when I entered the next night. Not good fish, either. Fish that had been forgotten in a garbage can. I scrunched up my nose as I made my way into the large central room where the monthly HOA meetings were held, wondering why it always smelled like bad food but no one thought to mention *that* at these meetings. Brooks was already there, dressed in a black button-down shirt and dark jeans. His sleeves were rolled up, and I caught sight of that tattoo that I really wanted a good look at. He was talking quietly near the front table with Leland and Hazel. Shayla, the treasurer, was in her seat and working to open the metal box she always had with her at meetings.

Brooks looked up as I walked by to a seat on the front row. His dark eyes followed me, and I remembered the open and curious way he'd taken me in the other night. Tonight he looked sort of okay with me being there, unlike how he'd been in the past. The realization pleased me, which then worried me, which made me feel grumpy, which he noticed. He quickly looked away, and I couldn't help but sigh on the inside. Start war with a guy, warm up to the guy, scare the guy away—the Meredith playbook, ladies and gentleman.

I took a seat and waited as more people filed in. It was slim pickings tonight, which was no surprise in December. People had plans. Well, most people had plans. Lizzie's wedding was the next day, so I could have been steaming out my bubble-gum pink dress or painting my nails or something, but those things weren't going to take all day. Brooks and his committee took their seats, signaling that it was time to begin. No one was sitting near me. In fact, there was a definite circle of emptiness around me, which probably should have hurt my feelings but didn't at all. I found it oddly amusing, and a small smile lifted the corners of my mouth. Brooks saw, and his lips softened before he opened his mouth to call the meeting to order.

"Leland, do you have the minutes from last meeting?" Brooks asked.

Leland frowned. "I don't take minutes. That's Hazel's job."

Hazel began vehemently shaking her head. "No, Leland. Last month I had hurt my right hand when I accidentally shot it with a nail gun, so you took minutes."

Wait. I looked around the room, and no one else seemed to catch the fact that Hazel had been using a nail gun and shot herself. Were things so strange around here lately that this wasn't even worth blinking at?

Leland was shaking his white head before she'd finished. "You have no business using nail guns."

Thank you, Leland, I thought.

Hazel's blue hair shook with fury. "Leland, don't you lecture me about power tools. How else was I supposed to build my indoor gazebo?"

"We don't care what odd contraption you're building this month. I didn't take minutes in November," Leland harrumphed and folded his arms across his chest.

Brooks looked at me as though to commiserate, and I was so caught off guard by him wanting to have a little eye conversation with me that I missed the cue and left him hanging there. In my defense I was used to him giving looks to others when I was the one talking. I fidgeted in my chair, wanting to get his attention back so that I could send him a 'these people are losing it' look, but the moment was gone, and he was working to regain the room.

"Leland, Hazel, how about we move on?" he said kindly. "Shayla, do you have any business from last month to discuss?"

Shayla looked up at Brooks and immediately blushed. She smiled big, and I expected her to deliver something earth shattering. But she only shook her head and said, "No, but thank you so much for asking me, Mr. President."

"Mr. President?" I scoffed under my breath.

The committee heard me, and I got scathing looks from Leland and Shayla. Hazel rolled her eyes, seemingly at Shayla. And, well, Brooks's expression wasn't scathing, exactly. If I was reading it right, he seemed amused. This whole thing was suspicious.

"Please, call me Brooks," he said to Shayla, who seemed to take this the same way she'd take a request to go out with him—extreme joy. Addressing the room at large once more he said, "I believe we have a few items on our agenda tonight."

"Can we start with the fish smell in here?" someone interrupted from the back.

"It's like a mildewy skunk carcass," another called.

At the word skunk Brooks looked at me and a full smile bloomed on my face as I remembered Rocky. Had he been rescued from my place only to take up residence here? It would almost be too much beautiful justice. Brooks fought an answering smile of his own.

"I haven't smelled anything this bad since I went into a high school locker room," Hazel agreed.

I raised my eyebrows and pushed down a giggle. Top points for descriptions tonight. And why would Hazel be in a high school locker room?

Brooks held up his hands. "Yes, it's bad. I think we can all agree that if someone uses the kitchen here, they need to clean it thoroughly and take out all garbage."

"Who was it?" Leland asked. "No one would be using it without reserving it. I say we find the person responsible and charge them a fee."

"A fee for what?" Brooks asked.

"For sensory damages," Hazel wrinkled her nose, "and the cost of fumigating the building."

"It's not that bad." Brooks stated. "And we can't suddenly make up new fees."

"It's like broccoli and tuna had a baby in the office lunch area and then someone microwaved it," Shayla argued, waving a hand in front of her face.

Well, points for Shayla. I didn't think she had a creative bone in her body. Brooks laughed at her description, which had her beaming from ear to ear, and my smile completely disappearing from my face. I refocused on Hazel as she banged her fist on the table and wondered why I cared about Brooks sharing a little friendly moment with a member of his board.

"I'd like to motion that Leland finds the responsible party, and they receive a fine." Hazel raised a hand and glared around the room until two more people raised theirs, too. She nodded her head. "Perfect. I'll make a note of it in the minutes."

"No nail gun injury this week?" Leland asked her in a sarcastically sweet tone that was so low I was probably the only one close enough to hear it. I stifled a laugh while Hazel shot him a look. "Just glad you can write again."

"We'll readdress the fine later," Brooks murmured down the table to Hazel, who pretended not to hear him. He looked up again and sighed. "Alright. Now that the matter of the smell has been addressed, let's move on to our actual agenda," Brooks said. Hazel handed him a paper from a knitted bag. It was folded a few times, and he patiently unfolded it as he thanked Hazel. "First up on the list tonight. Fines for . . ."

He paused, and I watched as he cleared his throat and rubbed at his beard-covered cheek for a split second. I observed him closely, realizing that in the past I'd have assumed he was annoyed, but now the tight line of his mouth seemed to be . . . struggling not to laugh? No . . . I had to be wrong. He cleared his throat and bit at his lip once more before pushing on.

"Uh, setting fines for homeowners with felines weighing over fifteen pounds." He didn't look up immediately, and I wondered what he was thinking. When he did look up, he seemed to be looking over everyone's heads at the back wall. "The floor is open for discussion."

His voice sounded strained, not with the cockiness I'd have accused him of before, but with hilarity trying to break free. While I agreed with him that it was hilarious, I also found it to be a gigantic waste of time to even be discussing it. Sure, he had to discuss the items put forth by people, but come on. I turned to see if anyone wanted to say anything before I jumped in with a question. Yes, a question, even though I wanted to kick it off with open mockery.

"Maybe we could get a little clarification on that, Brooks." Mrs. Parker called before I opened my mouth. She didn't bother to leave her seat or raise her hand. "What exactly are we discussing here?"

Brooks looked back at the paper and sucked his lips into his mouth so hard they disappeared. It hit me again, clear as day, that he was trying not to laugh. The realization took me a moment to process even though I'd already had an inkling moments before. All this time I'd thought he was fighting *for* these people and it was my job to stop this runaway train, but really he was just doing his best to fulfill his presidential role by letting people have their say. I suddenly decided to do something I'd never done before. I was going to sit back and watch. Observe only and see where Brooks took things.

It was only logical, after all, to test my theory.

"Well, Ann, it seems that whoever submitted this request has left off that level of detail. Uh, just that if people own a cat and that cat weighs over fifteen pounds, they would be noncompliant with the HOA codes and owe a fine," Brooks responded with remarkable calm.

"I don't understand the problem," Mrs. Parker murmured to her husband, Dennis. "Are fifteen-pound cats terrorizing the neighborhood?" Dennis shook his head and shrugged.

"Does anyone have anything to add here? If not, we'll take a vote," Brooks said.

"Is fifteen pounds heavy for a cat?" another woman asked. I'd been watching Brooks, so I wasn't sure who.

"Ms. Atwood has a cat," Brooks replied, looking to me. "Maybe she can answer that."

If I hadn't been watching, I wouldn't have noticed that his eyes were crinkled up at the corners. He was having fun redirecting it at me, and, suddenly, I felt like part of an inside joke—something I had only experienced with my friends and never expected to share with him. He was teaming up *with* me rather than *against* me, and my mind whirled.

"She's probably the one who put this on the agenda," someone grumbled behind me, bursting the bubble a bit.

I spun around to stare everyone down before I remembered I was trying to play it cool tonight. I hurried to change my expression to something less threatening. "Anyone who comes to these meetings knows this is exactly the kind of thing I'd consider frivolous. I didn't submit this request. To answer the question, my cat, Betty, is around nine pounds."

"Is Betty heavy or thin?" Mrs. Parker asked.

"I'd say she's neither. She's at a healthy weight," I replied.

"Okay, well, fat cats have nothing to do with anything as far as I can tell," Hazel spoke up. "Let's have a quick vote so that we can dismiss this and move to the next item."

She jotted a few things down, and as Brooks opened his mouth to call for a vote, Linda Jackman, an outspoken older woman with too much time on her hands, jumped to her feet and raised her hand.

"Having an overweight cat shows that you don't care about the health and well-being of your animal. Studies have shown that people who are cruel to animals are cruel to humans and often destructive to property. It's a measuring post, and an important one." She was nearly out of breath when she finished.

There were no words. Others apparently agreed with me, based on the silence that reigned for a few heartbeats. Enough heartbeats for things to get uncomfortable.

"How would you recommend we enforce this policy, Mrs. Jackman?" Brooks asked with total sincerity.

The man was made of steel or something even stronger than that. I'd had to turn around and face forward again, tucking my chin down and firmly holding my shoulders in place to keep them from shaking with laughter. This was absurd. These meetings got worse and worse every month.

"I'm not sure," Linda stated. "I just know that fat cats are a symptom of a bigger problem."

"What about old cats? Sometimes when things get old, they get heavy," Hazel pulled a face. "Do we punish pet owners for the natural progression of life?"

"How do we even know how many people have cats in this community?" Leland asked. "I'm certainly not going door-to-door registering pets. I vote no to this one. It's a waste of time. Let's move on."

"I get my vote like everyone else," Linda pursed her lips and folded her arms. "It's the law."

Brooks took a deep breath. "It's not necessarily the law, but it is proper procedure. So, all who vote in favor of, uh, pursuing the fat cat issue, please raise your hands." Linda's hand was the only one that shot up. She looked around, trying to get people to join her, but most of them wouldn't even meet her eye. "I'm sorry, Linda, but we'd need at least three votes to take this to the next step," Brooks said.

Linda left in a huff, and this time when Brooks glanced my way I was ready to share in that 'what on earth is going on' look he sent me.

"Let's hear what's next," Leland barked.

Brooks had apparently already looked because this time he couldn't stop the movement of his lips. He was losing the war against laughter. To buy some time he looked down at the list Hazel had given him and smoothed the paper on the tabletop before addressing the room.

At last he said, "There's some concern that our bylaws don't clearly state that no airplanes are allowed to land in our community."

This time I couldn't resist saying something. "I'm wondering where there's room for a plane to land around here?"

"Yeah. I'm picturing the entire community in my head, and there's no open field or street big enough and long enough for that," Hazel agreed.

"Who submitted that?" Leland tried to pull the page away from Brooks, but he snatched it up.

"It doesn't have names," Brooks said, and I wasn't sure if he was telling the truth or not. "But if it did, it would be my job to protect their privacy."

Leland recrossed his arms. "This is nonsense."

"I'm not totally familiar with all the details of the bylaws," Brooks said to the room at large, "but I'm happy to look into them and report back what I find. I'm guessing, though, that this would be an issue for the Federal Aviation Association and not an HOA group. I don't personally feel like there's much risk of a plane landing in our neighborhood."

"Someone's worried about it," Shayla supplied in a honey tone. "So, maybe it's a real concern?"

"My thoughts are that in the event a plane makes use of our streets, it's most likely an emergency situation and there were no other options," Brooks responded.

Shayla giggled. "Of course."

"Vote on it," Leland stated. "My show starts in thirty minutes, and I don't want to still be here when it does."

"What's your show?" Hazel asked with some surprising snark. "The Bachelor?"

Leland hardly spared her a glance as he replied, "Cold Cases. It's about people who get away with murder for decades without being suspected."

Hazel scoffed and looked away. I covered my mouth and tried not to laugh. How had I never noticed how much those two didn't like each other? This was comedy gold. I'd missed so much with my laser-focused quest for justice. Brooks piped up before they could get into a real rhythm, calling for a vote on if we needed to include airplane landings in our bylaws. It didn't go through.

The last few items were small things. Recycling schedules, questions about a community New Year's party, nothing big, and, before fifteen more minutes had passed, the meeting was closed, and Leland was on his way home to watch whatever show he loved most. Hazel was right behind him, but Shayla lingered as Brooks spoke to a few people. I'd noticed her crush on him before, but now I watched as she touched his arm repeatedly, at one point holding on when his attention was diverted. Tonight seemed to be the night that blinders came off for me, and I saw this whole HOA situation in a different light. I had a lot to think about.

I gathered up my coat and beanie, tugging the warm wool down over my forehead as I bundled up for the walk home. No one said much to me, which wasn't surprising, and before long I was walking down the sidewalk headed for home. It was dark and cold, and, even though I had on my trusty mittens, I tucked my hands deep in my coat pockets to keep them warm. My mind swirled, making me smile as I thought about all the silly things that had come up for discussion that night. In the past I'd have fought tooth and nail to keep them from going through, but now the fight seemed to be gone. I'd thought that if I was the HOA president I could make a difference, but maybe people didn't want a difference made . . . maybe they just wanted to air their little grievances and strange ideas and the HOA president had no real power at all.

"Meredith, wait up." I recognized Brooks's voice before he reached me. I didn't turn to watch him close the distance, but I did stop walking. "You were quiet tonight," he said as he came alongside me.

It shouldn't have made me happy that he'd noticed my silence or that he'd come looking for me, but it did. I started walking again, and he fell into step with me.

"I decided to try an experiment and simply observe tonight."

"And?"

"It was very educational. Maybe I've been fighting the wrong battles."

He chuckled. "You mean *me*?"

I darted a glance at him, and my own smile, although smaller than his, made my mouth curl. "Yeah. It occurred to me that maybe we're on the same side here."

"I've never been your enemy, you know," he said in a soft voice that sounded a little hesitant.

"That remains to be seen," I quipped, but there was no heat behind it.

"Truth moment, was that fifteen-pound feline actually your idea?"

I huffed out a laugh. "Oh my gosh, no. But the airplane thing? Totally me. The worry keeps me up at night."

"I can appreciate that. Want to know what keeps me up at night?"

"Sure."

"Wondering what people will want to discuss at next month's meeting. Is it me, or is it getting worse?"

"It's getting worse."

"So, maybe it is me. Maybe I bring it out in people. Sometimes I want to lose my cool and tell them they're being ridiculous and wasting everyone's time. It's getting harder and harder to take this seriously. At least I've had you all these months, fighting me, yes, but mostly fighting back against the strange requests. I know we haven't seen eye-to-eye, but it's nice to know someone agrees with me."

I glanced at him again. His profile was hard to see in the dark, but he looked honestly stumped, which matched my general feeling. He'd seen me as an ally of sorts?

"I thought you really didn't like me," I said quietly.

He shrugged. "I didn't like that you were out to get me. I was confused about why. But I've appreciated that we feel the same way about a lot of what goes on here. Now if you had any ideas on how I can stop it from going on like this, I'd be interested in hearing them."

"You could stop being so nice and actually discussing the ridiculous things people submit," I stated.

"I'm pretty sure I have to discuss them. I think it's the code," he scoffed. "They should have put Leland in as president. That man is just not interested in hearing it."

"He was the president when I moved in."

Ice crunched under his boot, and he stepped behind me for a moment, falling into single line to avoid an icy patch before coming back to my side. "Really? What was that like?"

"Well, no one talked about having towel police or weight limits for cats. But not much got done outside of the bare minimum."

"I know you wanted to be the president. I didn't really understand why you were so intense about it. I said some pretty rude things to you in the past. I'm sorry. My parents drilled politeness into my brother and me with exactness. I know better."

We'd reached my house, and I turned to face him as we stood on my driveway. His eyes were lost in shadows, but I could tell he was sincere by the tone of his voice and an intensity in his posture. I licked my lips, unsure of how to respond. I was better with sparring than I'd ever be with sincerity.

"I gave you plenty of reasons to be rude to me. Besides, it's probably for the best that I'm not president," I half-whispered. "I have a really unflattering tendency to turn into a dictator."

He smiled, his teeth bright against his dark beard. "These people might need a tyrant to lead them."

"Maybe. Or maybe they need a nice guy who will let them vent a little."

We fell into silence, but it wasn't uncomfortable. I wiggled my toes in my boots, feeling the creeping chill but oddly loathe to break up this little peace talk we'd stumbled into.

"So, your parents were big on manners, huh?" I asked.

He blew out a laugh. "Huge. They hosted parties a lot, and us boys were expected to be perfect little gentleman. Or when they took their summer travels to Europe and left us in the care of a sitter, they expected glowing reports of our behavior."

"They didn't take you along?"

He shook his head. "That was normal where I grew up. Expected, even. It's okay. My love of nature came from long summers either at sleepaway camp or with sort of negligent sitters. It gave me hours to explore."

It almost sounded like maybe he'd been a little lonely as a child, too, something I tucked away to think on later.

"I haven't done a ton of nature stuff, outside of skiing and this river raft adventure I did over the summer in Moab."

"That's in the southern part of the state, right?"

"Yeah. Red sand, desert."

"I went there once with my ex when I first moved out here. Pretty cool place. I should go back sometime." He tucked his hands in his pockets and seemed to be looking back at a memory as his gaze became unfocused. "Lots of off-road-vehicles and mountain bikers, right?"

I was still a little stuck on the ex comment, but I nodded. "Where are you from, originally?" I asked.

"Connecticut. I moved to Salt Lake about six years ago with my ex-fiancée when she found work there. After we broke up I wanted to stay in Utah because there's so much great outdoor recreation, but I didn't want to stay where she was. Logan was a good fit. I've been here about four years."

An odd lump had formed in my throat. "So, you didn't get married?"

He shook his head. "Nope. She needed someone a little more intense and creative. I'm neither of those things, apparently. Her words."

"You do woodwork," I managed. "That's creative."

He chuckled. "It drives the ladies wild, a man who measures twice and cuts once. Real hot and heavy stuff."

I laughed, too. "Well, someday you'll find someone who appreciates your truly boring personality."

115

He tipped his head slightly in acknowledgment. "And someday you'll find a guy who doesn't mind your crusade for ultimate power."

"Oh gosh, I hope not. Nothing would be worse than someone encouraging me," I mocked, making my eyes big. I walked toward my house. "Good night, Mr. President."

"Good night, Ms. Atwood. May you avoid obese cats and stray planes."

"And may you never get between Leland and his television programming."

I heard him laugh as I closed the door behind me, and the sound followed me into my dreams that night.

CHAPTER 16

I pedaled along on a bike at the gym early the next morning. Working out always helped clear my mind, and, with today being Lizzie's wedding, I knew I'd need extra patience. Big crowds and events were hard for someone like me who needed to feel in control. Wearing pink was also hard for me. But while Lizzie's color theme of dark pink, light pink, and green—with fancy names to dress it up—wasn't my cup of tea, I could admit that as far as pinks and greens go, it wasn't terrible. That said, I would never have worn those shades for any other reason.

My mind was whirling as quickly as the pedals on the bike, going around and around, thinking about my conversation with Brooks last night. It had been so normal. Almost like people would talk to a neighbor, or, you know, someone they were friends with. I hadn't felt uncomfortable with him. And there may even have been a few moments of jealousy regarding Shayla that were regrettable but still worth analyzing. I shot off a text to Hailey.

Me: Brooks VanOrman walked home with me last night. I think we might not be enemies anymore. I got jealous of the committee treasurer.

My phone rang five minutes later. Seeing her name flash on the screen, I picked it up.

"It's bad form to return a text by calling the person," I stated, out of breath.

"Why do you sound like you're dying?" Her voice was hoarse, and I realized that at 6:43 a.m. she'd probably been sleeping.

"I'm riding a bike at the gym. Let's be grateful I'm alone in this room, or I'd be getting a lot of dirty looks for talking on the phone."

"You're alone because it's too early."

"Science has discovered that exercise helps quiet down the worried parts of our brains. It's Lizzie's wedding day, and there's a lot going on. For starters, she's making me wear pink, and I hate pink. So, I'm exercising away my worry that I'll look like a giant cloud of cotton candy."

She yawned before responding. "First of all, it's not cotton candy colored. The shades are called rose and rosewood as you already know. You at least got rosewood, which is darker."

I laughed. "All I'm picturing is that scene in the move *Steel Magnolias* where they tease Shelby about choosing blush and bashful as her wedding colors. Rose and Rosewood are literally the same name!"

"Meredith?" Hailey called over my continued laughter. "Your laugh is morphing into a cackle."

"Sorry. I find facts wickedly delightful."

Hailey chuckled. "You looked pretty when we had that fitting, so stop fretting about it. Just because you don't usually wear a color doesn't mean it looks terrible on you. In fact it brought a little color into your complexion."

I slowed the pace of my pedaling and entered the cooldown phase. "Seeing as you're regularly the best dressed person I know, I'll take your word for it."

"Thank you. Now, I believe your text said something about Brooks and you getting cozy with a possible side of jealousy?" I heard some shuffling and a click. "I turned on the lamp; my eyes are open. Tell me everything."

"Cozy is a strong word," I said. "But last night was the HOA meeting, and I think I had an epiphany while I was sitting there. It was like, wait, I don't think Brooks actually likes having to listen to all this drivel any more than I do. So, instead of arguing, I sat back and watched to see what he'd do. He shot down their terrible ideas, and I didn't have to look like the resident ogre. Then on the way home, he walked with me."

"Has he walked with you before?"

I scoffed, "Hardly. He usually walks the exact opposite direction. Although . . ."

When I had paused for too long, she nudged me along. "Although, what?"

"A little while ago he was shoveling driveways and spreading ice melt, and I sort of went along and helped."

"Hold up. Are you telling me that the animosity between you has been de-escalating for a while?"

"Then there was the whole skunk ladder situation." I shrugged and stopped pedaling. I let my feet dangle and wiggled them around, stretching out my ankles and calf muscles. "The animosity is fading. Has faded. A little? I'm unsure."

"Have you stopped getting HOA tickets?"

"Well, yeah, but that's because I took down the decorations. They were a little much."

Hailey giggled. "They were terrible. So, what made you jealous?"

I blew out a breath. "This girl, Shayla. She's the treasurer, and she flirts so hard with him. When we were enemies I used it as more proof that Brooks is an evil-doer, but last night it made me feel . . . stabby."

"Stabby?"

"Like, I wanted her eyeballs to be on the floor."

"Okay, stabby over a man. That's new for you. What are you going to do?"

I stepped off the bike and found the small hand towel I'd brought. I used it to wipe down my head and neck. "Well, she still has her eyes, so nothing, I suppose. Chalk it up to an uptick of fiber in my diet?"

Hailey laughed. "I'm talking about Brooks, and you know it. What are you going to do about him?"

"I'm going to exercise a lot and ignore the fact that he said he likes how we think the same way about the HOA issues."

A cough and then, "What? This whole time?"

"Yeah." I gave her a quick rundown of the conversation. "But I don't think it's something I need to take too seriously. Hazel feels the same way. It's just a thing."

"He likes your mind, and he has this total, I don't know, like lumberjack vibe that's really intriguing and . . ."

At her hesitation I piped up, "Oh, I can't wait to hear what adjective you come up with here. Keep in mind I'm noting it and will use it as blackmail. Ford would probably love to hear you speak so flatteringly of another man," I teased, laughing when she made a huffing noise.

"Fine. I'll just say that I'm going to keep an eye on this developing situation."

I grabbed the spray bottle of cleanser and sprayed down the spin bike, using a provided cloth to sanitize it for the next rider. "Well, keep a close one on it for me, because I am completely confused."

"Like Ruby would say, this might be the beginning of something wonderful."

*****

I watched placidly as Willow curled my short hair and twisted it into what she was calling a 'faux wedding updo' later that afternoon. I was sitting in a beautiful upstairs room at an old Victorian-style home where Lizzie's wedding would be taking place in an hour. My friends were buzzing around me, each of them working on hair and makeup at different stations. They were all totally capable of doing their own hair. I, however, was not and never had been interested in learning how to do more than tuck my bobbed hair behind my ears. Willow, having been told I had no plans to get dolled up for the wedding, had insisted on meeting me here to fix the situation.

"I sometimes forget how stick straight your hair is," Willow laughed as she made a second attempt to get a curl to hold.

"We have the same hair," I replied.

She gently shook her head. "Our hair is representative of who we are. We may have the same color, but yours is much less cooperative than mine. Mine is more flexible with a slight wave."

I gave her a look in the mirror. "So, you're saying my hair is rigid and unable to change?"

She giggled. "Take it however you want to, sis."

"I'm taking it literally, like I always do."

Lizzie burst into the room, followed closely by her mom, who was holding her wedding dress in a bag across her arms. Lizzie's curls bounced around her head like a bunch of tiny slinky toys, her eyes were big and happy, and her smile was about to overtake her entire head.

"It's my wedding day," she said, throwing her arms out. "Finally!"

Willow released the lock of hair she'd been attempting to curl and allowed me to rise with the rest of my friends. We congregated in the middle of the room, all of us stepping naturally into a big group hug while somehow keeping our heads from touching. Wedding hair was not to be mushed. It was a moment of pure connection for me. I always participated in the hugs, but I didn't always do it with such a nostalgic feeling flowing through me. This was the beginning of big changes for our little troupe. Lizzie was leaving on her honeymoon tomorrow and then moving away.

I surprised them all when I said, softly, "I'll miss this so much when you go, Liz. This group has meant everything to me."

Lizzie's face crumpled, followed, like dominoes, by everyone else, including me. While I didn't get quite as teary as the rest, my throat closed up, and my eyes grew wet. Soon, sniffles filled the room and then some laughs and murmured, sentimental words. I'd started an avalanche that we were having a hard time recovering from.

Lizzie's mom clapped her hands after giving us a few precious minutes. "Ladies, we'd better pull it together and get moving. Makeup repair must be added to the list now," she chuckled warmly.

"Thornback dragon warriors," Aryn whispered fiercely.

We all snapped to standing, wiping at our eyes and offering a few final hugs around the circle before moving back to our respective areas. Willow was waiting with a knowing glance, and I pursed my lips as I took my seat and she picked up my hair again.

"You sentimental little thing," she joked. I rolled my eyes, and she grew serious. "Really, though, I think it's so lucky that you have these women in your life. I'm a little jealous, to be honest. Not everyone gets so many bonus sisters."

I nodded with a gleam in my eye. "Yeah. It's a wonder I was willing to take them on after growing up with you and Ash."

Willow tugged extra hard on a piece of hair she was pinning into place. "Uh, I raised you, if you'll remember correctly. Why do you think I'm still childless?"

At this I laughed and surveyed her handiwork in the mirror. My face looked softer with my hair curled and pulled back, and when Willow helped me into my dark pink—ahem, rosewood—dress, I had to do a double take. I looked approachable and warm. Two words that had most likely never been used to describe me.

"Well, well, well, Meredith Atwood, you are a stunner," my little sister whispered close to me. She wrapped an arm around my waist, and I did the same in return. "Do you think it'll ever be one of us?" she asked.

I shook my head slowly. "It's not something I've ever wanted, even if I had a man I loved and trusted," I stated matter-of-factly.

"The scars run too deep," Willow stated rather than forming it as a question. "I'll manifest some healing for you."

I grinned. "Even then, I may never want to marry."

"That's fine. I understand your reasons. But I'm still manifesting you a companion, anyhow."

"How many things can you be manifesting at the same time?" I asked, pulling my arm out of our embrace to adjust a hair that was tickling my nose.

She reached up to help me. "As far as I know, there's no limit to the good things we can bring into our lives."

"Great. Well, how about manifesting me a big diet soda?"

Willow put her hands on my shoulders and pushed me down onto the seat again. "And mess with the perfect lipstick I'm about to apply? Never. You know, the color of this dress really brightens up your face."

"I've been told."

*****

At exactly four o'clock in the afternoon, on December 20th, Elizabeth "Lizzie" Duncan married Jackson Walker. His daughter, Sally, stood at his side, and it was so adorable that even I had a hard time keeping steady. I stood in a line behind Lizzie with Ruby, Aryn, and Hailey, each of us clasping a small bouquet and watching with wet eyes and goofy grins as Lizzie's long-time dream came true. The vows were perfect, the guests weren't many, and the setting was peaceful and intimate.

I thought about what I'd told Willow upstairs, about never wanting to marry. It was a choice I'd made a long time ago, based on the fact that I didn't see the value in it. I had only a few prized memories of my mother. All of them were of ways she'd interacted with me or things I remembered her doing around the home. I didn't have any of her and my dad together. I didn't know how they'd functioned as a couple. All I really knew was that when she'd died, our dad had disappeared.

That's what love did in my viewpoint. It made promises that were left unfulfilled. People could say anything they wanted, but the proof came in their actions. And if a man's actions didn't match his words, then I'd be stuck trying to navigate a divorce and separate myself from the life we'd built. Yet, as I stood there listening to the promises Lizzie made to Jackson, I wondered if there was something I hadn't fully understood about the power of vows.

Much to my delight, the couple had decided to forgo a formal reception and instead had a light buffet dinner. Guests were invited to come socialize and eat an assortment of finger foods. It was casual and festive, and as I stood off to the side munching on a plate of veggies, I realized I felt a lot more at ease than I'd expected to. It was the first wedding that hadn't made my skin itchy. Because the group was smaller, I knew a lot of them. Lizzie's extended family, not so much, but they were pretty easy to avoid. People from work already knew I wasn't a small talker and simply offered friendly waves. My friends were being more social, and I was content to watch them.

In fact I was currently watching Hailey slip her hand into Ford's and pull him through an open doorway. Looked like Jackson and Lizzie wouldn't be the only ones stealing a few kisses tonight. The thought made me smile just as Ruby slid up next to me.

"Something is going on with Aryn," she leaned close to whisper.

Ruby was wearing the lighter rose color, and the pastel looked amazing against her darker skin. Her curvy figure was made for the flowing material. I doubted she had any idea that she was catching eyes tonight. So, I told her. She tilted her head at me and smiled softly.

"Thank you," she said. "Now, play it cool, but shift your eyes to the two o'clock position."

I did as she said and saw that Aryn was standing near the buffet table talking to a tall, lean, blond man. "Oh, love in the forecast tonight?" I asked.

"It's Wesley. From school."

"Oh." I looked again. He turned slightly, smiling at something Aryn had said, and I made a face. "He's seriously so bland. What could they possibly be talking about? Computers? Hardly Aryn's area of interest."

Even though he and Aryn had known each other in high school and she swore he was a good guy, I was completely unimpressed by him. Aryn was vivacious and active, as bright and fun as her red hair, and Wesley was like a faded photograph in glasses. He was always nice when I needed help, but there was no spark inside that man.

"Look at her face, though," Ruby replied. "She doesn't look bored."

Ruby was right. Aryn laughed, and I knew her well enough to see the heightened color in her cheeks. Aryn, who was always surrounded by guys but eternally bored by them, was glowing.

"Holy Toledo. No."

"You might not think much of him, but Aryn seems to," Ruby stated. She stole a carrot off my plate and bit into it with a crunch. "I'm interested to see where this will go."

Together, Aryn and Wesley found a table and sat next to each other. Their heads tilted toward one another as I watched, surprised. "Where it will go?"

"Yeah. They were friends in high school, remember?"

I nodded. "Yeah. She said something about that. But she never talks about him."

Ruby raised her eyebrows at me, still chewing the carrot. "Of course she doesn't. Every time his name comes up you make it pretty clear that you think he's not worth discussing."

"Do I?" I bit my lower lip. Was I accidentally shutting down Aryn's ability to share by being a harpy? "I mean, he's so . . ."

"I believe you once called him 'vanilla.' As in, the most boring flavor of all."

I blinked. "Well, in my defense, he looks like he's never seen a spot of sun or eaten more than one meal a day. He's so very skinny. And tall. And those glasses don't help. I'm not sure he's able to grow a full beard, but maybe that light scruff is a choice."

"You're doing it right now. Talking down about him." Ruby took another carrot. "He's a perfectly nice guy."

"Yes, nice is good, but don't you think Aryn would do better with someone as athletic and charming as she is?"

"Maybe. Do you think you'd do well with someone as snarky and closed-off as you are?"

"Hey." My eyes shot to hers. "I'm not like that." She raised one eyebrow and snapped off another bite of carrot. My mouth tugged up. "Fine. I get your point."

"It's the same reason I'm not going to bother dating someone like me. At least one person in the relationship has to have their feet on the ground."

I patted her arm. "That shows a high level of self-awareness." I laughed when she hip-bumped me. I glanced back at Aryn and Wesley. They did seem comfortable with each other, and nothing in Aryn's body language said she wasn't enjoying the conversation. For his part, his smile wasn't fading one iota. "Do you really think Aryn likes him?"

"Yeah. I do. It might be as nothing more than a friend right now, but it'll be interesting to see."

"I guess it's time to pay a little closer attention and keep my mouth shut."

"Great advice for all situations."

Ruby wandered off, attention caught by the announcement that cake-cutting was about to begin. Aryn stood, and Wesley followed. I watched as they gathered around. Being two of the taller people in the room, they hung back, able to see over others. They stood close, not like strangers but like friends. Hailey and Ford wandered in, his arm around her waist, a smile on her face, and I knew in that moment that there would probably be another Thornback wedding in the near future. Ruby stepped up next to Hailey, and they gave each other's hand a squeeze. For a split second I felt slightly out of the loop. I didn't have someone, and I didn't believe in the fairy tale. But Ruby turned to me, waving me over, and as I took my place next to her, she took my hand and gave me the same squeeze she'd given Hailey. In that moment I knew that no matter what happened, I'd never truly be alone.

*****

It was extremely late when I dragged my exhausted body into the house that night—or maybe it was morning already? I flipped on lights and made my way to the bedroom, tugging at the zipper on the pink dress as I went. I'd been smart enough to have Ruby unzip me halfway before leaving the venue, and I was grateful I did as it slid easily off my body to the floor. I reflected on the events of the evening, smiling and feeling content as I hung the dress and placed my shoes perfectly in line with the others in my closet. I sluggishly got ready for bed and into soft pajamas that felt like a hug on my aching body. When I reached into my purse to get my phone out for charging, I noticed two missed calls and a voice message.

Not many people actually left messages these days, and, when I saw that the missed calls were from Brooks, I couldn't wait until morning to listen.

"Hey, I'm making a broad assumption that since you like to exercise and you participate in Turkey trots that you also ski. If so, I have two ski passes, and I'm free tomorrow. Let me know if you're interested." His voice was hopeful and friendly with a thread of doubt like he wasn't sure that phone call had been a good idea.

This was a massive development, and my initial reaction was to back away. Men and I did not have a stellar history. But his face came to mind, followed by thoughts of the things I'd observed about him. Brooks was kind and dependable. I thought of Lizzie and Jackson exchanging vows and Hailey and Ford sneaking off to kiss and Ruby holding my hand while the cake was cut. Suddenly, remarkably, for the first time in a long time, I was willing to crack open the door and consider letting a new person in . . . letting a man in.

I didn't bother to call, because it was so late, but I shot off a text.

Me: Yes to skiing tomorrow. But pick me up at nine. I'm sleeping in.

I was asleep the second I hit the pillow.

CHAPTER 17

The snow was powdery perfection as the sun glinted off it and warmed my face. I took a deep breath and observed the skiers who were working their way down the mountainside. Skiing wasn't cheap, and I typically saved up enough to ski a few times a year, so I was very grateful for Brooks's generosity in bringing me today. After the hullabaloo of Lizzie's wedding day, I was craving the sound of skis hitting snow and no conversation at all.

My attention was pulled away from the view as Brooks skied up next to me. He slid to a stop, snow covering my own skis as he did, and wiped some powder off his goggles.

"You ready to get on the lift and go again?" he asked. I nodded, and we got in line. "The powder is perfect today," he said as we shuffled along.

"It really is."

I silently patted myself on the back for that spot of small talk. In fact, I'd been with Brooks all morning and hadn't broken out into a total sweat. I'd been quiet on the drive up the canyon, and if he found it odd that I'd encouraged him to do the majority of the talking, he hadn't let on. It wasn't that I was uncomfortable; it was more that I was unsure what he wanted or what this meant. I'd paid attention my whole life and noticed an unfortunate trend among women, where they created stories in their minds and put more meaning into things than men intended. A guy might invite you out, but it didn't mean he wanted to date you. He might even buy your dinner, but he simply thought he was being friendly. Meanwhile the woman is thinking they're exclusive and giving the stink eye to other girls he talks to.

I wasn't about to start giving stink eye unless a man specifically told me where our relationship stood. Well, okay, I wasn't actually known to humbly wait for someone to give me directions, and I'd definitely given stink eye to Shayla at the last HOA meeting, but that's because her flirting had been syrupy and clearly one-sided. It wasn't because I was trying to mark territory. I was defending a friend. Yeah, we were friends. I guess.

Anyhow, I had asked more questions about his family during the long drive and confirmed that his parents were kind but aloof. They hadn't batted an eye when he'd moved across the country but had applauded him for striking out on his own to create his own life. He'd always wanted to be a lawyer but also found it really tedious. He hated milk chocolate, only watched shows once all the seasons were wrapped up and he didn't have to wait for new episodes to come out, and preferred to fly under the radar rather than be front and center. He was a natural optimist and figured things would always work out.

Probably my favorite thing I learned about him, though, was that he was an impatient driver. It was another thing we had in common, and I'd fought down smiles as he'd passed people and grumbled about their driving or spoken out loud to other drivers about their choices. There was a flaw—a chink in his armor—and I liked him all the more for it.

We got into the chairlift, and I relaxed back against the seat, taking in the views and enjoying the fresh, cool air filling my lungs.

"I love the mountains," Brooks said.

"This is one of the only places I don't feel . . ." I paused, trying to come up with the right word for it.

"Trapped by the expectations of both yourself and others?" he suggested.

"Yep. That's about it."

"Well, it won't hurt my feelings if you want to do a few solo runs . . . with one request." He tugged at his gloves to pull them all the way on again. "If at some point you see two legs sticking out of a huge pile of snow, please check to see if I need any help."

"It's a deal," I chuckled.

We reached the top, and we got off the lift and skied over to the beginning of the run, where he threw me a salute with a grin as he zipped away. It took me a second to realize that I was watching him with a goofy look on my face. I immediately flattened my mouth, but I kept watching as he expertly made the run. He'd said he was an outdoorsman, and from what I was seeing, he hadn't fibbed. He looked completely at peace with the snow and the mountain, and I found it ridiculously attractive.

Another thing I was fangirling over? Him suggesting I may want to do a few solo runs. Other people felt hurt by that, but he had suggested it and then happily gone on his merry way, leaving me to it. Who was this unicorn of a human?

When he was out of sight around a bend, I pushed my pole tips into the snow and pushed off to follow the same path he'd taken, and before long I was smoothly coasting along, feeling the wind against my face and enjoying the push and pull as I shifted my stance to move in a side-to-side motion. The snow was fresh and light with no icy spots having formed yet. These types of days were rare, and as my mood lifted, I began wondering if we'd hang out again after this. I'd be up for it.

When I got down to the lift line, I could see Brooks's bright red hat and lean form. He wasn't in line but waved when he saw me coming. I waved back, and he met me as I got in line.

"You looked good coming down that hill," he stated in an easy compliment.

"You, too," I replied almost bashfully.

"Do you want to share a ride back up?"

I nodded, and we fell into silence as we shuffled along, trying not to cross our skis or bump into someone else's. The lines were still short, and we were on the lift quickly. Our shoulders brushed, and I leaned in, enjoying it.

"You grew up in the area, right?" he asked, breaking the silence.

"Yeah. In a really little town called Paradise. It's like twenty minutes away from Logan."

"So, you've probably been skiing forever then?"

I scoffed. "Hardly. I think it's a common misconception that all Utahns ski. Skiing is expensive, and we didn't have the money."

He held up two gloved hands. "Sorry. Assumptions are bad, I get it. Take it as a compliment. You look like a lifelong skier. So, when did you get started skiing then?"

"I've always really been into exercise and activity, so after I graduated and got a job teaching, I decided to learn to ski."

"How long have you been teaching?"

"Around twelve years, give or take."

"What made you decide to be a teacher?"

Rather than immediately answer, I glanced toward the top of the mountain, wondering how to answer that without going too deep for our budding friendship. I'd chosen the profession because school had felt like safety as a child. People there had shown up day in, day out. Lunch was always served. Lessons made sense. I'd gotten to almost be a child for those few hours each day. I'd wanted to do the same for other children.

He misinterpreted my silence as annoyance and said, "Sorry. I'll stop bugging you. You're here for quiet, and I'm being chatty."

"It's not that," I responded. "Just deciding if I keep it surface level or tell you the truth."

He nodded. "It's a dark and sordid tale, then?"

I laughed. "No. Let's say that as a kid my life was unstable, but school provided a foundation. I wanted to pay that forward to other kids who needed it."

"I'm going to tell you this because I think you're the type of person who can understand what I mean by it. I chose to be a lawyer because I thought it would be good to always understand my rights and never be taken advantage of."

I blinked and glanced at him. I did understand it. Deeply. "But you always come off so relaxed and unworried."

He tapped the tip of his nose. "Because I'm confident that no one is bamboozling me."

I chuckled. "Smart."

"I usually tell people I chose to do it for the money," he grinned.

When it was time to get off, we lifted the tips of our skis and I raised the safety bar over our heads. We stood in unison, but, as I began to ski away, I felt a tug on my coat. I looked over in time to see that the side of my coat had become tangled in the chair and, as the lift was going around to begin its descent, it was tugging me along with it. I stumbled to the side, trying to find my footing, but skis weren't built for that type of motion, and I started to go down as I was dragged along. I reached one arm out to break my fall while still tugging on my coat with the other, trying to free it.

Out of nowhere I saw a flash of silver, and suddenly I was released. The motion caused me to fully fall on my side, and Brooks dropped next to me to avoid getting clipped by the chair behind ours circling around. We laid there, face-to-face, me blinking away some confusion and him breathing hard. My goggles had gotten knocked off, and the sun was bright, making me squint.

"How . . ." I blinked, still a bit confused.

"I kicked off my skis, whipped out a pocketknife, opened the correct blade with gloves on, and saved your life, all in a five-second timeframe," he said.

"You had a knife in your pocket?"

He made a face. "What kind of Boy Scout would I be if I didn't? I'm practically an Eagle scout, I'll have you know."

"Practically?"

"The cooking badge gave me some difficulties."

He rolled onto his hands and knees and stood, offering his gloved hands to me. With skis still attached to my feet, I appreciated the help. He tugged, and I popped right up. Still a bit dazed, I looked down at my coat to find that it was now missing a chunk off the back side. It was bad luck. Good snow coats were hard to come by, and I'd expected this one would last me several years. I glanced to where I could see a flap of blue still attached to the chair as it moved downhill.

"Well," I straightened my shoulders and leaned down to pick up my goggles. "Thanks for that Indiana Jones move there."

"You bet. Someday you can return the favor."

I tugged my goggles on and straightened my coat. We moved together to where his skis were still lying in the snow, and I watched as he put them on. When he was finished our eyes met, and I had a sudden urge to tug him up against me for a kiss. The feeling flared bright, and it stole my words as I watched his eyes shine. Unable to speak, I moved to the side of the hill where the ski runs took off from. He followed, pointing at the run he was planning to do, and I specifically shook my head and pointed at another, waving at him as I pushed off and got moving. I needed space and time alone to process this newfound feeling.

That wasn't the first time I'd felt that draw to him. Only moments ago, as I'd laid on my side and looked into his face, I'd wanted to slide forward and snuggle close, to press my cheek against his and have him wrap his arms around me. That need was almost completely new. My lack of physical affection had always been an issue in all my relationships. So, why now, and why with him? I did not appreciate thoughts and feelings that came out of left field. I focused on the sound of my skis pushing against the earth until my mind was as blank as the snow.

*****

Brooks pulled his car into my driveway several hours later and cut the engine. I was wiped but also relaxed and warm. We'd eaten lunch in the lodge and skied until my legs begged for mercy. Sometimes we'd done a run together, and some runs we'd done separately, but I'd begun to notice that the choice was always mine.

128

Brooks never nudged or suggested; he simply asked with an open expression and willingness to go with the flow.

I wasn't sure what to think about that. Did he genuinely not care? Was he trying to appease me? The motivation mattered, and the curiosity stuck in my head all through the car ride home. I'd kept it buried, figuring it was silly to interrogate someone over why they'd be kind. Instead, I'd been chattier and told him some of the few funny childhood stories I had plus some classroom anecdotes that had him laughing.

Neither of us opened our car doors, and the silence felt significant, as though we were on a precipice and whatever happened next would decide our fate.

So, I made it weird. "Why did you invite me today, and why were you so nice about everything?"

I swiveled in my seat to face him and leaned my back against the car door. He mimicked my repositioning and shrugged.

"I've been told I'm a nice guy."

"Sure, I get that. But why me? There must be other, friendlier women to invite skiing."

He didn't immediately answer and, as his eyes moved over my face, I felt self-conscious enough to reach up and smooth my hair. Only I was wearing a knit cap. I had no makeup on, and I was sure that my goggles had left red marks under my eyes. I certainly wasn't in any shape to be eye candy.

"Forget I asked," I said.

It came off annoyed, even though it was driven by embarrassment and a terrified realization that, at some point, he'd started making an effort to understand me. Guys didn't do that, and, if they did, it ended badly for everyone involved. Before he could reply I pushed open the car door and got out. I popped open the back door and gathered my snow gear as he climbed out his side of the car.

"You might have the shortest fuse of anyone I know," Brooks muttered. "I take one second to think about how to reply, and you're huffing out of the car and stomping around."

I slammed the back door shut and marched up to my front door. "I am not stomping."

"My apologies. You were *tromping* around."

I pushed the key into my door, and in my frustration I tried to turn in the wrong way. "This was a mistake," I said, jiggling the key with one hand while I tried to hold onto my gear with the other. "Just, I knew it was too good to be true."

His chest pressed against my back as he reached around me and turned my key the right direction. I closed my eyes, fighting off an intense need to lean back against him and feel his heat. I froze, rigid and confused, as he pushed my door open.

"What was too good to be true?" he asked against my ear.

I reminded myself to take a breath and hustled in through the front door. When I turned to slam it in his face, he was already through. I rolled my eyes and spun around to go down the hallway to my kitchen.

"You and this whole ski day. Trying to make sure I had a good time, letting me do solo runs, bringing a picnic lunch. It was all to lull me into a false sense of security. You've been faking it all to try and tear down my walls so that I'll stop bothering you, but I'm onto it now."

I set my gear in a messy heap on my kitchen table and tugged off my coat before turning to find that he'd pulled off his knit cap at some point and it was sticking out of one of his coat pockets. His hair stood on end as he unzipped his coat and started dragging it off.

"Do not take that off."

"I'm taking it off."

"You're not staying." I folded my arms and glared.

He moved past me and added his coat to the pile of outerwear on my table before turning to face me.

"So, you had a good time today?"

"Until I realized that this was a giant scheme."

"You had a good time; you enjoyed the lunch I packed; you felt a sense of security," he listed.

"All lies."

"You thought I was nice."

"Stop repeating everything I said, and go home."

He took a step closer to me, and I stepped back. "You know, Meredith, you're right. There are other, friendlier women I could spend time with."

A sharp pain in my chest had me gasping. "That was rude."

He lifted one shoulder. "Only repeating what you said. And, sure, maybe there are women who would have wanted to do all the runs together." He took another step toward me, and I backed up, feeling the kitchen wall press against my back. A tiny smile tugged at his lips as he took another step until we were close enough that he was in my personal space. It was like I'd stepped into a sauna. "But I find I'm a lot more interested in unpredictable, grumpy, secretly kind-hearted, intelligent women." He closed the space until our toes touched, and I could swear we were breathing the same air. "To get real specific, I'm sort of a little preoccupied with one in particular."

"She sounds like a lot of work," I murmured as I courageously tilted my head back to meet his eyes.

He smiled and raised one hand to toy with a lock of my hair. "She can be." He leaned down and pressed his mouth against my ear. The feel of his breath against my skin, his beard tickling my earlobe, made my eyes close, and I pressed my palms to the wall on either side of me to avoid reaching for him. "I think she's worth the effort." He bent further, placing a feather light kiss below my ear. My toes curled in my shoes and a shaky breath escaped. "I was hoping maybe she'd be willing to let her walls down a little with me."

I swallowed hard and only managed a whispered response. "Why?"

His nose rubbed along my jaw line until his lips were directly in front of mine. "Because I have never found anyone more . . ."

"Frustrating, annoying, difficult?" I supplied shakily.

His answering laugh was low, and I felt the vibrations of it in my chest. "Intriguing, vibrant, strong."

My hands moved to his chest, and I opened my eyes to find his eyes right above mine. I shook my head as uncharacteristic tears gathered. "What if you're wrong?'"

He moved his head back and forth, leaning forward so that his lips moved side to side against mine in a weightless caress that had me fisting his shirt in my hands. "I'm not," he said.

I ached with the need to hear more while also fighting the vulnerability of this moment as he reached around me, pressing warm palms to my lower back, and gathered me close. His mouth took mine fully, and I closed my eyes. I held on tightly as he kissed me over and over, coaxing me to relax and be open to this. My hands slowly released his shirt and skated over his shoulders until I was standing on my toes, arms wrapped around him. The last of the space between us was gone, and a satisfied sound rumbled in his chest as his arms more fully tightened.

I was lost in him. The scent, the sound of his breathing, the feel of his broad shoulders and strong arms, the way his beard grazed my chin and his mustache tickled at my nose. The flannel of his shirt was soft against my palms as I slid them along his shoulders and then up his neck to delve into that curly, riotous hair that I'd secretly longed to touch. My fingertips scraped against his scalp, and he sucked in a deep breath, breaking the kiss and looking at me almost accusatorily.

He bent down, swinging me into his arms, and moved us to my couch, where he sat with me on his lap. I moved to start kissing again, but he tucked my head against his shoulder and wrapped me tight in his arms.

"Let's hold on a second here," he said with a rasp.

I shook my head and nudged up under his chin, pressing a kiss to his throat. The force of my reaction to him was startling and fierce, like a wave I had no control over. I didn't want to stop, ever. His hands tightened on my waist as I maneuvered around to look into his eyes. The dark chocolate was molten, and the tension in his body spoke volumes as I leaned in closer. His eyes closed right as I got to his mouth, and, with a tiny zing of victory, I picked up where he'd left off, grabbing his shoulders and showering his mouth with all the myriad of emotions I'd felt for him over the months. The kiss was angry, passionate, and tender, and my entire body seemed to be lighting from the inside.

I tugged off my hat, feeling like a chimney as heat climbed, and Brooks moaned once before pulling his mouth from mine. I shook my head, but he deposited me on a separate cushion and slid to the arm of the couch. He pushed out a big breath and ran his hands through his hair before looking over at me.

"I, um . . ." he shook his head. "Wow."

I celebrated a little, you know, cause he said 'wow,' as I ran my hands through my own hair. "Yeah."

"I . . . wasn't planning on this." He gestured between us, and I noticed his hand was shaking.

131

I was shaking, too, filled with more emotion than I really knew how to handle. "I know."

"Is it, are you okay? That was not normal for a first kiss, in my experience."

I swallowed, coming down off the high and feeling a little unsure about what, exactly, had happened. All I knew was that Brooks had just kissed me and lit a fire that had no business burning like that, and he was totally right that the experience was not normal. I bit my lips, tasting him on them still, and looked at him. He nodded, accepting my inability to say anything as my mind whirled. He stood, tugging his shirt into place.

"I really should go." His expression was serious, his voice raw.

I stood, too, walking with him to the kitchen where he gathered his coat and hat and then to the front door where we paused for a moment. I wasn't sure what he was thinking, but for my part I was still soaring beyond what my logical mind could grasp.

"Sorry I lost my patience earlier," I said at last.

"Being around you is a little like playing with fire," he replied as his fingertips made a trail down my arm.

"You afraid you'll get burned?" I asked, teasingly.

"Scorched," he replied as he walked through the door and closed it behind him.

CHAPTER 18

"He saved your life?" Ruby squealed over brunch the next morning. "That's so romantic. One time I was doing the monkey bars at school, and my hand slipped off. As I was falling, I hit my head on the post, and it knocked me out cold. When I came to, there was this cute boy from my class sitting next to me. I still have a little bit of a crush on him."

"How old were you?" Aryn asked, smiling.

"Fifth grade, so ten or eleven. Man, he still makes my heart pitter-patter. I love a good rescue."

"I'd rather be the one doing the rescuing, thank you very much," I replied as I buttered a warm biscuit. "But yeah, it was unexpectedly attractive."

Aryn, Ruby, and Hailey all stopped to stare at me with big eyes.

"Did you admit he's attractive?" Aryn asked.

"Mm-hmm." I took a bite of biscuit.

"Well, well, well." Hailey smiled.

We were in Hailey's sunny kitchen, the four of us enjoying a preholiday get-together. We'd be busy with family for the next couple of days, so we'd brought gifts to exchange and cooked a delicious breakfast. I didn't really like cooking much, but I was proficient enough to contribute something. Today it had been bacon and orange juice. Staples, in my opinion.

Hailey passed me some jam for the rest of my biscuit and said, "The idea of Ford jumping in to help me does kind of make my heart race. Remember when I was on that ice-skating date and he helped me home after the guy gave me a concussion? I think that's when things shifted for us."

"Yeah, that is romantic. But we're not in love or even headed that way," I replied, proud of myself for keeping my tone light and not blushing.

While I didn't think last night's kisses meant we were headed for an actual coupleship, I couldn't help but remember how his lips had felt against mine, how firm and strong his arms and shoulders had felt as he'd wrapped himself around me. I took a bite of biscuit and had to chug some juice to get it past the tightening of my throat.

Aryn poured herself a glass of orange juice and leaned back in her chair to sip it. "Him having a knife and cutting you free is seriously masculine, and I'm strong enough to admit that I'm here for that kind of thing."

Ruby grinned. "There is nothing more attractive than a man who knows a woman can do anything but still wants to help her out because he loves her. Give me a macho guy who's a big old cuddly bear on the inside, and I'll love him every day of the week."

"You know, Rubes, it's going to be very interesting to see what kind of guy you end up with," Hailey said with a soft smile.

Ruby clapped. "Ooh, I like this game. Let's make predictions. Aryn is going to end up with a sports star who lives for basketball and goes to find her in the crowd for a kiss when his team wins. He'll be super outgoing and up for anything she wants to do. King of the adventure jocks."

Aryn laughed. "I wouldn't hate that."

Hailey shook her head. "My guess is that Aryn ends up with a quiet type to balance out her sports-crazed, outgoing, sarcastic personality. He'll be soft-spoken, a little shy, but totally devoted to her in every way. In sports terms, she'll be the bouncing basketball, but he'll be the hoop she always comes home to."

She'd said it in a teasing tone, but Aryn surprised me by ducking her head and blushing. It wasn't a deep blush, but it colored the tops of her cheeks and made her blue eyes stand out. I wasn't the only one to notice, and we all set down whatever food we'd been eating to lean forward.

"Aryn, is there something you want to tell us?" Hailey asked in a coaxing tone.

Aryn bit her lips and looked up. "No, it's just so far off when it comes to what I honestly want in a partner. I like to put on a good show, but those guys that Ruby described aren't for me. I'm surrounded by them all the time, and I find them off-putting."

I pointed at her with the jam knife. "Okay, we accept that, but that is not why you're blushing like a twelve-year-old. I think it has something to do with Wesley."

"Wesley?" Hailey asked.

"Didn't you notice them together at Lizzie's wedding reception?"

Hailey shook her head and looked to Aryn as she tossed her red curls over her shoulder and rolled her eyes. "Well, what about Meredith?" Aryn deflected. "If Ruby's guy will be interesting, Meredith's is going to be one in a million. He has to respect her as a fierce woman and support her need to control everything and understand that she doesn't mean half the things she says."

I frowned, a little stung. "I'm not a monster." Even if some of her description rang true.

Hailey patted my hand. "Of course you aren't. Aryn is striking out because we got a little too close to something she isn't ready to talk about yet."

Aryn's jaw dropped. "Stop analyzing me. There's nothing to tell." She looked to Ruby. "What do you think about Meredith's future guy?"

Ruby leaned forward and rested her chin on her hands. "Meredith's guy is going to be really simple. He'll be kind, and he'll be dependable. We'll all worry that she's going to run roughshod over him, but at the core he'll be as strong as she is and be able to spar a little bit—because she'd be bored without a tiny bit of drama and wouldn't respect a weakling. She's had enough of the roller-coaster life. She wants steady, dependable, and nice with a few occasional sparks."

We fell into silence as the truth of Ruby's words landed in my heart. Brooks sprang into mind immediately, and I thought about how he'd said his ex had hated that he wasn't a little more creative. I couldn't understand that. Having been raised by a flaky, non-dependable, borderline neglectful parent, there was nothing in the world I craved as much as steady and firm. Firm like Brooks's hands pressed against my back.

"I, uh . . ." The words stuck in my throat, and I cleared it. As they all looked to me, I felt my own face heat. "I had an interesting conversation about that with Brooks the other day." Their eyes grew round as I told them about his ex-fiancée and what she'd thought of him. "So, it made me think that, yeah, I can't imagine faulting a man for being too steady. Ruby is right. Boring is my idea of a total prize. Boring shows up every day of the week, and I like the idea of that a lot."

They smiled kindly at me, and I watched as Aryn's shoulders relaxed. "I'm sorry, Mer. I was rude. I know that you're strong and determined because you've had to be. But I also know that you're so much more than that. You'll find someone who will see it."

I fidgeted with a slice of fruit on my plate, poking my fork tongs into it lightly. "I'm not sure if I want to find someone. Relationships are a big risk, and I'm not good at being open."

Ruby reached over to squeeze my shoulder. "And that's okay, too. You only have to do what makes you happy. You're a Thornback woman, what else do you need?"

Hailey suddenly giggled and looked to Ruby. "Okay, my prediction for Ruby is that he'll be a pampered prince. He'll never have shot a gun or camped or eaten something he didn't buy from the store. He'll be picky about food and squeamish about blood."

I grinned. "No way, you're way off base. Ruby is going to marry a guy that drives a big old truck with deer antlers attached and knows ten different ways to stop bleeding."

Aryn joined in, waving her hands, her smile big. "On their honeymoon he'll trap a squirrel and cook it over a spit while they have target shooting practice."

Ruby pointed her nose in the air. "I'm going to be the happiest out of all of you because that guy you just described actually exists somewhere, and he'll treat me like a queen." We laughed, and she went on. "Also, I'm returning all your Christmas gifts because I got you squirrel seasoning, and I can tell you don't have the palates for it."

That really cracked us all up, and we dove into teasing and chatter that lasted for the rest of our meal. While I participated, I only half listened as I analyzed why I hadn't told them about Brooks kissing me and my own volcanic reaction to it. Over the years I'd learned to trust my friends and their advice and genuine love for me, but what was happening to my heart was something I'd never experienced, and, maybe if I said it out loud, the magic would all disappear.

*****

"Why are you alone?" a deep voice startled me in the aisle of Walgreens drugstore.

I jumped and spun, nearly dropping the armload of magazines I was holding. Brooks smiled at my reaction, clearly the one he'd been going for, and I scowled at him. He looked too put together for Christmas Eve in a jacket, t-shirt, and faded jeans—at least compared to the reindeer-print pajama bottoms and Aggies sweatshirt I was sporting. I was wearing boots as a concession to the weather, but I was already missing my fluffy slippers waiting at home.

"Why are you?" I retorted.

"You first," he said. "It's Christmas Eve, and you actually have people around to spend it with."

"My friends are with their families, and my family is only good for one day of celebration per season. That's tomorrow." I turned back to the magazine rack and debated on what else I wanted to grab. "What's your excuse?"

"My people live back east."

"You have no people here?"

He shook his head. "Not holiday-level people, but I'm working on it."

I nodded. "Fair enough."

"I'm honestly surprised that your friends don't invite you to join their families," he said casually.

I pulled a face. "They did; they still do. Only it's kind of hard on me. Sitting in a warm, cozy, stereotypical Christmas setting pinches a little. I try, but I'm hyperaware that I'm a guest. It's easier to use the night for my own thing."

"Is this the time of year you catch up on celebrity gossip while sipping cider by the fire?" he asked, leaning in to see what I was carrying.

I caught his scent, and flashes of our kiss the other day skated to the forefront of my mind. I'd not spent much time thinking about . . . okay, I can't even finish that lie. I'd thought very little about anything else for the past three days. I was a little embarrassed, to be honest, about basically throwing myself at him and begging him to keep kissing me. It was not my style. I always held a part of myself back and never threw caution to the wind that way. It was the reason I'd gently rebuffed his offers to see each other again.

He'd texted the next morning and asked if I was interested in watching a holiday movie at his place. I'd begged off, telling him I had plans with my friends, which had been true but hadn't taken up my entire day. And in spite of my best efforts to retrench from my passionate reaction to him, here he stood smelling so amazing that I could practically feel his arms around me again. If I didn't know better, I'd say my lips were about ready to attack his without my permission.

I snagged a copy of Good Housekeeping and shifted down the row to grab a poster board. "No," I responded to his question. "I'm prepping for a project I'm

136

going to do with my students. I like to do a trial run first to see how it goes and if I need to make adjustments."

For the record, that was a total lie. But it was a great lie, being both believable and practical. This project was for me alone.

"Smart. What's the project?" he followed me.

"My students really love to create a board with their New Year's Resolutions on them in pictures. So, I ask parents to donate a bunch of magazines, and we spend an afternoon creating them. After they hang in the classroom for a week, the kids get to take them home to hang in their rooms and keep their goals in mind."

This part wasn't a lie. I really did do this with my students. Only today had nothing to do with them. I was creating my own vision board for the new year. It's what I always did on Christmas Eve. It had become kind of a special time for me to be honest. A night I knew would be mine alone. I listened to Christmas music and took my time with the magazines, reading articles and clipping recipes to give to Hailey or Lizzie—because I'd never actually cook them. Sometimes my project overflowed into the days after Christmas, but I didn't mind.

"Sounds like you've done it before, then. Don't you have an example from last year? Or do you like making a new one for yourself too?" I looked at him over my shoulder to find a knowing gleam in his eyes. I shook my head and took a deep breath. He held up his hands. "Hey, I'm not here to judge. Make your Christmas Eve vision board."

"I will, thanks."

"How do they work, exactly?" he reached for a poster board after I'd already grabbed one for me. "Do you have to do it alone or something?"

"I just told you I do them with my entire class."

"Oh, sarcasm, I must have hit a nerve."

He waved his poster board at me until I shook my head and smiled. "I usually spend Christmas Eve alone doing this. I'm embarrassed to be caught because vision boards are very cheesy, and I prefer to live a life of logic. No one would believe I did them."

"Great. It'll be our little secret. Should I grab some magazines of my own or . . ."

My eyes grew large. "Are you trying to horn in on my tradition?"

He nodded. "Definitely. You're alone, I'm alone, there's an entire pile of magazines that needs reading. I'll bring over the cinnamon rolls I made this morning. You've probably got a mean frozen pizza to cook. Sounds like a dream."

I gazed thoughtfully at him. "You made cinnamon rolls?"

"In the spirit of honesty, you should know they're from the freezer section. I just let them raise and then baked them."

What could it hurt to invite him over? That smell of his combined with his everything else was drawing me in and tempting me deeply. I'd had a great time skiing with him, and just because we'd kissed the other day didn't mean there was any pressure for something to happen again. We could be two neighbors sharing cinnamon rolls and gossip mags. I'd had worse nights.

I nodded. "Fine. Bring the rolls. I don't have frozen pizza. I have frozen corn dogs."

He grinned. "I'll meet you at your house in twenty."

He scooted away before I could take it back, and I had to laugh at the fact he knew enough to dash before I changed my mind.

Twenty-three minutes later he knocked on my door, and I swung it open. "You're late."

"I had to frost the rolls. Would you have really let me in without frosting?" He waved the rolls under my nose, and I took a deep breath. "See. Now you're glad I'm late." He followed me in, closing the door behind him. "So, how much glitter should I expect? I went ahead and changed into leisure pants, but I'm not sure if I should also wear an apron or . . ."

"No glitter. I'm against it on moral grounds."

He laughed. "Yet another reason I like you so much. Glitter is the worst."

My oven dinged, saying it was heated, as we entered my kitchen. I grabbed the sheet pan of corn dogs to put inside. "I'm oven baking these rather than microwaving them, so I hope you feel appropriately grateful."

He nodded. "Microwaved corn dogs are soggy. It's clear you feed to love."

I laughed out loud at that and shook my head. "My sisters would not agree with that statement, at all. Food is not my love language."

"What is?" he asked, setting the rolls on the counter.

"According to Hailey I'm an acts-of-service girl. She's probably right."

"So, me bringing you rolls and saving your life the other day are scoring me points?"

I shrugged. "If you're hoping to score points, sure."

He smirked. "I'm definitely looking to score points."

We fell into easy conversation as I cut carrots into sticks and warmed apple cider on the stove. He was so relaxed and cheerful, with no hint of the awkwardness I was feeling toward him, that I started to wonder if the reaction to our kiss had been completely one-sided. Was his stomach not in knots at my nearness? Was he not worried about any of this? Based on the fact he ate three corn dogs and a heap of carrot sticks and sipped three mugs of cider, I assumed his stomach was doing just fine.

An hour later we sat in my living room with magazines spread all around us along with a growing pile of trash, each holding a pair of scissors in our hands. He was currently involved with a recipe for a pineapple carrot cake while I was learning about the latest British royal gossip. He snipped his scissors unconsciously while he read, and I took the chance to watch his face. He was entertainingly expressive. His eyebrows moved around a lot, telling me if he was surprised or confused about something he was reading. His mouth occasionally formed a little O or moved into a flat line. As a person who was guarded, it was fun to watch his shifting demeanor.

"What do you know about buttercream frosting?" he asked, looking up to catch me watching him. He grinned.

"Nothing," I stated, tearing my eyes from him.

"Hmm. I think I need to try this cake, but I'm not a frosting expert."

"There's probably a recipe in there for it."

He was silent for a moment, flipping pages. "What are you cutting out for your vision board?"

"I don't want to tell you," I replied honestly. I'd been really open with him recently, but even my friends didn't know about my vision board. It was private, so I'd been clipping things, but I'd tucked them behind me somewhat under the couch to keep them from his prying eyes. "It's personal."

He closed the magazine and wiggled his eyebrows at me. "I like personal stuff."

"Pass."

He put the magazine off to the side and sat his scissors on top of them. "I double pass your pass, which negates it."

"What?" I frowned, furrowing my eyebrows. "That isn't a thing."

"In my world it's a thing."

"We're not in your world right now."

He moved to hands and knees and started crawling toward me. "I just want a tiny peek at your pictures. Just to get my mind thinking. I won't steal your ideas."

I pushed the stack further under the couch. "Not happening. I'm setting a firm boundary here. I'm not even going to glue them on until after you leave."

"How firm is your boundary?" he asked as he came around me and bent his arms to look under the couch.

I leaned forward, blocking him with an arm. "Very, very firm."

I should have seen it coming when the smile crept onto his face, but I still managed to be shocked when he knelt upright, grabbed me, and threw me on top of my couch before diving down to snag the pictures. Having not grown up with brothers or guy friends, I had no idea what this meant. Was he teasing? Did he genuinely not care that I'd said no? Did he think he could use his physicality to get his way? Anger whipped through me, and as he went back down onto his stomach, I launched myself off the couch, landing smack on his back.

He let out a grunt and laughed. "Get off me."

I grabbed at his arm as he reached under the couch. "No way. Those are private."

When it became apparent that his arm was longer and stronger than mine, I used the best weapon I had in my arsenal. My pointy joints. I scrambled up into a kneeling position and pressed my kneecaps into his lower back. As expected, he reacted as though I'd stabbed him.

"Did you bring knives to this fight?" he cried out, doing his best to roll over and unseat me.

I held on tight and doubled down, pushing my elbows against his shoulders. "Get away from my pictures."

He was shaking and rolling back and forth, and I realized that he was laughing. He found this to be great entertainment. Confused and unsure, I eased up enough that he managed to flip both of us over. We lay on our sides facing each other, and

I watched as he laughed and reached for my arms, wrapping his hands around my elbows.

"Jeez, those things should be registered as weapons. You are seriously boney."

My anger dissipated like drops of water, a little at a time. "You weren't actually going to breach my privacy?"

He shook his head. "As much as I like the phrase 'breach my privacy,' no. But it was totally worth it to find out you fight dirty."

I licked my lips and fought a grin. "You started it by launching me onto the couch."

His hands slid up my arms and wrapped around my back as he scooted me toward him. "Worth it to break down that wall you've been hiding behind."

I rolled my eyes. "What wall?"

"The same one you built after our ski day." He stroked one hand down my spine, and tension eased out as awareness crept in. "Is there a reason you're avoiding me?"

I nodded. "Yes."

His eyebrows raised. "Care to share it?"

"Nope."

His hand moved up to my neck, where he kneaded softly. "I'm a patient man. I'll figure it out. In fact, I already have a theory."

"You do not."

He simply hummed in his throat and leaned down to kiss me along my jaw. Flames licked up the side of my neck as he did so, and I closed my eyes. My arms had been wedged between us, but I moved them around his waist. His lips pressed to mine, and even though I was unsure of just about everything, I sighed and relaxed into it, experiencing that same sense of powerful connection that I had the first time. He smelled like cider and tasted like sweet frosting and cinnamon, and I didn't have one hesitation as he pulled me flush against him and deepened the kiss. It was pure bliss, like a sweet reunion my body had been craving.

We spent several minutes like that, lying on my hard living room floor with magazines beneath us, before he pulled away and ran a hand over my hair.

"You could put a picture of me on your vision board," he whispered against my ear.

I laughed and shoved at him, rolling away and standing up.

He stood, too, eyes dancing. "Consider this your warning to knock that wall down. I don't want to have to keep wrestling you." He bent and scooped up the magazine with the cake recipe he'd liked. "I'm leaving, and I'm taking this home with me."

"Fine. But the extra cinnamon rolls stay."

I walked him to the door, smiling the entire way. When I returned to the living room and surveyed the mess we'd left behind, I shook my head and allowed the happy feeling to flow through me. I couldn't promise the wall would stay down, but I could promise to leave a doorway open.

CHAPTER 19

I was awakened Christmas morning by texts chiming on my phone. I smiled to myself, keeping my eyes closed as I reached to my nightstand and picked up the phone. I already knew that it would be my sisters, and this was the very reason that one night a year I slept with my phone in my room. One of the few traditions I remembered from when our mom was alive was something called "Christmas Gift." The first person to say the words "Christmas gift" to someone on Christmas morning received an extra present. It was something small like a coloring book and crayons, but we loved sneaking up on each other and trying to be the first to say it.

When Mom had passed away, I'd been careful to keep the tradition alive. As a six-year-old it had been hard to find a gift for the winner, and for a few years it had been a toothbrush or some other silly thing. But when we'd gotten older and I'd started working, the gift had been things like movie tickets or new earrings. Now, with Ash living so far away, we resorted to texting each other or calling, and it was less about receiving a gift and more about the reminder of happy times.

I read their texts and sat up, tugging my covers with me and pulling my knees against my chest. My fuzzy pajamas were soft against my chin as I read through their texts.

Ash: Christmas Gift!
Willow: I don't accept. The moon is still up
Ash: We go by time, and my clock says it's 6:30, which is within the rules.
Willow: Who made these rules?
Me: I did. Someone had to set limits or you two would have stayed up until midnight on Christmas Eve just to be the first to say it
Ash: Probably true
Me: Merry Christmas, Ash. Wish we could see you today
Ash: Miss you two
Willow: Love you Ash. Tell Jake hi

While Christmas had never been my favorite holiday, I could appreciate that it was a time for families, and I allowed myself a rare moment to feel nostalgic about my sisters. Normally I was pragmatic about the fact that Ash was far away. This morning I remembered the years where I did manage to pull off something for

Christmas and their happy, surprised faces. It hadn't been easy to be the adult in the family, but I couldn't say all of it had been bad.

I gathered up my clothes and padded to the bathroom where I ran a hot shower and got ready for the day. I'd be meeting up with Willow and Dad for a meal and gift exchange. Willow was bringing Steve to meet the family, which really meant me, because he'd already shoveled my dad's walks. Then again, maybe he hadn't actually met my dad. Just because we were there taking care of him didn't always guarantee a sighting of the man.

As I blew my hair dry and straightened it into a slick bob, I couldn't help but think about the fact that both my sisters had brought men home in the past months. We'd gone from famine to feast in our family. I was proud of both of them for being brave enough to give it a real try. I'd done it once, and, after a year of emotional tug-of-war with one Ron Blanchard, it had been a relief when he'd broken up with me and moved away. Ron had been driven, hard-working, and logical to a fault. In the end our similarities had pushed us apart. We had both needed someone a little less like ourselves.

Brooks's name popped into my mind, and I couldn't help but catalog the differences between him and Ron. It was almost laughable how much more easygoing Brooks was, how quick to smile. His sunny personality should have clashed with my more pessimistic nature, but the man was managing to get under my skin in a way Ron had only hoped to. Actually I still wasn't sure Ron really wanted to. We were more like two power people fighting for domination. It made me realize that Brooks might actually be the strongest one of all, in that he didn't need to fight to prove anything, and there was something truly powerful in that.

We'd kissed two times now, so we were probably starting to be something, maybe. Sort of. I didn't go around kissing people, and I doubted he did either, but I also knew a few kisses didn't automatically launch you into a place that was clearly labeled. So, maybe we were nothing more than flirty neighbors. That idea had me wrinkling my nose in distaste.

Ugh. Before I could think better of it, I texted him.

Me: Merry Christmas

As I moved into the kitchen to get food prep started, I shot off a text to my friends.

Me: Merry Christmas, you filthy animals

I didn't have to wait long before replies started coming in.

Aryn: Which one of you made the naughty list and got coal in their stocking?
Hailey: I've never heard of this naughty list. Probably because I'm so nice
Me: I don't even hang a stocking. It's too risky
Hailey: Do you hear what I hear? It's the sound of bacon frying. I'm definitely on the nice list

Ruby: Ho ho ho.

Aryn: Did you call us a mean name?

Lizzie: Guys, you should all go on a honeymoon. Christmas is definitely meant to be spent on a tropical island

Ruby: Wearing nothing but stockings?

Hailey: Rubes!

Aryn: Speaking of ho ho ho . . .

Hailey: Santa is now rethinking who made the naughty list

Me: Well. This went straight down the chimney

Aryn: As expected

I laughed.

Me: Yes. I wouldn't like you all so much otherwise. Hope you have a wonderful day

They all signed off with their own well wishes, and, as I mixed up muffins from a box and sliced some fruit, I found myself whistling carols. When my food prep was finished, I loaded up my car and made the drive to Dad's house. The snow had held off, and I was grateful for that. Shoveling sidewalks on Christmas seemed like a borderline criminal activity. I pulled along the gravel drive to the back of the house and parked. Dad's truck was in the carport, and Willow's was nowhere to be seen.

My phone dinged, and I took it out of my purse, smiling when I saw Brooks had replied.

Brooks: Merry Christmas back. With family today?

Me: Yes

Brooks: All day?

Me: Yep

Brooks: Call me if things change

I tucked my phone back into my bag and headed for the house. Smoke curled up out of the chimney as I carried my first armload of things inside. The muffins were still steamy, and the fruit bowl was heavy. It smelled delicious. The kitchen was empty when I pushed open the back door, but I was happy to see the lights were on. Maybe Dad had remembered it was Christmas today and that we'd be coming. I went back out for a second load of gifts, and before I knew what was happening, I heard a cracking sound and fell straight through the back steps, landing with a jarring thud on one foot and lurching forward. The step below caught me on my shin, and I tumbled, catching myself on my hands before I could land on my face.

"For the love!" I cried out, looking backwards to see that one leg was in a hole while I was kneeling on the other. My shin throbbed. "Ugh!"

I tugged my leg out of the stair hole and managed to shimmy around to a standing position. My shin ached, and I was angry that I'd fallen through at all. I rubbed my hands on my thighs to dry them and then scoured my palms for any cuts. Thankfully, they were okay. Hands are important for a lot of things, after all. I pulled up my pant leg and took a look at my abused shin. The skin hadn't broken, but it was definitely going to bruise, thanks to the fact that bone against stairs never fared well.

Satisfied that I wasn't in mortal danger, I surveyed the broken stairs. I stomped on the stairs above and below where I'd fallen through. They seemed sturdy enough. I figured, if I gave Willow some warning, we could work around it for the day, and I'd come back tomorrow to fix it. A noise from Dad's workshop had me marching in that direction. I found him there, sanding something with goggles covering his eyes.

"Dad?" I called.

He turned, not bothering to lift the protective eye gear. "Willow?"

"No, Dad, it's Meredith. I just fell through the back steps. When was the last time you checked them?"

He smiled a soft, dazed smile that told me he was only half listening. Home repair was lower on his list than almost anything else. "Oh, Evergreen, don't fuss."

I swallowed hard. I was going to get called Evergreen all day, and I hated it when he told me not to fuss. I clamped down on heated words as I watched him continue to run his hands over whatever he was working on.

Then, with no warning whatsoever, they leaked out. "Guess what, Forest Atwood? Somebody has to fuss, and that somebody has always been me."

He stopped, and his head raised. "Nobody asked you to do that."

My jaw tensed, and I folded my arms. "Nobody had to. I did it to keep my sisters from suffering because you couldn't be bothered to care."

His eyes sharpened, and I watched as his face crumpled. Regret and recrimination passed across his expression and were mirrored in mine. I'd tried to talk to him several times over the years, and when nothing had changed I'd stopped. Today, of all days, was not the time to resurrect this issue. It was Christmas, and this was pointless.

I cleared my throat. "Well, it's Christmas morning. Time to come inside and have some food and exchange gifts."

He looked down at the object in his hand, and my eyes followed. "I thought I had a few more weeks." He held it up, and I could see that it was a cutting board with the beginnings of a beautiful tree etched into it. "I was going to give each of you girls one of these. See the tree? It represents our family. The Atwoods. All my girls have tree names."

Mixed feelings rushed to the forefront. Tenderness for his attempt to do something thoughtful for us. Annoyance at the fact that it was always too late and usually too little. Chances were that was the first one he'd even started. I watched as he stood there, his hair gray and his hands scarred from the life he'd chosen. Did he realize how alone that life had made him? Was he like this when Mom was alive? I fell into the comfortable pattern of gruffness to hide the range of emotions I was experiencing.

"I'm sorry, but you're too late. Maybe next year?" I stated.

His nod was slow. "I guess so."

"Why don't you set it down and come inside to clean up?" I gestured outside as I heard the crunch of wheels on gravel. "Willow's here. And she's brought someone special for you to meet."

Dad set the cutting board down on the workbench and tugged off his goggles, making his hair stand on end. "I met him, but I don't remember his name."

"It's Steve. What did you think of him?"

Dad shrugged and dusted off his shirt and pants. "Don't remember that either."

Had I grown up with a father who remembered things, I may have found this conversation troubling and wondered if he needed to be checked for dementia. As it stood this was nothing more than a regular morning, trying to get Dad to tune into the world around him.

I led the way out of the shed and waved at Willow as she got out of the driver's side of her vehicle. She waved back, and I watched as the passenger door opened and the mysterious Steve climbed out. He was average height, not much taller than Willow, with dark hair and a mustache that made me think of Tom Selleck in his glory days. Thinking of Tom Selleck made a forgotten image of Mom pop into my head. She was a fan of his show *Magnum P.I.* and watched reruns at night. She'd given me a bath and then combed my hair while we watched the show. She'd joked about how if she ever left my father, it would be for him. How ironic that this look-alike was who Willow had manifested into her life.

"You must be Steve," I said as I closed the distance and held out my hand. "I'm Meredith."

Steve smiled, making his mustache lift in a way I found incredibly entertaining. I was going to get to watch it all day. "Hi Meredith. Willow has told me a lot about you. I'm happy to meet you."

Willow came around and gave me a hug, and I was enveloped in her special Christmas scent of cinnamon and nutmeg. "Happy Christmas, Sis."

When she straightened I pointed to the back steps. "So, yeah, fell through the steps this morning. There's now a missing one we'll have to hop over as we go in and out. Try not to break something."

"By 'something' she means any food items and gifts." Willow winked at Steve. "She's not that worried about our limbs."

I grinned. "Your limbs are always at risk here. Seems redundant to keep mentioning it."

Willow and Steve laughed, and I moved to my car to gather the remaining items. Dad was nowhere to be seen. Somehow, while I'd been meeting Steve, he'd slipped away. The back door was open, so I hoped he'd gone that way and hadn't meandered back into the shop. I watched Willow and Steve go ahead of me into the house, stretching out to miss the hole. As my turn came I felt a drop of something cold and wet splat on the top of my head just as I leaned forward to bridge the gap. I looked up in time to catch another drop on my cheek. The rain gutter dangled above me, dripping melting snow as the morning warmed up.

Another day in Paradise.

*****

My legs dangled off my bed as I lay on my back looking up at my ceiling later that night. My belly hurt from laughing as I regaled Ash with tales from family Christmas.

"First, Dad wouldn't stop calling Steve by the wrong name. It was always something that started with an S, but never the right name. 'Stan, can you pass the butter? Stuart, can you hand me the juice? What do you do for a living, Simon?' By the end of the day, Steve had stopped trying to correct him, and Willow was shooting death laser beams out of her eyes at Dad," I giggled. "It was actually truly funny for once."

"He didn't do that to Jake," Ash chuckled.

"Because you're his baby girl, so he pays more attention to you. Willow is the middle child of a habitually distracted man. Let's just be glad he isn't calling *her* by the wrong name all the time."

"What did you think of Steve?"

"I'm . . . impressed, I think."

Ash gasped dramatically. "Wow. High praise from you, Big Sis."

"Well, he's really . . ."

I wasn't sure how to describe him. Steve was articulate and confident but didn't need to be the center of attention. He seemed cheerful and flexible and willing to take what was thrown at him. He owned an auto part store a few blocks from Willow's boutique, and they'd met at a city business owners' meeting, which told me he had a good head on his shoulders and wasn't flaky. I'd been happy for Willow, who in the past had only dated odd-balls who mostly forgot she existed— basically she'd been dating versions of our father.

"He's put together," I finished.

Ash, immediately understanding that this was the same as me saying he was a superhero, sighed. "Willow needs put together."

"We all need that."

"What did everyone get for gifts?"

"Willow gave me the dress she'd loaned me for Lizzie's bachelorette party. It's a really pretty dress, and it looks good on me, which is hard to find because I'm somehow short and tall at the same time. It's an expensive dress."

"Did Dad pull something together?"

I told her about the cutting boards, and the fact that I'd actually snapped at Dad. "So, you might get a Forest Atwood original cutting board in a few years. Maybe."

"Poor Dad," she said. "It's got to be hard to live in a world that moves so much faster than you do."

I'd never heard either of my sisters describe Dad that way, and I'd certainly never had the thought myself, but, as I pondered those words, I found it gave me a new sense of empathy for him. She was right. Even though his actions had hurt me deeply over the years, Dad probably wasn't having a great time, either.

"What did Jake give you?" I asked brightly, changing the topic like the pro I was.

"Well, it's a gift that I'm not sure how to feel about, actually."

Interest peaked, I sat up. "Really?"

"Yeah. It's scuba diving lessons."

"Oh." I instantly understood her hesitation. The Atwood family did not do water, and there was one solid, simple reason. Our mother, Judith, had died in a drowning accident at Hyrum Reservoir on a sunny family beach day. Deep water had always been the enemy. "Where would you even go diving in Boulder, Colorado?" I asked.

"I mean, assuming I'd be brave enough to do it, there is a reservoir here."

I nodded even though she couldn't see. "Does he know? About Mom and water?"

"Yeah. He knows."

"So, why the gift, then?"

"He wants to help me overcome my fear."

I cleared my throat. "I guess that's kind of nice of him."

"The thing is, Mer, I don't really have any memories of Mom at all. I was only two when she died, so I don't remember her drowning. I just remember not having a mom. I'm only afraid of water because I was raised to be afraid. I don't like that about myself. It's strange to be traumatized about something that you didn't actually experience."

"Understandable."

"And yet, even knowing all that, it doesn't make the trauma less real. I'm truly frightened of big bodies of water."

"So, what are you going to do?"

She chuckled, but it wasn't a sound of amusement. "I'm going to do what we Atwoods always do. Overthink it, avoid discussing it, and then freak out when I'm pushed on making a choice."

I huffed. "We're not that bad."

"Let's not start lying to each other now, Evergreen," she teased.

We fell into a short silence, and I took a deep breath. "I think you should do it, Ash. If you have a chance to get over something you're afraid of and someone by your side who cares enough to help you, you'd be silly to turn that down."

"Yeah?"

"Yeah. Be sure to send me pictures."

"Mer, when you decide to face one of your fears, I'll have your back, too."

I smiled. "Thanks, Little Sis, but my fears are too many to mention, and you only have one life to live."

"Eh, Willow tells me I can manifest anything I want, so I'll manifest eternal youth." She laughed. "She tells me she's manifesting a man for you. How's that going?"

"Don't encourage her."

"No men around? No one strikes your fancy?" Her voice was playful. "No one, maybe, with a beard and curly hair who bought something from Willow on Black Friday and who regularly pops up in conversation."

"Nope. No one."

"Not an HOA president with sculpted abs and gigantic biceps?"

"Good grief. Sculpted abs and gigantic biceps? His muscles, or lack thereof, are a mystery I have not unlocked."

Ash laughed out loud. "Who is he?"

"A figment of Willow's warped mind."

"She gave me some pretty specific descriptions of him, so don't pretend you don't know who she's talking about."

I made a growling noise. "Yes. I do. But she did not manifest him into my life. I've known him for months, and until, like, two weeks ago, we were mortal enemies."

"His name?"

"Not happening."

"I want to look him up online," she pressed.

"No way."

"Typing it in now. B-r-o-o-k-s . . ."

"What is happening?" I flopped back onto my bed and pressed my arm over my eyes. "Ash Atwood, you're a devious woman. What do you know, and who told you anything about it?"

"I know so many things," she crowed. "And, from his picture online, I'd say you might want to find out some things for yourself."

Warmth started at the back of my neck and crawled into my face as an image of him leaning over me flitted into my mind. "He's a monster," I said weakly.

"Really?"

"Yep. Mean and nasty. Always has to have his way."

"I see."

"He hates my cat, Betty."

"Betty is kind of a jerk, actually. She tried to eat Jake."

I scoffed. "Betty is the best person I know."

"Mer?"

"Yeah."

"I'm going to let you go because it's late and I have hot cocoa and a hunky man waiting for me in front of a fireplace. But your cat is not a person. Merry Christmas, Sis. May all your dreams come true."

"Brooks is not my dream!"

"Uh-huh. Bye."

Thanks to my sister, Brooks VanOrman was actually my dream . . . because he took up residence in my dreams for the entire night.

CHAPTER 20

The next morning I was loading groceries, cleaning supplies, and tools into the trunk of my car when Brooks casually walked up my driveway. Thanks to Ash and my humiliating dreams the night before, a tugging, wary feeling appeared in my chest as he approached with a smile. It felt unsafe to like him more than I knew he liked me even as I couldn't ignore the happiness I felt at seeing him. I put the bag full of freezer meals into the trunk and turned to face him. So much had flip-flopped, and I was a wreck of roller-coaster emotions.

"Merry Christmas," he said, offering a green bag to me. It was tied with a red bow and felt light as I took it out of his hand.

"That was yesterday," I replied.

"Christmas spirit lasts even after the 25th," he replied with a chuckle.

I opened the bag and took out a small, homemade, wooden ornament. The wood itself was a light-colored disc shape with an angel silhouette cut out of the center. It showed skill, and it was thoughtful. I looked up at him.

"You made this?"

"Yeah. I like to give them as gifts to friends and neighbors."

I dropped it gently back into the bag. "Wow, I made the list this year. I've reached neighbor status," I joked.

"Maybe next year you can reach friend status, but I don't think we should set unreal expectations."

I rolled my eyes and put the gift bag on a shelf near the house door. "Thank you. I'll take that inside when I get home. I'm sorry I didn't get you anything."

"No problem." He looked into my trunk and then back to me. "That's an interesting collection of items. What are you up to today?"

I wiggled my toes in my shoes, wondering how much I wanted to share. If Ash hadn't pestered me the night before, I probably wouldn't be having these erratic thoughts as I stood there staring at my feet. In the end I decided to try to keep that wall down like I'd promised.

"Oh, just over to my dad's house to help with some cleaning and get his freezer stocked up."

Brooks looked at the tools and back at me. "Does he need some help with home repairs, or are those his tools that you're returning?"

"He needs some help with repairs."

"Could you use an extra hand? I'm free, and, as you know, I have a few Boy Scout credentials that are pretty impressive."

"You planning to cut his shirttails off?"

Brooks laughed. "Really, let me come lend a hand."

I wasn't sure how to reply. Would my dad care? No. He probably wouldn't even notice we were there, depending on what he was working on today. Did I want Brooks to see the reality of my life and put some more pieces together about me? Not especially. He might see it, feel pity, and then things would get all messed up. I liked getting to know each other without all this childhood baggage coming front and center.

At the same time it sounded so nice to not face this task alone. I knew Brooks had the skills to help, and it was hard to look at him and not want to spend the entire day around him. I was drawn to him, thinking about him incessantly.

So, I said, "Okay, jump in," and watched with a crooked grin as he clapped his hands once and jumped into my car. I stayed outside for a few heartbeats before I willed my hands to close the trunk and pull my keys out of my pocket. When I did get in the car, it smelled like Brooks, warm and comforting and actually the yummiest scent in the world.

Stupid Willow and her manifesting and Ash and her meddling. Brooks had never smelled *yummy* before this.

I turned to him, my hands gripping the wheel. "Look, you asked me to take down the wall, so I'm trying. But there are things you need to understand. Like how I'm thinking about kicking you out of my car."

He shook his head. "I'm cool, Atwood. I've already gathered that your childhood was different, and your dad needs help. I'm an impartial community volunteer."

"This can't be something you use against me."

His entire face shifted from one of happy community volunteer to serious courtroom drama. I wondered if that's how he looked when he was arguing cases in court . . . if property lawyers did that. His jaw flexed, and he speared me with a look.

"I'm not looking for weak spots to exploit. Frankly, I'm kind of hurt that you'd think that after getting to know me better."

I'd seen him annoyed many times, but this was probably the first time I'd seen him hurt, and I felt terrible about it, so I admitted something that was hard to admit.

"If you had any idea how many times as a young person I was convinced to trust someone and then they saw my situation and ran off to tell others about it, you wouldn't blame me for being overly cautious and seriously worried about it."

He took a slow breath, his eyes on my face, and I watched as his expression smoothed out. "That's fair. If you're that uncomfortable with me helping, I'll get out and won't have any hurt feelings about it. However, I have a free day and would love to pitch in." He wrapped a warm hand lightly around the back of my neck. "It's as simple as wanting to spend time with you, and if I can help you out

151

a little in the meantime, that's a double win. I promise to keep any secrets you need me to keep."

"And no pitying me."

"No pity."

To recap: he wanted to be with me and help me with repair work at the same time, and he was down for secret keeping. He had inadvertently said the hottest thing any man had ever said to me, and I was quickly filling with warm goo.

"One of his rain gutters fell off, and I could use an extra set of hands to screw it back into place," I said.

"Great. I have hands." He released my neck and wiggled his hands at me.

"I fell through the back steps yesterday, and I could use someone to help me sort through the woodpile for pieces to replace it with. Some of the wood is hard to move by myself."

"I'm basically an expert wood sorter and shifter."

"I think the last time his house was cleaned was like a month ago. In fact, I know it, because it was me who did it."

"I went to college; I lived with five other guys; you can't scare me."

A smile twitched, and I turned to start the car. "Okay. So, we agree that you know what you're getting yourself into and will keep blinders firmly in place?"

He crossed his heart. "I hope my pay is good. I'm not cheap."

"Ah, sadly, you're a volunteer, and the pay is lousy."

I was tense on the drive, both regretting letting him come along and incredibly grateful that he was there. His light chatter and easy vibes should have helped me settle down, but the way I'd catch him watching me with a little smile made me antsy. Ron had been understanding and open at first, too. I think he'd thought with his powerful personality he could whip my family into shape. Instead, it had become one more sore point between us, and I'd never brought another man to my dad's house with me. This was a big leap of faith.

We talked through what needed to be done, and Brooks didn't argue with the game plan I'd already laid out in my mind. In fact, he said he thought it sounded good, and I chanced a glance at him to see if he was trying to appease me or if he really meant it. He smiled back, and I relaxed a little further. He was fine with me running the show.

Seeming to understand my disbelief, he chuckled and reached for my hand. "Meredith, it's *your* dad. Why wouldn't I be okay with doing things your way when you're the expert here?"

Once again, he melted my heart with logic.

We pulled up to my dad's rickety little house, and I had to concentrate to keep from watching Brooks's reaction to the place. I tried to see it like a first-timer, but there was too much history for me to be able to look at it with anything other than the taint of experiences. The gravel crunched as I eased my car around back. Dad's truck was gone, and I momentarily wondered where he could have gotten off to. However, in some ways it made things easier because he didn't like it when us girls got into his wood stash.

"Okay, this is the place."

"Great. So, we're starting with the stairs?" Brooks shoved his door open and climbed out. He pushed his arms into the denim coat he'd taken off while we'd been driving. "Your dad has a lot of land."

I looked around and back to him. "Compared to the city, yeah. But this is how all the houses are out here. Well, at least how they used to be when I was growing up. There's a lot of new growth now, but it's still a small town." I popped open my trunk. "I need to get these groceries inside first, so give me one second." I made short work of depositing the food in the freezer and then led the way to the workshop and around the side to where the wood was stacked. "It's good my dad is gone. He hates people sorting through his wood. Never know when one of these might be the perfect piece for a project. He wouldn't want to waste it on making a new stair."

"Your dad's a woodworker?"

I glanced up and saw that his expression was interested, maybe even a little excited, thinking he'd found something we'd have in common. I tensed but did my best to keep my tone nonchalant as I replied, "My dad's an artist. The medium shifts constantly. He does a little of everything."

"The arts can be a tempting field but a difficult one at the same time."

I pulled gloves out of my coat pocket and tugged them on before reaching for the top board. "And that's all we'll be discussing about my father today. Baby steps."

He nodded and grabbed the next board down, lifting it to inspect it before tossing it aside. "Can I at least know his name?"

I gave him a speaking glance. "Why?"

"Seems impolite to move a man's woodpile without knowing his name."

"His name is Forest."

"And your sister is Willow?"

"Yep. My other sister is named Ash." I shifted a few things and pointed. "I think I see a board there that would work."

Together we moved a few larger, long tree limbs that Dad had put there when he'd been really into carving larger objects. Once a flat board was freed, we restacked it all and headed into the workshop to get a measuring tape before using Dad's tools to trim it to size. I paused with a hand on the door and turned to face Brooks, who was holding the board.

"Do not get all googly-eyed when we go in there. You're going to think you've entered a wonderland, but you're actually going down a rabbit hole of doom. All is not how it appears."

"I wouldn't have pegged you as a poet. You paint such a pretty picture."

I tilted my head. "I'm serious. Do not engage with the Forest Atwood treasure trove."

"Yes, ma'am."

I pushed aside the door, and we entered the space. It smelled like it always did—a mixture of freshly cut wood, turpentine, paint, and burning from whatever he'd been working on. There was heat radiating off the kiln in the corner, and some dirty rags nearby showed he'd been working with pottery earlier.

"Oh my . . ." I heard Brooks start.

I turned quickly to him. His eyes were large as he took in all the half-finished projects leaning against walls and hanging from hooks along the exposed rafters. His gaze touched on the tools and stacks of artistic elements gathered in piles here and there. Lastly, he looked back at me. I shook my head, and he quickly flattened out his expression.

"This is probably the most boring place I've ever been," he said in a monotone voice that made me smile.

"Exactly." I gestured to the big workbench. "Put the board there. I'll go tear out the remains of the broken step and measure for the new one. Feel free to drool over everything while I'm gone, but be sure to pull it together when I return."

I grabbed a measuring tape and a hammer and didn't wait for a response from him. When I returned to the shop, he was running his hands along the workbench as his eyes wandered. It was so strange to have him there, appreciating everything in the shop. It was hard to reconcile the Brooks of HOA rule enforcement with the guy dropping his jaw over this artist's haven.

"I have the measurements if you'll plug in the saw?" I called.

He spooked a little and shook his head as he spun around. "Sorry. I was accidentally drooling still. But I'm all better now."

We made quick work of cutting the board and nailing it into place. I jumped on it a few times for good measure while Brooks watched with half a grin, his arms folded across his chest.

"You know that's not the safest way to test a new build?" he said.

"Probably not, but I've been doing it this way since I was eight, so why change a good thing?"

I could tell by the way his mouth moved that he wanted to ask some clarifying questions about why I'd have been building steps at that age, but, thankfully, he kept those questions to himself.

"At eight there was probably less danger of you breaking the board," he said instead of whatever he'd wished to say.

I stomped once more with one foot. "True. But I figured if I did my best to break it and it held, it was good enough for normal use." I pointed above my head. "That's the next project."

I headed back into the shop, leaving the hammer on the newly fixed step, and grabbed a big ladder to get started on fixing the rain gutter. When I emerged from the shop, ladder tilting dangerously, Brooks jogged over and took an end from me.

"You have to make use of the community volunteer," he stated.

"Who do you think is going up on this ladder?" I replied. "I hate heights."

We propped it on the corner of the house where the gutter was supposed to be attached, and Brooks climbed up to survey the damage and give me an update so that we could make a game plan for repairs. I watched as he made his way up, and, when warmth bloomed in my chest, I realized that I found it super attractive to watch a man doing home repair work. Not flexing in the gym or dressed up in a pressed suit or rescuing me from some villain … or whatever else was always happening in romance books and movies. I was going ga-ga for a man climbing a ladder to inspect a rain gutter. My mind was warped.

He came down and brushed his hands against his pants to remove some of the dirt and debris.

"So, what's first?" I asked.

"We'll need work gloves and some nails to start with," he said.

We walked together back to the workshop, and when his hand brushed against the back of mine, my dusty heart seemed determined to go pitter-pat, which was something it had never done in the entirety of my existence. I told him where to find nails, and I went in search of gloves while I tried not to stare at the fit of his jeans and the way his jacket stretched across his shoulders as he moved.

Is this what physical attraction and chemistry felt like? If so, I was starting to understand why people seemed to lose brain cells when they were dating someone new.

"Do you have trash bags?" he asked from behind me. "I think it would be a good idea to get some leaves and branches out of the gutter while we're up there."

"Good idea." I grabbed bags and met him at the door of the shop.

Ten minutes later I had a bag full of soggy leaves and pointy branches. Brooks had taken advantage of the hanging rain gutter and used it as a sort of track, pushing leaves from the far side of the house gently enough to keep the gutter from breaking further but hard enough to funnel them directly into the bag I was holding. The process had been much easier than I'd anticipated, but the smell of moldy decay had me wrinkling my nose as he climbed down the ladder and walked toward me.

He was smiling when I finished tying off the bag and looked up at him. "What?" I asked.

He took off his glove, which was now wet and muddy, and reached toward me. I flinched. He pulled his hand partway back and chuckled. The sound was different than anything I'd heard from him before. It was low and soft, tender and amused. He reached out again, and this time I held still as he lightly worked through my hair, pulling out leaves that had fluttered into the midnight-colored strands while I held my head chin-down.

It didn't take long for him to tidy my hair, but a curious silence had descended as he worked. I dared to look up at him, only to find him watching me closely, analyzing and pondering. I wasn't sure what to do with that type of attention, and, yet, he seemed determined to give it. He was asking me to let him in; he wanted to learn more, but old habits made me want to scramble backwards as fast as I could. As though he could see my spooked reaction, he finished by running a finger over my outer ear and then dropped his hand.

"Baby steps?" he questioned.

"Yeah."

155

"Ready to hammer something?" he asked, his light tone so different from the look in his eyes.

"Uh-huh."

When he was back atop the ladder, I was able to fully breathe again. My mind whirled as I held the ladder steady for him. One leg of the ladder seemed to be a little off, and when he'd hammer something it would wiggle slightly, so I held tightly to the legs while he forced the old, rickety rain gutter into submission. My head, however, was thinking about what a nice color his eyes were and how intriguing the one or two gray hairs in his beard looked.

"Evergreen?" I hadn't heard the approach of my dad's truck, so I was completely caught off guard when he called my name.

I turned to find him coming around the corner of the house. He must have parked out front. "Hey, Dad."

"What's going on?" he asked, shielding his eyes from the sun as he looked up to Brooks, who had stopped hammering and was looking down at us.

"My, uh, friend and I are fixing a few things around the house this morning," I replied.

Brooks pounded in one last nail and worked his way down the ladder. He tugged the work gloves off and held a hand out to Dad.

"Brooks VanOrman, sir. Nice to meet you."

Dad shook his hand, but his eyes were on the new porch step. "Was this broken?"

I bit down on my lips to keep from replying in a snarky tone. "Yes." It said a lot about the normal functioning of his life that he'd not only just stepped over a broken porch stair and gone about his business without even registering that there was an issue, but that'd he'd forgotten me yelling about it the day before. "And the rain gutter was hanging down."

"Evergreen always takes care of me," Dad said to Brooks.

I cringed so hard I thought my teeth would pop. Brooks, for his part, managed to keep his face open and friendly, but, from the side-eye he shot me, I knew there was going to be a whole slew of questions coming about that one.

"Okay, Dad." I jumped in. "We're going to go inside and do a little cleaning. Have you eaten?"

"Willow took me to lunch," he nodded, already turning toward his precious shop.

"I'm leaving some meals in your freezer," I called after his retreating form. When he didn't reply I looked up to the heavens and muttered, "I'm trying, here. I'd better be getting some points for all of this."

"Who you talking to?" Brooks asked as I moved back to my car to pop the trunk.

"My mother. I like to imagine that she's watching over us and rolling her eyes as hard as I do sometimes." I grabbed the cleaning supplies and led the way inside, where I shrugged out of my coat and reached a hand out to take Brooks's when he'd done the same. "I'm going to clean the bathroom and replace the bedding.

My dad keeps a stack of woodworking magazines in the living area. I won't be long."

He looked around. "What can I do?"

"Nothing, really. I'll be back down in a minute."

I hustled up the stairs, suddenly wishing Brooks was anywhere but here, seeing it all, seeing me and where I'd come from. All those looks he'd given me and the kisses we'd shared, I knew they were about to become ancient history.

CHAPTER 22

Twenty minutes later I had finished the bathroom and was working on removing the sheets from my dad's bed when I heard the ancient vacuum start up on the main floor. I paused what I was doing and leaned against the wall for a minute. Brooks was vacuuming. I analyzed the way my heart had started pounding and wondered if there was anything more alluring than someone helping with the housework. I pictured him vacuuming and realized there really was nothing to top it—at least not to me. Had I known I found this attractive? Nope. Because no man in my life had ever, ever started randomly vacuuming things. Without being asked. Okay, I'd never asked a guy to vacuum for me . . . but still. I grabbed my phone out of my back pocket and speed dialed Hailey.

"Hello?" she answered after a few rings.

"Brooks VanOrman is vacuuming my dad's living room, and I've started feeling really warm all over. Inappropriately," I said in a rushed whisper.

"No way."

"Yes way. This is really happening, and I'm having feelings about it."

She made a sound. "I love feelings."

"I don't."

"I'm aware. But that doesn't mean you can stop them from happening. Why is he there?"

"Aside from the fact that we've become friendly and he wanted to help me out, it's probably more because we've been kissing a little."

"What?" she cried.

I gave her a brief rundown of the ski day and the fight we'd had and hanging out at my place on Christmas Eve. Then that morning and his Christmas gift and pulling leaves out of my hair and that weighted silence.

"Why is my stomach feeling strange?" I moaned.

"Those are called butterflies, and we all get them sometimes," Hailey replied. "This must mean you enjoyed the kissing parts?"

"Yes, it was like we'd set my brain on fire, but I don't do butterflies. I'm pro caterpillar." I started pacing, one hand pushing my hair away from my face. "The vacuum is still going. He's doing an incredibly thorough job of *cleaning my dad's house*!" I whisper yelled. "What am I supposed to do with this? Why am I so attracted to him right now?"

"Because it's playing into your deepest wish of having someone see your needs and help take care of things."

"Willow already does that."

Hailey laughed—okay, scoffed. "Willow is not a guy with great eyes and sort of a mysterious bad guy vibe going on, and she doesn't fulfill your needs that way."

"He's doesn't have a bad guy vibe."

"Speak for yourself on that one. From where I'm sitting he looks like a bad guy, but he's not. Those guys are . . . What?" A masculine voice from the background said something and Hailey laughed. "Ford thinks he needs to monitor my phone calls from now on. He's feeling a little jealous over my descriptions of Brooks."

"Maybe Ford has something to worry about since this is the second time you've tried to convince me that Brooks is . . . a hottie." Even saying the word made my mouth feel sour.

"Did you just call a man a hottie?"

"I'm in a stressful situation. Words aren't coming to me right now." The vacuum clicked off, and I stopped pacing. "He's done."

"Now what's he doing?" she asked. "Is he slowly climbing the stairs, building up suspense, only to find you helpless against his charms?"

"Hailey," I hissed. "I'm freaking out."

"Ford says to lay one on him. Again."

"I'm not going to keep kissing a guy when I have no idea what it means."

"Why? Kissing is fun," Ford's voice came in close to the mic. Hailey must have put her phone on speaker.

"I'm not like that. We haven't even gone on a date."

"You've gone skiing. You've made vision boards together. You're cleaning your dad's house. Those are basically dates," Hailey replied.

"What's a vision board?" Ford asked. Then he made an impatient noise. "Nevermind. If he's vacuuming, he's into you."

"This is terrible advice." I swallowed, listening to make sure Brooks wasn't about to bust in on this conversation.

Hailey sighed, and her voice lost its playfulness. "Mer, enjoy the fact that you've got a nice man helping you with some work around your dad's house who also wants to kiss you. At the very least, it cuts the work time in half. At the most, you're working toward something new. Let the rest of it figure itself out."

That sounded logical. I heard footsteps on the stairs and fumbled with the phone. "Bye," I said hastily and shoved it back in my pocket.

I dove toward the bed, stubbing my toe on the bed frame as I reached for the sheets. I ended up face down on the mattress, moaning as I tried to wiggle my toe back to life. I looked over to see Brooks lean against the door frame and push his hands into his pockets. His sleeves were rolled up and that tattoo on his arm was peaking out again.

"What's your tattoo of?" I blurted as I pushed myself to standing.

"What's up with your dad calling you Evergreen?"

I pulled a face and yanked the sheets off the rest of the bed. "Never mind. Questions are a horrible idea. Secrets are the way to go." I wadded up the dirty sheets and tossed them toward the door to be carried down to the laundry room later. "Thanks for vacuuming. I hope no rodents were harmed."

He grinned. "Do you usually end up vacuuming rodents?"

"No. I'm cracking jokes to break up the humiliation of you seeing all of this," I said without thinking. Then, realizing what I'd said, I shook my head and made my way out into the hall to grab fresh sheets. "Ignore me, please. I think I'm having an aneurysm."

"Your dad's house isn't nearly as bad as you act like it is." He stepped to the side to let me pass, and I pushed down a shiver as my shoulder brushed his. "It looks like a bachelor pad. No big deal."

I made a popping sound with my mouth. "Except he was married for a decade and raised three daughters here, so it should look a little less that way."

Brooks stepped to the bed and began helping me put the fresh bedding on. "Are you a military corner person? Because you strike me as one. I have a quarter if you want to do the bounce test," he teased.

"For my own bed, yes. For Dad's, no. I'm more of the 'Congrats, he's not sleeping in filth' mentality." Again, I spoke without thinking. I stepped back from the newly made bed and took a deep breath. "I'm sorry. I'm really freaking out right now, and I'm acting strange. Give me a second to get my head back on straight."

I left the room, my hands shaking, and sat on the top stair. I wrapped my arms around myself and ducked to sit with my forehead on my knees. I could not figure out why I felt like my sturdy, rock-like foundation was teetering today. It was like Hailey said, Brooks was a nice guy helping me out. He wasn't here to judge anything or to pity me or whatever. I didn't need to feel so off-center. But when he sat on the stair next to me, everything inside of me went on high alert. Because he wasn't a nice guy anymore. He was the guy taking up a lot of headspace and making me rethink my deodorant brand.

"Hey, um, are you a person who can talk when they're upset or a person who needs to be alone to process?" he asked quietly.

I let out an unamused laugh. "I think you're the first person to ever ask me that. I'm usually a processor."

"Okay."

He fell into silence, simply sitting there. He was warm, and he smelled nice, and he gave me the same type of feeling I got from my cat Betty on hard days when I hugged her to my chest and stroked her fur. I closed my eyes. I was comparing him to my cat. I found myself matching my breathing to his, and soon a peaceful feeling stole over me. Enough that I was able to sit up, although I continued to stare straight ahead.

"Okay." I cleared my throat. "So, my family is a whole thing, and I don't really let people over to see it. When I was little, I got pity, loads of pity. I hate pity. I've worked really hard to build myself a fully functioning life, and I've always kept it tightly together and very separate from my dad. I believe I'm having a little freak out session over the fact that I've fought so hard to have you take me seriously, and now you're seeing all this and hearing my dad call me Evergreen, and I can't stand it."

He took his time answering, and I appreciated that he was thoughtful about what he'd say. "Sure, this situation is messy, and I've been imagining what that was like for you as a child with the weight of it all on your shoulders. I'm guessing you were responsible for your sisters, too. I have to tell you, I've never taken you more seriously than I do now, after seeing this. You're pretty incredible to have built the life you have. You won't get pity from me. You'll get admiration."

At that I dared to look at him. He was so close that my eyes met his chin, and I had to tilt back slightly. "Really?"

He nodded. "I'm glad you let me come today."

Tension flowed out of me. "Okay."

He pulled up his shirt sleeve to give me my first full glimpse of his forearm tattoo. "My tattoo is a compass. I got it when my fiancée left me. It symbolizes finding your true north and navigating the unfolding journey." It wasn't very big, maybe two inches across, and beautiful in its simplicity. I reached out to run a fingertip over it, and his arm tensed slightly under my touch. "I think it's brought me good luck."

"What about the one on your chest?" I asked.

He pulled his collar down to give me a view. There was a light dusting of dark hair that tried to catch my attention, but I pulled my eyes away to inspect the design. It was a thin circle with a single pine tree in the middle. Chills raced down my spine when I saw it, and a lump rose in my throat. It felt meaningful in a way he couldn't possibly understand. If Willow were here, she'd be dancing and cheering, but my heart almost refused to beat.

"It represents the ability to grow and adapt," he whispered, clearly picking up on my emotion.

I shocked myself by laying my fingertips across it. His chest was warm and firm, and I could feel my own heartbeat in my fingertips where they pressed against him.

"It's my name," I whispered back. "Evergreen. It's my first name. Meredith is my middle name." I looked up at him, still touching his chest. "I've never told anyone that. Even my best friends don't know."

"It might be an unusual name, but evergreens are survivors. I think it suits you."

I wrinkled my nose and started to pull my hand away, but he snatched it and pressed it against his chest. "I'll never call you a name you hate, and I won't tell anyone else. But you are not who I thought you were, Evergreen Atwood." He watched me closely. "I've been paying attention for a while now, trying to figure you out, and every layer I peel back makes you more and more interesting to me."

My head felt like it was floating off my body as his eyes closed and his head came towards mine. I knew that this kiss was going to be different. It was going to mean more. Walls had come down today, and, while I wanted the connection with him, I was terrified right up until the moment his lips pressed against mine. My head immediately reattached to my body and brought with it a rush of heat and wonder. The hand against his chest grabbed at his shirt and made a fist of it even as my other hand worked around his shoulders to run along the back of his neck. His kiss had been soft and questioning, but when my hand ran into the hair curling at the back of his neck, he deepened it. He wrapped both arms around me and tugged me close, and I leaned into it. I wanted to climb into his lap and make sure there was no space between us.

The strength I'd always sensed in him came to the forefront. The things I'd pushed against and fought with were now surrounding me in a cocoon that felt at once exciting and protective. This was so much. Too much, maybe. Our other kisses had been exploring and discovering, but this kiss felt like melding and accepting. I released his shirt and put my hand against his face as I pulled away, both of us breathing hard.

"Just . . . one second," I mumbled.

His arms immediately loosened, his hands becoming soothing as they ran along my spine. "That was . . ."

I nodded. "Definitely. And if you, uh, don't want this to mean anything, I'm really good at . . ."

He playfully pinched at my waist, and I jumped. "Don't do that. Especially after a kiss that clearly meant something. You can't shove what's happening between us into a little logical box."

I dropped my hands from him and scowled. "I do not force things into boxes."

He grinned and released me. "You do. Right now, you're wondering what to do with me. I've jumped from 'annoying neighbor' to 'hunky, great kisser,' and you're trying to shove me back into 'neighbor,' but I won't go."

I stood and tugged my shirt down while fighting a laugh. "Hunky, great kisser?"

"Hey, I don't make the labels, that's your job." He stood too and pushed my hair back behind my ears, causing a shiver to skitter across my scalp.

"I'm thinking more along the lines of 'nosy, know-it-all.'"

His hands slid to either side of my neck, and he bent with a smile to press his mouth against mine once more. This time it was light, playful, comforting. As the kiss lingered I wrapped my hands around his forearms and held on tight.

When our lips parted he leaned his forehead against mine and said, "How about if you label my box 'superhuman dreamboat?'"

His joke created some much-needed distance, and I headed back into my dad's room, retrieving the comforter from where it had been draped across his rocking chair. Brooks followed me, reaching for one side to help me spread it out. It was so domestic I felt like I needed a slap across the face.

"That doesn't feel accurate," I replied, biting my lip to keep from grinning like a fool.

"You object?" he asked, stepping into my personal space. "Because I can give you another sample if you'd like."

"It won't change my mind. I already have you pegged as 'thinks too highly of himself.'"

Quick as a striking snake, he had his arms around me and lifted me off my feet, pulling me up against him and hugging me close. His beard tickled at my face, and I wrapped my arms tightly around his neck, sinking into the feeling. This was the guy who climbed ladders and vacuumed floors and asked me if I needed space to process things. If there was a box for him, I'd simply label it 'possibilities.'

CHAPTER 23

I flopped down on the soft rug near Aryn's yellow couch and looked up at the ceiling. The sun was down, but Aryn's apartment was lit up like noonday. She was obsessed with light and always had lamps in addition to the overhead lights. Her furniture was bright, her throw pillows were bright, and all I wanted to do was crawl into comforting darkness.

"Hailey?" I waved a hand in the air to get her attention in the tiny, two-butt kitchen where my friends were packed in like sardines as they tried to prepare dinner together. "Hailey?"

"What?" she called back.

"I need you to psychoanalyze me," I whined.

"I'll do it," Ruby piped up, pushing her way out of the kitchen, carrying a tray with fresh bruschetta on it. "Yep, you're psycho."

"Ha . . . ha." I groaned. "You guys aren't taking me seriously."

Ruby's face popped into view over mine, and she squinted her eyes down at me. "Guys, she might actually mean it. She doesn't usually get so dramatic. In fact, this might be the first rug flop of her life. Maybe we should listen?"

Aryn glanced over the back of the couch as she stirred a bowl full of what I hoped was a cheese ball. We were having our own little between-holidays dinner, and the theme was bring whatever sounds good. I'd brought a bag of chips and a jar of queso that I was hoping someone would heat up in the microwave. I was too busy having an existential crisis to do it myself. The crisis involved—big shocker—Brooks and his delicious kisses and funny conversation and general swoon worthiness.

Aryn blew a strand of hair out of her eyes. "She looks pretty mopey. Did you guys know Meredith could mope? It's kind of interesting to watch."

"Leave the poor thing alone," Hailey called from the kitchen. "She shared a few moments with Brooks that weren't filled with scratch marks and emotional bandages, and she's questioning her entire existence."

I couldn't see what she was preparing, but something smelled like barbeque sauce. "Are you making hot wings?" I asked her.

"Yes," she replied.

I sat up. "I take it back. I'm healed."

I pushed to standing and shoved my way between Ruby and Aryn to stand near Hailey. Watching her toss perfectly cooked chicken wings in her homemade sauce

164

was enough to cheer up even the most morose soul. I leaned over and stuck a finger in the sauce bowl, licking it with a smile.

"I love dinner nights."

"Of course you do," Hailey swatted my hand away. "You always bring something microwavable."

"It's not my fault I didn't have a mommy to teach me how to cook," I pouted and made puppy dog eyes. They all groaned, which made me laugh. "I'm sorry. I'm tired."

"From being chased around town by a clearly very interested Brooks VanOrman," Hailey said. "With his lips."

That stopped Aryn and Ruby dead in their tracks. They turned slowly to face me and Hailey, which meant the four of us were basically standing shoulder-to-shoulder in a circle. A splat of barbecue sauce hit the floor, and Hailey hurried to turn around and put the wing in the bowl before facing the group again.

"I'm sorry. Did you say Brooks VanOrman is interested in Meredith?" Aryn spluttered. "And by lips are you saying they've kissed?" Aryn leaned over and pushed her bowl between me and Hailey to set it on the counter and then stood straight again, hands on her lean hips. "I'm sorry. But I need the entire story, from the top, nothing left out."

"Well, a moment ago I was lying on the rug moaning, and none of you were very curious about that," I replied, enjoying the moment.

"That was when I figured you had stuck your finger in a light socket or something," Ruby replied. "Do you need to lay back on the rug?"

I grinned. "I could use a hot wing."

They all groaned for a second time and shoved me toward the living space, bodily putting me on the couch before gathering around and demanding I spill it.

"Brooks kissed me," I said. My expression was smug, but only because I knew how much they'd be freaking out about this news and not because I was proud of anything. "At my dad's house." I let that settle. "After helping me make repairs." Another pause. "Two days ago."

Ruby exploded. "Two days ago?"

I held up my hands. "And also after we went skiing together."

"You went skiing together?" Aryn cried. "When?"

"The day after the wedding. And he also might have kissed me on Christmas Eve."

Their questions overlapped.

"He was helping you at your dad's? You hardly let us go there!"

"On Christmas Eve? And you couldn't text us?"

"We've seen you since then, and you didn't say anything!"

"Was it hot?" This last one from Ruby.

Aryn held up a hand, and they closed their mouths. "How dare you not tell us?"

"I told Hailey." I pointed a finger at her.

She placed a well-manicured hand against her chest. "I figured that was a secret, and you'd tell everyone on your own time."

Aryn waved a hand. "What on Earth is happening?"

I leaned back in my seat and folded my hands in my lap. "We've been kind of hanging out and sort of aren't enemies anymore."

"So, he called a truce by kissing your face off?" Ruby asked. "This must mean he's your boyfriend now. Right?"

I sighed. "As you can see, my face is still intact, and I have no idea what we are."

"Did your toes curl?" Ruby wiggled her own toes. "I love it when the toes curl."

I shrugged. "Maybe?" *Yes, yes, yes.*

"It's nice of you to admit that rather than shooting me down." Ruby grinned, and I grinned back.

"I'm going to need a lot more information than that." Aryn slapped my knee.

So, I told them all the things that had shifted and changed, and while Hailey knew some of it, all three of them sat with their mouths open and eyes big as I shared the transformation I'd gone through recently and the things that had happened with Brooks.

"I'm sorry I kept it to myself," I said at the end of the whole story.

Aryn waved that off. "You've always been this way. You tell us nothing and then suddenly, bam, a year's worth of information gets dumped in our laps. Only usually it doesn't end with your mortal enemy kissing your face off."

"Once again, my face is . . ."

"We get it," Ruby and Hailey said in unison, prompting them both to laugh.

"So, help me make sense of this. I've never felt this way before," I moaned.

"Brooks is a smart, good-looking guy with a job who finds you interesting. You jump on this," Aryn said.

"Do you realize that at our age it's really hard to find a guy that doesn't have serious baggage? Or leprosy?" Ruby added.

"I . . . haven't been that concerned about leprosy," I replied.

"But the baggage concern is real," Aryn stated. "And Brooks probably has some, but he's really coming across like a prince."

"His ex-fiancée dumped him because he was too boring," I offered. "That's kind of a red flag."

The three of them looked at me with identical expressions of disbelief before Ruby said, "Didn't we recently talk about how you find boring really attractive?"

"Well, yes, but what if all he wants to do on a Saturday night is separate his lights from darks and reorganize the pantry?" I held up my hands. "Can I live that way?"

Hailey nodded. "Only if he doesn't take you away from your own pantry reorganization on the weekends."

I threw a pillow at her, and she laughed. "I'm not that boring."

"We all are," Aryn replied. "Seriously. The days of partying are far behind us. We're exhausted after teaching all week. Honestly, if I came home on a Friday night and there was a guy here sorting laundry and cleaning out the kitchen, I'd jump on that so fast his head would spin."

"Oh and maybe he'd want to watch a movie afterward and then get to bed nice and early," Hailey sighed and smiled. "It's my favorite when Ford isn't busy, and we can hunker down at one of our houses."

"I think this is great news. You two are going to be fun to watch," Aryn teased.

"I am not in this for your entertainment," I replied.

"And yet, here I am, very entertained. I'm guessing, with a few more kisses, you'll be putty in his hands. Can't wait to meet Marshmallow Meredith."

My friends stood, sharing knowing looks, and it made my skin feel too tight. "Guys. I'm kind of freaking out about this."

"Why?" Aryn asked as she picked her bowl back up. "He seems perfect for you."

When they innocently returned to the kitchen to continue prepping their food in silence, I caved with a huff.

"Fine. The issue is that I like him a lot, okay, but I'm sure I'll scare him away because all the others were terrified of being with me, and I don't want to scare this one away because he makes my toes curl so hard."

I was practically out of breath by the time I finished admitting everything. They came back to where I was sitting, and I didn't miss the self-satisfied expressions they were wearing.

"I love it when the truth finally bursts out of you," Hailey smiled and patted my knee. "It's okay to hope things develop further, but I understand why you're feeling unsettled about it based on your history."

I frowned. "Do you think he already regrets it? I haven't heard from him in two days."

"Maybe the feeling of total confusion is mutual," Aryn offered with a shrug.

"Or maybe he's waiting to see if you'll reach out to him," Ruby added. "Guys have feelings, too, and it's not fair to assume they should do all the chasing. They're as vulnerable as we are when it comes to worrying over how the other person is feeling and what they're thinking."

I thought on that. What if I didn't like the idea of him having the same crisis of thought I was having? I wanted him to want me, no holds barred. Doesn't every woman deserve that? Okay, and Ruby was totally right to say that every guy deserved it, too. It was fairly hypocritical of me to assume he wouldn't care if I was indecisive about my feelings. Ugh, all this thinking was making it worse.

"So, what do you think you should do?" Hailey asked me.

I thought back to Ash's response to that same question from me about scuba diving and parroted her words to my friends with a grin on my face. "I'm going to overthink it, avoid discussing it, and then freak out when I'm pushed on making a choice."

Hailey slapped at my knee and rose with a laugh. "Then you deserve whatever's coming to you."

*****

167

The doorbell rang two nights later, and I looked over the top of Betty, who was lying flat on my chest, toward the front door. It was seven o'clock at night. I was in my flannel pajama set with the TV remote in my hand, very happily watching reruns of my favorite sitcom from my college days. Tomorrow was New Year's Eve, and I was saving up energy for that, so I had specifically avoided any plans this evening. My hair was held back on the sides with two bobby pins that were slipping out, and I'd not bothered to put on an ounce of makeup.

The doorbell rang again. I sat up, gently helping Betty onto the couch cushion next to me and rubbed at the cat hair that had collected where she'd been resting. This was not a great look for me, but this surprise visitor seemed pretty committed. I opened the door in time to see Brooks lift his hand to knock. He almost knocked on my forehead but luckily snatched his hand back in time.

"Oh, hey," he said with a big grin. "Glad you're home."

He was wearing a button-down shirt in forest green, that amazing pine tree tattoo peeking out over the undone top button. His hair looked fresh from the shower, and the jeans he was wearing were worn and comfortable looking. His ever-present work boots had left prints in the snow dusting the walkway up to my door.

I wasn't sure how to react to him being there and grinning at me. Mostly because it had been several days since we'd gone to my Dad's house, and I was feeling shy about everything. Was it normal to share information and connect like that and then have no communication?

"I brought stuff to make ice cream sundaes," he said, holding up a shopping bag.

I sighed and leaned against the door jam, deciding to go with honesty. "After four days of silence?"

"After four days of the flu. Well, okay, three days of the flu and then a day to make sure I was over it. I'm not looking to puke up ice cream in front of you. We aren't there yet."

"You were sick?" I stepped aside and let him in, closing the door behind us. "Why didn't you tell me?"

"Phones work both ways," he called over his shoulder as he entered my kitchen.

Okay, that stung. I wanted to apologize, but when I stepped up next to him, he was grinning at me with his usual teasing look. He didn't seem upset, so I dropped it.

"How do you even know I like ice cream?"

He shot me a glance. "That's going to be a friendship ruiner if you don't."

"I like ice cream. A lot."

"Good. Because after the way you've been kissing me, I was pretty confident that friendship was on the table."

My jaw went slack as I stuttered out, "Oh, so that's how you're handling it then?"

He tamped down on a smile and turned to open my cupboards, looking for bowls. "I figure if your method is to ignore and avoid, then mine should be to

168

shine a light on it. That way we'll end up somewhere in the middle." I moved to where he was and opened the correct cupboard, getting down two large bowls as he continued. "It happened three times, and I'm not sure I appreciate you taking advantage of me without making your intentions clear," he stated as he brushed past me. "I thought that we could have some ice cream and discuss it like two grown adults."

Well, that was new. None of my previous dates or short relationships had ever wanted to discuss anything.

We worked in silence for a few minutes, peeling bananas and loading them up with vanilla ice cream and various toppings. I didn't eat a lot of sweets because they weren't a healthy choice, but when I did I tended to go a little overboard. The nerves weren't helping either, and I ended up with a sundae that was easily twice the size of his. We made our way to my small table and sat down, both of us digging in. I was a slow ice cream eater. Sensitive teeth combined with my desire to truly enjoy any dessert I partook of meant I swirled it around and let it melt on my tongue before swallowing. I tried to simply enjoy it, but I was wondering too much what he was thinking.

He leaned back in his chair and folded his arms over his stomach. "So, I think it's pretty obvious that things between us are evolving, but I'd like to know where you see things going from here."

I shook my head. "Oh, no, you first. I can't answer that without knowing what it is you want from me."

He made a sound of amusement. "I'm sure you believe that you don't know, and I understand why you're playing dumb."

"I've never played dumb in my entire life," I responded with some heat.

He stood and took our dishes to the sink. "You're smart and driven and incredibly capable, and I've discovered over the past weeks that you're also a person of deep feelings and strong morals. I like you, a lot." He turned and leaned against the countertop, facing me. "But you also have a tendency to back off when I put on a little pressure. I'm not interested in staying in a cycle of occasionally seeing each other and sneaking some kisses then having you disappear. Those games worked when I was a teenager and maybe even into my twenties. Now, though, it's a waste of time."

"I'm not playing games."

His eyes sparked, and I felt pinned to the spot. "Maybe not on purpose."

His digging in made me want to push back with some sarcasm. "So, you're saying you want an actual relationship?"

"I'm saying that, yes. I'm also saying that you're going to have to say what you want, too, and I'm wondering how long that will take."

I stood and marched toward him, irked at both myself and him. Probably mostly myself, because he'd nailed it on the head when he'd said I was playing the chicken.

"What if I say that I want to never see you again?" I stood toe-to-toe, challenging him with my stare.

"I'll believe you're lying, but I'll walk away."

Our gazes tangled, and I could see the sincerity behind the strength. I sighed, and my stance softened. He leaned down, pressing his lips to my forehead. I closed my eyes and fisted my hands in his shirt, taking in a deep breath through my nose, inhaling his scent that had already become familiar. When I let it out, his mouth moved to coast over one of my temples.

"And if I say I want to explore this?" I whispered.

He gripped my shoulders and pulled me closer until my cheek was pressed against his chest. The feeling of it skittered through me, so calm and sweet, and I wrapped my hands around his waist.

"Then I'd ask what you're doing for New Year's Eve tomorrow night," he answered.

"I'm going to my friend Hailey's party. Her and her boyfriend are throwing it at his mansion."

His chuckle vibrated against my cheek. "Her boyfriend lives in a mansion?"

I nodded, still distracted by the concept that with one word, one sentence, he could be mine. He'd admitted he wanted to pursue a relationship with me and that the only thing keeping that from happening was . . . me.

"Cool. Is there a theme or something?" he asked, stroking light fingers down my back in a soothing way.

"Uh, no. We'll play games, watch TV, eat food. I think. I didn't really pay attention to the specifics."

"Big crowd?"

"I don't think so."

"So, what do you think? Am I your plus one, or am I packing up my ice cream and saying goodbye?"

He was teasing, and I knew it, but there was an undercurrent of truth there, too. He didn't want to play games. He'd seen me at my worst and he'd taken my shots and, somehow, he'd found something inside of me that he wanted to be close to. I'd be a fool to let this man walk away.

"Are you sure you want to come? You'll be in the hot seat," I said at last.

He nodded. "I'm good with that. I've lived through worse."

"Okay."

He squeezed me and then let go, moving away to meet my gaze. "This is me, double checking that this is what you want."

I nodded, pressing my lips together as a look of triumph flitted across his face. I scowled at him. "Are you gloating? I thought we were done with the attempts at annoying and bothering each other."

He laughed and started gathering up his sundae supplies, that smirk still on his face. "Listen, Tigress, I've made it clear that I will never be done trying to bother you."

"Don't call me that." I made a gagging sound that only made him smile bigger.

"This is going to be fun."

CHAPTER 24

It's been pretty firmly established that I'm not a holiday person. I'm not out here trying to harp on my childhood, but it was enough to keep me from being much of a believer in the magic of celebrations. However, New Year's Eve was one I could totally get behind. As a major goal setter and big believer in fresh starts, this time of year was my jam. Hailey and Ford were throwing a joint party at his house. I knew it started at something like seven p.m., but other than that, I hadn't really bothered to look over the invitation. I already knew I wouldn't be asked to provide food, so I figured I didn't need to stress much over the details. In years past we'd all sat in our pajamas at someone's house, sipping bubbly drinks, eating lots of junk food, and lazily having a great time. This year would probably be the same.

So, at six p.m. I pulled up the invite on my phone to confirm Ford's address and the time and then froze in my tracks. I scrolled through the invite, zoomed in, closed the image, rebooted my phone, and looked again. There was a theme. It was Winter Wonderland, whatever the devil that meant, and we had been asked to come dressed in semiformal wear. Um, excuse me? The local couch surfer had not been consulted on this. I sat on my bed and pulled up the internet on my phone to look up what exactly one would wear to a winter wonderland semi-formal event. As I scrolled through the images, I took a moment to mourn stretchy pants and pizza rolls. I had a feeling tonight would be very different than other years.

I'd been bamboozled by this visible proof of the changes our group was going through. We were down to four this year with Lizzie gone. And Hailey was throwing this party with Ford, not with the rest of us. And formal wear was involved.

I sat up straight, took a few deep breaths, and got back to investigating clothing ideas while I reminded myself that I could flow with change. Change was inevitable, and it was only logical to go with it. I couldn't always change the currents, but I could learn to swim along with them rather than sink. I was a survivor.

I shot off a text to Aryn and Ruby.

Me: What are you two wearing to the party tonight?

They texted back as I was digging through my closet to see if I had any heels that would work. Everything I was finding online said sparkles would be a good idea, and I had zero sparkly dresses, but maybe I had some shoes I'd forgotten about.

Aryn: A long, green dress. Flowy
Ruby: Navy blue cocktail dress
Me: Do either of you have something I can borrow?
Aryn: It starts in an hour
Me: I know that. I didn't read the invite until now. I had my snowflake pajamas already laid out
Ruby: I am literally several sizes bigger than you and a few inches taller. There aren't enough safety pins in the world
Me: Fine. Tell me if your dresses have sparkles
Ruby: Yes. So many
Aryn: No. I'm not a sparkle girl. Call Willow

It was good advice and exactly what was going to have to happen. So, after tossing aside all my useless shoes, I sat on the floor cross-legged and called my sister with an SOS. She picked up after my third attempt to get in touch with her.

"What is so important?" She sounded a little too huffy for my taste.

"Dress emergency. I'm supposed to wear semiformal for a Winter Wonderland themed party at Ford's mansion tonight, and my snowflake pajamas aren't going to cut it."

"So, you call me the night of and expect me to drop it all to help you with inventory from my personal business?"

Wow. I'd really irritated her. "I'm sorry, Willow. I'm up a creek."

She made a noise. "That's pretty unusual for you."

"I made an assumption rather than paying attention to details."

"Hmm. You love details. What's got you off your game?"

"I'll tell you while we try on dresses," I wheedled. "It involves your manifesting."

"Oh." She sucked in a breath. "Well then. Steve's here, so you have to be quick. We're having an intimate New Year's Eve, and sisters aren't invited."

Eww. "The party starts in less than an hour, so, yeah, it'll be fast."

"How do you feel about maroon and sparkles?" she asked.

"Grateful?" I attempted to placate her with the fib.

"I have the perfect dress, and I think I have it in your size. Bring your shoes and makeup. You might not have time to go home first."

"Thanks, Sis."

"You owe me."

"I think we're probably even because of how many times I cleaned up your barf as a kid."

"You still owe me."

She hung up, and I hurriedly gathered up all the supplies I'd need to get ready at Willow's shop. I threw it all in a tote bag, slipped on my boots, and rushed out to my car. I was backing out of the driveway when I remembered that I'd need to tell Brooks. I slammed on the brakes and squealed a little at the oversight. I hurried to dial his number.

"Hey," he answered on the fourth ring, right as I was getting antsy.

"What are you doing right now?"

"I'm making a bird house. A big one. Maybe more like a bird apartment complex. I'm curious if multiple bird families will use it or if birds don't like to live that way. It's an experiment."

"A bird complex, huh? Sounds fun."

"You sound rushed. Did I lose track of time?"

"It's worse than that. I was wrong. It's semiformal tonight." I blew out a breath. "We've always done pj's and comfort food, but, apparently, there's a theme this year."

"When you said mansion I had a feeling there'd be a theme."

"Yeah, well, my bad for not reading the fine print. I'm on my way to Willow's shop to borrow a dress and get made up before I ascend into the mountains. Why do rich people always live on hills?"

"I always figured it was because of the views."

I backed out of my driveway and started heading his way. "I'm coming over now. I don't think I'll have time to go to Willow's and get all ready and come back here again."

"Okay. See you in a second."

I pulled into his driveway and put the car in park as his garage door opened. I needed to get moving, but as he made his way to my driver's window, I had a sudden desire to skip the party altogether and see if he wanted to split a pizza. It was the first time I'd ever wanted to choose a guy over my friends, and it caught me off guard enough that I could do nothing but stare at him. I took stock of his face and the little things that were wrong about it but that somehow came together to create something intriguing and attractive. His hair—curly and always a little messy—plus his beard gave him a certain look that I found appealingly masculine. His build was lean but not thin, and his hands were kind of beautiful.

"Meredith?" he tapped on the window, and I startled.

I rolled down the window. "Sorry, I'm trying to figure out why I was suddenly considering ditching my friends and asking you if you wanted to hang out tonight."

His eyes grew large, followed closely by his smile. "I like that plan."

I laughed. "It definitely sounds better than this themed party with its sequined dresses and fancy hair styles. It makes me feel squirmy."

"I think it sounds fun to get dressed up and go party in a mansion overlooking the valley."

I wrinkled up my nose. "Of course you do."

"What's so wrong with it?"

I turned to more fully face him and leaned sideways. "I guess it's more that I had a certain expectation that I'd be lazy and happy tonight. Now I have to dress up and have good manners. A theme night also suggests that it won't only be my friends. Some of Ford's people will probably be there, too. So, no licking my fingers after eating Cheetos."

He grinned. "So, do you want me to go grab my suit and tie?"

"That would probably be good."

His eyes crinkled as he pushed away from the car. "I'm going to go grab it before you change your mind. I'll get changed at your sister's shop, too. Does she have a bathroom where I can get cleaned up?"

"Yeah," I replied, noticing the sawdust on his clothing and in his hair.

"Give me two shakes."

Willow opened the back door of her shop as I was pulling up to park ten minutes later and gestured to me to hustle inside as the air was freezing. She opened her mouth to say something, probably snarky and very sisterish, when the passenger door of my car opened and Brooks got out. Her mouth froze in an open O, and her eyes darted between us. I saw the moment she realized who he was and imagined that her meddling manifestations had worked.

"Welcome to my home," Willow said warmly to him, shaking his hand. "Come on in."

Brooks stood aside to let me enter first and then took the door from Willow, closing it behind us as we made our way through the back storeroom. Willow pinched my upper arm as we walked and leaned close to me to whisper how happy she was to see that the universe had come through. I told her to zip it until we were alone.

"Brooks needs to get cleaned up and changed into his suit," I said to Willow as we moved through the backroom doorway and onto the sales floor. "Do you want him to use a changing room or go upstairs?"

Willow smiled at Brooks. "There's a restroom over there. But hurry up so you can still chat with us while we get Meredith situated."

I doubted Brooks was excited about that, but, in typical fashion, he smiled and agreed. Ugh. He was so agreeable all the time. I secretly loved it.

"How nice to find an agreeable man," Willow said as though she'd read my thoughts.

"It's annoying," I replied under my breath.

She laughed. "Liar."

I rolled my eyes and followed my sister to the rack of maroon sparkly dresses she'd mentioned. She pulled out my size and directed me to go to the changing room.

"You have maybe five minutes to give me all the details and leave nothing out," she said under her breath through the curtain.

I smiled, surprised to feel excited rather than hesitant. As I changed into the dress, I talked as quickly as I could, telling her all the things I thought were highlights, saving the little details for another time. She made happy noises or little squeals, and, when I was ready to be zipped into the dress, she pressed me into a hug.

"This has made my day. You have no idea. When I met him on Black Friday, I felt something, and I knew he'd be important in your life."

I spun around, giving her access to the zipper. "Well, let's try not to start monogramming anything. We only decided last night to be a couple."

Brooks came into the room, and Willow pulled aside the curtain so we could see each other.

"So, Brooks, I didn't realize you'd be attending the party with Meredith tonight," Willow chirped. "That's fun."

"I wasn't actually invited," he replied, happily. "I'm crashing."

"Oh." Willow clapped her hands together. "Even better."

"Hailey and Ford won't care," I responded as I folded my clothes.

"Tell me, Brooks, do you consider yourself a hard-working person?" Willow asked.

"Stop it," I hissed, recognizing that she was starting down the list of attributes she'd manifested to me. "Brooks does not need to be grilled by you."

Willow only laughed. "Smart? Kind? How do you feel about exercise and lifelong learning?"

"Willow," I growled.

At this point Brooks was laughing. "I'm not sure about intelligence, but I appreciate physical activity and continued learning." There was a short pause and then, "Is that the right answer, Meredith?"

Him and Willow both laughed when I scoffed. "Yes, Brooks. Thank you."

"You know, I've been telling Mer that she needs to date, and I think the two of you will get along well." Willow's audacity knew no bounds.

"Oh my gosh," I muttered.

"I've been telling Meredith the same thing," Brooks cracked.

Willow's eyes grew large and delighted. "Really?"

I closed my eyes and shook my head. "This is a nightmare."

"Meredith is notoriously stubborn," Willow stated.

"I'm like a pebble in her shoe. It took a while, but I wore her down," he replied.

"That's a terrible way to get a woman's attention," I rolled my eyes.

Brooks's smile was playful. "I tried less annoying ways, and you were resistant."

Willow was grinning back and forth, enjoying this immensely. "Less annoying ways?"

I shook my head and deliberately broke eye contact with Brooks as I felt a flush move up my face. "Do you think you can help me with my makeup?" I asked Willow.

"Come on upstairs. It'll be good for Brooks to meet my boyfriend, Steve."

Brooks smiled and stepped to the side. "Lead the way. I'd love to meet him."

Willow's skirt swirled around her ankles as she turned toward the back of the shop. Brooks waited for me, and, when I came to his side, I made a face.

"Sorry about her," I said as we started walking.

"Don't be," he chuckled. "Her and I are on the same team. I like her."

"Do I even want to know what team that is?" I asked, shivering slightly as his warm palm met the small of my back.

He leaned down and brushed an airy kiss to the top of my head. "The winning team."

We arrived at the small staircase that led up to Willow's apartment, and he let me go first as we had to climb single file.

"You're pretty sure of yourself," I said over my shoulder.

He nodded. "Pebble in the shoe."

More like shark in the water, I thought.

I stopped at the top of the staircase. Willow had left her apartment door open, and I could hear her talking to Steve inside. Brooks came to stand near me, crowding against me on the tiny landing. I looked up at him, and a swell of rightness caused my breath to tighten.

"I wasn't ignoring you. I'm still a little scared."

One side of his mouth tugged up. "I know. You simply need more time to trust it."

I felt breathless at him once again seeming to see through me. "Oh."

His hand came to my shoulder, and he ran light fingertips down my arm until he took hold of my hand. "I'm planning to kiss you at midnight."

I licked my lips and nodded, already feeling the pull toward him and the desire to have those words come true. "Okay."

He smiled. "No arguments?"

I shook my head and released his hand to enter Willow's apartment. "I know when a battle is worth fighting and when to graciously surrender."

He made an unintelligible noise as we crossed the threshold into Willow's cozy living space. Brooks and Steve hit it off, talking business and local hiking trails, etc. While they talked, seated casually on Willow's couch, Willow threw me an endless stream of knowing looks while doing my makeup and putting a few curls in my hair. She managed to keep from saying actual words, but I knew she was thrilled.

When she was finished I stood and hugged her close, thanking her for her help.

"He's worth opening up for," she whispered in my ear.

I looked to see that he'd stood also and was watching us. Gone was the way he'd looked at me months ago. Exasperation had been replaced with admiration. Annoyance had turned into interest. Skepticism had faded into an open watchfulness that honestly made me feel as though the conclusion to our story was already written in his mind. I couldn't understand how he felt that way after such a short time, but knowing he wasn't worried helped me feel a little more sure.

"You look incredible," he said, and I believed that he meant it. "Ready to go?"

He held out his hand to me, and there was hardly any hesitation as I wove my fingers through his.

CHAPTER 25

I'd never been to Ford's house. Probably because he and Hailey had only been officially dating for a little while, and this was their first couple event. I'd spent some time around him, and he didn't come off as the guy with all the money and blingy things, but, as I stepped into the foyer of his castle, I had to slightly reorder my opinion of him. I stood in the center of the huge entryway and gazed up, up, up while spinning in a slow circle.

"How disappointing it must be to come home to this every night," I said to Brooks who was watching me spin. He reached out for my coat, and I stopped spinning as he helped me out of it. "I have no idea what Hailey sees in the guy."

Brooks chuckled. "I can think of a few million things."

I squinted at the chandelier and wondered how many Christmases that would have bought for my sisters. The thought was bringing down my mood, so I turned to look at Brooks instead. It was the right choice. He cleaned up real nice . . . and I'm talking *really nice*. He'd slicked back his hair, but a few curls were starting to spring back up. I wouldn't mention it to him because I found it ridiculously adorable and hoped the rest of those curls made an appearance as the night went on. The suit was well-fitted, which made sense because of his lawyerly occupation, and pressed perfectly. It highlighted broad shoulders and a lean waist and legs that didn't look that long in the other clothing I usually saw him in but now seemed to go for miles. I know men talk a lot about legs on women, but I'm a leg girl myself. Give me a glimpse of some healthy male thigh muscle and I'm a goner.

"Hailey's pretty down to earth, and I wouldn't have guessed Ford lived like this," I said, pulling my eyes away from his chest and up to his eyes. "Money isn't everything."

"Are you ogling me?" he asked with a grin that made his beard shift and my fingertips go numb.

I raised one eyebrow. "I'm inspecting you to make sure you'll fit in with this upper-crust crowd."

"There's a lot of pressure, for sure. It's not every day you walk in with a boyfriend."

The word boyfriend made my chest feel warm, and I nodded.

He wiggled his mustache. "Do you like what you see?" He gestured to me. "Because, I have to tell you, Mer, I like what I'm seeing very much." Now his eyebrows danced, and he did a slow wink that startled a laugh out of me.

I'll admit, it was a pleased laugh, but still. I was wearing a short maroon concoction with see-through sleeves and so many sparkles the stars were jealous. It managed to make me look like I had some feminine curves, and the coloring was good against my dark hair and fair skin. Willow had insisted on putting some waves in my hair and really going to town with my makeup, giving me smoky eyes that made the blue of my irises really pop. I didn't look much like myself tonight.

"Do I need to have a talk with you about party manners?" I asked.

He nodded and moved closer, still holding our coats. "Probably. As long as we seal it with a kiss."

I laughed again and turned toward all the sound and light coming through an archway. "Come on. Let's get this over with. Prepare yourself for my friends having a freak-out session over you being here."

"Why would they freak out?"

"Oh, mostly because at one point they expected to meet you at your funeral after I committed homicide." I shot him a look over my shoulder and added, "They're understandably not sure whether to go to war or welcome you to the club."

His eyes had grown large, but he responded with the same wit I'd come to appreciate. "I'll be on alert for both flying butter knives and attempts to hug."

We entered a big room that was filled with people. So many people that I stopped, and Brooks bumped into my back. His free hand landed on my waist, and I lightly leaned back against him while I took stock of my surroundings. His fingers tightened as he leaned down next to my ear.

"These are simply nice people celebrating the end of the year together."

"Strangers," I replied stonily. "How lovely."

"And with me to play buffer."

Aryn stood across the room, her deep green, almost black, dress catching my eye at the same time she waved. Her eyes coasted over me, smiling in welcome, and then over my shoulder where they froze in surprise.

"Friend one has spotted you. Green dress, red hair, tall, and pretty."

"Where?" he asked.

"The one all the dudes are hanging around. She's an athletic sort who looks like a model, so, yeah, find the guys, find Aryn."

He made a noise and ran his thumb over my ribs, eliciting a chill. "Still not seeing her."

I scoffed. Knowing he was lying to be cute about it didn't stop the goosebumps from rising on my skin, though.

I started moving toward her. "Come on, then."

He followed behind me, the room too crowded to allow for us to walk side-by-side, until we stopped where Aryn was standing. Sure enough, at least three guys were talking to her with dopey looks on their faces. Aryn wasn't ever interested in any of the men who hit on her at gatherings. She was good at talking like a guy and had a lot of the same interests, so they all thought she was into them. Let's just say, based on how well I knew her body language and vocal tones, none of them had a chance.

"Mer, you look stunning," she said, reaching for me to pull me close and give me a hug. It wasn't that unusual to greet each other with hugs, but it was still rare enough that I took it for what it was—a cry for help. These guys were bugging her. "Looks like things with Brooks VanOrman have hit a new high," Aryn whispered as we stood cheek to cheek. "If you can get rid of these guys, I will owe you for life."

I pulled away with a sweet smile at Aryn and gestured to Brooks. "Aryn, this is my lawyer. I invited him along tonight because he's doing a little investigating on harassment in social settings, and a New Year's Eve party is a great way to do some research in a crowd."

Brooks grunted as I elbowed him lightly. "Uh, yes. At what level would you say a line has been crossed and it qualifies as stalking?" I chanced a look at him, and his face was very serious. He looked around at the men who were listening in. They'd all lightly shifted away from Aryn. "What do you fellas think? Where is the line?"

They basically evaporated from sight, leaving their best wishes for a lovely evening. Aryn and I laughed, and Aryn gave Brooks a high-five.

"Brooks," Aryn said warmly. "I can't tell you how glad I am to have you here."

"Meredith said you'd be surprised. So, on a scale of one to ten, where are you?" he smiled.

Aryn rubbed at her chin. "Honestly, I'm torn. Never thought I'd see the day you two made peace, but I've also been noticing a certain besotted look on Mer's face when you're mentioned, so . . ."

"Oh, we're still at war," I replied. "Brooks jumped in my car and tagged along in an effort to take things to the next level."

"Excellent. Then tonight should be fun." Aryn's grin was smug and satisfied.

"Any idea where I can deposit these?" Brooks asked, lifting the arm where our coats were still hanging. "I do love spending time as a coat rack, but . . ."

Aryn pointed across the room where some sort of hanging rack was standing. He nodded and moved that way. Aryn grabbed my arm, watching him over my head as he walked away. She kept her eyes on him while she talked to me.

"He looks amazing; you look amazing. Please tell me this means you've decided to let something brew between you two, because the sparks are definitely there."

I nodded. "We had the talk last night. You're looking at a brand-new girlfriend. Even saying the word sounds strange."

She looked down at me. "Thank goodness you decided to snap that man up."

"How is it possible that I fell for a guy that's in a good mood all the time? It's unhealthy."

"Maybe. But he is seriously into you."

I shook my head and clucked playfully. "It's the absolute worst that I feel the same about him."

She rubbed one of my arms and said softly enough that I knew he was returning, "You're one of my very best friends, and you deserve love. Please start believing that."

Brooks reappeared, and we decided to go greet our hosts and then check out the food spread. We only had a few seconds to thank Hailey and Ford for the invite before more people took our place, but Hailey gave me a knowing look and squeezed my hand, a promise that we'd talk later.

At the buffet table we loaded up plates and moved to a section where some small, round tables were set up. We chose one that wasn't already taken and sat down in the intimate space, digging in to the delectable catering that Hailey had provided. I people watched, and it seemed like Brooks did, too. But when I looked over to point someone out to him, he was watching me.

"Why are you looking at me?"

"I'm thinking over a few things," he replied, wiping his hands on a napkin. "First, I wish we'd gotten a better start and not immediately become enemies because of something I had no knowledge or control over."

"That would have been nice."

"Why did you come at me with the heat of a thousand suns? We could have talked it out from the start, you know."

I pulled a face. "Are you suggesting I could have potentially handled things differently or that other people my age aren't literal big babies when they don't get their way?"

He chuckled before growing serious again. "Were you that hurt about it?" I nodded, looking down at my plate and pulling a roll into little pieces. "I'm sorry. I hope you understand by now that I had no idea what had gone on behind the scenes. I didn't even know who you were until that first meeting when you came in with your big words and righteous anger and tried to rake me over the coals."

"Well, you responded in kind," I grumbled.

"I was under attack and scrambling to understand everything. All I knew was that I couldn't retreat and show weakness. I was supposed to be the new president."

I popped a piece of soft roll into my mouth and chewed. "Yeah. Sorry. I wasn't in a good place about it, and in my life I've had to fight tooth and nail for everything. So, it came naturally to go to war."

"Yeah, you really dug in your heels," he chuckled.

I made a noise and put my head in my hands. "Hey, I have regrets, okay? You're sure you want to take me on?"

He put a warm hand on my knee under the table. "I'm a thirty-four-year-old man. I can make my own choices about what kind of woman I want."

"Thirty-four?" I gasped, lifting my head. "You're too young for me."

He laughed. "You're thirty-five, Miss Atwood. In fact, if I remember right from all that background checking I did on you, for two months of the year, we're the same age."

"I have so much baggage."

"We're in our mid-thirties, of course you do. We both do. That's part of life."

I shook my head. "You have to stop being nice."

"I know. It's the worst when you want to be thought of as a witch, but I insist on seeing good in you."

"It won't last, though. We're in the infatuation stage, and before too long the blinders will come off, and you'll see the real me under there."

He quirked a brow. "I'd like to remind you that we started this situation by seeing the worst of each other. We did it backwards. So, I'm not really scared about discovering skeletons in your closet, considering you chucked them straight at me on day one."

At that I clasped his hand where it rested on my knee and laughed. "I really did."

He squeezed my knee. "Um, I think your friend Ruby is spying on us. Wearing a navy-blue dress and watching you with big eyes?"

I looked up to find Ruby standing behind a potted plant looking at me. I waved. She ducked and then popped back up and began marching toward us with a bright smile on her face.

"Brooks VanOrman," she said when she reached our table. "You are a sight for sore eyes."

Brooks smiled and took her hand. "Thank you, Ruby. I'm glad you think so."

She plopped down in the free chair next to me. "I have to tell you that the way Meredith was freaking out about your epic kiss, I thought for sure she'd ghost you. But this is a very pleasant surprise."

"Epic kiss, huh?" Brooks looked at me with a sly grin. "Guess it's a good thing I promised to kiss her at midnight."

"You're smart. Meredith prefers to not be surprised." Ruby smirked.

I stood. "I'm going to let you two get to know each other. I'm going to find Hailey and have her help me analyze why my best friends continue to torture me."

They laughed as I walked away. Ruby would keep him entertained, and I needed a big, long breather.

✳✳✳✳

I was standing at the back window, looking at the moon and stars when the countdown to midnight started. I felt Brooks approach before he said anything. His chest, warm and firm, pressed up against my back as he slid his arms down around my waist and closed the space between us. His head rested against mine, his chin lightly touching my temple, and I nearly smiled at this man's confidence. He wasn't the young men I'd flirted with who were all about the push-and-pull and mixed messages. No, he was clearly stating his desires in a way that left me no room to pretend ignorance, even though I'd tried to do exactly that for weeks. The men I'd actually dated were either too intimidated by my strength to be themselves or too determined to bend me to their will. Yet here was Brooks, gently but

181

persistently staking his claim while allowing me the freedom to be me. It was novel—that was certain.

He'd been chatting with Ford and some other businessmen for the past half hour. I hadn't minded. In fact, I'd liked watching him in that element as I'd never caught a glimpse of him in a professional role. He was funny and charming, quick with a witty phrase but also able to talk shop. It was another piece to the puzzle of who he was, and, so far, every new piece I discovered only made me like him more. I'd left the group no more than five minutes before, wanting to end the year with my own thoughts.

As I looked back over the past months, I couldn't help but catalog the major course shift that had happened in recent weeks. I was ending the year a different person, and I knew I couldn't credit myself with every adjustment that had taken place. I'd thought it before, and the thought circled back, that with Brooks there were possibilities. I could be a whole person with limitless potential.

"If I didn't know you better, I'd think you made a tragic picture over here by yourself looking at the stars. But the reality is that you look peaceful and beautiful," he said quietly, turning his face to press a light kiss to my cheek.

I leaned back more, resting my head against his shoulder. "It hasn't been a terrible night."

A chuckle vibrated in his chest. "The karaoke room was a little touch and go."

I laughed, remembering him accepting Ruby's invitation to partner with her and the horror on his face when he realized that Ruby had choreography in mind. It was an image I'd never forget, and, while they'd won the prize, it had clearly scarred him for life.

"I probably should have warned you."

"I might not have believed you."

I laughed again. "When it comes to Ruby, please know that regardless of how odd it sounds, we aren't making it up."

"You laugh more these days," he whispered against my cheek.

It was something I hadn't really noticed but was certainly true. I felt lighter with him around. The crowd around us was chanting the last of the countdown now. "Ten, nine, eight, seven . . ." Brooks spun me in his arms, and I lifted my own to wrap around his neck.

"I toyed with saying something cheesy right now, but I think it might taint your view of me, and things are going so well," he said in a low voice.

"It doesn't hurt to try," I replied with a teasing grin.

"Being with you is the best start to a new year I've had in a long time."

I smiled. "That wasn't too bad."

Our eyes held as the others around us counted down the last two seconds, and then he was lifting me slightly up, and I was closing my arms tighter around his neck until we were kissing like two people who had nothing to lose and everything to gain.

CHAPTER 26

Something new I learned about Brooks the next day was that if you gave the man an inch, he was going to try to take a mile. I'd received no less than three phone calls and ten text messages asking me to come out and play that day, but I had to turn him down for several reasons.

One: school started back up the next day, and I was planning to spend the day in my classroom prepping everything. School rooms did not run themselves, and it wasn't an excuse to not spend time with him.

Two: my heart was no longer a recognizable piece of my body, and I needed some space without his eyes and curly hair and hands and lips . . . yes, those lips needed to be far away from me . . . in order to process and prepare for the next logical steps in our relationship. Steps I was ready to take, yes, but without jumping in willy-nilly. I'd agreed to date him but not to totally lose myself.

Three: January 1st was the day I planned out my year, and I had a date with a journal and a still-unfinished vision board.

Brooks finally stopped pestering me after I promised I'd have dinner with him that night—with the understanding that this teacher had an early curfew.

I wasn't the only one back at school that afternoon. Other teachers and office staff had arrived after sleeping in. The lunchroom was even lit up as food was delivered in preparation for students returning. I went around my classroom wiping things down and clearing out any garbage that I'd forgotten about. I put up a "Happy New Year" bulletin board with spaces for the children to hang their own mini-vision boards we'd be making and prepped out my lesson plans for the week.

Around four o'clock, some internal clock had me heading for Ruby's nurse office. I hadn't actually spoken with my friends yet today, but I thought there was a chance they'd be there, and if they were, they'd find their way to Ruby, too. It was the best place to meet because no one else went there after school. There were no parents popping in or students who'd forgotten their backpacks. It was small and quiet.

The light was on and the door was slightly ajar when I rounded the corner. So, I tapped lightly and pushed the door open. Ruby was sitting behind her desk, and Hailey was sitting on the exam table. They both looked up with a smile when they saw me.

"Well, hello, Miss Atwood," Ruby said. "I'm surprised to see you today. I thought you'd be with your new boyfriend."

"It was certainly a surprise to see Brooks there with you last night," Hailey said, patting the place next to her. "You seemed to have fun together."

A silly grin broke out on my face before I could stop it. "Yeah."

I pictured him in that suit, his arms around me as he told me I was the best way to start the new year. When they didn't tease me, I snapped out of my daydream and looked around the room. They looked identically delighted and really unsure about mentioning it.

"What?" I grumped.

"Mer, your face was so dreamy," Hailey said.

"I think the wall crumbled," Ruby stated. "You used to love the idea of punching his face, but now you love his face. It's the absolute best turn around I've ever seen."

I held up my hands. "Okay, I'll admit that I'm happy to be with him. But only because it's logical and not based off an emotional response. We have a lot of the same goals and ideals, we're both successful people who work hard, he's into serving others and so am I."

They were silent for a heartbeat before Hailey said, "Baloney. You have chemistry. There's no reason to take that out of the equation when it should be firmly planted in the middle of the whole thing. Logically, you work, yes, but that's not as important as that pull you have toward each other against all reason."

"Hailey is right," Ruby nodded. "Ford and her don't make logical sense, but they keep sneaking off to have special time together. The heart wants what it wants."

Hailey was blushing, but she pressed on. "She's right. Ford and I are opposites who are mad for each other."

"Great. So, when that chemistry fades?" I asked.

"Then you still have all those logical reasons you listed." Ruby smirked, throwing my own words back at me.

"Do you like Brooks?" Hailey asked. "And I actually mean like as in enjoy him as a person and find him pleasant to spend time with?"

"Yes," I admitted.

"Then it's icing on the cake that he makes your heart sing," she offered.

"My heart isn't singing so much as . . ." I began.

"Lies," Ruby called over me. "She's singing."

"Fine," I rolled my eyes with a smile and waved my hands. "I'll keep you posted. Now, can we talk about literally anything else?"

"I caught Ford's secretary trying to sneak two jars of Nutella out of the kitchen last night," Hailey laughed. "I came into the room as she was shoving them into her purse. We made eye contact, and she froze and then slowly pulled one jar out and set it on the counter while holding my eye. I could see a second bottle in there, but she turned and strolled right out with her head high. I didn't try to stop her or bother telling Ford, and I'm still laughing about it. Why would she do that?"

That got the ball rolling, and we delved into funny things we'd seen, heard, or participated in at the Winter Wonderland New Year's Eve. I admitted I'd not read

184

the invite, which got them both howling, and Ruby admitted that her dress had been held together with safety pins after it tore during her exuberant karaoke performance. Overall, we complimented Hailey on a smashing party and then begged her to let us go back to pajama night the next year.

An hour later I was driving home, thinking about my friends, my students, my dad, and Brooks. My mind was full with ideas for resolutions and setting up a schedule with Willow for meals and cleaning at Dad's house. As I got close to my neighborhood, I had the thought hit me that maybe it was time I did something nice for Brooks. He'd ice melted my walks, shoveled my driveway, helped me with my dad's house, brought ice cream sundaes, and generally lifted my spirits over the past weeks.

So, I made a quick turn and headed to my favorite sandwich shop. When I parked along the curb, I shot off a text letting him know I'd be bringing dinner with me. The sandwich shop had been around for as long as I could remember, and it had smelled the same for years. I ordered two roast beef heroes, two Jackson Hole sarsaparillas, and two bags of potato chips. I bounced on the balls of my feet as the local college students put my order together and nearly jumped when my phone buzzed with a text from Brooks.

Brooks: Thank you
Me: Hope you like Logan's Heroes
Brooks: Love that place

A smile lit my face, goofy and way out of proportion, but I couldn't tamp it down even when they handed me my food and had me pay. I drove straight to Brooks's house, anxious to be there, missing him even though it hadn't even been a full day. He opened the door as I parked, waving when I looked up to see him there. I felt an overwhelming sense of coming home as I walked toward him, and, when I reached the porch, I found that same big, silly grin had reappeared.

"How was setting up your room?" he asked, stepping aside to let me in.

"Great." I gave him a light play-by-play as I followed him into his kitchen.

I sat the sandwiches on the counter, and he helped me shrug out of my coat and hung it over a bar stool. Then, I turned to face him, and, in a move I'd never imagined I was capable of, I launched forward and took his face in my hands, tugging it down to meet my lips. I pressed firmly against him, still cradling his face, as his hands came to my waist to steady both of us. It didn't take long for him to catch up and join fully in the exchange. His lips were warm and soft, and he tasted sweet as though he'd had syrup recently. I ended the kiss and pressed my forehead against his chin momentarily, breathing heavily from adrenaline and something deeper, before straightening up and stepping out of his arms.

"I think we should date," I said.

He licked his lips and a smile bloomed. "I thought we already were."

I laughed and put a hand on his chest, where I could still feel his heartbeat racing. "Right, but we should set some ground rules."

He shook his head. "No ground rules."

I rolled my eyes and turned to get our sandwiches off the table. I reached into the bag and pulled everything out while I spoke. "Yes, rules. Like, I prefer to go to bed early, and I wake early, so no late nights. And you have to respect me if I say I need some space." I handed him his sandwich, chips, and sarsaparilla bottle and moved to take a seat on his couch. "Are you okay with food in the living area?" He nodded. "Great. So, other rules. No phone calls during business hours. Texts are okay. If we make plans to do something, we honor them. I will always be where you expect me to be, and I'd appreciate the same in return. We don't loan each other money or ask each other for money." I unwrapped my sub and took a bite. "What rules do you have?"

He was still holding his wrapped sandwich in one hand and drink in the other. "Mer, we aren't children. We've both had relationships. We do not need to set up a governing body of bylaws for this. We simply need to communicate and care about each other's needs and feelings. All of your rules fall under those simple parameters, which is simply how people should treat each other."

I kept chewing, and he unwrapped his sandwich and joined me. We watched each other as we ate, and I knew that he knew that I was thinking over what he'd said. It's just, I wasn't sure he fully understood where I was coming from. I was going to have to be brave here. I sat my sandwich on my lap and took a swig of my sweet drink before clearing my throat and diving in.

"Okay, so you know my childhood was a little unstable."

"I got a general feel for that, yes," he replied kindly.

"Rules helped me feel like I had control in a life that felt very out of control for my entire childhood. Rules still help me. In this case, they help me know that you'll behave a certain way, and that helps me relax enough to give this a try. If I have to totally rely on blind trust, well, I'm really bad at blind trust." My hands had started shaking, so I took another bite of sandwich to distract me.

"You must trust me a little bit, or you wouldn't be here having this conversation," he said.

I nodded. "I do. And I, um, actually like you enough to want to be having this conversation."

At that he smiled and bumped my knee with his. "Look, those rules you listed, I can understand why they give you boundaries and safety. So, I can agree to the ones about being where we said we'd be and not borrowing money or calling each other at work too often because they make good sense. But I'm not going to agree to never keep you out past your bedtime or to never push into your space. You have to leave room for spontaneity, too. And frankly, I think if I let you totally run the show, you'd lose all respect for me, and I'd become a resentful doormat."

"Yeah. That's happened before."

"So, how about we keep it this simple. Meredith Atwood, I want to spend every waking moment with you until I know you inside and out. Someday, when you realize you can trust me with your entire heart, I will feel like I've won the biggest prize in the universe. Until then, I plan to generally irritate you, laugh with you, tease you, and kiss you every single day." As he spoke heat curled in my belly and swirled up into my chest until my entire body felt like I was on fire. "Can you accept that?" he asked.

Honestly, that's all I'd ever wanted from someone. I swallowed, unable to speak over the lump in my throat, so I simply nodded.

He sat his food aside and then gently took mine out of my hands. "Come here."

I crawled across the couch and into his lap where he tucked me against his chest, and I proceeded to peel away several layers of my protective shell as I shared some of the dark places in my heart. He stroked my back and arm as I spoke, running his fingers lightly through my hair and murmuring words of comfort when I shivered over some particularly painful memory.

When I was done, he returned the favor, telling me about the loneliness he'd felt as the child of busy parents who spared little time for him. How he wasn't close with his brother but was trying to build a relationship with his brother's children. He talked about how devastated he'd been when his fiancée left and the harsh reality of moving to Logan and not knowing a soul. We found comfort in understanding the feeling of being outsiders and both desperately seeking a safe place to land.

I pressed my hand to his heart as he spoke, feeling each heartbeat as though it was my own.

After a long time, sandwiches cold and forgotten, he bundled me up and walked me to my car. We paused with my car door open, and I realized how much lighter I felt standing there in the moonlight.

"These first days of our official relationship have been pretty intense," he said. "I've never started out with a good old-fashioned soul baring like that."

I liked that he didn't skate around issues and was finding that casting light on things scared away shadows. "I warned you that I'd be a lot to take on."

"A little thing like you?" he laughed, putting a hand around the back of my head. "Nah." He pressed a kiss to my forehead. "I'll see you tomorrow after work?"

"Yeah."

"I'll make dinner here. Six o'clock okay?"

"I hope you realize you might make an unfair amount of meals because I'm not a good cook." I turned and sat in my car, and he leaned down.

"Consider it me bribing you to spend time with me."

I smiled. "I think I'd do that for free."

He held up his hands. "Pardon me for saying it, but with you I'm not taking any chances."

I rolled my eyes as he closed the door and waved at me as I pulled away with a smile.

CHAPTER 27

The next week was the most wonderful week of my life. Brooks and I had dinner every night, and during the days he totally broke the no contact rule by repeatedly texting me things all day long. Of course, my phone was off during the school day, but at lunch and after school I'd discover multiple texts with funny sayings or jokes. I was all but ignoring my friends at lunch time, but they handled it with good grace and supportive smiles.

Monday's texts were pick-up lines, like, "I'm no photographer, but I can picture us together," and "Kiss me if I'm wrong, but dinosaurs still exist, right?"

Tuesday was all about fun facts: "Apparently, it's only supposed to take four minutes to decide if you'll like someone. We were slow on the uptake."

Wednesday was terrible puns. "There might be other fish in the sea, but you're my sole mate."

Thursday he called the front desk at school and asked them to please have me call my boyfriend. This caused no end of delighted questioning by the entire office staff, which left me both amused and determined to pay him back. I'd responded with a text.

Me: I got a message asking me to call my boyfriend.
Him: Spoiler, it's me.

And so on. I had a perpetual smile on my face, and even my students noticed. When I told them I was dating someone new, they insisted on cutting out hearts and writing messages on them for me to give to him, so, after school on early-out Friday, I taped them all to his front door for him to find when he came home. That had been a memorable night leading into a weekend filled with mindless togetherness. Chores were scrapped in favor of playing board games. Dinner ended up being frozen pizza and ice cream. I'd read once that your brain literally stopped working logically during the early phases of infatuation, and I could see that in the way that I didn't care about dirty clothes or grocery shopping, only about teasing him and finding ways to make him look at me like he'd won the lottery.

And I laughed. I laughed more than I knew was possible. I laughed until my throat was sore and my eyes were watering, and then it turned into sobbing because I didn't know someone could feel this much euphoria and survive it.

Monday morning found me on a happiness hangover. My mind tumbled over memories of the weekend, and a mixture of dread and excitement over what today would bring. Today was a special day. It was my birthday. I was turning thirty-six and couldn't remember the last birthday I'd celebrated with someone I was dating. Willow and Ash were always sweet to send cards and call, and my friends always took me out for dinner, but today, I had a boyfriend. An actual boyfriend. I wasn't sure what to expect, which Brooks knew gave me hives. The thing was, I hadn't really told Brooks about my complicated feelings surrounding birthdays and holidays. I'd hinted at it but not admitted the full scope of emotion. I tended to have a knot in my gut every birthday morning even though the days of being forgotten were behind me. But those types of feelings were hard to shake. I didn't know if he was a big birthday person or a low-key celebrator, and I was trying to be Zen about it.

When I entered my classroom promptly at 8:00 that morning, my friends were waiting for me. They had party hats on and blew whistles as I walked through the door. My initial foot-high jump followed by startled screaming quickly turned into laughter and smiles.

"Happy birthday," they called, clapping and cheering.

"We brought you birthday breakfast since we know you have plans with *your boyfriend* tonight," Hailey said, holding up a tray of cupcakes.

I wasn't against cupcakes for breakfast, even though I'd already had my overnight oats with fresh fruit and chia seeds. "Yum. Thank you."

We ate around the back table, our knees banging up against the edges, and talked as we licked frosting off our fingers.

"Three dozen years you've been on this earth," Ruby said. "How does that feel?"

"Like a lot. As the grandma of the group, I'd like to thank you all for keeping me young," I replied.

"Three years doesn't make you the grandma," Aryn responded. "But something tells me we do keep you young."

"I think I was born old," I said, picking up a second cupcake.

"My parents say that about me a lot," Hailey piped in. "They say I have an old soul. Probably why finding a good group of friends was hard until my twenties. I didn't relate to boy-crazy, poster hanging, giggling girl drama in my teens."

"Good thing you relate to that now," Ruby teased, "or you'd never be friends with me."

"Any advice, oh wise, elderly friend?" Aryn asked me.

I nodded with a serious expression. "Trust dogs. They're good judges of character. Never trust cats. They hate everyone."

They burst out laughing, and I joined in. We cracked a few more jokes until it was time for us to all prep for students to arrive. They all hugged me on the way out and wished me luck with whatever Brooks had planned.

The phrase 'whatever Brooks had planned' was what worried me.

Brooks picked me up at half past five, sharp. He was freshly showered with a newly trimmed beard and curly hair. I stood in the open doorway looking at him, amazed once again that this man had turned out to be basically perfect for me. He smiled and opened his arms, and I stepped into that familiar place, snuggling my nose into his neck as my arms coasted around his waist.

"Happy birthday, my little tiger," he said.

I shook my head. "Don't call me that. It's demeaning."

He squeezed me close. "Lioness?" I shook my head. "Slayer?" This time I scoffed. "The Ripper?" I pinched his back and laughed as he squirmed. "Warrior Princess!"

I leaned up and pressed a kiss under his chin. "Nicknames aren't my thing. But I could start using one for you if you'd like."

He nodded. "I have one prepared, already. I'd love to be called Hunky Monkey."

I plopped my head against his chest and laughed. "No. That is not happening."

"Just Hunky is fine if you'd prefer to shorten it."

"How about Brooks? It is your name after all."

He tickled my sides, and I squirmed in his embrace. "I'm like the pebble in your shoe. You will eventually cave."

"I've already caved enough. I'm standing firm on this. No Hunky Monkey."

"Not even on special days? Like my birthday or Christmas? Or when I've done something especially boyfriend-ish?"

I raised my arms to wrap around his neck and pressed a kiss to his smiling lips. "Okay. On your birthday."

He kissed me back. "In that case, seeing as it's your birthday and all, I'd like to make you happy by calling you Chipmunk for the rest of the night."

I laughed and let go of him, turning back to grab my coat from the hall table. "Absolutely not."

I closed the door behind me and locked it. Then we made our way to his waiting car. He held the door for me to get in, and before long we were on our way.

"I'm hoping the little bird who told me that you like Chinese food wasn't lying," he said as we pulled out of the neighborhood. "I was going to take you to Mandarin Garden."

"You were told correctly. I love their food."

"Great. And then, afterward, I thought we could go to my house for dessert." He threw me a playful look. "And I'm talking actual dessert, not the kind Ruby means when she says that."

I chuckled. "It should frighten me how well you already know her."

"She's fantastic. All your friends are. Although Aryn's sarcasm occasionally confuses me."

"You'd think that as my boyfriend you'd be immune to sarcasm, cynicism, and general pessimism."

He took my hand and linked his fingers through mine. "Those are your love languages. I'm becoming fond of them."

Dinner was delicious and perfect, just the two of us at a corner table with noodles, chicken, rice, and shrimp steaming between us. We talked more about his upbringing and family, and he shared with me that he'd started woodworking when he'd moved to Logan after his engagement broke up. He hadn't had friends, and the winters kept him indoors, so he'd found a way to keep busy. I was slowly starting to separate Brooks's hobby from my dad's passion and realizing that the art itself had never been the issue. It made me happy to hear about his projects, which was pretty huge for me.

When we were finished I looked around the table and realized we hadn't eaten even half of the food.

"Brooks, there's enough here for two more meals," I said, looking at him with wide eyes.

His responding smile was all-knowing. "I did it on purpose. This is your first birthday present from me. I know you hate cooking, so you'll have another day or two of meals that only need reheating."

I sucked in a breath. "Are you serious?" He nodded. "Why am I so excited to get leftovers as a gift?" I bit my smiling lips.

"I pay attention to things."

We packaged up the remaining food and carried it out, me practically skipping at the thought of more tiny spicy chicken and imperial shrimp being available tomorrow night. I hugged the bag on my lap on the drive home, and Brooks laughed at me.

"If I'd known this was the way to your heart, I'd have started bringing you takeout back when our war began."

"I would have suspected poison," I replied.

"Really?"

I nodded. "I wouldn't put it past me."

"Good thing I never tried. There were a few times I wanted to reach out to you and see if we could mend fences, but I wasn't sure how to go about it. Everything about you screamed 'Electric fence—approach at your own risk.'"

"That's the basic message I was trying to convey."

"It was hard, though, because the first time you came to a meeting, I couldn't stop sneaking peeks at you. I thought you were the prettiest woman I'd seen in a long time, and I wondered how I'd never seen you before."

I looked over at him, my face softening. "You're making that up."

He shook his head and took my hand. "No, Chipmunk, I'm serious. I was going to ask Leland or Hazel to introduce us after the meeting."

I licked my lips, ignoring the chipmunk thing. "And then I opened my mouth."

He nodded with a smirk. "Yeah."

"For what it's worth, I honestly felt sick to my stomach after most of those meetings. I hated the way I acted. I think part of me understood all along that nothing was truly your fault. I'm sorry."

"Did you secretly find me wildly attractive, too? That would go a long way toward full healing on my part."

I squeezed his hand. "I'll admit to a certain level of interest."

"I'll take it."

We pulled into his garage, and I carried the takeout inside while he followed along with his arm around my waist and said, "Now, for actual gifts."

"You know dinner was enough, right?" I said as we entered his kitchen.

"I know. But if I can't spoil my lady then my life is incomplete."

"It's just, I've never been spoiled. So, the idea of it makes me a touch squeamish. I'm not sure how to feel or react."

He took my takeout bag and put it in the fridge while I took off my coat. Then he gripped my fingers in his and led me to the living room, flipping on lights as we went. When I saw what was waiting on the coffee table, I stopped walking so quickly that he ended up yanking on my arm.

"Presents," I stuttered.

"Yep," he chuckled, tugging on my hand.

There had to be six or seven of them. Basically, the same amount as my entire family ever got for Christmas. This was extravagant and unnecessary, and a swirl of unease loosened in my gut as he sat me on the couch facing them.

"Happy birthday, love."

I couldn't make any words come out as I surveyed the gifts. They were various sizes, all wrapped neatly, stacked just so. He was watching me with a smile, clearly excited to shower me with this offering, but I wasn't sure I could accept so much.

"This is too much," I said.

He grinned and picked one from the top. "This is nothing compared to what usually happens on birthdays."

I blinked and took the gift with numb fingers. "What do you mean?"

"I mean this is slim pickings. I know holidays and birthdays were never big at your house growing up, so I tamped down on it. No balloons or streamers and no party hats. I kept the gifts to a minimum." He was chipper to the extreme, clearly oblivious about the slight meltdown I was having. "I didn't spend as much as you think I did, so enjoy."

"This is slim pickings?" I asked, the numbness spreading to my lips.

What was he going to expect from *me* for special occasions? Was I going to have to remember a set of celebration rules I'd never been instructed on? Was he going to be disappointed when he realized that thoughtful gifts and party planning were so far outside my wheelhouse that I often had to be reminded when a gift was required? Did he understand that on my salary I was barely making ends meet?

"Yeah. My parents went way overboard for my brother Grady and me. It was almost like one present for year of life. By the time I was eighteen, I had to beg them to stop. I was running out of room, and there are only so many pairs of hiking boots one guy needs, you know?"

I shook my head. "I'd have been happy to get one pair."

My voice was low, and he must have finally noticed my ice-like state because his hand came to my back, soothing in warm circles.

"Hey, Chipmunk," he said in a light tone, clearly hoping to snap me out of it with the absurd pet name, "Breathe. They're only presents."

I managed to meet his eyes. "Only presents. Is this, um, the type of thing you're going to expect out of me?"

He frowned. "No. I'm not materialistic. I don't expect anything."

"But you'd be disappointed if the traditional gift haul didn't happen for your birthday or Christmas?"

He shook his head. "I mean, to be honest, it would feel kind of strange, but I'd live."

"You'd live."

"Yes. I'd manage; I'd be fine; I'd survive."

"If you got less than you're used to, you'd survive?" My voice was creeping up at the same speed as terror was rising. I wasn't sure what had triggered it, but I felt claustrophobic and panicked, and I wanted to throw the gifts across the room and run away. "But you'd be disappointed. In me. I would let you down. I *will* let you down."

I put the gift back on the table, and he pinched his lips.

"What's happening here?"

"I can't accept those gifts because I'll never in a million years be able to reciprocate. I don't have as much money as you do, and any extra I manage to eek out usually goes to taking care of my dad. I manage to pull off exactly four gifts per year. One for each of my sisters, my dad, and one for a gift exchange with my friends."

"I don't see what this has to do with me giving you gifts."

"We'll never be even. I'll always owe you, and I'll always come up short."

He blew out a breath. "This is a complete overreaction."

I hated that word being associated with me, and it caused me to sit back away from him and watch him with raised eyebrows. "This is not an overreaction. I'm telling you that you went way overboard and are setting expectations I will never be able to meet."

"So, are you going to make this one of your rules, then? No gifts over five dollars? No occasional spoiling of each other?"

I gasped. "You aren't even trying to see where I'm coming from."

"Because I spent days looking for little trinkets or things I thought you'd like. I watched a stupid online tutorial on how to wrap gifts. I knew you preferred simple birthdays, so I tried to keep it that way. And honestly, I think I did a fantastic job doing something so different from what I'd normally do. Everything about this night took you into consideration. You haven't even opened the gift, Meredith. How do you know it's more than you could ever reciprocate?" He stood. "And who said relationships are about reciprocation? It will never be totally even. Maybe one week I'll need to hold you up. Maybe I'll get hurt, and you'll nurse me for a month. The point is that we both give whatever we have, and, together, it's enough."

He stormed out of the room, and I sat back against the couch cushions, my hands bunched into fists, my arms shaking. I was miserable and angry, surging with righteous indignation. How dare he give me that speech? I wanted to follow him and give him a taste of his own medicine. I wanted to hurl the gifts at his hard head. Then I wanted to tear them open one-by-one, so I could shove it in his face that these were more than mere trinkets.

In fact, I leaned forward and grabbed the gift he'd handed me first. I tore at the wrapping and sucked in a breath when I saw what was inside. It was a tiny skunk figurine, the type you'd find at a dollar store, nothing real special, but still meaningful. Some of my anger cooled, and I set it to the side to open another. The second one couldn't possibly be that small. Yet, it was. It was an obviously homemade knit cap that looked identical to the one he'd said Hazel had made him.

"It's so we can be cheesy twinners next time it snows," he said from over my shoulder and across the room.

His tone was hesitant and still a little cross as I spun around to look up at him. His arms were folded, his sleeves pulled up, and I remembered running my finger over that compass tattoo.

"I kind of love it," I said over the lump forming in my throat.

"Hazel made it."

"So, you commissioned it for me?"

He shrugged and didn't move from his position leaning against the wall, so I turned back to the gifts, almost hesitant to see what else he'd come up with. The next gift was one candy cane and, as I laughed, remembering how hard he'd laughed when I'd told him about the candy cane hat trying to strangle me, I hugged it to my chest. These gifts were inexpensive, but they were so very dialed in to me and us and our story.

The fourth and fifth gifts were an ice cream sundae kit (minus the ice cream) and work gloves I could use at my dad's house.

"I got a pair for myself, too. Thought we could keep them over there for when we go help with things," he mumbled.

He'd said 'we,' and my heart positively shattered. I didn't care what was in the last box. I jumped off the couch and hurried to where he was standing. I gave him no warning at all before I launched at him, wrapping my arms around his neck and pressing my cheek to his. He caught me with a grunt and held me close.

"Forgive me, please," I said against his ear. "I'm such a jerk. I was scared and mean and totally reacted without thinking. This is the most thoughtful thing anyone has ever done for me, and I love it."

"I stand by my statement that you must have the shortest fuse of anyone I know."

I tightened my hold. "I know. It's the worst trait."

"I know you, Evergreen Atwood, better than you think. And what I don't know, I'll learn, hopefully without an argument every time."

194

"I don't know what triggered that."

He walked over to a chair with me still clinging to him and sat down. I was on his lap facing him and leaned back to look into his eyes. They had shadows that I'd put there. I'd hurt this man, and I felt sick about it. He'd been nothing but patient with me and happy and understanding, and I'd somehow forgotten to take his feelings into account. I'd deserved him storming off; in fact, I possibly deserved worse, but I was so grateful he'd come back into the room, back to me even when I'd been ugly.

I sighed. "The honest truth is that even though the years of deprivation and neglect are a decade behind me, the mental effects are still there. Thanks to people who've come into my life over the past couple of years, I'm improving, but I still have a ways to go. I didn't mean to hurt you. I never want to hurt you."

His hands skimmed up my back. "New rule. We need a safe word. When I've done something that triggers or overwhelms you, you say the word, and I'll give you a minute to process it before we discuss. That way I'll know not to put on pressure, and you'll know not to start accusing me of things. It'll be like a pause button. Then, we'll chat like adults until the issue is resolved."

I bit my lips. "I like that a lot. It goes both ways, though. You should use the safe word when I've done something to upset you." He nodded. "I have the perfect safe word in mind."

"What's that?"

"Hunky Monkey."

Those shadows faded from his eyes and were replaced by something magical. "You need to open your last gift."

I stood with his help and snagged the last box off the table. I opened it to find a house key inside. I looked up to see him grinning.

"That's a key to my house. No, I'm not inviting you to move in. But I am informing you that my fridge is always full, and I have better television options than you do. So, I guess what I'm saying is that my door is always open."

I blinked, fighting back tears, and nodded repeatedly. "Can Betty come, too?"

He motioned for me to join him back on the chair, and I did, sitting sideways so that my legs dangled over the arm.

"Meredith, I love you, but your alleged cat is not invited."

I put my head on his shoulder and hugged the key to my chest. "You love me, really, or you love me like one loves hamburgers?"

"It's probably too early to admit, but I love you more than I love hamburgers."

I nodded. "Good. Because I really, really love you back."

CHAPTER 28

The next day I felt a little sheepish when I thought about the argument I'd started with Brooks over birthday gifts. I'd put the skunk figurine on my bathroom vanity and looking at it had me squirming a little. We'd made peace and gone on to have probably my best birthday ever, but I still felt slightly nauseated over my behavior and reaction.

A prickle of fear tried to weave its way into my thoughts, telling me that he'd grow tired of that and I needed to change myself if I wanted him to stick around. My shoulders sagged at the thought I'd had so many times with so many people. I'd rarely felt worthy of commitment and love, and after some therapy sessions I did understand how that tied back to feeling ignored by my parent. I'd grown enough to find worth in myself, but my relationship with Brooks was quickly becoming necessary to my happiness in a way that was making me realize how much I had to lose.

I was still a little mopey throughout the morning, and by lunch time I was pretty much sulking as my friends and I gathered around a table in the faculty room. They all launched into their usual chatter while I used chopsticks to sculpt something out of my leftover birthday dinner. It was a chicken, shrimp, and rice masterpiece.

"Okay, we've been patient. How did last night go?" Aryn asked, interrupting my morose thoughts

"Brooks is perfect, and I'm a horrid monster," I replied.

A hand lightly landed on my shoulder. "Do you really believe that, or are you exaggerating because you're feeling upset about something?" Hailey asked.

I looked up. "I know I'm not a horrid monster. But Brooks is perfect, and I was a super big jerk last night."

"Nobody is perfect," Hailey said gently.

I nodded. "Well, he can be pushy sometimes. I'm not sure he's ever picked up an iron in his life, and his hair is a little messy." I felt oddly better listing out a few of his imperfections, actually.

"Spill it," Ruby said. "Then we'll tell you how to fix it."

I shrugged. "It's already been fixed. We talked it out, and things are fine."

Aryn gestured at my slumped body and pouty expression. "Obviously."

That had me rolling my eyes as I launched into the whole story of the night before. When I'd laid it all out, I said, "I'm falling in total love with him, and I can clearly see some behaviors and issues I have that might drive him away. So, today

I pout." They were nodding and chewing on their food as they thought. "Excellent, you all agree."

"That you have issues? Definitely," Ruby cracked. "This is like the worst-kept secret in the universe. You're messed up, my friend."

A smile cracked through my defenses. "Thank you for validating me."

"But the important thing is you know you're messed up. The people who really worry me are the ones who don't realize it." Ruby tapped the table with a long fingernail.

"To paraphrase Dr. Seuss," Aryn said, "we are all a little weird, and when we find someone whose weirdness matches ours, we join up and fall in mutual weirdness."

We chuckled, and I took a bite of my chicken. "I'm definitely strange."

"Honestly, Mer, if you are still feeling this way after school, go talk to him. Communication needs to become your new superpower," Hailey advised.

"But snark has always been my superpower," I joked.

"Don't forget striking terror in the hearts of your enemies," Aryn added.

"I've always been a fan of your ability to silence a room with one eyebrow lift," Ruby said, attempting to move her eyebrows separately.

I arched one and gave them all the teacher stare. Ruby fake shivered. "That's the one. Ooh, it's creepy. Maybe don't lead with that."

"When in doubt, always lead with chocolate," Aryn said.

******

I showed up unannounced at Brooks's house that evening. When he answered the door, he was loosening his tie, and the top buttons on his shirt were undone, exposing that evergreen tree over his heart. His suit jacket was hanging off one arm, and he looked like a man ready to call it a day.

"I gave you a key, love, remember?" he teased, stepping back for me to enter.

"I only plan on using that when you're away so that I can eat all your food in peace," I replied, tilting my head back to receive his greeting kiss.

He closed the door behind us and finished taking off his tie. "How was your day?"

I followed as he walked into his kitchen and draped his suit jacket over the back of a barstool. "Good. Um, I'm here with a peace offering."

He unbuttoned his cuffs and rolled up his sleeves. "A peace offering? Hmm. In my family those come just before someone is about to share bad news. So, I'm not sure how to react."

I smiled. "In my family they come after the fight."

He nodded, his face relaxing into a smile. "I like your way better. But I thought we were good. Are you still feeling bad about yesterday?"

I nodded and handed him a chocolate bar I'd snagged at the gas station on the way home since I didn't typically keep junk food handy at my place. "My friends told me to always offer chocolate."

"I like your friends. What else did they tell you?"

"That I have issues and need to learn to communicate better."

He leaned back against the counter and looked at the chocolate bar, toying with the wrapper. "Probably good advice for everyone I know." He looked up at me, his dark eyes solemn. "You know I was engaged before, right?" I nodded, hating the reminder but also accepting that we both had pasts. "So, I can tell you with total accuracy that couples argue. In fact, I'd be more worried if we never argued because that would mean one of us wasn't being honest."

"I'm very honest," I nodded, my mouth tugging up.

"I don't need a peace offering after every argument we have. All I need is for you to keep coming back and keep trying with me."

"I can do that."

"In a very short time you've come to mean a lot to me, and if you think you're the only one who is a little nervous about that, you're wrong. I've been doing a lot of woodworking, using the time to make sure my heart doesn't run away too fast."

That small confession made a huge difference in how I felt, and I smiled at him. "I used to be afraid of loving too deeply. I watched my dad and thought that I'd never want to love someone so much that when they were gone, I'd become a shadow. It was important to me to be a whole person myself and not fall into the trap of thinking I needed someone to complete me."

He stood up from his leaning position and came close to where I was standing. "And now?"

He put his hands on my waist and tugged me close. I rested my hands on his forearms. "Now, I think loving someone can mean safety. Like I can finally relax because I don't have to be on my own anymore."

His lips were warm on my face. "I know how capable you are, Mer, but I'm here to help you shoulder the load, every single day."

"I love you so much," I said through wobbly lips.

"Love you too, Chipmunk."

I didn't have time to tell him to take it back before his mouth was pressed to mine, and he showed me without words precisely how committed he was to taking me on.

*****

Two hours later I pulled into my driveway to find Hazel waving at me from my front porch. I parked my car and met her on the driveway. Her blue hair was wrapped in a scarf, and she had on oversized, crocheted mittens that looked like they would fit a giant. Her face was unreadable, which was kind of unusual for Hazel.

198

"At first I thought this happened because you're dating Brooks," she stated with a shake of her head, "but now I think you might be the luckiest person in the world."

"Wait, you know I'm dating Brooks?" I asked.

At this her eyes sparkled. "Everything is on the interwebs, Meredith. There's no such thing as privacy. I know you've been kissing."

"What?" I asked. "How?"

She only winked. "That's for me to know." She reached inside her coat and pulled out an envelope. "Word spread that you'd been fined over your holiday decor, and some anonymous person started a donation to cover the fees. Guess my social media campaign worked."

Confused, I took the envelope from her and tore it open. Inside was enough cash to cover what I'd given Hazel several weeks ago. My knees felt weak, and I gasped.

She smiled. "I think it's kind of twisting the rules a little to have other people pay your fines, but I also know that you're trying to do good things and that you don't make a lot teaching school. So, I'm going to be happy for you and warn you again to stick to the bylaws."

I nodded. "No inflatable hearts for Valentine's?"

She grinned. "Try me."

THE END

EPILOGUE

One year later. January.

The clubhouse was already filling up as I took my seat a few rows back. Gone were the days of me sitting up front and bellowing out arguments over every, single thing. Now, I submitted topics through the proper channels—that being my boyfriend—and respectfully discussed my ideas with the HOA board and community. Thanks to my improved behavior, along with Brooks's obvious campaigning behind my back, people didn't run from me anymore. It had been a solid two months since I'd even heard a snide remark behind my back.

Brooks, Leland, Hazel, and Shayla took their seats at the head table. Shayla gave Brooks a warm look, and, when his amused eyes met mine, I wiggled my eyebrows at him and made a kissy face. He blushed a little, and I considered it a small victory. Turns out, making that man blush was one of my very favorite activities. Making up after an argument was up there, too.

"Welcome to the new year," Brooks called the meeting to order. "We have a full agenda, but I'd like to kick it off with discussing nominations for next year's board. When I came on as president, I took on a two-year term. I've done a little over that now, and elections are coming in April. Our community has three months to nominate and prepare for elections. I'd like to kick off the nominations for HOA president by putting Meredith Atwood on the ticket."

There were a few mumbled conversations in reaction, but my entire heart plummeted to my shoes, and I didn't understand a word of what was said. I clasped my hands together in my lap, watching him meet everyone's glances but mine. In the last year of dating, I'd contributed a ton behind the scenes. These people didn't know it, but Brooks and I were practically copresidents with me discussing ideas and him presenting them in meetings. We'd found a lot of fulfillment in the secret partnership, and it had been meaningful to me to contribute. But I'd thought my hope of being HOA president was a dead one, and I'd made peace with it.

However, based on how anxious I felt sitting there, my toes curling and my heart racing, it would appear that I still very much wanted the position. I hadn't said as much to Brooks in a long time, but I shouldn't have been surprised at all to find out the man knew what was really bumping around in my heart.

"Meredith is capable and wise. She understands the needs of our community and regularly has suggestions on best use of funds and time. Meredith grew up in Cache Valley and understands the people and traditions. She'd be a fantastic asset here," Brooks added. "No voting happens now, but I would encourage you to take the next several weeks to visit with her and really get to know who she is. I think you'll be surprised by what you find."

My heart was hammering against my chest as people turned to look at me. I tried to smile, but I was sure it came off like more of a grimace as I was fighting off tears over this development.

"You have to say all this because you love her," someone called from the back of the room in a teasing tone.

Others laughed and joined in, "You might be a little biased, Mr. VanOrman."

Brooks smiled and replied, "You're right; I do love her. And I know you will, too."

Leland cleared his throat. "Now, can we please discuss the twelve-foot skeleton that the Leslie's have in their backyard? They have to know we can all see it from the street."

"That's a $200 fine," Hazel called, lifting her knitting needle and using it to slam the table like a gavel.

Brooks finally met my eyes and shrugged. *Business as usual*, his eyes seemed to say.

I hoped it would be business as usual for a long time to come.

AUTHOR'S NOTE

Dear Reader,

I wish I'd thought to do this in earlier books, but here are a few of the "true tales from my life" that made it into this book.

The first grader kissing Ruby on the bum at lunch, and the third grader calling her Big Booty Judy are both things that happened to my coworkers when I worked in an elementary school.

The HOA meeting agenda items I put in this story are *true*. Yes, towel sharing, and cat weights, and airplane landings, etc, were found by me on various forums where people discussed funny HOA rules, or things people had submitted in monthly meetings. Two of them - the giant skeleton and seeing trash cans from the curb - were told to me by a reader through Instagram. Thanks Leslie!

The skunk ladder is a true story from my own life. That situation with the skunk falling under a sunken trampoline happened to my family while I was writing this book! My husband and sons built a skunk ladder and set up a camera. Apples were used as bait. The skunk got out and all was well.

The ski day incident where Meredith gets her coat stuck on the lift and Brooks cuts it off with a knife truly happened to me too. My coat got caught when I was a pre-teen skiing with my dad. He honestly thought quickly enough to grab out his pocket knife (dads in the 90s always carried these!) and cut my coat free before the ski staff even realized what was happening.

Ruby hitting her head on the monkey bars and passing out. Me again. Ha ha. In fifth grade that happened to me and when I came to recess was over, but my friend was sitting by my side on the empty playground waiting for me to wake up. Adult me wants to know where ground duty (recess adult person) was??

Lastly, "Christmas Gift" is a real thing my husband's family introduced me to when we got married. The first person to say it on Christmas morning gets a "gift". The gift is just bragging rights, but it makes for some amusing situations with phone calls, or yelling it as soon as the front door opens at someone's house. It's a fun tradition we all get into and enjoy.

There are a few others, but I'm not going to give up all my secrets. Just know, that occasionally when you wonder how I came up with that idea . . .truth often is stranger than anything from my imagination.

COMING SOON

If you've been enjoying reading about the Thornback Society friends, you'll be happy to know that Back To Class, Aryn's story, is set to release June 1, 2023.

Aryn Murphy loves her family and friends, sports, and teaching school. What she doesn't love is all the wrong attention she receives from men who don't know the first thing about her.

When her childhood friend Wesley moves to town and lands a job working at the same school where she teaches, she has the perfect idea – he can be the decoy that keeps all the men away while she focuses on her otherwise perfect life. After all, Wesley has always been someone she's felt safe with.

Wesley Baker harbored a secret crush on Aryn in high school, and when he arrives at his new job to find Aryn there too, that crush comes raging back. Now she wants him to play the part of doting boyfriend by night, and forgotten coworker by day.

But he had enough of playing pretend all those years ago. This time, he's looking to play a different game – one with high stakes, and the potential to make them both winners.

Back to Class is now available for preorder on Amazon.com

ACKNOWLEDGEMENTS

As always, I have to thank my family because they bear the brunt of my distraction. I get pretty laser focused when I'm writing a story and you just roll with it. My husband, Steve, and our four children, who always understand and support. I love you more than all the books in the world!

I have to once again thank the author community, especially my friends who have my back with constant support and kindness. Writing is a solo journey in many ways, as you sit alone at your computer and attempt to tell stories. However, my author friends remind me often that I'm part of something big and wonderful, and it's a gift to be here.

My extended family – every time I write about difficult family situations I feel incredibly grateful for all of you and the happiness you bring me.

My besties – you know who you are. Thank you for our daily conversations, and the unending support and cheerleading through one of my roughest years. I'm so grateful for the place I have with you.

And with humility and deep gratitude – you readers are awesome! A million times, thank you!

ABOUT THE AUTHOR

Aspen Hadley loves nothing more than a great story. She writes what she wants to read: sassy and romantic novels that give you a break from real life and leave you feeling happy.

Outside of writing, Aspen's number one hobby is reading. Number two is sneaking chocolate into and out of her private stash without being caught. Other favorites include: playing the piano, traveling, a good case of the giggles, kitchen dance parties, and riding on ATVs.

Aspen shares her life in the foothills of northern Utah with a patient husband, four hilarious children, and one grumpy dog who make her laugh every day.

You can find Aspen on social media.
On Instagram @aspenhadley_author
On Facebook Aspen Hadley Author

She also sends a newsletter twice a month where she shares updates and hosts flash giveaways. You can sign up through her website www.aspenmariehadley.com

Made in United States
Troutdale, OR
05/14/2024

19858314R00120